THE HORMONE JUNGLE

ALSO BY ROBERT REED

The Leeshore

THE HORMONE JUNGLE

Robert Reed

DONALD I. FINE, INC.

NEW YORK

Library of Congress Catalog Card Number: 87-46033
ISBN: 1-55611-066-9
Manufactured in the United States of America
10 9 8 7 6 5 4 3 2 1

This book is printed on acid free paper. The paper in this book meets the guidelines for permanence and durability of the Committee on Production Guidelines for Book Longevity of the Council on Library Resources.

Library of Congress Cataloging-in-Publication Data

Reed, Robert.
   The hormone jungle.

   I. Title.
PS3568.E3696H6   1988   813'.54   87-46033
ISBN 1-55611-066-9 (alk. paper)

To Natalie

1

I've been to Kross, our innermost world, and seen the sprawling strip mines and the fantastic cities and the princes and princesses of Kross, the poorest of them richer than a hundred of me. I've seen the high sulfurous clouds of Morning and played poker with its cyborg inhabitants, listening to their human laughter and their matter-of-fact stories about the wastelands below, cruel and unforgiving. And of course I've been to the Earth, homeland to us all, and to its sister world, Luna. And then there is Cradle, the first major world to be terraformed, with its violet plant life and its tiny childlike people, happy artists every last one. And there is the multitude of Belter worlds, each unique. There are the worlds of Jupiter, sparse populations and fantastic scenery . . . I have reached clear to those far-flung bits of humanity in the Oort Cloud and to some of the places set between the major places—those tiny man-built worlds of Kross metals and Titan plastics—and people, knowing my compulsion to travel, ask me which of those landscapes is the most beautiful. The most intriguing. The most complex. The most rewarding. And always, always I smile and look straight at them and explain, "There's only one landscape that fits the bill. Only one." Which one? they persist, puzzled and eager and smiling at me. "The human face," I say. "Of all the landscapes, without doubt, I would claim the human face is easily the best. I would."

—excerpt from a traveler's notebook, available through System-Net

THERE are a bunch of whores in the back, playing edible chess. Steward can see them by the light of their big bright skullcaps, and he hears them chattering and then hears them turn quiet, waiting for someone to make a move. Then some of them start to cheer and clap. One of the pawns gives a high squeaky scream, and one of the whores laughs, saying, "You're mine. All mine."

Steward sits alone at a little round table, one of his big hands holding his glass while he sips and thinks that he's dry enough and the rain has quit and maybe he should go now. He thinks about getting home. He thinks how he hasn't been busy enough lately because he sure isn't tired and maybe he should go somewhere besides home. Get some work done. Do those boring chores he's been putting off till whenever. Like running a check of his inventories. Or testing his security systems for flaws. Or maybe just spending a few hours with his high-placed contacts, sniffing out any news that might mean something to him.

He hears the front door open and close, then he turns and sees a girl come inside. She's a strange girl. He knows it at once and yet he has trouble deciding why. From a distance, through the pasty smoke and gloom, she seems pretty enough. With big eyes she surveys the bar while she moves halfway in Steward's direction. Another pawn screams, and she hears it and jerks and watches the whores for a second, something showing in her face. She's wearing a sheer white dress with precious little underneath and expensive white shoes and double strands of Garden pearls around her perfect neck, and both hands hold a purse made of some living snow-white leather. It's a wardrobe for casual wealth. She's much too much for this kind of place. One glance is enough to prove her wrongness. Even the whores and patrons turn down the volume a notch, watching her settle at a table close to Steward. The barmaid comes and the girl orders a drink. She's too much. Steward hears a dusky voice. He sees something in the barmaid's face. What is it? Then he takes a long deep breath, feeling a hollowness high in his chest and smelling a delicate musty scent that makes his head wheel. Something is going to happen, he thinks. Something tells him something is coming. Wait. Just wait.

There are a dozen patrons, tops. They're a scrubbed and liquored lot, all Terran, of all shades, wearing rumpled clothes and uncertain smiles. The whores not playing chess are sitting with them and drinking with them and laughing when they think it'll do them some good. Steward looks at all the faces, measuring moods, and then he looks above them and takes in the bright old-fashioned holos advertising beer, and the swirling smokes rising through the holos and toward the high-arched roof. Buildings in the Old Quarter are dead and durable and typically more than a thousand years old. This particular building is made from dead woods commercially perfect and tarnished steel pulled into elegant shapes, and the bright green moonlight pours in through the glass roof and softens everything it touches. Normally this place is lit up by its own lights. Steward has been here with clients and with people who never quite became clients. It must have been the storm, he thinks. Someone must have turned off the lights so they could watch the storm pass, and now they've forgotten to turn them back on. Half the sky is eclipsed by a tall stone building. A line of floaters cross the other half—saucer-shaped craft carrying their passengers from place to place—and he notices a rainboy higher still, its bright body streaking towards the Gulf. He breathes and thinks how he should be working. He isn't a man accustomed to idleness. All the years he has lived in Brulé City, and still he can't be comfortable or contented or even relax for long. Like now. He looks down again and turns toward the girl, not really thinking about her, concentrating on his inventories and security checks and whatever; yet all of the sudden his head is full of her pretty face and the poreless skin and the white of her dress showing the brilliant cool green of the moon.

The barmaid returns with a simple fruit drink.

Steward watches the two of them and sips his own drink and wonders what is strange about the girl. He knows what's wrong. She doesn't belong in this place, not at all. But there's something strange too, and he can't for his life identify the trouble.

Opening the leather purse, the girl removes a single green glass bill. The barmaid looks at the girl while she makes change, and then she spies Steward staring at them and decides that he must want something now. She comes over and asks if he's thirsty for another one. He says, "Thanks, no." He swirls his chilled liquor and asks, "How's it going tonight?" without ever actually taking his eyes off the girl.

"You see the storm?"

"I was in it," he offers.

"That's right. You came dripping in, didn't you?" She is a big woman with a flat round face and big hands showing the miles. "You see it too, don't you?"

"What?"

"The girl," she says, laughing in a funny harsh way.

Steward looks up at the barmaid and waits.

"Or don't you?" She has an odd expression. She's curious or she's angry or she's amused about something. He can't quite tell. "I've seen them on World-Net a few times but never here. Not in Brulé." And then she blinks and says, "What do you think?"

"I'm never sure," he says.

"Well," she tells him, "if you thought you were in a storm before, you just hold on. Okay?"

"I'll try."

"Wait and watch," she warns. Set next to the girl in the white dress, the barmaid seems huge and graceless and nearly ugly. "She should have never come in here."

"No?"

"I wonder why she did." And she leaves him, working her way to the back and the chess-playing whores.

Steward tries to piece it together. Nothing fits. So he looks down at his glass and sees a big swallow waiting for him. He tilts the glass and looks through its thick bottom while the girl glances from face to face to face. She's got a nervous quality. Mostly it's hidden, but sometimes some of it seeps out around her edges. Like now. She sips her own drink, fruity and dark, without shutting her eyes. A thin dark mustache forms on her upper lip, unnoticed for a moment. Then her tongue darts, pink and moist, and Steward has to take a breath. He wonders what the barmaid has seen. He wonders why a girl of her apparent worth and character is in this kind of place. She sure didn't come out of the rain. That's his excuse. A couple of whores had made their sales pitches when he arrived, and he thinks about whores and money and breeding and how anything can become dull when you get too much of it. Maybe that's it, he thinks. Maybe she's waiting for a sales pitch or two. She's come to see how the census figures live and love. Sure. And the big barmaid is simply . . . what? Jealous? Offended? What?

Steward lingers for the moment, curious.

He is a tall man who doesn't look tall when he sits, his long legs folded beneath the table. He has a dark complexion, deep dark brown eyes, and surprisingly bright red hair—curled and cut close to his scalp. His face is thin and wind worn, bones giving angles to his cheeks and chin. His arms and shoulders are thick and toned by exercise and an athlete's genes. He's wearing a simple shirt and trousers and shoes that are little more than slippers. He's still very much a young man, barely fifty. People who meet him tend to label him as being private or aloof, or even shy. But if they learn how he was born and raised up in Yellowknife, up in one of those crazy Neoamerindian Freestates, he becomes an instant creature of mystery. Everyone has heard stories about the Freestates. Everyone has an opinion. Steward's long silences, once judged to be shyness, are now reason for respect. He is a warrior, after all. The various Freestates have been fighting their wars for the last thousand years. Yet no one dies. Not typically. What

brought Steward down to Brulé City? What kind of man can make
that transition? They stare at him, saying nothing, not daring to ask
him anything personal. Suddenly, little noises make them nervous. It's
almost funny, he thinks. Almost. They want to know how these
strange endless wars are fought. They want details. Nothing personal,
but they'll ask Steward the methods of the fights. Pain. It all revolves
around pain, he'll explain. Then he will tell them some good studies
on the subject, their titles and their authors, and sometimes he will tell
them the exact catalog codes so they don't have to wade through
World-Net. Most don't bother. Most don't care enough. Pain is an
ample answer. The rest of it—honor and trust and relentless bravery—is likely beyond their reach.

He sighs and goes back to studying the mystery girl.

She isn't watching anyone anymore. She's got her eye on the doorway and both hands around her glass, and she drinks and licks away
the thin mustaches as they form. Steward pulls a weathered round box
out of his shirt pocket and opens it and finds a long ornate needle
laying between the folds of a soft cloth. He twirls the needle in one
hand and eases the pointed tip into the meat between two fingers, into
a tender region, then twists the needle until the pain is white-hot and
coming up his arm. Inside himself, in a secret place, he makes a hollow
and fills the hollow with the pain. And now he feels none of it. He puts
the needle back into its box and the box back into the pocket and finds
that his head is absolutely clear and that his senses are heightened to
their limits.

It's a Yellowknife trick, channeling the pain.

It's funny. The mystery girl and Yellowknife seem joined somehow.
He has to consider things for a minute before he remembers a certain
girl with the same blonde hair and those big eyes. Sure. Not nearly
as pretty, but the same kind of looks. Steward remembers the circumstances. He had been out on a boy's patrol. He and his Shadow, Chaz,
had separated in a woodland not far from the main compound. He had
gone into a glade like a real warrior, sober and alert, and then all at
once he had stumbled onto the girl. She was several years his elder.
She had been watching him and hiding. He was embarrassed not to
have seen her sooner, but remembered her name and said it several
times. She confessed to having noticed him in the past, smiling in a
funny way; they were talking for a little while before Steward thought
of his duties. By then it was too late. The spell was broken. He was
no longer a warrior, young or not, and something else had begun to

take shape while they sat talking in the long grass. It was cool that day. But when they were naked and pressed together both of them were sweating hard; and when Chaz came looking for him, walking past him, Steward put a hand over the older girl's mouth and said nothing and waited before continuing with the deed. It's all right, he had told himself. I'll feel guilty about everything later and that will make it all right.

But of course it hadn't. It never does.

And now, thinking about the Yellowknife girl while he watches this girl, he feels the old guilty ache as if he's let himself down, and Yellowknife, and his poor, poor Shadow. Sweet Chaz.

Now the girl isn't staring at anyone or anything. She seems halfway lost, her big eyes round and glassy and one hand playing with the empty glass while the other one lies on her white purse. Steward starts to use his senses now, focusing on her until there is nothing else but her in his mind. Her scent is thick in the air. He has never experienced that exact scent, and yet it seems familiar. It has a certain power. A real punch. Those big eyes blink and he thinks about them and everything else and something goes *click* in his head. She can't be, he thinks. Is that what the barmaid saw? he thinks. So he breathes and blinks and turns his attention to the back of the bar, to all the whores sitting around the big chess set and the barmaid talking to them, telling them something about flowers. "Flowers," she says, and for an instant Steward doesn't make the connection. He can't help but think about blossoms. Roses and carnations and so on. Then he remembers the word's other meaning. Twenty-five years in Brulé City and never once has he seen her likes. Not before tonight. Where's she from? he wonders. New Brasilia? The Jarvis Seamount? Quito? If he had to guess he would guess Quito. That's where you find most of the Flowers. Damn! he thinks. What's a Flower doing way up here anyway?

Is she absolutely insane?

Or what?

◆ ◆ ◆

She had a name when she was alive, and then another name when she turned into a Ghost and was only partially alive. But then the Magician gave her this body and a Flower's life, plus a third name. Miss Luscious Chiffon. And she's loyal to the new name as if she's had it all of her life, the past hidden away by the Magician's tricks and her glad for that as well.

It's a functional Flower name, sensible for commercial reasons. Miss Luscious Chiffon. She has fine, butter-colored hair flowing down on her wide shoulders, and a face and figure that are even better than the dress and gloom allow. But she's glad for the gloom, of course. Maybe they know what she is and maybe they don't, and won't, but if the place was bright and they saw her baby's skin and her feral blue eyes a few of them would be sure to point and say, "There goes a Flower. Would you look?" and that would make it all the tougher. If it was possible to be tougher at this point.

She came in here to escape for a few minutes.

She sits without moving, thinking about everything at once and trying to collect herself in the process. They'll be looking for her soon. She can be sure of that much. And if the boy didn't show at the rendezvous point, maybe he isn't going to make it at all. She feels angry and betrayed. Now she has to escape on her own. But how? A Flower would be noticed in a tubetrain. Floaters can be traced in a dozen different ways. The Quito boy was bringing several people with him, plus a fast unregistered floater, and they might have gotten out undetected. *Might.* But where was he? I did my part, she tells herself. I did everything expected of me, and more, and he wasn't waiting like he promised and I watched and that damned rain came over, me hiding in that shelter beside the pad, and I thought he must have wanted the storm for cover, sure, only no one came even still. So it's a mess, she thinks. Everything is a mess. It's gone sour and now I just need to sit and think. I've got to get it straight in my head somehow.

Dirk and Minus are probably back at the apartment now.

Dirk is screaming. Minus is sniffing for clues. They'll be chasing me once they get their bearings, and they can have me cornered in no time. If I let them, she thinks. I can't let them!

God!

Sweet sphincters of God, what a mess!

And now, to make matters worse, the gloom isn't helping like she had hoped. The barmaid in the back is talking to the whores, and the whores are starting to talk among themselves. She hears someone say "Flower," and her thigh starts to ache. The ache is like a warning. No one points, but the patrons are looking at her in a different way now, their smoke-washed faces showing curiosity and lust and a trace of anger too. A real resentment. Brulé City is a conservative town. It's got restrictions on things that are ordinary in Quito. "People are always people," its people might say. "Furred or finned or covered with machinery, they are still people."

Some of the men show glancing interest in Miss Luscious Chiffon.

She has a palpable urge to seduce one of them and coax him into taking her home. She needs a sanctuary for the night. She imagines Minus out in the shadows, crafty and armed, and she tells herself that she needs an ally. But who would be best? There are ways to find out. After all, she is a Flower and it has its advantages. She looks around the room, at the men and the women too, trying to judge their relative worth. Smile, she tells herself. Smell enticing. Maybe a hero will come out of the crowd. Sure, she thinks. The Magician gave you these gifts. Use them. Turn this mess around somehow.

No one is talking anymore.

The whores have quit their game. She can see them looking at her while they sit around the chessboard, the playing pieces silent on their pedestals and the empty pedestals set in two ragged lines. The barmaid is standing beside a pretty-faced male whore. He's wearing flashy clothes and the cock-on-the-trot posture of a proud stallion. He says something to the others. Then he stands and starts to walk in Chiffon's direction, a little bit of a swagger showing, and he gives her a sly smile before he sits at her table and stares at her face and the smile turns into a challenging frown. He has no true hair on his head. The glass skullcap is a local fashion, or a legal requirement, its colors and patterns changing while he sits facing her. The whore's face is lit by the skullcap and the soft moonlight. The patterns within it are curling and complex and absolutely senseless.

She does nothing and says nothing.

He asks, "Why don't you get up and leave?"

She takes a long breath and starts to lift her glass, forgetting it's empty, and then she sets if down again and unconsciously licks her clean upper lip.

"I'll tell you why you won't get up and leave," he says, one fist knocking at the tabletop. "You know why?" His voice is a little drunken and careless. He looks older than she would have guessed at first, a fine net of wrinkles radiating out from his eyes. She has to wonder how many years he has been holding court in drab little places like this place. Probably for more than a century. Sure. "Do you know why you won't?" he asks.

She says, "Tell me."

"I won't let you leave."

"And why not?" she says with her voice cool and level.

"Because you'd go somewhere else and if you weren't stealing our business here, you'd likely steal business from our friends." He waves at the other whores, one or two of them nodding in response. "So you see, we're not letting you go, darling."

Inside her snow-white purse, hidden, is a small pistol carrying a full charge. She stole that from Dirk, too.

He says, "A shit-fed Flower."

She can feel the gun inside her purse and wonders what kinds of noise that would make around Brulé. A Flower pokes holes in some working people, killing several, and the police are hunting night and day to find her. Lord, she tells herself, that's not what she needs. Things just keep getting worse and worse.

"I'm sitting with a shit-fed Flower."

"Please just let me go." She works to make her voice sound helpless and confused, a little, and she says, "I'm not here to steal anyone's business."

"Then why?"

"To meet my owner. I'm supposed to meet him soon," and she shrugs. "But fine. I'll go."

The whore is profoundly disgusted. He snorts and spreads both hands on the tabletop and presses downward. "What would you cost someone?" he asks. "No, no. Don't think of standing. Just sit and tell me what you'd cost."

For an instant she has a foolish thought about charming him. She tries a weak, beguiling smile. The smallest expressions on Flowers are enticing. A good Flower's smile can melt the sternest countenance, and she shows her small perfect teeth and makes a delicate purring sound designed to steal away tensions and a person's will.

"Don't fuck with me, precious."

She lets the smile melt away, feigning injury, and she squeezes the purse and decides where she will shoot him.

"So maybe you're special. Maybe we're nothing." He nods toward the back of the bar, saying, "We were talking between ourselves and decided that maybe someone's trying to press the rules, putting something special into the marketplace, and maybe they won't stop pressing until we stop them. Do you see what I'm telling you?"

She waits.

The whore's face shows blood. He breathes through his teeth and begins to stand, glancing over a shoulder and gesturing. "I bet you're worth a fortune. Huh? We're talking about what? Artificial genetics, sure. A brain that learns quick. Tutors and taxes up the butt and the etceteras. Well," he says, "too fucking bad."

She's gotten up out of her chair. Her legs are telling her not to try outrunning him. She can't. And the cut on her thigh is all flames and razors.

The whore's coming around the table. "An artificial cunt," he says. "Brulé is clean and simple, and people are people. You see?" She has a hand inside her purse, feeling its natural warmth and the cool butt of the gun. He is reaching towards her without hurrying, without concern, unaware of the gun's barrel as it noses out at his crotch. Then a stranger's hand takes the whore by a shoulder and turns him. The whore mutters, "What—?" He is completely turned. He says, "Who the fuck—?" and starts to wrestle with the strange sudden man, grunting and growing madder by the moment.

She sees a sharp dark face and the leggy body keeping the whore at arm's length. The pretty-boy muscles look marvelous but they can't connect. The whore swings and the tall man lets him take his swings, ducking them without really working. Then the whore rushes him and the tall man grabs a wrist and turns him and jerks the arm up and twists and puts the whore's face to the floor, delivering pain so fast that there's only a muttered cry before the body goes limp. The glass skullcap, sensing injury, starts to flash red. The bar is filled with blood-faced whores who come at them, and the tall man stands over the unconscious whore and looks at Chiffon, saying, "Can you run like the wind?"

She shakes her head, stepping away from the table and taking her hand out of her purse.

"Okay," he says. "Relax." The other whores are furious but uncertain, their mouths open and fists clenched. They glance at one another, trying to decide on what to do and how, and the tall man looks at them and says, "How are you going to make livings when you're broken? Huh?"

The whores form a half-circle. One of them throws a chess piece, and it comes at them spinning, hitting the bar and screaming louder than the pawns. Chiffon sees the smashed piece laying on the floor, leaking a sweet alcoholic sap. The big male whores are coming at them, encouraging themselves with glances and harsh words. Chiffon gets behind the tall man, thinking of the gun again, then the whores rush them, keeping low, and the man puts his foot into their faces and throats and cuts several of them down. But others get close, shouting. They swing and connect, and they curse and move and swing again, and the tall man works hard on their faces. He uses closed fists and crisp swings. She hears the skulls *pop* and each of them goes down with a strange sudden grace, then he puts one of his big hands to Chiffon's neck and squeezes gently, the grip light and dry.

"Come on," he says. "Walk slow and easy."

The whores are melting away. Skullcaps are throbbing with the bright red light, coloring the smoke and washing out the old-fashioned holos. The two of them leave the bar, walking, no one daring to give chase, and they find themselves in a strip of parkland sandwiched between tall buildings. There are trees around them and streams threading their way through the darkness, and the moon throws speckled beams down through gaps in the canopy. She can smell the rain drying. She turns and turns. A couple Morningers are in the distance, huge and dark and shiny black. They mean nothing. They work in the mantle mines and they mean nothing, and no, she can't see a willowy man or a rainbow-colored man. No Dirk. No Minus. And the boy is still nowhere. She doesn't know where to look, or how, or even if she should.

"You know, you shouldn't go into a place like that again. Not in this town." The tall man sounds like an adult instructing a child not to trust spiders. It's a common voice for people who have never been in the company of a Flower. "It's not particularly safe."

She thanks him, smiling in a large way and telling him that he saved her life. No doubts. "I was stupid and I know it. But lucky," she says. The man's face is stained by the moon, and he seems a little angry even when he sounds patient and knowing. His eyes are narrowed and his breathing is deep and slow, and he regards this odd Flower while the two of them walk together. "Anyway," she says, "let me pay you for your trouble. I should."

They're walking beside a little stream, half-exposed.

"Anything of mine is yours," she says. It is one of the greatest lies ever told, she imagines. And again her thigh begins to ache.

He says nothing.

She says her full name.

He says, "Indeed?" He repeats, "Miss Luscious Chiffon," and seems to halfway laugh.

"You're a brave man," she swears, wondering why he did it. Maybe it was his glands making him do it, except he doesn't seem the kind to be won so easily. "What's your name? What do I call you, Brave Man?"

He is wondering what to do. She reads it in his face.

"I can pay you. I have a little money, plus these pearls." She strokes her necklace and says, "Real ones. Garden made."

He says, "Steward," with a simple flat voice.

"Steward?" She repeats it several times, working for that perfect cadence and color. "Why don't you take me home, Steward? I'd let you. I'd like you to, or something." She touches the back of an arm and opens ducts in her fingertips, extruding a crazy mix of pheromones and assorted subtle potions. They're absorbed through the skin and make the humid hot air intoxicating. "Please," she says. "Please?"

"Who's to miss you?" he asks.

"Pardon?"

"You mentioned an owner. Before." He pauses. "Were you waiting for your owner?"

"No."

"Then who?"

"No one." She wonders what she can say and succeed with now. "I'm not waiting for anyone," she tells him.

He blinks. His face is tough to read. He's not going to be easy to win, and that's good. Difficult is best. Difficult means he is a man accustomed to being strong, in charge, full of conviction and security with everything in his life. Very good. If she handles everything right, making him her ally, then he won't even realize what has happened. Like she did with Dirk. It will be the first time in his tough-minded life—

"All right," he says. "Payment. It was a tough situation. I got you out. I think . . . oh, five hundred is cheap. Okay?" He stares straight at her eyes and gives a little shrug, pretending not to notice the cocktails running through his bloodstream. "Is that fine?"

"I'll give you these," she says, one hand touching the Garden pearls, and her leg feeling awful. No more painkiller, she thinks. She thinks about the depth of that cut, bandaged and treated with clotting foams, and it's amazing to think what she is carrying inside herself. She wants to shiver. She wants to cry out for joy, telling the world. "Is that enough?" she asks.

"Too much," he answers. "One pearl and I'll give you change. Okay?"

An honest man. She coos and agrees to the terms.

"So where's your owner?" he persists.

"It's complicated." Putting on a needing face, she works with the moonlight and sounds strained and tired, all of those qualities true, and she tells him, "I'd love to go with you, Steward. For tonight. If I could." She says, "I can be very good with you."

He says nothing, tempted by the proposition.

"The two of us and such pleasure," she promises. She smiles brightly and bravely and touches him once again.

Steward resists. They walk and he shakes free of her hands once, then again, and finally he pauses and says, "There's a floater pad ahead. I'm going home and I guess I can't stop you from following me." He smiles, his face and all of his body suddenly shy.

She has won. She knows she has won, and she follows. They go up the pad's stairs and she thinks again of the Quito boy, wondering if he is waiting here for her. There might have been a mistake. Several Terran women come down past them and giggle among themselves and then pause to watch Chiffon, simply curious. The boy isn't waiting here, either. She knew he wouldn't be waiting, she tells herself, and she looks into the shadows for anyone odd or out-of-place. It's critical not to be followed. She has to get away without complications . . . if only to the other side of Brulé. They're alone on the pad, its glass surface rough and rubbery and damp from the hard rain, and a little wind comes up and they turn their backs to it and she asks Steward what it is that he does for a living. He doesn't seem like the sort of person who lives on investments.

"I do this," he volunteers.

"What?"

"Troubleshoot," he says with that matter-of-fact voice.

She asks, "What? Are you some kind of professional . . . what?"

He says nothing.

"A professional hero? Is that it?"

He admits, "I've got some skills," and in the fashion of all good heroes, he gives a humble shrug and says no more.

A floater is descending.

He looks up at it and she looks at him, wondering what he could mean to her, her hero, and wouldn't it be wonderful if everything worked out for the best? It might. It just might, she thinks. And while her leg aches to the bone, and while they stand together and wait, she tells herself that this might be her chance to find something sweet and lasting. That's all she's ever wanted. At least during this lifetime, she thinks.

◆ ◆ ◆

The Old Quarter is directly below—an assemblage of archaic buildings and the crosshatched patterns of old streets. The Earth is famous for its relics and the tangible sense of history, and Brulé City does what it can to preserve what it can with tax breaks and rent supports. Nonetheless, the Old Quarter tenants are mostly low-profit or low-profile businesses like the smoky bars and brothels, plus some cheap hotels and tiny secondhand shops. Most of its permanent residents are entities like the AIs and Ghosts—things that appreciate cheap, stable housing and don't particularly care about their surroundings.

AIs live everywhere, in truth. They are the miniscule descendants of old-fashioned computers, sophisticated and tirelessly quick. They exist within World-Net and System-Net. They *are* the various Nets, in truth, each of them linked with every other AI and all of them serving mankind in an endless array of ways. Like now, thinks Steward. This particular floater is piloted by an AI. He has entered into a contract with it—service in exchange for a small fee—and it will do its job efficiently and gladly, no doubts in its mind as to who is servant and who rules the System. Me, thinks Steward. And he laughs without sound.

Ghosts are tied into World-Net and depend on it utterly. They are people whose bodies have died for whatever reason, but their minds have persisted as so many hard crystal chips and encoded patterns and memories and maybe the human soul, too. It's their humanness that stirs controversy. Some people consider them odd AIs, while others pretend they are nothing more than complex tombstones meant to mimic dead souls. Certainly they aren't alive, whatever their state. At least most flesh-on-blood people believe they're something else. The Ghosts below—and Steward knows more than a few by name—depend upon World-Net. They employ banks of AIs that work hard to build them lifelike sensations, creating a vague kind of reality out of nothingness, and normally Steward will look down on the buildings and feel sorry for them. He does. Alive or not, Ghosts are smart enough to know what they're missing. All the AIs in all of World-Net couldn't produce a true Brulé City. It's too complicated and crazy and fickle and beautiful for mere machines to generate. It is.

Tonight, however, he doesn't feel so sorry for them.

He halfway wishes he could be Ghost so he wouldn't have to breathe every so often, sucking in the heavy scent of the Flower beside him. He feels his body tingling and his glands being teased, and some voice deep inside him warns him, reciting just some of the capacities attributed to Flowers.

Steward mistrusts pleasure.

Pain he knows. Torture and suffering he can manage in a host of ways, but he isn't even sure how to stay wary with Miss Chiffon. Their little floater is climbing up into traffic and heading east, and she is staring at all of Brulé City, saying nothing, Steward breathing and watching her ample body and the delicate face, thinking back to Yellowknife again. When he was growing up, day after day, the Elders spoke of suffering and survival. They swore pain wasn't just their means of waging war, it was a great instructive force too, and to prove the sanctity of their philosophy they stuck talons into Steward's chest and burned his toes and fingers with hot metal brands. Everyone underwent the same training, male or female. It was an essential part of their education. Pain can be channeled and focused and used for a variety of tasks, from defeating enemies to bolstering your own resolve. It was a question of understanding its usage, the Elders maintained. With practice and more practice a person won skills and the iron-hard discipline required.

Chiffon? he thinks. What a preposterous name!

A Flower's name, sure. Right-sounding in Quito, sure, but not in little Brulé.

The Old Quarter has dropped behind now. The rest of the city is dark and low by comparison, built from rounded living shapes looking smooth under the moon. There are no streets, just paths intended for walking and bikes. Floaters move commuters when feet and pedals are unwilling. And underground, at several spots, stations exist where the tubetrains pause, the tubes empty of air so the trains can run at supersonic speeds—linking Brulé to the populated lands in the south.

The city began as a dirt-and-wood hamlet where farmers came to sell crops and trade gossip. That was a couple thousand years ago, or more, and Brulé was just as remote as it is today. In a relative sense. The seaports were the hubs of the world in those times. Times change. Now the hubs are built around the skyhooks—towers of hyperfiber rising to the lucrative geosynchronous orbits—and some ninety-plus percent of the Earth's population is shoulder to shoulder on the equator. Quito and Jarvis and Singapore are some of the hubs. New York and Havana and Cairo are drowned and eroding under the deep warm sea. A billion people live in the smallest hub city. Industry and commerce are centered some forty thousand kilometers over their heads. Brulé City, by comparison, is a baby with two million citizens. Plus the Ghosts, of course. And the ever-present AIs.

Yellowknife, now and always, has a few thousand citizens.

No Ghosts. No World-Net links. And the AIs are minimal and quite simple in their nature.

Steward thinks how he used to know every Yellowknife face, if not every name, and how it felt to be in a crowded room and know some fact about everyone. A hamlet like Yellowknife is built from people. Brulé is built from strangers leavened with people, a few, and sometimes it is all he can do to be out in public and not feel the strangers pressing in on him. Even now. Even after spending half his life in this place, trying hard to purge himself of these alien feelings. This sense of not belonging. Like a Flower might feel, he thinks, and he laughs to himself.

The floater is descending now. Chiffon makes a sound and turns to him with her hands folded around the living white purse in her lap, her breath fragrant and cool and nervous-quick. Her dress is clinging. He hadn't noticed it before. He can see dark nipples muscling their way up through the fabric, as broad and long as the tips of his little fingers, and she makes the sound again and looks up through the round canopy, confessing, "We don't have so many in Quito."

"So many?"

"Stars," she says, looking at him and smiling again.

"No?" He glances at the moon, emerald green and cloaked in a deep newborn atmosphere that's sheathed under a monomolecular cocoon, the moon's water and soil manufactured from Belt materials and assorted comets. Below the full moon, stretching in a neat glittering arc from horizon to horizon, are an assortment of factories and fusion plants interwoven with hyperfiber tubes. The skyhooks themselves are slender and dark and rise up out of Quito and New Brasilia to link with them. Spinning wheels and cylinders are in even higher orbits, and beyond the moon, scattered through local space, are the Apollo asteroids and several thousand captured comets, all of them settled, all of them wet and warm and dressed up in their transparent coats so nothing boils or drifts away.

"You're from Quito," he remarks.

She nods and shoots him one of her patented smiles.

Kross—once called Mercury—has set. Morning—once called Venus—is down too. Cradle—still Mars to the astrologically inclined—may be up but it's too dull and dark to show. Jupiter is and has always been Jupiter, King of the Gods. It's high and bright and attended by its various bright terraformed moons. Steward wonders about Saturn. Probably hiding somewhere. He wonders what Flowers know about the System's geography, deciding they're probably not ignorant. Somewhere he has heard that their nervous systems are designed to be programmed with a minimum of fuss, and their AI tutors work them while they're still inside their artificial wombs. Geography makes sense, he thinks. Sure. A Flower needs to be able to chat with customers, filling the quiet gaps, and there must be a lot of varied travelers coming through Quito. From everywhere, he thinks. Probably homesick, too.

Steward doesn't feel like a customer.

He remembers Chiffon telling the whore that she was waiting for her owner, lying then or lying later to him. Or maybe lying both times. He recalls someone saying that Flowers, like all expert lovers, lie easily and well. There's no better proof of intelligence, he reasons. He tells himself to be careful, don't treat her like some simpleminded child. And always be careful, don't take every word as the absolute truth.

He glances to the north and sees a lumpy chain of clouds moving away from Brulé, rainboys herding them. Sometimes the clouds fill with lightning. They turn pinkish and orange and a hard sharp blue at their cores, looking like strange living creatures for those moments. The rainboys themselves are shaped like enormous teardrops, perfect as that sounds, and they twist and dart around the clouds. This is the storm that hit earlier. The wind is helping it north, but the rainboys use lassos of plasma to adjust the direction and speed—dispensing rain to whichever Freestate or City-State or Farmstead pays for the privilege.

The cool seamless voice of the pilot announces, "We are landing."

Steward's home is inside a long shaggy building, low and rounded and flanked by identical buildings. Everywhere are the same square floater pads on the roofs and the same tiny swimming pools full of green moonlight. Bushes and trees and vines grow half-wild, tangled and mysterious, and most of the visible windows are darkened. The scene doesn't require people, or invite them. It's all a poor neighborhood likely never to improve again.

A woman—a *human* woman—would insult what she saw if she knew better, or she would say nothing at all, and either way Steward would feel an obligation to explain or apologize. But Flowers are set apart from human values. Or so the advertisements on World-Net claim. They give love and companionship without making judgments . . . another reason why they're so popular wherever the laws allow them.

Not in Brulé, he thinks. So what is she doing here?

And the floater sets down, the AI thanking Steward for his patronage. He glances at the tab and pays, then he uses a special green-black card and code number to blank the AI's memory of this trip and transaction. It's his custom. No one can trace him home now. The glass canopy opens and the air turns summer-hot and damp. They climb out and Steward grips Chiffon's arm, and the floater crackles and lifts. Then they walk down a staircase, and the hallway senses them, teasing awake the lights in the ceiling. The hallway is endless and curling to afford the illusion of privacy. Its walls are white and scuffed and dead in spots. The carpeting is dead down the middle, killed by feet. Chiffon is alert. Tense. He glances at her eyes, big and impossibly blue and darting, and he notices how the dress clings to her body like a white, white layer of skin. "This way," he offers. "Here." He finds himself squeezing the arm, feeling an unexpected firmness laid over her delicate bones.

His door recognizes him. It says, "Steward—"

"—with a friend," and the big mag-locks, massive enough to serve a vault, cut their power and release. It's a very secure home. *Very.* "Make yourself comfortable," he says.

"I am." Her tone implies there is no other state besides comfort. "I'm just fine, Steward. Thank you."

He feels giddy. He came here telling himself that he would leave and do some work for himself, only here he stands, numbed, thinking about turning on a light or doing some small host-type thing. Why would she ever get herself into this mess? he wonders. Alone and surviving on a stranger's kindness. A Flower knows no pain. It's a sobering thought. The typical Flower is raised in a special brothel where candles burn scented wax and the foods are rich and sweet and there is no suffering. He thinks of the whores and their poor chessmen. He doesn't agree with the whores, not in the least, but his Yellowknife sensibilities tell him that a Flower's life is no way to acquire an education. He has half an urge to lift her and shake her hard. He wants to show her the honest shape of the world.

She says, "Steward?" and he turns.

Miss Luscious Chiffon is kneeling on the floor, on the healthy living carpet, with the hem of her dress in both hands and a knowing, wide smile beaming up at him. She has such a pretty face and big eyes, her hands lifting the dress and the fabric crinkling and sparkling. That's why it's clinging, he thinks. There's a potent static charge being generated. Not for the last time, he remembers the girl in Yellowknife and the smell of the crushed green vegetation mixing with the smell of her loins, and the big eyes watching him then and waiting, trusting in him. He blinks and breathes deeply, once and again, aware of his heart beating too high in his chest. He has been uncontrollably aroused for nearly half an hour. His penis hurts and the dress is off and he stares at the swollen nipples, like plums, and the wide hips and a Flower's magnificent clitoris, fan-shaped and glistening and huge. Chiffon is folding the dress and watching him. She seems so pretty, yet there is something hard beneath the pretty features. There's a toughness that he can't quite explain. And there! What is that? He sees a bandage on the inside of her leg, and the white crusted clotting foam, and he wonders what has happened and feels such an enormous ache for her. Something is going on. He knows it now, and he wonders what is happening, everything so crazy and his heart filling his chest and her dropping the folded dress to the floor and pressing it down with one hand, a few staticy sparks showing inside the white fabric. He thinks of lightning inside distant clouds. He remembers something he once read about ordinary static charges being brighter and hotter than the surface of the sun—for a moment, in a miniscule space—and he starts to kneel and then reaches for something too cool to burn. That's how he thinks of it. It's silly, but that's how he thinks.

Garden is a gemstone. I love it. It is peaceful and warm, blessed with
skies like few others, deep and blue like its seas, and jade green
where the land drifts in the gentle currents. Life and life and more
life. Beautiful life. *Inspired* life. But what makes it truly precious to
all of humanity is its people and their unique foundation . . . The
Prophet Adam's descendants are good and kind and full of love. The
typical Gardener knows the value of leisure, of noncompetitive fun,
his or her tailored genes designed to accent those qualities that lie
dormant and unrecognized in so many of us, sadly . . . I admire these
people. I spent several weeks with them, sharing their feasts and
their boundless love, and when I left them I cried and they cried and
I went away with my self empty of jealousy and aggression and all
those terrible emotions that poison the soul. And I found myself
more in touch with the worlds around me. More perceptive. More
understanding of those things that seemed at odds with me and my
world . . .

*—excerpt from a traveler's
notebook, available through
System-Net*

TOBY—the future despot—wakes up feeling crushed by the stale
air of the little room. So he stands and opens the window and lies
down again, drifting away to the chattering sounds of monkeys. He
starts to dream. He dreams about walking on the island where he was
a child. He sees himself cloaked in a strange black uniform, eerily
familiar, a black sack drawn over his face, the fabric made of some
slick and pliable hyperfiber. He walks down a trail that twists around
a stand of whitesmear palms, and Toby's family is waiting in the glade
beyond. He sees his father and his mother, plus his assorted cousins
and such. The family looks at him and wonders about his identity,
pointing and growing a little scared.

But it's me! he says. Me!

They don't recognize his voice. They begin to cower in his presence.

I'm Toby! he swears. Toby! Don't you know me?

Apparently not. His father comes forward—an old man, gray and a bit feeble—and says: *What's your name?*

Toby! Toby! Toby!

But no, his father doesn't believe him. With a strange sharp voice he repeats himself: *What's your name?*

I'm your son, Toby! TOBY!

Come on! Wake up and tell me your name!

Toby opens his eyes and sits up in bed, sweating, his head swimming and his stomach full of nothing. A voice from the window asks, "What's your name?" Toby looks. A large black bird is perched on the ledge just outside the window, its head tilted and one black eye giving a curious stare. "Hey!" it snaps. "What's your name?"

Toby says, "Shoo!"

"Mr. Shoo!" says the bird. "I have a message for you, Mr. Shoo." It pauses, the head rolling from side to side, and then it tells him, "Eat my green donkey dick."

Toby throws his pillow at the window. The bird waits calmly and watches the pillow hit the rigid screen and fall away. It's some kind of gene-tampered bird, he thinks. *Someone* has given it a mouth.

"Suck my saggy tits, Mr. Shoo!"

Toby rushes the window, shouting, and the bird wheels and flies away with a crowlike squawk and bearing. Toby pauses and tries to listen past the chattering monkeys. He wonders who did it. Vandals might have done it, he hopes, and just ignores it. He shuts the window and tells himself that it must be vandals, random and perverted, because it has been a long time since *he* has done anything. Weeks, or maybe months. Or does it just seem that long?

Toby begins to pace.

Wiping his sleepy face with both webbed hands, he arches his back and cracks his joints and picks at his nose while he speculates.

What if it is *him?*

What then?

It makes him shiver just to think it might be so.

◆ ◆ ◆

The apartment is cramped and miserable for anyone born on watery, warm Garden. It's two rooms and a bath, plus a short empty balcony. The bedroom has a single window, facing north, and a bed and hideaway closets. The yard below seems constricted. Underneath the balcony is a round swimming pool with a narrow soft-coral deck and a fringe of half-wild fruiting bushes. The fruits are ripe. Birds and monkeys are waging a noisy war over the prizes. Toby stands at the window and looks across the yard, feeling typically sad about his sad life. Each building is a gene-tailored tree. The walls and floors and roofs are indifferent to sunlight but still vegetable in nature. They feed on electrical currents carried through a fine mesh of buried wires. The gene-tailoring allows them to use energy from Brulé's own power net, their wood fixing carbon dioxide into long-chain carbohydrates. Miniscule pipes are buried alongside the wire mesh, assuring a kind of vascular system. Workmen had set up the wires and pipes ages ago, laying out the pattern of curved rooms and curling hallways, leaving gaps for the doorways and sewage lines and grocery lines and the World-Net linkups.

All the essentials.

The buildings don't grow anymore. The living wood is fed enough to maintain itself, no more. Broadest at their base and flat where the floaters perch, they are covered with a thick, durable bark, rough and dark, and layers of infesting vines and epiphytes and an assortment of odd parasites. Where sunlight is strongest, the outer walls resemble steep, jungled hillsides. Birds nest and rats nest and all sorts of peculiar invented creatures hide in the cracks and little holes. Just by living here, by sheer osmosis, Toby has gotten to know the local fauna. He recognizes species and sometimes individuals and wonders what they would say on Garden if they heard him tell how nature is corrupted on the corrupted old Earth.

He picks up a pair of shorts and steps into them.

His arms ache and his right knee complains as he walks into the bathroom to enjoy a good long piss.

Later, coming into the front room, Toby thinks of eating. He sits and leans back in one chair and looks at the empty ceiling, no need to hurry. No place to go. Most of the wall and ceiling is covered with panels of acoustically and optically active proteins. The panels are linked to AIs rooted in the Old Quarter, and those AIs are themselves part of World-Net. There is nothing resembling World-Net on Garden. There are no million channels involving drama and sports and arts and fantasy, not to mention the millions of subsidiary channels linking with libraries and data pools and scholarly AIs using their rapid computer brains to manage and manipulate every small thing.

Through World-Net, Toby can call any of his fifty billion immediate neighbors or arrange delayed conversations with any of the two trillion people scattered throughout the System. Or, should he wish, he can summon any painting or photograph, tri-dee or not. The artistic accomplishments of every human and AI and Ghost are permanently recorded. He can even do his own work and put it into the common memory, his limits set only by his will and talent and patience.

World-Net confuses Toby and oftentimes bores him, and there's very little that he does or feels comfortable with doing.

There's one interactive fantasy, yes, and there are certain links to libraries and ancient records . . . but not much else. Garden and its people don't have this kind of equipment. They don't need it and the Prophet forbids its needless use. So Toby won't invest the time or energy to master the potentials. He won't let the Earth touch him any more than he can help, his presence here something forced on him. Something entirely against his will.

The panels are a neutral bottomless white. In the front room, at times, the whiteness threatens to swallow the two small chairs and the scattered dishes and clothes. Toby presses buttons on his little remote control—a native Terran would have a larger version of the same tool—and now the entire west-facing wall dissolves into a flat image nearly two thousand years old. An ancient nuclear rocket, massive and filthy, stands on a concrete plain. A voice is talking in a dead language, and Toby decides against an AI-supplied translation. He has watched the documentary many times, and he certainly knows the subject better than its original makers. What interests him are the old videotapes from which it was drawn, authentic scenes and the spirit of the times captured. A pioneering spirit. The documentary begins with the launch of the rocket, fire and poisoned smoke and a ripping roar that he feels in his bones, and he looks at his little prison cell and shakes his head and stands and walks into the kitchen-corner. He wishes for the rocket's kind of freedom. He envies its power and primitiveness, muttering to himself, "If only I could get loose." Saying, "Gabbro, did you do it? The bird? The wicked black bird?"

He works his sour-tasting mouth and punches up an inventory, the selections stored in a communal set of freezers and bug-free closets somewhere underground. He chooses and punches and waits, listening to the ridiculous rattle of old machinery struggling to serve him breakfast. Something moves above him. He sees a large steel-colored bug clinging to the wall, a white skull-and-crossbones on its carapace.

It's supposed to be a gene-tailored cockroach, predatory and certain doom to the pests that come into its realm. The management introduced them last month. Toby's Garden training and Garden temperament make him suspicious. The Earth is home to countless species. More are born every minute, each to serve aesthetic or economic roles for their makers. No reason to the process. No vision. None of what the Prophet in His wisdom saw for Garden, surely. Standing on his toes and extending, Toby gives the bug a hard swat and leaves the wall stained.

His breakfast is meant to mimic a Garden meal. The juice tastes like whitesmear palm milk and the biscuits are dough around a soft boneless fish. AIs are the cooks. He has no trust in their work. What if the wrong roaches have gotten into the kitchen? What if there are diseases freshly tailored by some ill mind? It makes no sense to believe in the boxes of circuits. His fifty billion neighbors are fools. And he vents his frustrations by sipping on the juice, white and thick and warm, then pronouncing, "Too tart," while punching the AUDIO ON button.

The AIs hear him.

Next time, sure as sure can be, he'll say, "Not tart enough," with the same conviction. Maybe that confuses the AIs. He likes to imagine them confused, sitting pretty in their Old Quarter homes, or wherever. He knows it's unlikely, but he pictures them cursing whenever he makes his requests.

It's too hot again. He opens the glass door out to the balcony, feeling a hot, fresher burst of air curling through the gap. He sits and balances the plate and watches the yard while he eats, the Portuguese voice and ancient space scenes forgotten momentarily. The fish is mostly to his taste. Toby chews without haste, watching a big water rat come shuffling out from the bushes. It's the one with the bobbed tail, fat and old and grizzled. He studies how it bends and the way it drinks with long lazy swallows, the body still capable of a kind of grace. A delicacy. It's a ragged creature, ugly and absolutely wrong. It serves no function, no matter how obscure, and he wonders how the Terrans can let such things persist. It makes no sense to him. None.

The swimming pool is deeper than it is wide, the soft-coral covering the deck and steep sides and the flat bottom. Like the wood of these buildings, the coral are fed by electrical currents. They serve to clean the water and seal the pool and produce food for the fish. He can see fish flicking about in the bright water. Once, he supposes, they were pretty enough . . . the sorts of fish you'd see beside an ocean reef. But now they're junk species, carp and goldfish and tiny sharks and pulsating eels. The management doesn't care. His neighbors are ignorant. Toby shudders and shuts his eyes and sees the clean perfection of Garden—the clear blue sky and sea, the wild white clouds oozing gentle rains, the artificial sun rising and setting every few hours, and those equally brief nights when Father Jove and its attendant moons were brilliant, shining down on the Souls of Eden.

The Earth is a terraformed world, as is Garden.

Sometimes Terrans think otherwise, buoyed up by their pride. It seems to Toby that they have a special smugness when they boast how their home is still the only sure haven for mankind. No other world can support them without trickery—machines and controlled climates and artificial suns—and that's why they can claim a special status among all the worlds.

What a tub of shit, thinks Toby.

Absolutely!

Fifty billion vulgar, ugly people are squeezed into this biosphere. The technologies making it possible are imported. Like rainboys shepherding the hyperdense clouds—that's a Cradle skill. Or the way buildings are made from living woods—a Lunar trick used to snare carbon dioxide, minimizing greenhouse effects. Water and heat are the cruxes of managing the world. In the last couple millenia, or more, fossil fuels and changing ocean chemistries have caused a sharp warming of the climate. The Earth hasn't been so tropical since the Coal Age. People and AIs and Ghosts, plus the Earth-based industries and power plants and such, all serve to produce more heat and to change weather patterns. Concentrating the people at the equator only adds to the problems. Effects have to be spread around the globe, and the result is a world oddly uniform seen from space. The Earth has darkened in recent centuries. The continents are a rich, rich alfalfa-colored green from the mega-cities to the sparsely populated poles. Deserts are gone and icecaps are gone and even communities like Brulé are obscured by, and even include, the rampant vegetation. And the oceans, too, have been transformed. Once bright and blue—an inspiration to the Prophet—they now resemble a thick pea stew, kelp forests supported by foam-metal buoys and hyperfiber nets, and sucking up sunlight to fix more carbon dioxide and feed fish that feed people that lie to themselves, telling themselves that this enormous balancing act is eternal.

He takes great pleasure from wishing the worst.

Stop the rainboys, he thinks, and the deserts return. Clouds blossom and run wild and reflect sunlight away from starving plants. Heat begins to linger at the equator and the poles cool and the difference in airborne temperatures causes storms and chaos and hardship, too. If the fusion plants and geothermal plants were closed, the wood of the buildings would die and dry and become liable to burn. Toby imagines the cities in flames. All this rich land turns to ash and the ash stains the atmosphere and the seas experience massive die-offs, rotting kelp staining the water and fifty billion people facing extinction.

Toby sees it clearly.

He paints it in his head and paints himself safe on Garden, watching the show, and if he were in the mood for compassion he would feel a slight pang of regret for the pain and the waste. But when he's upset and uncertain, like now, he loses all sense of proportion; his bright colorless mind takes a vicarious pleasure from the images, playing them over and over and never becoming bored.

◆ ◆ ◆

According to World-Net, there are one hundred and twenty-six distinct worlds named Garden or some derivative of Garden.

Many are in the Belt. Most of the rest are miniscule comets and tiny worlds manufactured by various means. The largest, most important Garden is a moon of Jupiter. Two thousand years ago it and the entire Jovian system belonged briefly to the old Amazonian Empire. It was then known as Europa. The Empire had claimed it and its neighbors for military reasons as well as for the usual gray justifications set in the realm of prestige. The innermost major moon, Io, was and remains a dense body rich in ore. In those times it was bathed in hard radiation and its metal guts were stirred by tides. The Empire tried mining Io. It used adapted military robots and geothermal power, plus help from European and American partners, tapping the richest veins; for a couple of decades the Empire tried competing with the Belter mines and the Kross strip mines and the ocean-floor operations on the Earth.

It took a beating.

At one point the Europeans and Americans, possessing the clear eyes of all junior partners, pulled out of the venture. The Empire had to find new capital and fresh enthusiasm with other peoples. Toby's documentary was made in those times. He looks at the images and hears the muted Portuguese voice running on and on with a well-coached verve. Io was a harsh landscape of sulfurous volcanoes and molten lakes. At some point, pressed into a desperate brilliance, the volcanoes themselves were adapted to serve as mass launchers. Jupiter's extensive radiation belt and magnetic field were milked for their energy, the technologies new and crude. Toby blinks and studies the typical mining camp squatting on a flat ruddy plain. The voice has quit. Marching music has replaced it. Jupiter, banded and rather subdued, hovers permanently on the horizon. A lone robot passes near the camera, fat tires throwing up fountains of the sulfur dust. Toby sighs. Those were glorious times, he believes. In spite of all the things grating against his Gardener sensibilities, he feels a desire to live in times when people and their nations are in flux. Like when the Prophet was alive, he thinks. When an individual with vision and drive could rise above all the mediocrity . . .

The documentary ends, credits rolling and the nearby robot giving a clumsy salute to the viewers.

Toby touches a button, and the wall turns white.

Several years later, he recalls, the Empire went bankrupt. Prestige has its limits. Its people had limits. Leaders in Old Brasilia faced a wicked set of choices—sell out to the Belters or the Luna City-States, or act tough with one of their competitors and hope no war resulted. The Empire was cowardly, thinks Toby. Instead of toughness, it took money. Cash. The Belters purchased the entire Jovian system just as they had done Mars, ensuring secure borders and deep buffers and resources to rely on in the remote future. But those same Belters, proud like all Belters, boasted about their good sense and their good fortune and made certain that the Amazonians noted their pleasure.

Part of the terms included existing facilities and the supporting deep-space shuttles.

The Earth-based ships were prepared and launched under tight security, and their robot pilots sent them on a curious course. What's this? asked the Belters. What's going on? The fleet passed suspiciously close to Vesta, hub of the Belter Empire. What are you planning? they asked. Nothing! the Empire responded. And indeed, the shuttles went on to Io and braked into orbit just as the Belters had expected. But before their people could arrive and take possession, each shuttle fired its rockets one last time and fell onto the sulfurous moon. Nuclear weapons, archaic and potent, were secured in their holds. Flashes of brilliant dirty light signaled the destruction of mines and power facilities, and great clouds of poisoned dust were kicked loose and flung in every direction.

The Belters screamed. They asked, How could you do such a thing? Where's the sense? You yourselves spent billions on what you've ruined! Why? Why?

Why not? responded the Amazonian Premier. Why not?

They had the money, Toby knows. And they had something better too. Satisfaction. A great and lasting satisfaction stretching from the halls of government to the simplest peasant in the most obscure cornfield. No, he thinks. The Empire should have fought to keep what belonged to it. He has no doubts. But what happened was the next best thing. If he had been that Premier, he would have laughed and laughed while the Belters raged on about the waste and destruction. Let them make something of it now!

◆ ◆ ◆

The Belters were the first people not truly Terran. They were the first colonists to rename worlds to suit their own sensibilities. And they were the first to tailor their own genetics, bending themselves to fit the new environments—low gravity and as crowded as ants' nests—yet never losing that imprecise, undeniable quality of being human.

In the centuries after the Great Vengeance, the Belters increased their population a hundredfold.

It was a time of expansion everywhere. Terraforming became relatively quick and marginally cheap. There was a steady pressure from the Earth and Luna for new worlds to absorb the excess populations. The Belters had no use for gravity and robust worlds. They still shun them whenever possible. Mars and the Jovian system were neither profitable nor habitable to them, so they made the prudent choice of picking their neighbors and selling each place according to the buyer's purse.

Harmless causes and toothless cults were preferred. Mars became Cradle and the Cradlers built a society dedicated to song and dance and similar pursuits. Io became Chu's World—a harsh, half-tamed place famous for high-grade ceramics and its simple, long-lived people. The moon outside Europe, Ganymede, was renamed New Siberia. Terraforming gave it icy seas and wintery continents and tiny populations of ascetic Russians living like monks in the scattered villages. The final major moon, Callisto, was purchased by Terrans who were moved by charity. Its icy crust was melted and its deep, deep sea was colonized by the tailored descendants of whales and porpoises. Its name became Cetacea, appropriately. From space and the other moons it resembles a drop of green water lit from within by ten thousand tiny suns.

Europa was renamed Garden.

The name, like everything else in the world, was revealed to the Prophet Adam in a series of great visions. Toby knows the story better than any other. The Prophet founded the Souls of Eden long before terraforming was possible. Adam was a mystic and a thinker who had seen the future, and with perfect clarity he described the look and feel and smell and sound of His paradise. He told of the new creatures that would live on it and in it, and how the people themselves would look, and by what codes and principles each would live day by day. Few believed in the Prophet in those times. *Not in your lifetime,* thought his charitable skeptics. But there was money collected just the same, and supporters gathering in small numbers, and when the man died without seeing his vision come to fruition as he had reportedly promised it would, soon, soon, and he asked them to hold his body in waiting for the coming day.

The Belters had practically handed the moon to the Souls, rightfully judging them harmless.

It had seemed miraculous, and the Prophet had been proven a true Prophet, and suddenly there was no shortage of money or followers.

Toby can't count the times he has seen the mummified corpse of the Prophet and the first Souls—a few thousand of them in lifesuits, in rows, the icy landscape spreading around them. From every angle he has watched the Prophet dissolved into a scalding acid bath, then poured into the dark cold dead sea below them. And he has studied the history like every native Gardener, understanding the sacrifices made in the next years, the sea melted and the artificial sun built and the warming atmosphere wrapped inside its monomolecular sheath, then the tailored lifeforms added with care, and finally themselves: rebuilding themselves in the new perfect form described by the Prophet, His atoms flowing in all of their veins.

Toby, like any Gardener, is a functional androgyne.

He is tall and slender and thin by Terran standards, his face narrow and handsome and his eyes cool and lightless. He has a high forehead and a delicate sweet chin. All of his face and body is covered with an apricot fuzz that thickens on top of his head and around his groin. His skin is a soft dark color, darkest on his backside. A subcutaneous layer of fat serves to make him buoyant and keep him warm. His feet and hands are webbed, the flesh of the webbing pink and laced with delicate blue veins, and he sits in his chair and picks his nose and listens. Listens. He tips his head and listens very carefully, his breath held.

Downstairs.

He hears them moving now. There are small noises straight below, motions casual and someone talking—on World-Net?—and then the sliding glass door pulls open and words come to him. A conversation. A man and then a woman are speaking in the crisp, measured tones of unhappy people.

"Well?" says Gabbro. "You hear anything?"

"What do you mean?"

"When I was working." In the mines. He works all different hours, out of reach of night and day. "Did it come? Did you hear it?"

"I must have missed it," she says.

"Did you listen?"

"Hey!" she says. "I listened."

"I just asked."

She says nothing. Toby waits and listens, imagining their faces, and she says nothing. Sometimes they fight. He wouldn't mind a fight now, thinking of the black bird.

"What do you want to do?" he asks.

Maybe she shrugs. He imagines a shrug.

"Want to swim?"

"No."

"Wash me off first? The grit?"

"I don't want to."

He says, "Sweetheart," with a hook in his voice.

She says, "What?"

He stays quiet.

"What do you want?" she asks.

"Are you going to get mad?"

"Don't tempt me," she warns. "I just might."

The door is slid shut again. Toby breathes and thinks about all the ugliness around him. He has lived in this poorhouse neighborhood for an entire year. Just like the bobtailed rat, he recognizes the people around him. There's a family of Cradlers, for instance, with their singsong voices and their otterlike fur, muscular builds and nervous manners. And there's a Lunarian next door, very tall and fragile and usually gone for weeks at a time. He doesn't know where. Mostly it's Terrans around here. It makes sense. Many of them are ancient people—two and a half centuries old, or more, with their collapsing faces and the glass eyes and the cheap synthetic organs sighing and wheezing beside their tired bones. On Garden, where the Ideal according to the Prophet is the only Ideal, people live shorter lives without the feeble years and the cursed synthetics. It's a consequence of their genetics and their disdain for unnatural practices. Purity. It means everything to Toby. Purity of the Ideal. He came to the Earth fearing that he would be tempted, attacked and conquered, but it hasn't happened. Not in any meaningful sense. He won't let it happen, he thinks while he sits in his chair. Never. He feels strong and righteous as the sweet-smelling perspiration comes seeping out of his pretty face. Enemies around him, yet he perseveres.

Arching his back, he looks across the yard and spies a neighbor standing at his own glass door, hands on his hips.

The man is a tall, redheaded Terran. He is wearing only shorts, as usual, and his bare chest shows the gruesome scars, like claw marks, and the way all of his skin has been abused by wind and UV light from wild sunshine. The man lives alone. Toby has watched him more than he has any other neighbor. He has seen him watching World-Net or napping on his ragged couch or eating simple meals or doing nothing but sitting or standing by the glass door. He lives like a prisoner, thinks Toby. The two of them seem to share something, and more than once he has wondered how they might meet and talk. Just talk. The only time they were face-to-face was during a night that Toby doesn't care to remember now. There wasn't an opportunity for conversation. He shudders just thinking about the incident.

He breathes once. Again.

And he tilts his head and listens for anything in Gabbro's apartment. As if on cue, the ultimate ugliness begins to move, setting the floor to vibrating. For some reason, Toby thinks of a dream he had this morning and then he loses it. Leaning back in his chair and staring at the white, white ceiling, he halfway falls asleep again. He imagines Garden. The sun rises—a nickel-iron asteroid on which the Souls have fixed an array of lasers, brilliant without cutting at the eyes—and the blue sea and the deep blue skies are warm, slow gentle waves beating against a wide sandy shoreline. The islands were built from honeycombed stone reinforced with hyperfiber and coats of tailored coral, and their green forests are what the Prophet saw in his visions, the animals just as perfect, and Toby is asleep now, dreaming, his father having called him back from his exile and he is coming into a glade where a dozen people, all friends, are busily engaged in a Necklace of Paradise.

A light, dry motion comes to the balcony.

A familiar voice, sharp and sudden, shouts, "Mr. Shoo! Look! You've got turds on your face!"

Toby is awake.

"Poor Mr. Shoo!" cries the bird. "Did I wake you?"

Toby bolts onto the balcony, waving his arms and shouting and then thinking to quit. To listen. The sound of Gabbro's voice comes up at him, the voice not loud but large somehow. Massive.

"Did you hear it?" he asks the girl. "Called him Mr. Shoo!"

The girl says something. Their door is open again, but she isn't close enough to be heard clearly.

"I bet I got him going," says Gabbro. "Got him mad!"

The girl says she doesn't care. "You and your goddamn jokes!" she cries, hooks in her voice. "Aren't you listening to me?"

"Were you talking?"

"Was I talking?"

"Now what are you doing?"

Something breaks.

"Don't do that!" Gabbro is screaming. "Hey! Not that!"

Something heavy tumbles into a wall.

"Fucking quit that!" he says.

And Toby retreats. He shuts the door and sits on the floor, in one of the white corners, curling into a ball and pursing his lips and wishing he could be anywhere else, by any means, halfway wanting the white walls to do him a favor and reach out and swallow him whole.

⋅⋅ 3 ⋅⋅

Masking Glass was developed in twenty different places at approximately the same time, on the Earth and elsewhere, and it spread through most of the available markets in several decades. Not too many inventions of the last several centuries have done so well so rapidly . . .

. . . It's a technology of deception. One or more AIs produce an entirely fictitious scene in order to deceive passing eyes. There are limitations, of course. There's the obligatory sameness to the scenes. AIs have only so much capacity. And there's the expense involved, but many find the money well spent. Several tricks can allow the modern burglar to probe past the Masking Glass, but isn't that true with every safety system? The primitive burglars will be stymied, and they're the ones who are clumsy and dangerous and frequently vindictive—envious of your wealth, angry with their lot in life. Think about the Glass as a filter which allows only the most professional thieves into your midst. If it keeps everyone away, fine. But if not, your lives will still be safe, and isn't that the most important factor . . . ?

—excerpt from a Masking Glass text, available through World-Net

In Quito, funny as this sounds, the Glass is used in two ways. The wealthy use it as a sophisticated, nearly flawless camouflage. That is its original function. But people with considerably less in the form of bulky goods, like antiques and expensive furnishings, will nonetheless spend enormous sums to acquire and maintain their Glass. The Glass produces the illusion of wealth within their walls. The rarest antiques in the System can be shown sitting in the middle of a room, and people passing by in floaters or on foot will glance indoors and be amazed. Of course a watchful crime lord, knowing the neighborhood and its people, will not believe his or her eyes. But the others will stay amazed long afterward. "Gemstone furniture. I mean it! As big as that ugly old couch, and so brilliant!"

—excerpt from a traveler's notebook, available through System-Net

S HE remembers the last time she spoke to the Quito boy. He told her that Dirk and Minus were suspicious, that Minus had made inquiries back in Quito and the inquiries had shaken the Magician pretty good. Had she heard anything from Dirk? No? Anyway, the Magician wanted all of them to pull out now and cut their losses. He's lost his nerve, the boy swore to Miss Luscious Chiffon. Are you sure Dirk doesn't suspect? You're sure? Well, he said, maybe. Maybe. But things down here are sure odd. Chiffon, he said, I don't like the feel of it. None of it.

The Magician's a coward, she said.

Isn't he? he said. He does half the planning and the hardest part of the work. Besides the front-line risks. That's you, Chiffon. Bless you! And now he's scared. You should see him. Him and his high-velocity brain, so damned clever and foolish at the same time. You know him. He thinks it takes brains, nothing more, to beat Dirk. Except now he doesn't feel so smart, and now he's going to kill us all.

You make it sound like he's turning us in, she said.

If he bolts, he does just that. Believe me. Minus is already sniffing around. He'll see a suspect run and figure the rest for himself. He will.

She believed him. A cold feeling came into her chest, and she sat in the dark and listened to the quiet around her while she looked down at the shadowy projection. What do *we* do? she wondered.

This line's secure? he asked.

Chances are.

And you're sure you're safe?

Minus may suspect. Not Dirk. I know for certain.

You do?

And she said nothing. The boy would realize as much for himself, she knew. She studied him, what she could see of him, and decided he was talking from a public booth somewhere in the East Skyhook region. The architecture. The constant street sounds. He was to serve as her contact and savior. He was a human-shaped slice of shadow, sensibly paranoid. She said to him, I've got news of my own. The biggest!

Yeah?

Today he got in a conversational mood. Dirk, I mean. He got to bragging like he does and do you know what he did? Talk about him suspecting nothing. He opened the safe. *He showed me the safe!* That's what I've been waiting for, finding where it's hidden. And the bigger news is that he and Minus are going to be gone tomorrow. Dinner at the Mayor's. A good chance to make my move.

The boy had no response.

She listened to him breathing. She wondered if he heard her just now. A dozen quiver chips! she wanted to shout. Imagine them! I saw them sitting pretty inside the safe! But she took a calming breath and asked, What are you thinking?

About the Magician exposing us.

He showed me the chips!

Just the same, he said, maybe you should break it off now.

Now? Who's losing his will now?

Chiffon, he told her, I don't know. I'm scared for you. If they find us out, and they will anytime, you'll be the first one caught. Not the damned Magician. Not me. You.

And what are my prospects otherwise? she asked. Tell me.

Let me come get you, he said. Now.

Tomorrow.

They're not home tonight? Do it tonight.

They won't be gone long enough. I'm not even sure where they've gone . . . for a walk, drinks, I don't know . . .

All right, he agreed. I'll come tomorrow night. Like we planned.

Good.

Unless the Magician bolts early.

Chiffon didn't want to think about that prospect. It was out of her hands, and fuck the bastard, she thought. This business was a helluva lot more important to her than to anyone else. It was everything. Twelve IA quiver chips, fully charged and worth . . . God, she couldn't put a number to their value . . . and if she held on till tomorrow night and if she could keep Dirk snowed with her charms and body, then they were hers and the boy would come snatch her away to safety, like they practiced, and then she'd have all the options that her new-won fortune would ensure.

She told the boy where they would meet and what she'd be wearing. She warned him about the AIs that were watching everything. Floaters. The tubetrains. Almost every way out of Brulé, or in, and he asked:

Wear something less potent, would you?

It's all I have, she said. I know what I'm doing. Don't worry. (She came to Dirk nude. The dress was the most public part of the wardrobe that Dirk had purchased, and she hadn't worn it twice in these last months. No one saw her but him and Minus, plus the Mayor once. By accident.) I'd dress in his clothes, only that would look silly.

The boy was jealous of Dirk. She knew just by listening to him say nothing. She knew his own job tomorrow wasn't going to be easy. An unmarked, unregistered floater without an AI pilot or governors on its speed . . . she pictured him and maybe some hired muscles riding in over the Farmsteads, keeping low, the big corntrees clipping the floater's belly. He needed encouragement. He needed to believe that she was waiting for him. So she said:

I've missed you, lover.

Chiffon.

She said, Two people with twelve fortunes between them, working as a team, can run a long distance. You and me. *Us.*

The boy confessed, I dream of you. Every night.

I dream of you, she lied.

Maybe it'll all turn out right . . . like it was at the first.

It'll be better.

You think? he said.

I promise.

That Quito boy was the purest product of the streets—tough and typically wise and utterly reliable when the reasons were good. In the early days, just after her "birth" from the plastic womb, the boy and she had spent some time together. Not much. Just enough so she could play with her new body and so the Magician could make some tests. Now the boy was suffering for their fun. She could tell. She knew enough about her talents to imagine his dreams, and the sweats, his nervous system swearing to him that he was in love. Thoroughly and forever in love.

Sitting alone in Dirk's enormous apartment, sharing space with Dirk's other possessions, she had a sudden but obvious thought that came up out of the depths of her brain. Twelve quiver chips divided between one person only . . . imagine that!

Chiffon, he moaned.

I'll be waiting for you, lover.

He said, Just get out alive. Promise me that much.

I will. I do, she said, lying to him with perfect ease. She blinked and took a long breath and looked at him while smiling; she thought how there were trillions of people and millions of Flowers in the System, but only one individual had had the experience of being both things.

Only one. And here she sat, the honest voice in her head telling her that she would do anything and everything to survive. But no, she wasn't coming out of this apartment without the quiver chips buried in her leg. Never. She told the Quito boy:

Promise me something too. Please?

He said, In a second. You know that.

Come save me. Whatever happens, come pull me out of here.

I promise.

Thank you.

Count on me.

I knew I could.

They said a few more things, letting nothing to chance. Then she kissed his projected face—the boy mistakenly letting his features show for an instant—and she said good-bye and killed the image and stood and listened to the silence, no one yet coming home. She had already written off the Magician. It was easy. He had brought her out of her Ghost life, giving her this new chance, yet she didn't waste time or energy on his behalf. The cowardly shit, she thought. Then she looked at herself in the room's bad light, noticing how her hands trembled, and her insides made a nervous noise and she farted softly, the air suddenly full of the smell of honeysuckle.

◆ ◆ ◆

Steward is standing at the Masking Glass door, permanently sealed and secure. His hands are on his hips and he watches a man who screams at some black bird—a Gardener, isn't he?—and Chiffon listens to the show and thinks this is some neighborhood. Steward has a microphone strung outside. He says he likes to keep tabs on the world. Chiffon can now hear other voices shouting too. This is some wild neighborhood. She looks at the wide bare back, the cords of his muscles showing, and she hears him telling her, "I don't know why. I tell myself every year that I'm going to move. Find something better. But this is all the home I need, I guess. I've been here since the start."

"Really?" She is sitting on the living sofa, her thoughts a little tangled and slow. No sleep, she thinks. But her leg feels better today. She rubs the cut and makes certain that she can't feel the buried quiver chips, and she breathes and looks at the tiny room without saying anything more. The furnishings and the etceteras make it feel smaller still. But at least she's safe. The Masking Glass hides her presence from all these loud neighbors. Somewhere an AI hired by Steward does nothing but paint a picture of him living in a pauper's room. A sophisticated trick, she knows. A private man. He lay on the floor all night, neither of them sleeping, and he explained all the ways in which he had made this modest home a fortress.

A pure Freestater.

She is in the presence of a born-and-bred warrior.

Steward turns now. Chiffon thinks to smile and twinkle her eyes— the bright overdone expression designed by teams of biologists and human psychologists and perfected by more than a century of Flower commerce—and she can't help but stare at the scars on Steward's broad chest, remembering when she saw them in the moonlight and his sensing that something was wrong.

Warrior rites, he explained.

She had kissed him on the mouth while he spoke, pulling him down on top of herself. Thinking of the tough Quito boy, and Dirk, she used her charms. The scars were nothing. She canceled them from her mind. She thought she was getting somewhere with Steward, but then he looked into her face and explained:

In Yellowknife. I got them a long time ago.

Warrior rites? she echoed.

They don't bother you, do they?

No, she lied. I don't mind.

Do you know anything about the Freestates?

Very little, she said. (Not much of a lie this time.)

I didn't think you would, he responded. Then he nodded and kissed her mouth and asked with tenderness if she was comfortable. Was the floor comfortable?

I'm fine.

Because I've got a bed. If you want a bed.

Do they use beds in Yellowknife? she asked.

And he had hung over her in the moonlight, thinking, his face sober and a little hard and his eyes fixed on nothing, she deciding that no one, warrior or not, was going to slip out of her grasp. So she went on with her work and made him forget whatever he was thinking. She was everything to him, and even now he looks at her smooth legs and the dress and gives a sigh, deep and hungry, probably remembering last night.

The monkeys in the yard are quarreling, running and screeching and throwing bits of masticated fruit at one another. In Quito, she recalls, the best areas have monkeys that are tailored to sing if they need to make noise. Operas are the preferred nonsense. The wealthiest Quito traders and investors, and crime lords have a peculiar fondness for Cradler operas and the ancient Chinese works, milking status out of genetic tinkering. In another century or two, when those particular citizens are dead or Ghosts, some other kind of nonsense will come along. Dancing bears, say. Or big crickets harpsichording Bach.

People, she thinks.

God, she thinks, what a crazy species.

These last few months have been instructive, surprising and often-times bewildering. She has been a Flower and not a human being of any kind, and it's shown her vantage points, all right. Like the way people, any people, care desperately for what others think of them. Like Dirk, for instance. Dirk the famous crime lord. Dirk the alleged sociopath. Dirk the aging chunk of callous, brutal and unforgiving, who spends an hour every day sitting at a mirror while robot hands work at his face with healing creams and lotions and makeup. As if it matters. As if he has spent years cheating and killing so he can have the freedom to sit and worry about his face. About his looks. Dirk, the man who has done so well for himself in Quito that he doesn't dare step inside its borders again. Dirk, the fool who put the bulk of his fortune, unregistered and untraceable, inside a foolproof safe, and then thought to himself that a man of his staggering good looks and means deserves the best and so why not purchase a Flower from the best Quito brothel? A special, almost one-of-a-kind Flower all his own?

Chiffon nearly laughs when she considers everything.

Steward sits on the chair facing her, the big hands capping his knees and his expression lustful, yet wary. The sofa and the chairs are living dark leather. The shelves on the walls are full of curiosities, plus several hundred old books. While Steward was in the bathroom this morning, unaware, Chiffon had hidden her little pistol behind the dustiest ones.

"You've got interesting neighbors," she begins.

He shrugs as if to apologize for them. He says, "Another good thing about this area . . . there's a rapid turnover in the tenants. I've been here so long that I've outlasted their memories," and he shrugs again. "I can't afford to let anyone know too much. It's bad business."

"You were explaining your business to me." He had started telling it when the crazy Gardener began shouting at the bird. "Something about registration. Citizenship—?"

"I'm no citizen. Not of Brulé, or anywhere." He breathes, making himself seem larger. "No one knows where I live. Or how. Or even my name, for certain."

"Steward—"

"There's a few dozen Freestaters in Brulé City. Sometimes we do work for the government offices, and part of the payment is obscurity. It comes in a lot of ways."

"The Glass?"

"And a reinforced door. Hyperfiber mesh in the walls. Untraceable World-Net lines, very sophisticated and damned expensive, plus Freestater weapons hidden here and there. Just for us. The police promise not to notice so long as we obey the laws and do the occasional job."

She simply listens, offering no judgments.

"Most of what I do is . . . teaching, I guess. Some people pay me to show them how to fight. A few want to learn how to hunt wild game, and others find a kind of pleasure in dressing what's dead. You know what I mean? Cutting away fur from the meat." He pauses, then says, "Some of Brulé's good people are curious about Freestate mental training, its philosophies or whatever."

She nods.

"But a few months, a few years, and they get bored and forget to come to class." He has an easy warm laugh. "I bet they don't know about the Freestates in Quito. Brulé does. A lot of the people who started those little nations, back in the old Neoamerindian Revival, came from this area. And there are still some ties. Enough to keep impressions alive. Wrong impressions, often enough, but alive just the same."

"And what else do you do? How much are you a hero?"

He seems disappointed by her words.

But she persists. "You were my hero last night." The big smile comes to her face without effort, instincts taking hold. "Did I thank you properly?"

His expression is watchful and somewhat innocent. "Like I told you, you were stupid to go into that place."

"I know."

"What were you thinking?"

"That it would prove safe."

He breathes and seems to weigh her answer on his tongue. Then he nods and asks, "Why did you need a safe place?"

She says, "A hiding place."

"Why?"

"Steward?" She waits, then asks, "Have you ever spoken to a Flower? Before me, I mean."

"Hide from whom?"

"The misconceptions are enormous. Even in Quito." She pauses, then tells him frankly, "We aren't fucking machines. Or mindless, moronic robots built in factories. And certainly not *succubi* and *incubi* that rise up only when our masters are in bed."

"You're no freelancer—"

"Intellectually, we're close to human. More sophisticated, actually. In some ways."

"—so there's an owner pining away for you. Somewhere." He wonders, "Who is he?"

"I was conceived in a plastic vessel and born this size," touching herself. "I was in a brothel at the foot of the main Quito skyhook, Steward. I was *devised,* Steward. Besides my shape and basic needs— water and food and so on—I have no relationship to humans. None. My genetics are derived from single-helix nucleic acids. Not DNA. Not RNA. A synthetic nucleic acid. And all of my genes are the product of laboratories and wholly original."

"Devised," he echoes.

But she talks on, giving the history not for the purpose of dispensing information, but so her intellect can be showcased. A Flower is a graven image, she admits. An abomination. Most worlds of the System and most areas on the Earth itself do not allow them to be produced, and if Flowers travel through restricted zones, then their freedoms are severely limited. Local whores don't want the competition. Local sensibilities find them a delicious taboo—something most people half-way want to try, if only once, and halfway wish banned. Flowers are the perfect lovers in popular mythology. Nothing compares. And the public's ignorance only helps to enlarge the myth and help it sprout wings.

Flowers have been possible for centuries.

But possible doesn't mean something is done. There are a staggering number of technologies still in the cupboard waiting to be applied. Like truly intelligent AIs. Like world-cracking antimatter bombs. Like any new thing that might threaten the long-lived creatures of dominion—Mankind. Convention and social goals paint synthetic humans as a new danger to true people. Flowers, as a result, have been flesh-on-blood realities for only a little more than a century. Quito is their stronghold. In Quito, most people will swear that anything can be bought without the buyer or seller invoking any messy moral sensibilities. It's a corrupt and thoroughly wondrous city stretching from the hollow Andes to the Galapagos Islands. Two billion people live in its confines. Plus Ghosts. The better areas hold some of the wealthiest humans in the System. Only the royalty of Kross and certain old-money Belters could pile up their assets and stand taller on the piles, proud for the view.

Regardless of wealth, however, people can live but three centuries or so. Then they wear out and they die.

Tailoring and modern medicines have slowed the aging process as much as seems possible. Organs can be transplanted. Flesh can be grown anew and grafted onto the weary old flesh. The brittle calcium sticks devised by natural selection can be replaced with plastics or even hyperfiber bones. But the limit comes with the human brain. No one has yet learned a way to build the perfect cyborg body, then mesh it with that fatty lump of tangled neurons. And even if that trick were possible, she reminds her audience, there comes the steady erosion of the brain's capacities and its redundancies and its general vigor. Brains are the weakest link in any life-extending process. They're the seats of the soul, and unless you wish to be torn apart and made into a Ghost (Chiffon's true self made ill by the simple thought) the prospects are clear as to the destiny of all those precious thinking gray lumps.

A score of diseases, both ancient and modern, inflict themselves on the oldest living people.

A century and a half ago, without warning, some of the wealthiest elder members of the Quito community got ill and died with shocking suddenness. The source of infection was traced to a virus native to far Titan, usually beneficial to its hosts—but not to dusty old Terrans, it seemed, and before it was identified and killed it had claimed several thousand citizens worth billions. The main mode of infection was through delicious contacts. Certain popular whores were identified as carriers. There was a near-panic inside the exclusive clubs and health parlors. And even once the virus was gone and its living victims treated with success, a general sense of dread lingered on.

What if new diseases appear? people wondered.

What then?

Quito receives produce and people from all over the System. What if the whores became carriers of something worse? How can a true epidemic, the first in a thousand years, be combated before millions die out of sheer ignorance and lust?

Flowers were one answer.

Says Miss Chiffon, "I can't hold or spread any virus or bacteria." She says, "I am a functional alien in every sense," and she shrugs and looks at Steward, smiling her pretty smile and telling him, "You know that already. Even in Yellowknife they have to know about us—"

"You've got an owner somewhere."

She says, "I do." She says, "We're property, yes. In Quito and elsewhere. Our treatment is regulated, or it is supposed to be regulated, and the truth is that we live better lives than most average citizens." She sighs and tries to look small. No one could see her and not feel a measure of pity. "Since we're supposed to entertain some of the most cultured, well-educated minds in the System, we've got sharp minds of our own. And flexibility. And humor. And a demon's skill with pleasure." She sighs again, working to blend her charms with the visible helplessness. "Which is small consolation for being a slave, Steward."

He says, "I bet."

She tells him, "Yes, I've got an owner. And the truth is that I've run away from him."

"Why?"

"It's complicated."

"We're both smart," he says. "Try explaining."

"And yet it's simple, too." She smiles with a hint of embarrassment, this business so much dirty laundry. "I'll explain."

"Do."

"For my hero," she coos.

And he says, "I don't know. Tell me and then we'll decide what to call me. Okay?"

❖ ❖ ❖

The walls of the room are covered with shelves, and the shelves are alive. Steward listens to Miss Chiffon and looks at the various books and trinkets. They're part of what people won't see when they look inside his home, the Masking Glass more than a luxury to him. He installed it himself, at night and in secret. He built the shelves later, splicing into the feeding wires and the vascular pipes running inside the walls, extending them and then shaping the resulting structures with care. At first there was nothing on them. He had brought nothing from Yellowknife besides weapons, and those were stored elsewhere. But eventually, slowly, Steward added the antique books bought in the Old Quarter and the rare trinket or ornament—ill-labeled nothings with no clear value, each representing some portion of his life in Brulé.

She is talking about her mysterious owner.

"Where is he?" Steward asks.

"Now?" She seems uncomfortable, perhaps afraid that talking about the man will produce him from out of the air. She says, "Nearby," and squirms in her seat. Her bare toes dig into the carpeting, between pale brown and green stalks, and she tells him, "I was devised to suit him. Only him. He's wealthy and very special in his wants. Very unusual."

"Explain." He doesn't want to sound tough. He almost tells her as much, then catches himself.

"He's cruel." She sighs and reports, "He enjoys being cruel."

Steward tries to remain objective. Calm. Okay, he thinks. Cruel.

And now she draws a picture with words. She has a sober, careful voice when she describes what a Flower must suffer when her master is separate from the law. She mentions knives and electrical currents and droppers of warm acid, and when she doesn't tell him how these things are applied, Steward's imagination is sufficient. He tries to look at the shelves, tries to keep her hurting face out of his eyes, remembering the merits of cool estimations and sober assessments, Chiffon and her owner and Steward too—all mixed into this crazy stew.

And she breaks him down.

He can't say when or how. He wouldn't know how to resist, he thinks, and he finds himself staring at her toes, then her bare knees, and finally at her face with the sober voice coming out and wrapping around him and pulling some sort of knot around his poor insides. He knows pain. He's certainly experienced worse pain than she's known, and much of it he sought out for himself. But he is trained in suffering and surviving. A Flower isn't the same. This strange Miss Luscious Chiffon is near tears and being so brave about it, he thinks. He thinks back to last night when he mentioned the Masking Glass, that everyone saw a fictional Steward living in a bare room, that's all, and he had felt the relief come into her suddenly and all her nervousness before then making sense. Now, he thinks. She's crazy because of the bastard, he thinks. Look what he's done to her—!

"I'm sorry," he offers, recalling the cut on her leg.

"For what? You've done nothing wrong to me."

"There's a rich bastard somewhere in Brulé City—"

She says, "You've helped me more than anyone."

And a thought comes into his head.

She asks, "What is it?"

"Scars." He has to ask, "Why aren't you scarred?" His fingertips and tongue have been everywhere, nothing found besides that one healing wound and all the perfect smooth skin, scented and sweet tasting. "I don't understand," he confesses.

"Flowers heal."

"How do you mean?"

"We can't scar," she says. "Our beauty heals completely. For as long as I live." She gives a weaker smile and shrugs.

"Oh." He remembers how he was lost at the height of sex last night, and he can't count more than a handful of times when that kind of passion had happened to him. "Go on. I'm listening," and he leans forward in his chair.

"You know the rest."

"You ran away from him."

"Yes."

"That's it?"

"Yes."

And he has an urge to sit with her and hug her until she bursts. She's so lovely, he thinks. She carries herself as if she doesn't even know it. And still there's a toughness wrapped inside her beauty. He can catch it in her face and her posture. She's been injured, mightily injured, but she persists, undaunted by her circumstances.

He asks, "Does this happen often?"

"What?"

"Flowers fleeing their masters?"

She says nothing, crossing her arms and looking between his feet.

"You're loyal, aren't you? By nature?" He needs to make it sensible in his head. He wants it to become clear and reasonable, but he has to confess, "I've heard stories of a Flower's loyalty. It's fierce to an owner. It's in their genes."

"Running isn't easy," she whispers. "Oh, no."

"I'm sure."

"But you're wrong."

"How?"

"Anything can be inside our genes. We can be trained in any fashion desired."

"Okay."

She looks at him with her perfect mouth closed and grim.

"What's your blood and schooling telling you, Chiffon?"

"To withstand almost anything, then flee. There came a point when I had to flee—"

"Of course." He shakes his head, saying, "A brutal rich turd is somewhere in Brulé, and you couldn't live with him anymore. That's fine. You've been terribly lucky, Chiffon. I found you and you're safe, quite safe, and don't worry about anything."

She watches him, volunteering nothing.

On one shelf is a little globe. Steward remembers when he bought it for almost nothing in a secondhand shop in the Old Quarter, reconditioning its workings himself. He's afraid to touch Chiffon now—afraid her nerves are too tightly strung—but he needs something in his hands and so he picks up the globe, the roundness firm and pleasantly heavy. It's a Universal Globe. He bought it because in Yellowknife he had lived without World-Net or Ghosts or even talking AIs; he felt backward that first year, people saying so in his presence. Or saying worse. So the Globe seemed smart. Name a world, any world, and it projects the image with an old-fashioned holo arrangement. Like now. It's showing the Earth as it is today, this minute, with its several kinds of green, continents and sea, and the lines of rainstorms moving away from the equator, white as curdled milk and apparently solid.

She finally says, "Remember? I was devised by him."

He says, "Yes," with his most patient voice.

"He's done this before. Many times. He devises Flowers and does the same terrible things to each of them, and all eventually run away. He expects it."

"He wanted you to run?"

"He enjoys the good hunt." She smiles and hurts with the same expression. "Does this make sense?"

"A game?" Steward can almost feel his hair straighten. He doesn't know why he's so surprised, but he is surprised. Even stunned. He tells her, "In edible chess, the player who captures a piece gets to eat the piece."

"Yes."

"You're the only piece on the board, aren't you?"

"I just want to hide."

He aches to his bones. "As long as you need," he promises. "How long before he quits hunting you?"

"Five months." The answer is precise and immediate. Her voice has gone flat. She looks straight at him and reports, "My genetic material is not only synthetic, you see, it's unstable. The typical Flower lives a year, rarely more, and I am seven months old."

He hears himself say, "I understand."

"I'm scared."

And Steward glances at the globe. He can't remember the last time he used it or which of the tens of thousands of worlds he had wanted to see, but he recalls how he learned quickly that people in Brulé have no compelling interest in anything outside Brulé. He thinks how five months isn't any time at all. He thinks he should put down this stupid globe and say something or do something, only he doesn't know what. So he sits, saying nothing, telling himself that people are odd. They can learn so much and see so much and yet they care only about the things immediate. It's been that way from the beginning, surely, and it'll be that way to the end.

◆ ◆ ◆

A Freestater, she is thinking.

While she lies to him, telling him the fable she devised while lying awake in the early morning hours, she tries to decide how she might make use of him and his skills. She sees him as an opportunity, gray but potentially enormous. She sure knows enough about Freestaters to be excited. No one is more tough-headed. No one. They've been fighting the oddest, longest set of wars in human history. More than a thousand years of steady confrontation. Odd because there are so few fatalities and so little destruction. Warriors inflict ritualized pain and fear on one another, and battles are decided with all the ceremony and tradition of a grand wedding. He was talking about some of it last night. Now she tries to sketch in the blanks with what little she remembers. The Neoamerindian Movement had been a religious phenomena. A Revival, Steward had called it. It was a conscious attempt to mix elements of mankind's tribal nature and aboriginal faiths with modern technologies. Selective technologies, she thinks. Never World-Net. No. Each little Freestate is a nation unto itself, each possessing its own history and demanding faith and a unique sense of culture; its people somehow manage to hold themselves in isolation from the rest of the System—a wicked trick for remote comets and asteroids, a marvel for people so close to so much.

If they started killing one another, of course, the big City-States would put an end to their fun.

Immediately.

Wars can't be tolerated. Not when smart individuals with few resources can build and deploy weapons of terrible destruction. Not when tiny nations lacking status or real populations can fabricate nukes and gamma-ray lasers capable of eradicating billions. There hasn't been a major war in fifteen hundred years. There aren't even any standing armies anymore. And that's what makes someone like Steward so damned valuable, she tells herself. A warrior! A potent Yellowknife warrior!

What's he doing down here? she wonders.

Then she decides not to question her good fortune. Just think of ways where Steward can help . . . not that he'll be worth damp shit against people like Dirk and Minus, of course. Not nose to nose. But his home, his hideout, and his warrior sensibilities and all—

"Five months is worth a fight," he declares.

"I'll keep out of your way," she promises, making her voice sweet and submissive. "I'll pay for your trouble, too. Whatever—"

"No." A big hand cuts at the air. "Forget it."

She wonders what he would say if he knew the truth and how long his hero mentality would linger. She has no intention of including him, not like she would have done with the Quito boy, and she thinks about the boy and all the things that might have happened. Maybe he'll show in spite of everything? There's no knowing. She tells Steward, "Thank you," and he says:

"Stay for as long as you need."

She'll need some way out of Brulé. Some means that Minus can't find and trace. The clock is running, she thinks. Five months is an honest figure. She has plans. Living with Dirk meant time where she could dream up solutions to all of her problems. And that was with a quarter share of the fortune. Three IA quiver chips. Now she has twelve and maybe all of her partners are dead, the Magician and the Quito boy included, and what she feels isn't joy and she won't call it greed . . . no, she's not greedy . . . but she is a creature of opportunity and she won't give up what she has earned for herself. Five months to save myself, she thinks. Somehow I'll do it.

Outside, out past the living railing of the balcony and down, she can see a woman emerging from the apartment below the Gardener's. Chiffon wants to ask about the neighbors. Does Steward know them? How well? What do they know about him? What damage can they do? This neighbor woman is a firm kind of fat, youthful but not pretty. Her bland face is thick with emotion and red like some fruit. Someone's talking to her from inside the apartment. The voice is odd. Chiffon blinks and sees a dark figure in the doorway for an instant, the skin black hyperfiber and the entire man enormous. A real stew of humanity, she thinks. A cyborg from Morning and an assortment of Terrans, and then there's the Gardener who hates birds. Brulé is more tolerant than it lets on. It must be if it lets scum like Dirk make a home here, however temporarily, and she sighs and turns to Steward and thanks him once again.

He shrugs, lost in thought.

"Do you know how good sanctuary feels?" she asks.

He says, "Mostly," and sets down the globe. He is completely fooled, and helpless, and he wants to help this poor hurting Flower more than even he knows. She knows the symptoms. She sees them in his face, his asking, "So what's his name?"

"Whose?"

"The guy with the rude prick."

She says, "I can't tell," and looks at him. There is something in his expression, in his posture, and she asks, "What is it?"

"Nothing," he lies.

So she uncrosses her legs and uses her dress like a fan, shaking it, spreading a cocktail of bare-knuckled pheromones through the air. She has the distinct impression that he's contemplating something, that he's got some crazy nonsense in his head, and she arouses herself in a moment and invites him to come to her on his fine long sofa and tell her his concerns. She calls him "Lover." He takes a deep breath and holds it and touches a corner of one shelf, saying, "Five months," with a reverent tone.

"Come here."

He crosses his arms on his chest and seems to hug himself, straining, the fibers of his muscles standing out, and her saying:

"Why not join me, love. I won't bite."

He says, "You know, sometimes I forget you're a Flower."

And she says, "Well, I'll have to remind you more often," and she reaches, taking him and pulling him close enough so neither can see the other's face.

The IA class of quiver chips is distinctive for having no distinctions. It is plain; it is white and smooth; it has no marks besides tiny IAs on both sides; it is no larger than the nail on the average thumb, nor any thicker; yet any one of the chips, filled to capacity, would make a Kross prince salivate. It is worth that much . . .

—excerpt from an economics text, available through World-Net

I ate a lovely, quiet dinner with one of the Quito crime lords. She was a handsome older woman, small and fragile in appearance. She had cooked the meal herself. We sat on pillows and looked out her windows, all of Quito below us. Or so it had seemed. She asked about my travels. She asked intelligent, perceptive questions about many subjects. I was charmed. I have no reservations about making that claim. She was a thoroughly charming dinner hostess, her jokes subtle and her smile quite genuine, and the height of our evening was more intimate than this account can give. Suffice it to say that I left full of honest joy, glad for the opportunity and wholly unconcerned about the supposed line of work to which she had dedicated her life . . . yet several days later, by chance, I met someone who was familiar with the woman and her various reputations. He asked me about the events of the evening. He listened while I related some of the high points, his expression distant and quite sober and his head nodding steadily as if my story was one he had heard several times in the past. Finally, as if in pain, he admitted to me that he did not consider her such a good person. Indeed, there was one story told about the woman. True? He couldn't say. Did I enjoy the meal she served? Was there a meat dish? What kind of meat was it? I couldn't remember. And he paused, shaking his head, then muttered some crazy nonsense about her enemies and their sad fates . . .

—excerpt from a traveler's notebook available through System-Net

Minus is a thickly built man made thicker with some selective tailoring and several kinds of strength training, his hands broad and strong with squat fingers and his face flat and square and centered on a triangular nose. His wide lips are caught up in a perpetual grin, self-assured and humorless. He has a thick beard and masses of hair on his bare chest. The pigment inside each hair has been deleted by tailoring—a trait common to certain Quito neighborhoods—and inside the hairs' hollow spaces grows a wide assortment of algae colored metallic green and sky blue and sharp violet and violent red. The actual pattern of colors changes from day to day. The effect is heightened because Minus has no pigment in his skin. He is milky white with cold pink eyes gazing out at the world from behind a chaotic rainbow.

He's steering a private floater, thinking for the countless time that he never trusted the girl. Not from the first. He remembers them calling her a fancy Flower, a truly exceptional Flower, but he hadn't liked the way she worked with Dirk. Not from Minute One. In no time she had had him crazy. He was like a young bull again. More than once Minus thought about going to him and asking if he could check out the brothel, say. In case. Only he knew what Dirk would say. He would say no, don't, and don't worry about me either. Worry about you. If we're going to get a real home someday, Dirk would say, you've got to get on it. Find someplace worth living and get us in the door. All right? Understand me? All right?

It was stupid, his waiting like he had. In the end, entirely on his own initiative, Minus had checked out the Flower's origins. Just to make sure. He didn't plan on telling Dirk, and the funny part of the story—easily the funniest part—is that he had cleared her and the brothel on that very same day.

She was designed and grown and trained in the very best facility in Quito. Someday, or so said the brothel owners, the Chiffon series would become the emblem of worth to every aging stud, equivalent male and androgynous versions soon to be added to the stable. This was nearly the first one. Was there a problem? asked the brothel. No problem, he told them. My boss is just acting crazy sometimes, that's all. And the brothel took that as a compliment. They said that if that's a problem, maybe they should tone down the future Chiffons. Maybe a little?

All right, Minus told himself. I was wrong to worry. Where's the big harm if the old shit's happy? She came to us with nothing, after all. She was a Flower, after all, and they're tailored and trained to be sweet and harmless. So all right, so long as she doesn't tell him how to run the business, what is the trouble with Dirk having a playmate?

Nothing, he thought.

Everything's sweet and fine.

At least it seemed so. But somewhere someone got a case of shaken will. Minus had seen it happen before. A few questions and satisfactory answers, and maybe the issue seems cleared. Only one of the parties gets nervous. He or she gets to thinking, asking if someone's on their trail, then finally deciding that if that's the case it's best to make a break and hope to get clean away.

The brothel had this kid. The Magician.

A genius with tailoring the new nucleic acids. Last night, too late to give them warning, the kid packed up and left Quito. Minus was paying a couple AIs to watch the brothel and its people, in case, and they noticed the Magician's leaving and traced him through the night, watching him change names and put on new disguises and all sorts of ding-brained shit like that. They sent out an alarm, too. Early this morning, Brulé time, the kid was cornered on a fast-shuttle making for Luna. A couple of hired muscles had owed Dirk a favor, and so they did the work. It was way too late to catch the Flower, of course. That's the ugly truth of it. But the kid was caught and the muscles poked him twice, growling, and he melted. Just melted. Between the tears, he used some goofy story about a group of thieves forcing him to build a special Miss Luscious Chiffon, then he squirted the Ghost of some girl into the Flower's head somehow. Crazy as it sounds, parts make sense. Minus tries to imagine meshing two entities, a Flower and a true person, and he's sure it's never been done before. Nowhere. And of course parts of that story are lies. Like the poor Magician being forced. He *knows* that without having to ask. But he's told the muscles on the scene to talk to the kid with sweet words. Make him believe that they believe him and that he's alive to stay. Let him talk. Minus guesses that he'll tell everything without anyone having to ask questions. Give him room and the time, plus encouragement, and they'll know everything soon enough.

The stinking shit.

He's a genuis, they say. You know a genius, thinks Minus, because he can talk for days and not repeat himself. Most people don't have an hour of original noise in them.

And afterward, the interrogators will pat him on the back and offer him congratulations—"Isn't it better getting that garbage off you?"—

and maybe the kid, this Magician, will break into a weak little smile. Sometimes stinking shits have an easy giggle, he thinks. A giggle and a want to believe. And one of the muscles beside him will take the opportunity to break him into pieces, no warnings given, and Minus has already told them what to do with the body.

Take it to that brothel, to the nursery, and dismantle him.

Pipe the pieces into the nutrient tubes; feed the Magician to all those pretty young Flowers.

The Flowers will grow fast under the influence. Those atoms that belonged to the Magician will keep laughing among themselves, or so Minus likes to think, and they'll become part of some new Miss Chiffon and spread lust and joy throughout Quito and the world. It's a perfect end, he tells himself. He has half an urge to have them record the event. It's not something you want recorded, of course. But then it's not every day when you get so many billions stolen from you, either. Or when you can punish one of the ones responsible.

◆ ◆ ◆

The center of Brulé is the tackiest tangle of square and weathered old buildings. He hates this town, looking ahead to the tall broad building where Dirk rents an entire floor. Beyond it is the narrow tower where Dirk is waiting for him now, suffering a good deal of embarrassment at the proxy hands of a Quito physician. He was sleeping with a thief, after all. There's no telling what slow-acting toxins she might have carried, or the diseases encapsulated in her hair, or even subtle corrosives mixed with her breath and laid inside her ex-lover's lungs. He'd left Dirk several hours ago, business needing his attention. Now he's steering the floater toward the pad on top of the tower. Don't push the speed too high, he reminds himself. This is Brulé, not Quito. They're out of their element here, in foreign country, and it pays to keep that in mind.

Minus thinks about Quito. Someday, somehow, he intends to go home. Dirk's no young man, and if Minus can stay with him and keep him safe until he can die in peace . . . well, he figures he'll pocket a lot of the man's wealth by default. Then it's back home as a rich man, buying some sprawling home in the Galapagos district and retiring. It sounds good to him. When he was younger, he remembers, he thought about getting into Dirk's own line of business. He was stupid. Dirk's got this knack that Minus won't inherit. Never. Dirk got his money and power because he understands people and plays them and gets what he wants from each of them. He has a skill. All the money they whittled off the others . . . and all the while Dirk making alliances, playing games, making sure that he'd be able to get out of Quito untouched. That's what Minus admires and can't hope to do for himself. Play the game and then trick the other players to let you stand and leave the table. That's tough. It doesn't happen much in Quito. Until yesterday, the only trouble left for Dirk and him was to find a new home with enough to offer. Brulé was a stopover. Nothing more. So far Luna and Titan and Kross have turned them down, as have the Belters. It was politics. It was Dirk's reputation. And so Minus has been spending his days finding other possibles. Little worlds. Man-built worlds. Whatever. Draw up a profile and bring it to Dirk and stand back and wait for his judgment; then if the thumb goes up, start to investigate the chances and the costs.

Lately Dirk's been talking about building his own world.

He can afford it, sure. He could buy a comet out in the Oort Cloud, terraform it anyway he wanted, then spend his last years in peace. Sure. It had all sounded pretty good to Minus. He remembers imagining what those billions could do if they were applied with brains and skill—Dirk rich enough to hire both things—and he remembers the way Dirk sat there with the damned Flower on his lap, her hands stroking him all the time and her voice cooing in that special way, and all the time she was thinking that there were quiver chips somewhere close. Hidden but close. And she was waiting, watching, knowing her chance would come.

Minus hates quiver chips.

Wealth shouldn't be locked up in one place. Even if it's illegal. Even if it's protected. Even when it can't be traced, and even when it's been the mainstay of this business for better than a thousand years. In old times, he thinks, it was cash. Paper money. Gold. Jewels. But the legal money today is glass and computer coded. Gold is bulky and too cheap. And jewels are manufactured in orbit—made huge and perfect and suitable for furniture and kitchen counters. Which leaves people of opportunity with nothing but quiver chips. Tiny, yes. But utterly vulnerable.

It works like this:

Money in glass-form is traceable and precounted.

Taxes are an easy trick.

Seizure is too.

Money inside a quiver chip is just as real as any other, and maybe more so. The chips are recognized by World-Net as banks unto themselves, portable and impregnable and trustworthy to whoever holds them. At no time will World-Net or any other Net refuse payment from a chip. Yet they can't be traced or taxed. Everyone has them. Or should. Even the most average person keeps a fraction of his liquid assets in them. They can't be duplicated or counterfeited, not even badly, and any attempt to change World-Net so they would be refused . . . well, it would lead to chaos. Chaos, and probably economic collapse.

The chips are standard currency with Dirk and his associates.

They were stored inside a safe deemed unbreakable and invisible. Minus remembers coming home last night, Dirk behind him, and seeing their invincible safe opened and gutted and the Flower gone to parts unknown. For a minute, cunt crazy, Dirk had tried believing that Chiffon, his poor precious Chiffon, had been stolen along with his money. She wasn't to blame! he swore. Yet then the others parts fell together, the Magician skipping and the physical evidence conclusive, and Minus took time to rub Dirk's nose in the mess until he had to agree. The sweet perfect cunt was holding his life's work in her perfect paws, and Minus promised that he'd get back the chips and her paws and they'd have some fun with her, then finish her, and he'd have the body stuffed and mounted at the door to their new comet home. How did that sound?

Except he doesn't know where she might be hiding.

Except the money can buy someone a lot of freedom, too. Even for an apparent Flower on the run.

Like here, he thinks. It was wealth that made Brulé City open up to Dirk. It was the honorable Mayor Pyn with his investments, his causes, his good-hearted greed for his town. The Mayor's favorite nonsense is the enormous mantle mines—a dream involving novel technologies and Morninger labor and the remote prospects of rare and precious elements being brought up from several thousand kilometers below Brulé's deepest cellars. Minus has had to suffer through long, long promotional speeches and intricate holo plans and all the stupid rhetoric that seems to cling to such things. The Mayor has taken a certain heat for having let Dirk in the door. That's another part of the equation. The mines are strapped for cash, and Pyn is hoping against hope to get a piece of Dirk's money and turn into a hero. He's doing it for his town, sure. He's a good man, and weak. That's what they've been trading on these last months. How much

longer? Minus wonders. The Mayor is going to get smart. He has to.
And then what happens to the two of them?

He takes the floater down to the tower, thinking that this robbery
might turn out for the best. Maybe. It'll get Dirk's head away from
Flowers and dreamy schemes. Dirk isn't a senile fool yet. He should
be able to come to some arrangement with a Luna City-State. Or
Kross. Or someone. The trouble all along was Miss Chiffon. He can
see it now. But a schemer like Dirk, having beaten the best Quito has
to offer, should be able to pull a victory out of this mess. Sure, he
thinks. Sure.

The floater lands and out he steps with a hot dry wind coming from
the south. It pulls his colored beard and hair smooth against his face
and body. He looks around the roof with a professional detachment.
A tiny groomed forest looks sick of the heat. Below him, filling the
next several floors, is Brulé's most exclusive club—clean food and bad
drinks and some private party rooms—and Minus hunches in the
wind and hurries down a flight of stairs, wanting out of the burning
bright sun. To get to Dirk he passes through the main bar, drawing
looks even after this long. The local politicians and business types are
too conservative to accept his appearance, and too reserved to obviously snub him. Minus is important. They know it. He gazes out at
them and spots the Mayor himself—an average man wearing forgettable clothes and a perpetually worried expression, his life always coming apart at the seams—and the Mayor scrapes together the will to
nod at Minus and offer a tentative smile. He's sitting with moneyed
women and men. Things aren't going so well, his expression says.
Minus nearly laughs. Some of his companions take the trouble to look
at him—the frightful, nightmarish bodyguard—and they give a visible
shudder before looking away again.

Minus laughs aloud.

It's what he wants. Their fear. That palpable sense of mistrust and
loathing.

Dirk's the important, notorious investor from Quito. And Minus is
just a bodyguard to them. A hired lump of muscle. But the truth is
different. He's actually something larger, unlabeled and invaluable,
looking out not only for Dirk but for all of his organization and
keeping tabs on his enemies too . . . rather like a personal secretary
of state.

Minus is through the bar and in a narrow hallway with locked doors
labeled with the names of dues-paying members. The door marked

Mayor Pyn opens for Minus, some AI greeting him by name, and he enters a carpeted lounge too small to impress anyone. In the corner, alone, sleeps a willowy man lying on a reclining chair. The Mayor's personal medical gear, autodocs and such, is beside the man. A block-ish woman is displayed on the opposite wall, on tri-dee, and she sees Minus as he enters and says his name with less feeling than the AI used, nodding and telling him, "The sedative's still working. Let him sleep."

He asks, "So. How's the old warhorse?"

"Scrubbed. And blocked."

"What did she do to him?"

"Just ordinary Flower dope. Mood-changing stuff. Love potions, if you will. Those kinds of poisons." She is sitting in an office in Quito, the living picture of discretion. "I filtered his blood twice and got most of the physical stuff. The rest is being denatured now, slowly, and he'll piss it away in a day or two. Don't worry."

"Scrubbed, huh?"

"And blocked. Like you told me. I used forced hypnosis to help him suppress residual feelings." She explains the particulars to Minus, and the limitations. The past can only be obscured, not buried. Character? Nothing changes character.

"You should have seen him," he says. "Lovesick's the word."

"I know." Her expression is passive, her eyes held halfway closed. "For all intents and purposes, he was in love with that Flower." She has seen this kind of love many times and cured the wickedness. Or so her voice implies.

"Well," says Minus, "thanks."

"Watch him for a couple days. Closely."

"Yeah?"

"Denaturing pulls out his natural endorphins, too. He'll be in some pain and his mood might be ugly—"

"Normal enough."

"—because endorphins play roles in mood and controlling all kinds of pain. And the forced hypnosis, the blocking, may produce a few odd moments. Brains aren't things you can change at will, you see." She seems sorry that it's not otherwise. "He may have episodes of unreasonable fears. Unexpected bouts of crying. That sort of thing."

"No love left in him?"

"Too much love, really. But I've done everything possible."

"I know," he says. "And thanks."

"These sorts of things vary from person to person. How badly it hurts. How long it persists." No misunderstanding please. Her voice says it.

"Bill us," he declares, "and thanks again."

She nods, then vanishes. He wonders what Dirk might have said under hypnosis, and Minus sits beside Dirk and makes a mental note. Have an AI keep watch on the good doctor. Sure. The last thing they need now are their old enemies coming to get retribution. He breathes and looks at his boss, at his face and closed eyes, and he goes through the medical file and thinks back over these last months. Dirk had been suffering the love and everything had been so odd. There was a smoothness to Dirk, a tangible calmness, when he talked and when he moved. Maybe that's why I didn't press the Flower, thinks Minus. Maybe I liked Dirk smiling for a change. And when he decides that's the case, he feels angry. And a bit surprised. Maybe I'm getting old, he thinks. Soft and lazy, he thinks. Or maybe, just maybe, it's the world itself getting younger and tougher. That's the history of the world, he knows. It's always been getting younger and tougher.

No change in me, he thinks.

Never.

◆ ◆ ◆

"So who managed the safe for them?"

"Another insider. She's an officer in the company that built the thing. This kid, our magician, says she told them a simple way to ease open the mag-locks. Household tools and some special equipment that fit in a cavity in the Flower's thigh. The safe's big feature, after all, was its invisibility. Not its strength." Again Minus is rubbing Dirk's nose in the mess, glancing up at the wall where the chips were hidden inside the toughest hyperfiber on the market. Not strength, no, but it was plenty strong anyway. "There's a glitch in the way the safe recognizes its punch-in code. The builders found the glitch after the fact, and they've kept it a secret until now. Trying to find a patch for the damage, and all that."

"How many are we talking about?"

"The Magician. The Flower. The safe officer, plus minor players. Some workers at the brothel. A street kid with muscle and weapons skills. Too many players, if you ask me. Too many mouths. Too many shares."

Suddenly Dirk shifts his weight, his face turning pale. He says, "I hurt," and breathes gently.

"I bet you hurt."

"You read the doctor's report?"

"Twice," he says. "A Flower using Flower-style tricks. Nothing fancy. Strong doses, but nothing that could have spooked us."

"I feel shitty."

"I bet."

"Tell you what. Why don't you wear my pain a little while?" Dirk laughs and shifts in his seat, combing his hair with a shaking hand.

Minus finishes his drink and looks past Dirk, staring through the long Masking Glass wall. Its builders promise that it's impervious to lasers and impacts and any explosives short of nuclear charges. The floor and ceiling are both similarly reinforced. Even if something knocked down the entire building, they'd be safe. In theory. A high-density foam would spray out from the floor and cushion the impact for everyone indoors. Of course a squatter, windowless bunker might make more sense. But then this perch has visibility, a presence, the security systems all second to none—hardened senses and half a dozen AIs hired to do nothing but scan and notice everything in the area, guessing if anyone has any evil intents.

The AIs weren't watching indoors. Not last night. Not ever.

If they had seen the damned Flower, the reborn Ghost, whatever . . . she would have been caught. She wouldn't have stood a chance. But then the AIs would be privy to every private word and act, and that's the kind of knowledge you don't give to anything. Not to people. Not to machines. Never.

"You should feel my fucking joints."

He says, "I'll pass."

Dirk says nothing more. Minus studies his long, pained face with the big boyish eyes and the angelic chin and mouth and nose. He knows Dirk hasn't always looked so innocent. He's had surgery to retain the whiff of youthfulness and to enhance the sweet exterior. He claims it allows him to be liked by more kinds of people. They trust his face and eyes. The people who meet him expect something else, maybe picturing a Minus-style creature, and when they see the willowy form and the smiling face they tend to let down their guard for a little while.

"Is she letting me have anything for pain?"

"In stock and waiting." He punches buttons on the console beside him.

"And how's this pack of thieves doing?"

"Suffering. All but two." Minus describes the various captures, then says, "There's still the Flower and the muscle. The muscle left Quito a couple of nights ago, maybe later, with friends hired for a long trip. His job is extracting the Flower. The Magician says so."

"And is he here?"

"Not that I've seen. I got the alarm out soon enough to catch him fleeing, provided he made his pickup."

"And how are we hunting?"

Minus sketches the heart of what he's doing. He's got AIs watching Brulé wherever possible, and he's got other AIs scanning World-Net with the usual intrusive systems. They watch who watches what and keep tabs on the kinds of information requested from libraries and data banks. A thief on the run should have peculiar viewing habits. At least they can hope so. And then there's still another team of AIs eavesdropping on the nearby Farmsteads. Farmers use open channels. If they saw a floater filled with Quito types, coming in or going out, they'd likely tell one another and Minus, too. But so far there's nothing. "And suppose he tries coming in now. We're ready. We'll see him all the way." He asks, "And how long can a Flower hide? And how far can she go alone? Not long. Not far. So maybe we're out of bad luck, finally. Maybe."

Dirk shrugs. He has quit listening, his mind drifting and the expression on his injured face changing, growing darker. Minus knows what's coming and he doesn't so much brace himself as he makes himself relax. Let the fury sweep over him and past him and be finished. It's something he's learned through his years with Dirk. The man isn't smart in a lot of ways, and he'd probably be smart to refuse a good rounded set of brains. What he is is a survivor, cruel and tough and normally impossible to fool. The various ways in which he robbed and swindled his fellow opportunists prove what it takes to succeed.

"Why do I pay you?" he asks.

Minus waits.

"I pay you a good living so I'm safe from small-timers and new talents and similar flavors of shit."

Minus says, "Sure."

"You're a worthless sack of sphincters."

He has no response.

"What did you tell me? That she was a Ghost? That before they pumped her inside that Flower body . . . she was dead?"

"It seems so."

"And you know how I feel about Ghosts." He hates them, sure. But the terror on his face is something new. Minus is surprised until he remembers the doctor's warnings about mood troubles and such. "She was in here, and you let it happen. She was in my bed and had me so pumped full of chemicals that I couldn't think a straight line. And you just watched!"

The forced hypnosis is talking. His suppressed feelings are coming out along his seams, Minus tells himself. Ignore it.

"She sees me open the safe once. Sure. That one was my fault—"

"You couldn't help yourself," Minus offers.

"But you should have picked up on things before. That's what I'm saying."

"You're right."

"Even checked on her pedigree."

"I did."

"A day late."

"You're right."

"I should fire your hairy ass."

That's not the part you pay, thinks Minus.

And Dirk seems finished. Pain or exhaustion or maybe simple lack of interest causes him to turn quiet, sitting back in the cushioned chair so his aching joints can rest and recover. The painkiller arrived long ago. It's been checked and mixed and checked again, and Minus automatically checks it himself. It's a sweet drink, warm and dark. He hands it to Dirk and watches him take it all down and then asks if there's anything else he wants now.

"How long before we're cash poor?"

Minus makes a guess. A lot of the legal holdings are still in Quito, and turning them into Brulé currency might prove difficult. "When the time comes," he mentions, "Brulé and the dear Mayor are not going to be patient with us. If we're cash poor, they might reconsider our status."

"If they learn it."

"Sure."

"And suppose they do."

He doesn't like their prospects. No other City-State will want them. Maybe some minor world. Maybe they could acquire new faces and identities and give up hoping to live well again. Or they can invent a new way of raising capital. "Maybe this is too soon," he says, "but the kid, this Magician, is a real master of tricks. Some of them might mean big profits to us. For instance, Flowers can be more than Flowers in the future. Putting a person inside a functional upright body has never been done before now."

Dirk seems to think. Then he says, "You're right. It's too soon," and mutters something beneath his breath.

"We'll find the two," Minus promises. "Plus the chips."

Dirk mouths the word, "Ghost."

And Minus sighs and glances around the room—spacious and bright and decorated with the finest gemstone furnishings. He feels as if he's saying good-bye to the surroundings. It's an odd, unsettling sensation. He happens to let his gaze linger on a prominent panel along the far wall. It's more sophisticated, and much more expensive, than a World-Net panel. It possesses olfactory functions and limited tactile functions and they are latched to channels unavailable to most people. Just a few weeks ago, standing centimeters from that panel, the honorable Mayor Pyn had held a drink in one hand and some discrete drugs in his blood and complimented Dirk on his splendid tastes. Dirk's tastes, naturally, were purchased tastes. And when the Mayor sniffed the phony wind and pushed his free hand into the panel, stroking the rough blue face of the alien leaf, he asked what was this place and why did it look so familiar?

It was a view being broadcast from Tau Ceti. From one of the handful of colony worlds.

Dirk boasted like a proud parent. He explained how this was a new panel, very rare. So far as he understood, there weren't more than a few hundred outside Quito. Wasn't it worth the tab? he inquired. Huh? That smell is alien biology talking. Those mountains in the distance? And that sky? No synthetic views generated by AIs. Just watch and you can tell they're real. And it'll be centuries before World-Net gears up for any of these functions!

What a master, thought Minus.

What a way to work on someone, winning favors.

The next day, first thing, Minus ordered an identical panel to be sent to the Mayor's home. It cost a stiff fee, and it employed a bunch of AIs just to keep it working . . . but it had seemed smart at the time. A gift. Something unusual and desired, and the only trouble is that if things get tight in a week or two, whenever, they may have to quit making the payments. And if so . . . well, Minus doesn't have to be a student of human nature to know what happens next. Pyn finds the courage to turn to his Chief of Police, telling her, "Throw them out and today. No warnings and no gloves."

That's what will happen.

Sure.

5

Hyperfiber denotes our time. Remember the Bronze Age? And the Iron Age? Then the Age of Plastic? Well, now we live deep inside the Hyperfiber Age in all its splendor, in all its majesty, and every day still brings new forms and new uses and hints of new possibilities. It has been brought on with the creation of ultrapure compounds of intricate design . . . hyperfiber, flexible or rigid, massive or light, capable of standing on a world's waist or enclosing a man's body or armoring the nose of the newest starships . . . I can't quit applauding the stuff . . . !

—excerpt from a technical manual, available through World-Net

The angriest Morninger I have ever seen, without doubt, was a certain smallish woman who had just been insulted. A companion of hers, furious for obscure reasons, had screamed and thrown up his hands and called her a damned sack of machine parts. Not strong language! you might think. But to be accused of being a machine, in any context, makes any Morninger livid. And she was. Other companions had to restrain her. She roared and shot back her own saucy insults and finally was carried away, and after an hour or two I had a chance to speak to her and see the universe from behind her glass eyes . . .

"I'm no machine!" she maintained. "I'm as human as you! In my world I feel pain, I feel the heat, I'm mortal and small and cry in the night because of my fears!" She told what others had said in the past—that the flesh-on-blood you is merely enlarged by turning cyborg; that a small weakish girl remains a small weakish Morninger in adulthood; that an ugly face and form are retained with an honesty that Terrans and others might want to emulate; that Morningers, more than most people, know that what makes you or destroys you comes from within. Not from the hyperfiber, but from your soul. From your human character . . .

—excerpt from a traveler's notebook, available through System-Net

70

GABBRO is swimming. Or, rather, he has climbed into the pool and sunk to the bottom and now is working his muscles—the pliable hyperfiber muscles he relies on—running circles on the bottom of the pool. The water foams and churns and bubbles madly. He is the hub of a furious whirlpool. It's a glorious sensation. Turning his enormous black head upward and backward, he sees the blue sky strained through the swirling coral-rimmed water. Fish are swimming without actually moving, faces into the current. Other little things cling to any surface they can find. A single Cradler appears against the sky, his expression puzzled and happy in that Cradler way. Then there's April, hands on her ample hips and a scowl directed straight down at his happy heart.

He quits running.

Standing motionless, he lets the current die against his bulk. Then he bends and leaps with enough momentum to carry him up out of the pool with a rush, water spilling over the deck and April too, her shrill voice telling him what he can do to himself. She means it. She's still not over this morning's tussle, over his getting home late and no good excuse ready, but Gabbro doesn't let it bother him. He's gotten halfway used to her moods. He's had no choice. And he knows how to tease her when she's this way. He cackles like some goofy kid. He wants her to know how much fun he's having.

Two little Cradlers are standing nearby, watching.

They're laughing along with him, but he knows they're frightened. April says they're terrified of him. How silly, he thinks, and he shakes himself dry and sits on the oversized lounge chair and takes a chamois off the coral deck, wondering how many times he has told them he means no harm. Never. Don't be afraid of me, he has said. A billion times at least.

Oh, well.

I try, he thinks. That's the point. I make the effort and isn't that what matters in the world?

The chamois feels smooth and dry in his hands. He pulls it taut and drags it across his slick black skin, careful not to tear the leather, and he happens to glance at the calming waters. He can see the sky reflected, assorted birds wheeling and the upper floor of the one building showing too, all dressed up in its weeds. One glass door reveals a single face glaring down at the laughter, eyes angry and the delicate mouth angry and one hand with its pinkish webbing pressing against the glass. Let him steam, thinks Gabbro. He almost makes it too easy, he thinks. It sometimes seems the guy forgets what it's all about. Which is fun. Just fun. I do things to him, he thinks, and he tries to do them back. It's a goofy wrestling match between people with nothing in common.

He finishes with the chamois, pulling it across his broad bald head. Then he giggles and balls it up and throws it underneath the chair, April telling him, "Quit it."

"Quit what?"

She says, "Can't you see, darling? You scared them," and she waves at the little Cradlers. "You and your human-fountain tricks."

"They're scared and they're laughing?" he asks, playing stupid.

She shakes her head, frustrated. "Can't you just hold yourself back a little? Please?" She touches one of his knees. "Gabbro? Dear?"

Gabbro blinks and smiles, the muscles of his face letting the white ceramic teeth show in the sunlight. A few hours ago, in their apartment, she was flinging shit at him and screaming. In all of his life he has never known someone so quick to explode. If she didn't get over it as fast, he tells himself, he'd have left her long ago. Somehow. He'd go crazy under the pressure.

Relaxing himself and breathing softly, he tries flowing with the mood of the moment. "We should quit fighting," he announces. "Let's make a pact."

"Sure."

He says, "Never again?"

"Never," she promises, both hands on her closer knee. He feels her grip, the hyperfiber flesh laced with the synthetic nerves. "You know why I love you, Gabbro? You're such a little boy."

He can't count the times he's heard it from her. A billion or a hundred billion, and how many pacts have they made?

She calls him "Darling" and smiles, her face tanned and round. She's wearing her tight, tight black swimsuit. The ample flesh threatens to burst out in a dozen places. Her breasts are barely restrained, from the big brown nipples downward. The long black hair is streaked with lines of bright gold, regularly spaced, and the hair lays flat on her back and butt, ending just short of her good-sized feet. She sure has her reserves ready, he thinks. He resists the urge to use the joke. Later, he thinks. Our next fight. Then his mind wanders back to when they met . . . a year and a half ago? . . . in that narrow park down in the Old Quarter. He was just off the tubetrain from Jarvis, fresh from Morning, and she had looked respectable and tall and well built in the city lights. He had felt like a little lost miner against the lights and buildings. A friendly voice was what he needed at that moment, and she listened to him tell how he had been recruited to come to Brulé and work in some deep operation. Something that would put him near the belly of the Earth's crust.

In that heat? she asked.

I'm from Morning, he said. Or doesn't it show?

And she laughed and told him, Oh, it does. It does. I just can't see how people stand that furnace. You know? Even with hyperfiber around them.

We carry refrigerators on our backs, he said.

Hey, she said. I'm teasing. I know.

And we're strong.

Who doesn't know that?

I start work tomorrow, he confessed. Early.

They're hiring more and more of you, aren't they? She laughed and said, Listen. I know all about you people. Why you're here. All the good you're going to do us. Brulé City and everyone.

And he joked in turn, I'm doing it for me. Not you. When Small Fry pay me better money than I make at home, I do it for me!

Small Fry? she asked.

What we call you—

Because we're small, she said, and if we're caught outdoors on dear Morning—

—you fry.

See! I'm smart about these things.

He had come to the Old Quarter, he explained, looking for a certain bar. It was a rumored collection point for the Morning miners, and April confessed to knowing the address and why not follow her? So he did. And she mentioned, This has got to be something to see. All of this!

There's nothing like it on Morning, he said. He was amazed by all the people and the towering structures clustered together, his own home being a single building shared by three bachelors and set on an empty plain. He described it with hands and words, missing the place and missing all of Morning without actually feeling love. Funny, huh?

They weren't far from the bar. April led him and went inside with him, casual and self-assured, and it surprised Gabbro when he saw all the Small Fry spread among the miners. There were women and men both, Terrans and not. April said, Sure, sure. A lot of us come here. We like it here.

You do?

They say you're the shape of men to come.

Do they?

Absolutely. Didn't you know?

It was fun, him and her together. It seemed natural and easy and Gabbro nearly forgot to ask her to come home with him, expecting her to keep at his side till the end. And he wasn't too drunk, particularly after taking some sober-up pills. By the time they were in bed together, her wanting him on top, he was authentically scared. He was worried about his strength. In every meaningful sense, she felt like any woman feels. But what if he forgot that she wasn't like any he knew? What if he did her harm? This was his first night on the Earth, in an apartment bought and furnished by his employers, and he didn't want to think what would happen if he jerked wrong and cut the poor girl wide open.

I'm not worried, she had claimed.

You should be, he said. Anything can happen.

Gabbro, she said. You're a splendid hunk of flesh, yes, and I'm thrilled to be here. But I wish you'd put something into this venture. And now.

And if something goes wrong—?

Silly.

It might!

Oh, silly! She said, Don't you understand? That's part of the attraction!

❖ ❖ ❖

Venus might have been terraformed.

The tools and skill existed, sure. Even a thousand years ago. It could have been refashioned into an honest second Earth. Only there were limits with time and expense. For the greater bulk of the System, from Cradle to the cold Oort Cloud, heat could be applied to land and ice and yield a crude soil and easy seas with plenty of opportunities for organic trickery. But Venus had more heat than ten worlds could use, and barely enough water to make a good dew. Importing volatiles meant buying comets and other expensive freight. Lunar City-States had tried such a business, and they still do today. They're dry places. Brutally dry. Only their wealthiest citizens can swim in the stuff, or pee in it, or just let it run for the thrill of watching it.

When colonists finally organized and purchased rights to Venus, taking them from the old Luna-Kross Compact, it was seen at once that the best solution wasn't rebuilding the world. It was rebuilding themselves. So they renamed it Morning, thinking the word lent a certain promise and elegance to their endeavor. They borrowed cyborg technologies first used during the Anglo-Amazon Wars, in simpler forms, updating the designs and materials and capacities. Hyperfiber flesh was coupled with corrosion-proof electronics and power cells needing only minimal recharge. They encased themselves inside their protective shells, balancing strength with honest grace and sharp senses. The crux of it all was to retain their humanness. The feeling of being part of a machine, seductive or not, was strictly excluded. The hyperfiber flesh had something of the spring and look of real flesh, and the faces mirrored the flesh-on-blood faces below them—the glass eyes moist and the ceramic teeth a little crooked sometimes—and the more personal glands and their talents were neither more reliable nor pleasurable nor impressive—on a relative basis—than what comes with ordinary flesh and the maliciousness of genes.

Their culture was immediately controversial.

There were sects and established faiths that declared Morningers to be blasphemies of an ultimate sort. Arguments wouldn't sway them, and still don't. Logic or simple decency had no impact on blind perceptions. Monsters had appeared in the System. Demons! they cried. Treacherous demons! And still today, in many places and by different means, Morningers are restricted or outlawed or taxed unfairly. If they didn't have so damned many uses and talents, of course, all of them would live isolated existences. But a good cyborg is invaluable. Particularly since the easy and comfortable places have been conquered . . . and sure, thinks Gabbro, maybe it's fair calling us the people of the future.

Demons or not, Morningers are born in the sky.

As a boy, Gabbro was raised in a floating habitat anchored to a hyperfiber tower with the atmosphere's cold reaches all around. Like every Morninger, he grew at a galloping pace. His pituitary gland spat out hormones and his tailored body turned long and clumsy, his height finally topping out at a graceless two and a half meters before his sixteenth standard birthday. Then, as if on a signal, his body quit its growing. A small ceremony was held—a thousand-year tradition being played out—and he was deemed an adult-in-waiting.

The cyborg shell was built around him, slowly and carefully.

Terrans, friendly or not, cannot comprehend the complex and fickle processes involved. It takes time and a measure of pain to make the transition. You lose your natural teeth and eyes, and the inside of your mouth is coated so whiffs of acidic air won't scald it. And Gabbro suffered the usual troubles. Objects shattered in his new hands. He stumbled and broke walls and strong furniture. His body—the fleshy remnants of his natural body—weakened and shrank while the cyborg functions invaded and attached themselves to the muscles and nerve endings. It all seemed to take forever. It took him exactly four years to be transformed, which is fast; then Gabbro was pronounced an adult, officially and forever, and he was taken to the surface at the conclusion of a second ceremony—larger and more lavish, people honoring him for his courage and his persistence.

As if he had had a choice in it all.

His adjustments had only just begun. Morning was still very much a wilderness world, empty and harsh with its landscape of hard, broken stone and blowing dusts and the liquid-thick air greedily sucking up the sun's heat. But Morningers had a plan. They were in the process of building a unique biosphere, slowly and patiently, planting forests of photosynthetic machinery growing like brush and trees, then stocking herbivores that tapped them for electrical food and predators that in turn caught and fed on the herbivores. Robotic lifeforms, yes. Not a unique vision in human history, but it was the first time the dream of machine worlds had seen a practical application. Much as Gabbro cares. He can recall how he hated all of it—the barren places and the scattered forested places and the little place where he lived and the brutal mines where he worked hellish shifts, emerging exhausted and with nothing to do and no real friends as of yet. So he spent any free time walking the plains where the strange ceramic bushes struggled to grow. If his hyperfiber muscles grew tired, he would run an illegal tap and drain some of the bushes dry of their excesses. Then he'd continue, going in some wide sloppy circle with Morning spread around him, ugly and endless, its air as hot as flowing lead and as dense as deep, deep water.

Now Gabbro is staring up at the sun, eyes absolutely human in looks but indifferent to the glare.

April says, "Say. Listen."

"Yeah?"

She touches his nearest thigh and squeezes. "Let me make it up to you," she tells him coyly. "Let's go inside."

He thinks, then says, "Why don't we wait."

"Why?"

"I'm waiting for the bird to come back." The bird. He wants to watch it torment the Gardener. He wants the chance to laugh. "Just this once."

She says, "Gabbro," with a hook in her voice.

Not again! he thinks.

"I don't want to say anything, dear."

He readies himself.

"But what if the rumors are true? What if you're put off the job?"

He laughs and says, "I'll sleep for a change. And swim more." He shrugs again, thinking the chances were poor and Brulé wouldn't let it happen. "Just rumors," he says, his voice confident and sincere.

"What does a tailored bird cost?"

"What it's worth. What I paid," he says.

"You should save some of your money."

"I do," he lies. "But I'll save more. How's that?"

"I hope so. I do."

Words give him time. He looks at the swimming Cradlers. They're not paying attention to him any longer, his jokes forgotten. He looks at their smooth fur, matted and dark, and hears them talking in that songlike version of the standard System language, all squeaks and whistles. If you're going to tailor yourself, he thinks, that's the way. Make yourself cute. He sighs. He wishes April hadn't brought up that layoff business. He's heard enough rumors lately. Like after last week when the backers came through the mines—frowning men and women, Terran and a few lanky Lunarians, standing in those clumsy coldsuits and staring at all the big hardworking Morningers—and Gabbro had heard it from several directions that these backers had had enough. The project was too far behind schedule. The goals were too vague. It's brutal work to forget the pressures and just do your own job. But he's managed pretty well by his own estimation. Gabbro does all the shifts he can stand and makes no trouble for the bosses, and if he ever believes the rumors he also tells himself that he won't be laid off. Not him! Maybe the bird was a bad move. All right. But it's been his experience that planning for the worst makes it come to you. What he needs to do is keep laughing, keep happy, and work like a son-of-a-bitch. And what about April? He doesn't know. It's so damned frustrating to live with someone so long and realize that what you think is beyond her understanding. Not even a million years would make her know him. Not really.

"What are you thinking?" She smiles, pleasant and ignorant.

"I'm wishing I was rich," he lies.

"Not that *we* are rich?"

"We're rich."

"I'll try it, too, darling. Let's make it come true."

"Sure." He glances at her swimsuit, wondering where it will split first. He breathes and shifts in his chair, making it creak and grind. Then he looks at himself, relishing his thoroughly human shape and the foreboding blackness of his skin. The skin is mildly photovoltaic. That's the reason for the absorbing color. The apparent bones and muscle groups help the illusion, as do the phony veins and pores and even the creases on the tops of his big fingers. There aren't any statues on Morning, he reminds himself. Art doesn't have room in a wilderness. But he's seen statues on World-Net and in person, some of the best ever made, and he has come to appreciate his shape all the more. He's like something carved from obsidian, nude expect for the tiny clinging swimsuit that hides nothing.

"Gabbro?" she says with less patience.

"Yeah?"

"Why don't you come inside, please."

"Another minute." He had grown up hearing stories about hatred of his kind. When he arrived on the Earth, at first, he had expected resentment and hatred and possible violence from the Terrans. Yet the truth is something more complex, more elusive. For instance, he has all kinds of Terran friends. And the people who dislike him are typically too intimidated to make noise. At least most of the time. Most of his neighbors like him well enough. Brulé City ran checks wherever they put Morningers, choosing areas where people would accept the presence of the cyborgs. He's grateful. Maybe he's scared the Cradlers too much, but it's not on purpose. And the older Terrans like him because one night, in a driving rainstorm, he heard an odd something and went outside to find some kind of wild ape lost and trying to get under cover. The ape was at someone's window, clinging tight and slapping the glass, and Gabbro leaped high and caught it and shook it a little, making it more scared of him than the storm. Then he let it run away. The police arrived later, and he went out and said sure, it was a prowler of some kind. He had chased it off. And that's what the old people learned in time. Then for a long time, at odd intervals, food was left in his grocery chute, and someone sent April bags and bags of sweet candies.

He looks up, ignoring April. He hopes to see the Gardener, but now he's hiding or something, and so he looks the other way and spots Steward staring out at nothing. Steward, he thinks. They've talked a lot about all kinds of little things. Weather. Sports. The mantle mines. And foreign places. Steward doesn't give clues to his history—he keeps to himself without being unfriendly or tight-lipped—but he knows the System. He knows the names of worlds and the ways people live, and he carries himself like a man who's done some serious wandering. Sometimes Gabbro thinks they'd make good friends. One of them just needs to try.

"Your bird's not coming," says April.

"It's up there. It's waiting its chance."

"So what do you say?" she wonders, giving a bawdy laugh.

"I guess. Sure." The funny thing is that he doesn't care about the bird or the Gardener. He got an idea about tormenting one with the other, and so he reactivated their feud. Hell, he thinks, the Gardener, Toby, would probably feel lost if I forgot about him for too long. He probably expects this sort of abuse, he tells himself.

Only it's been getting old these last months.

Now he can barely care how it began.

And now April stands, picking up her towel and chair and starting for their open door. Gabbro watches her fat ass and the cottage-cheese thighs and feels nothing. He wonders what would happen if he changed everything in his life now. Cut it down to bedrock and start again. He thinks of healing things with the Cradlers, and maybe the Gardener too . . . and his mind drifts to April and him in the beginning, the way she'd lie under him and trust him completely. Now it's different. They still make love, sure, but now it's changed. He never loses himself in the act. He is in total control of his every motion. And the trust she felt at the first has turned legitimate.

He laughs to himself, realizing it's so.

◆ ◆ ◆

The crow circles and circles, then tires and comes in to land. It's on the facing building and keeps up the vigil while it rests, eating what happens to be close and drinking the warm stale rainwater in the cracks of the bark. Always, always it's aware of the window and glass door. It's possessed by its solemn task. The brain's set patterns are like a fever, and all that matters is tormenting this Mr. Shoo. Any means will do nicely, please. Mr. Shoo! Mr. Shoo!

Around dusk, either thinking it safe or suffering from the day's heat, Mr. Shoo decides to open the window a crack and gives the crow its chance. It drops to the window's ledge, looks inside and spies a figure reclining on a simple mattress. An entire bedroom wall is filled with a multitude of figures engaged in procreation. The figure is breathing softly, both hands gripping the edge of the mattress and a faint sheen of sweat showing in the gloom. "Mr. Shoo!" shouts the crow. "Mr. Shoo! Eat my milky gobs of shit, why don't you!"

Mr. Shoo throws the pillow.

And like before, the crow watches it slide off the screen. Then it cries out, saying, "I'll teach you, Mr. Shoo! I'll show you manners! I'm the Angel of Knowing and you'll wish you were dead—!"

He has stood. He moves as if pained, passing out of view and then returning with a big bowl in his hands. Too late, the crow sees him fling scalding water through the screen. The crow turns and drops, flying weakly down to the little pool. There it shivers and finds its senses. It looks up and sees only glass made dark for the night, all the seams sealed, and it feels a terrible frustration followed by a sudden hunger. The fever has left it. It forages by the moon's rising glow. The wild bushes have been picked clean by the day's monkeys, but a few rotting half-eaten fruits are enough to make a full belly. Then it belches with a soft, contented voice and hops up high and flies to the facing building, to the second floor, and perches on the wooden railing of a balcony.

Time passes.

It sleeps and then wakes to the vibration of people moving behind it. It feels them through its curling feet, and it pivots its head and looks through the glass door, moonlight illuminating a little empty room. The crow doesn't have the flexibility to be puzzled. It doesn't look twice, and eventually the vibrations cease.

Sleep comes over it again.

Below, unnoticed, are motions in the narrow yard.

A high, almost inaudible sound wakes the crow. It's a familiar sound, and the crow feels compelled to go toward it. A large figure is holding a humming box in one hand. Somewhere dim between its passions is the memory of this figure standing in the tailor shop where the crow was born and raised. The crow flaps its big wings and descends. It makes no sound. Yet the big hand knows where to reach, taking it by the neck and squeezing so fast that it doesn't seem to squeeze at all.

◆ ◆ ◆

Gabbro is dressed for the mines. His clothes are durable, and dirty in spite of the sonic cleanings, and the pockets bulge with tools and the various etceteras required for his job. Having killed the bird, he tells himself it's for the best. Live, he thinks, and let live. Whatever it was that started this feud . . . just forget it! He considers burying the corpse in the soft earth, then thinks, Why? If I'm calling a truce, why not tell Mr. Shoo what I'm doing?

He looks up at the Gardener's balcony, seeing no lights and no hint of motion. He considers notes and apologies and decides to simply show him that it's done. Let him figure it out for himself. With a small precise throw, he puts the corpse up on the balcony. A small quick thud and then nothing. And Gabbro squats and leaps high enough so he can see the bird laying against the glass door, good and dead, its black head turned at an unnatural angle and its crushed body leaking fruit meat and crow meat and drying blood.

All right, thinks Gabbro All right.

If that doesn't make everyone happy, I don't know what will!

The church was one of the oldest structures in Quito. Built of native stone and ancient European design, it seeped a distinct sense of Faith and Trust and Charity. I found it lovely. I studied its history with fascination. It was once Catholic. Then the Catholics were driven out and it became Fundamentalist. Then they were gone and several vanished sects took it over, each remodeling according to their needs, and now the Fundamentalists have returned—devout and traditional and full of fire and fire-tinged speeches. I sat through one of their services, in the back and out of view. I listened to the minister wail about the sins of Ghosts and the sins of cyborgs, the immortality of the human soul and the peace of God beyond our mortal understanding, and I watched a pair of gold-winged Angels building a nest in the highest reaches of the church, their tailored monkey bodies lovely, their steady voices like the ringing of small bells . . . and somewhere it occurred to me, somewhere in the middle of that fire and Faith, that those Angels had been inside the minister's private quarters because they were using her stolen robes in order to make their home for the night!

—*excerpt from a traveler's notebook, available through System-Net*

S OMETIMES he can hear the Ghosts.

Minus says he's wrong, of course. Minus swears the floor above is too much for any sound or sensation to seep through; he mutters something about the forced hypnosis, the blocking, and him losing his perspective; then he says that Dirk should relax, sleep and heal, everything is being done for him now. But Dirk has no faith in the soothing words. He knows what he hears and feels. Delusions indeed! This has nothing to do with the doctor's treatments or his lovesick mind. There are Ghosts nearby! Like now! He's alone in this place when this happens, always, Minus out on some errand and the AIs keeping tabs on the building around him, and here comes the clear soft eerie whispering of some disembodied soul. He hears it! Listen! Listen! What's it doing pestering him?

Maybe a few random shots will scare it away, he thinks. He'd shout, only he's afraid the damned thing would shout back, saying something horrible. And then what would he do? Piss his pants, probably. And he's not going to act that old. Not for anyone or any damned thing!

Dirk breathes.

He works to calm himself. Minus is right about one thing, he thinks. The doctor's left him in a real state. He feels a terrible cold insanity snug against his bones, and he breathes again and wonders if part of the problem is the chemical uproar inside his body. But he has always hated Ghosts, and feared them. It's just that he typically keeps control over the feelings. He breathes once more, aiming for bravery. Real or not, he thinks, you bastards aren't making me cower in my own home!

People would think it's funny if they knew. They might ask him, Why don't you mind AIs? Aren't they just a different flavor of the same kind of blasphemy?

But they aren't.

Not at all.

AIs were never human. Not even close. They're just computers with enormous speed and perfect memory, serving people's needs and not their own. Plenty of times, and for plenty of reasons, Dirk has talked to AIs. He's made arrangements with some of them. He's extracted favors, or they've done the same for their own clients, and sometimes it works both ways. AIs are supposedly intelligent. Which is a joke. Talk with one for one minute and you learn that they haven't any sense of humor, or any spark of good thinking, or anything. It's the way they've been built. It's the way they like to be, or so he's heard. They're fast and precise and each has its own identity. But they're indistinguishable from a room full of hyperactive bookkeepers or lawyers—bland and glad to be bland, tap water having more spirit and sparkle than their most radical members.

Ghosts are entirely different.

That's what has him worried now. Ghosts were once people, living and fornicating and mortal. The trouble began when it was time to die, whatever the reason, and they decided to live on by any means. It's not a cheap trick. A brain is disassembled one neuron at a time, and all the memories and tendencies and stupid quirks are encoded into a set of laser-interface circuits. They tie up enormous numbers of AIs just so they can pretend to be alive. And too many of them dream of technologies that will allow them true life again. Dirk shudders, the bitch Flower coming into his mind again. Leave me alone! A walking, talking, fucking Ghost and I slept with her! If ever he found himself with the power, he tells himself, he would break those crystal brains into dust. Without doubt! To him and to any rational person, Ghosts represent a true evil. The souls of Men and Women belong with God when it comes time to die, and tinkering to do otherwise is the ultimate crime.

Dirk is a religious man.

He was raised in one of the Fundamentalist homes so common in the oldest parts of Quito. His particular district is famous for its stoic poverty and its enormous faith. But it wasn't until he was an adult that his training took hold. That's when Dirk was working as an assassin, his name taken from his weapon of choice. He had a fondness for daggers. Quito is particularly suited for such things. Crowds and tiny curving streets and the constant press of bodies on bodies, plus the need to spread terror with the punishment, means a good dirk in good hands is always in demand. Dirk remembers the victims and how they struggled against him, kicking and screaming even when he had them bound and gagged; but then there came a point when they would give in, letting the end come easily, saying nothing and their faces softening and him shutting their eyes afterward, thinking it's right and they're with God now, and He was with them, and what could be construed as even a minor evil when all he had done was release a fool to where he belongs?

Dirk is lying on a gemstone sofa, not sleeping because of the pain and nerves and the nagging sense that he's being watched by half-dead entities. The Old Quarter stands outside, dressed in bright lights without seeming bright itself. He watches the quick, silent floaters moving in and out of their streams, and he spots a pair of rainboys shepherding a little cloud toward the north. He thinks about Minus leaving to pick up a couple men from Quito—they don't dare bring more, what with the need for secrecy—and he thinks how Minus has been taking care of everything while he's down and suffering. It's the one bright spot. That Minus is one tough, reliable animal. He is human enough when he needs to be, sure, but underneath his colors and his skin is something that makes even Dirk keep his breath to himself and watch what he says and does when he's in the room.

There was a problem a few years back.

For instance.

A married couple had come to them—a woman and a man—and made some promises. Teach us to sneak and steal, they said, and we'll give you a cut. A considerable cut. Absolutely.

Of course, cracking a home is work these days.

The AIs are everywhere in Quito and forever watching. They're the best watchdogs ever devised. And Dirk has always made a portion of his living because of those tight security systems. Centuries ago, a kid with gristle and balls could make reliable money. The same kid today has to get a sponsor and schooling and promise his or her teachers payment for their trouble and time and risks. That's custom. That's part of how a person like Dirk expects to make his money—teaching eager babies how to fool the AIs and survive.

Anyway.

There was this couple. The woman was the boss. She was good looking and willing to do anything to succeed, by any means, and her man was a weepy-faced boy with a genius for technical things. They made a dream team. Minus had seen it at a glance. He brought them to Dirk's penthouse high on the Ten Klick Tower, and both of them were impressed by the view through the Masking Glass and impressed with his place and the talk turned to business and how they needed some help. So Dirk told them, Fine. I'll give you the best help possible. And the woman thanked him. And he said there'd be costs, to which she said, Nothing's too much if it means steady employment. We're not greedy people, she swore. We just want a living share.

He gave them everything. They couldn't miss with their abilities and his hard-won knowledge, plus resources, and as part of the early payment plan, the woman returned to the penthouse for several private parties. It was she and Dirk and sometimes a Flower or two. Those were the days when he started using Flowers. He can't remember details from the parties—they're recorded somewhere, he supposes, and if he wanted to he could access them from here—but the funny thing is that he remembers the woman as good looking yet he can't picture a body or face or much of anything else. Not even color. The older he gets, the more he'll forget the bounce in an ass or the mouth giving suck. The only exception is in a person's character. No, he thinks, I *always* remember character. The first time she was up in his place, sharing the view with her weepy-faced husband, it took all of five seconds to know that she would cheat anyone by any means, big stakes involved or not.

Which was fine.

Knowing you can't trust is sometimes better than knowing you can. Like with her and her man. Dirk sent them out on jobs. Minus kept tabs on their performances, knowing what to expect. When the woman started to keep back too much, in the early going, the amounts were small. It was as if she were testing them, and Minus did nothing but tell Dirk the news. Certified antiques and occasional quiver chips—with she taking some of the extra chips—and her man entirely stupid to the situation.

She got greedy.

It took time, but Minus kept tabs on the greed. He found where she was stashing the chips, and when their worth was about equal to the harm the two might do in the future, Dirk said to finish them. Do something good, he said, and he left it to the animal inside Minus.

Minus caught them. He disarmed them and put them inside one of the unmarked, untraceable floaters they had kept in Quito for this kind of work, and then he climbed into the bright sky and talked to them while they sat, bound together, staring as much at each other as they stared at Minus. It was news to the husband that his darling lady was dipping twice. It came as a shock on top of shocks, and he was angry and scared and ready to turn her in himself. He'd never imagined this! And Minus took them south, keeping out over the Pacific and the pea-green kelp farms, then he swung back over the jungles where the world's storms are born, no one following them. No one tracking him or even aware of him. He found a nice fat storm, full of moisture and being towed inland by a mess of rainboys, and he edged the floater closer and cut loose the husband's ropes and put a one-shot pistol in his hands, telling him, Do her and the file's clean. Okay?

Do her? he asked.

That's simple, isn't it? Just do her!

His face filled up with conflicting thoughts. There was anger and there was fear too, and a kind of slow-boiling hope.

Minus said, And don't try aiming at me. He brought up his own artillery and made certain the man wouldn't confuse targets.

Minus said, Go on.

The wife started to talk just then.

She had this way of pleading and crying all at once, working on her husband's nerves. It was an effort for him just to put the tip of the barrel on her skull. She claimed to have done it for the both of them. Didn't he see her intentions? The husband started applying pressure to the trigger, crying too. He said she was a fool. She agreed with him. He said she should be thankful to have it this way. Fast and painless. She said, Take him! You can take him! But he didn't try. He managed to make the trigger click, the tip of the barrel glowing for an instant and burning her flesh in one small spot; then nothing more happened and he pulled the trigger again and again, frantic and sobbing, and Minus laughed and said:

Hey what? No juice?

They were like a pair of wet sacks full of nothing. Minus loved to tell it, and Dirk could still imagine it. His bodyguard made certain they were tied together. Then he took the floater straight up over the storm and opened the hatch and flung them down into the spinning air and water and blazing bright lightning. Storm clouds have been a reliable disposal system since the first rainboy. A freefalling body has enough momentum to break through the plasma walls. You don't die fast when you're inside one, either. The sheer winds and the suffocatingly thick clouds tear at you and choke you, and the plasma walls are doubly hard to puncture from inside. You die. You're torn to pieces, nothing larger than a raindrop, and you mix with the rain and vanish, pretty as can be, and then you come dribbling out. You're diluted and lost. Not even a world of blue-dressed policemen can ever, ever be sure you were there or who you were or what it was you had done to deserve it.

◆ ◆ ◆

He sleeps for a little while, then wakes.

This time he's absolutely sure that he hears a noise. It's got to be a Ghost, he thinks. He blinks and breathes and looks across the dark room, glancing at the big Tau Ceti panel—it's night there too—and then standing, his joints aching but not hurting so badly anymore, and he starts walking around the apartment, aware of his breathing and wondering how he can prove what he knows to Minus. Minus thinks it's nothing. Well, thinks Dirk, fuck him. I know. By stopping and holding his breath for a moment, he clearly detects motion coming from there. There! Across the room. He bends and starts to approach the sound, cautious and not a little bit scared. Sweat is under his arms and rolling down his face, burning his eyes, and he pauses again and stoops even lower and takes a long breath that he holds when a sudden vertical line appears before him, brilliant and thickening and sounding for all the world like voices.

The elevator comes open.

Minus emerges, followed by a pair of Quito-born men with the same kind of tinted hair and white, white skin.

"What's going on?" asks Minus.

Dirk tries to stand without seeming flustered. "I was resting," he lies. "Remember? I'm hurting." He sounds in control, but it's a wonder he didn't shit his pants.

Minus says, "Listen. Some Farmer up north saw a kid in Quito-type clothes. We intercepted the Farmer talking."

"You think it's the one we want?"

"One way to know," says Minus. In the pre-dawn gloom he merely looks pale and hairy. The men beside him are the same, only larger and younger and stupid in the face. Dirk doesn't know them. He stares at their pink eyes and tries to judge their character.

"Want to come?"

"I need medicine," says Dirk, thinking travel would do him good. "I've got to kill some pain."

"Here." Minus is punching the console's buttons.

Dirk drinks his fill, then more, then goes to the safe. It sickens him to look at the sprung locks and the thick useless door, the slick hard brand of hyperfiber impregnable to everything but brains. There's a single gun in the back of the safe. There used to be two guns, a matching set. He checks the juice in the one not stolen and takes a final gulp of sweet medicine and looks to Minus, saying, "I've got to talk to you."

"What about?"

"There's nothing wrong with my fucking brain, and I don't care what you've said. They're inside." He points to the ceiling so Minus understands. "Do something."

Minus shrugs.

I need allies, he thinks. "You fellows don't like keeping company with Ghosts, do you?" He squeezes shoulders and waits for affirmative nods. "Well, there are a mess of them upstairs. I'm not kidding, either!"

The men seem anxious. Dirk's attention makes them uneasy, the chatter about Ghosts unexpected and perhaps meant to test them.

He doesn't press. He says, "Any word on the girl?" and feels ill, emotions hidden somewhere beneath his skin. "Anything?"

"One possible," says Minus. "A disturbance in a drinking hole near us. At about the right time." He breathes and leads them into the elevator, pressing for the roof and saying, "A Flower or a girl dressed like a Flower, a fight and something about her leaving with a certain man." Minus has been talking to the Brulé police. Dirk's made some friends with them. "No official reports, so details are sketchy."

"What man?"

He doesn't know. As they accelerate upward, he says, "A guy with moves. And strength, too."

"Maybe it's this kid."

"Maybe," Minus allows. "Only the kid was seen walking toward us. Not away."

"Walking?" Dirk's joints hate the acceleration. But he's not letting himself bitch, with strangers so close. He works to hold himself like someone in charge, like someone they should respect. He wonders what's the cover story, because they sure can't learn what it is they're chasing. Not the chips, he thinks. "Anything else?" he asks. "Anything new?"

"Nothing."

"Don't tell me that."

"I'm paying for a bunch of tailored animals. Good eyes and wired into our AIs."

"Yeah?"

"They'll help us hunt."

"Maybe we won't need them," Dirk hopes. "Maybe this is going to finish things. This trip."

Minus says nothing. The elevator opens and they walk out into the hot, raw wind, down a short path and into the floater. Dirk's glad to be out of the apartment. He likes the distance and being rid of the Ghosts, real or imagined. Maybe Minus is right. Maybe it's the way my head is doctored, my crazy feelings for the Flower/Ghost still buried but not deep enough . . . except I've always hated them, was raised in a house where you cursed them instead of God . . . Ghosts—people set into crystal and laser light, no mobility, no escape paths. He thinks how they rely on the steady input of energy, and on all the machines and AIs and people around them. Maybe that's the worst of it, he tells himself. The trust. They trust us two trillion flesh-on-blood mortals, and I've spent my life disproving that faith. And at some point, like it or not, I'm going to have to choose.

Choose between being a Ghost and being quite dead myself.

◆◆◆

The Farmstead is a tiny town with homes for people and buildings for machinery and AIs, plus a little power plant and hospital and school. Maybe a thousand people. Not many more. Sitting with his back against a tree trunk, watching and thinking to himself, the Quito boy can recall hearing that Farmsteads are the most sophisticated communities on the Earth. They have every technology found in every city, only each citizen knows how to use the tricks. Not select specialists. Tailoring and climate control and AIs and so on—it's all part of their landscape. It's done every day. Farmsteads are private and proud and they have a strong, strong sense of territory. Each one is a little nation unto itself. Each has its own codes of conduct, its personal sense of right. A couple of days ago, out of the blue, the boy found himself dealing with Farmers a touch more predatory than he liked. And now he's still paying for the trouble, and so is Chiffon.

They circled around to the north and came in low toward Brulé. No one was following him at the start. He made certain. He kept them blended into the landscape, brushing against the trees as they passed, and only a wizard could have tracked them. Some of these Farmers, he thinks, must be wizards. Two of them riding a big rebuilt floater got on him and kept with him in spite of every trick he knew, and then they managed a crippling shot up their rear. A hard belly landing, ugly and quick. He and his muscles got out and got chased into some trees, the Farmers herding them with some careful gunfire. Then they hitched up his floater and were gone in a half minute. Neat and quick. And the boy told his muscles, Well, it looks like we walk.

Walk where? they asked.

To Brulé, he said. It's not so far, he said.

They looked at each other and then spoke their minds in a couple different ways. They weren't going a step south. Not after this start. This operation was too damned screwy and they wanted to stay alive and if the boy was smart he'd walk out of this mess with them, going north, getting to one of the City-States and tubetrains that'd take them home.

But he wouldn't go.

He thought of Chiffon needing him, and maybe it was the money too. He made a lot of heads shake, but of course he didn't explain it or make them do what they didn't want to do. He knew these people. He knew what was possible and what wasn't and how bad things could get if he tried to force them.

So since then he's done nothing but walk by himself.

All day yesterday the boy trudged through fields of corntrees and meat berries and wine flasks growing in the bright, bright sunshine. He ate when he thought it was safe, stealing where he thought no one would care. The wine was sweet. The corn was hard. One big meat berry wasn't ripe, its self-cooking enzymes too scarce, but he managed to wolf down the raw parts. He didn't care. Food had never tasted better. Not since he could remember, he thought.

He scarcely slept that first night, thinking about Chiffon waiting somewhere in Brulé. He wouldn't let himself imagine her captured. And there were times when he nearly forgot about the chips. God, he thought, he'd never felt such an ache for a woman. A woman, not a Flower. He wouldn't let her be a Flower or even a Ghost in his thoughts. He kept running it through his mind, picturing them leaving the Earth and finding a safe haven and using the billions to save her. If she had them. And if not, he thought, he would see her Ghosted again. To save her. Even if she said she'd rather die than live half a life . . . he couldn't stand the idea of losing her.

Miss Luscious Chiffon.

The Magician had looked a long time to find her. What the boy knows about her past lives is sketchy, partly because of security and partly because so much had been blocked out by the Magician. So she could better play the Flower's role, he knew. She was born rich and respectable, and she lived her first life with an endless parade of fur and suitors. She was still young when she became a Ghost. Too young maybe. When she concentrates, she remembers being a Ghost, the experience something like an old bad dream to her now. She remembers boredom. She remembers terrible fears. And of course Gray-time. The worst of it was Gray-time.

The boy had lain awake in the pasture that night, alone, remembering how the two of them had shared the brothel's ivory and living-feather bed, him spent and her tireless, her talking about the enormous things she would do with her quarter share of their earnings.

Then last night, all night, he had slept hard, dreaming of Chiffon while the pasture around him made noise. His flesh has been cut and sucked and masticated by hundreds of unseen mouths. He feels the long kilometers now, shifting his weight and watching the Farmstead, and he tells himself that today he will enter Brulé and he can sleep normally. One of his hands is holding a clod of soil. His Quito shirt and shorts are full of colors, swirling and mixing and never changing their patterns the same way twice. He wants to keep himself hidden. So he works the clod into the fabric, hurting the bug-chewed flesh below it.

The best course is to the west side of the Farmstead.

Stay alert, he tells himself. Forget everything else. This strange country has a way of wearing down his nerves, too much too new. Too many things startling him, or dulling him, or just plain leaving him baffled. He forces himself to stand, trying for quiet. The Farmstead itself is mostly silent in the breezy morning air. He hears birds in the trees and birds in the sky, but all that comes from the buildings and homes are a few scattered barks and whines—dogs of some sort talking among themselves, their voices assertive and grouchy with the hour.

He follows a row of unkempt jungle, keeping low and parallel to the closest buildings. Then he enters an empty field where nameless stalks lay crushed and rotting in the soft moist soil. He can smell the rich stink of it. The Farmers care for nothing like they care for their soil, or so he's heard. Not even for themselves. Any Farmer can stoop and lay a tongue to the stuff and tell if it's his or her land. They know it that well. And they never like city-bred hotshots walking it, which is why he needs to keep moving. Trotting. Now running. He works to stretch out the kinks.

Crossing back into the jungle, he follows a game trail, narrow and winding. Something ahead gives a low snort and leaps. On his right is a slow, clear stream, and he hears splashing and wheels to see a long brown head bobbing and dark luminous eyes alive and him thinking *roodeer* as he sees the glint of spray coming off the water. The roodeer startled him, too. His heart is startled. Running faster, he thinks this is too fast and feels his shoes slipping on the turns. He's down alongside the stream, the water shadowy and slick, and he sees logs rotting and reeds growing in tangled green masses and a school of silvery fish, like knife blades, scattering as his long shadow passes over them.

In a little while, and gradually, the stream widens.

The original trail is drowned by the water and mats of vivid green moss, but a second trail, newer and narrower, branches up into the trees and takes him to the top of a low hill.

He quits running when he's back in the hot sunshine, hands on his knees and his back bowed.

It's then that he senses something, smells it or feels it, and he straightens against the exhaustion and pulls out a big handgun and tries waiting, listening, listening, only he can't hear anything coming. God, he thinks, I can't tell what's a bug sound and what's a person sound. Listen to the racket! But he has this nagging sensation, enough to make him step backward, and then he forces a breath and turns so he can get off this open ground. Now.

The trail dips.

He follows it and comes to the shoreline of a small clear pond.

Trees are drowned in the deepest water. Squatting on the far shore, holding tools and looking straight at him is a Farmer in work clothes. He is smiling while he squints. It's an odd, knows-something smile.

The boy ignores him, running again and hearing nothing special and thinking that maybe he didn't hear anything in the first place. It's just nerves, he thinks. Following the pond around a lazy bend, the Farmer now out of sight, he sees a tangled dam of logs and junk plastic and the bodies of scrapped floaters, and he thinks of crossing the dam, sure, and watching whatever follows.

The dog takes a leg.

He doesn't hear the dog. It comes bursting out of the brush beside the dam, jaws snapping and the teeth neatly slicing every tendon in his lower leg. The boy shouts and wheels and collapses. The big farm dog comes up into his face, and the boy shoots it between its pale yellow eyes, removing most of its head, and three more dogs boil out of the brush and snarl and come at him. He shoots one of them and then cries out in pain. He tries moving the leg while the remaining dogs wrestle over his neck. He shoots one of them badly, clipping off an ear and a chunk of its skull. It gives a howl and runs, and the remaining dog has him by the throat, bad old teeth working for purchase and the boy too weak to aim, firing the gun again and managing only to burn a circle in the moist black earth. The dog is old. It's a slow feeble struggle between them. Hours seem to pass before the gun becomes light enough to lift, and he halfway aims and puts a dozen shots into the bright sun and then the gun clicks and clicks and rolls off his fingertips and into the smooth water of the pond.

The dog's breath is sickening.

The boy lies motionless, sensing nothing but the breath and thinking if only the smell would get out of his nose and then he wouldn't mind, a lapping sound coming now and the dog's hairy face red with blood. Red bright bubbles form on the end of its black nose, each one popping. A stupid set of eyes seem utterly evil. Those eyes would suit me in Quito, thinks the boy. In Quito they understand those looks and respect them.

Now the dog suddenly turns.

There comes a bark, remote and soft, and the boy feels paws pushing against him as the dog leaps, barking again.

Nothing happens.

Nothing happens.

He is staring up at the sharp blue sky, thinking hours must have passed, or days, and the twisted form of the dog crosses the sky with a kind of dignity, and it drops into the pond and kicks up spray and waves that feels so wonderful, so fine, and he stares up and sees a white face now, and bright-colored hair and a beard, and the face says something to him, something about Chiffon, and that makes him smile and he thinks back to Quito and he's happy and feels safe and the sun's still coming up and all the day is left him.

◆ ◆ ◆

"Dead," Minus announces.

"What fucking luck."

"The hounds really worked him over."

"So are they there?" Dirk is talking about the chips. He doesn't know why the corpse would be carrying them, but it might be and there's no sense taking risks. "You check him out?"

"Twice."

"And around him?"

Minus blinks and says nothing. Except his eyes say it.

"Just asking," says Dirk. He is standing on the hilltop over the pond, the wind hard at his side. His mouth is skeptical, seemingly doubting everything in view. He wonders, "Does the kid match the one we're chasing?"

"Probably."

"Where'd the others go?"

"Backtracking," he says. "They're making sure he's alone," and he adjusts the brim of his hat. Oversized clothes and the hat keep him safe in the hard sunshine. "What do we do with the body?"

"Find a rainstorm."

"Okay." Minus goes down to pick up the mess, carrying it up the slope and over to the floater. Dirk just waits. All the tangled vegetation is so green it looks black, and a thousand unseen things are screaming and singing from inside their hiding places. He hears someone coming and turns. The two new men are climbing the hill, struggling, cutting their hands on thorny vines.

"Anything?" Dirk uses his tight, don't-waste-my-time voice.

One of the men says, "Nothing now." Both are dressed like Minus, and both are sweating hard.

"Nothing now?" Dirk echoes.

"There was someone," says the other man. "He found the guy." He gestures at his partner.

"What happened?"

"I thought he knew something," says the partner, shrugging. "Maybe he saw something, you know? I don't know." He's a little nervous, unsure of his footing. "I figured he saw something and we can't leave him. Can we?" He shrugs once again and gives a little sideways smile.

"Where's the body?"

Both men point to the bend in the pond.

"Why the fuck didn't you bring it? We've got to dump it."

One of them volunteers, "We thought the pond was good enough." Both nod, sharing their conviction.

"You sunk it?"

"Yeah."

"And what if someone finds it?"

"It's a warning."

They think this is Quito, Dirk tells himself. They think this is home and they can do as they please. "What'd you think he knew?"

"He had this goddamned smile on his face. So I did him."

"Yeah," says his partner.

Dirk looks at their weak faces and weepy eyes and senses that they are afraid. So he keeps looking at them. With the sun behind him, they have to keep it in their faces. And the glare burns them while they stand, waiting for whatever Dirk says or does next.

A friend of mine, a noted mathematician, has assured me that what we have done with the System—its diversity, its sheer bulk—is the merest slice of a fraction of what is possible. He says Humanity comprises a creative force and an enormous potential beyond any reckoning by mere numbers and minds. We will continue to expand, he says, and new cultures will form out of our passions. He has no doubts. Ten billion years and a hundred million galaxies will not blunt our assault on the infinite. Someone like myself, he says, cannot hope to perceive anything more than the surface of this phenomenon. And I laugh, of course, not ever wishing to . . .

—excerpt from a traveler's notebook, available through System-Net

We kid ourselves. We do. We tell ourselves that genetics is bricks and mortar, that tailoring allows us total control over our offspring, that we can build whatever people and cultures we desire and then retain control over directions and destinies. The honest truth, however, is that several tens of thousands of genes interact in a multitude of ways. No computations can insure one result over every other one. No population can be declared immune from novelty at any level. And when one interjects the gray effects of development—the quality and consistency of a child's care, for example—you begin to see the enormity of the task . . .

—excerpt from a tailoring text, available through World-Net

H E isn't wearing black this time, and he's not on Garden. It's a place Toby doesn't know, and he soberly watches the flat featureless plain stricken with geometric shapes—severe and shadowless—and hears the mournful sound of a gusting wind. Toby is hunting someone. He wants to tell them something, only the message escapes him. Ahead, far off on the horizon, is a sharp pyramid that draws him. He walks and walks, finally reaching its base. On its peak is an enormous black head, hairless and smooth with its eyes and mouth shut. Toby says something to the head. The eyes come open. He repeats himself. The mouth breaks into a long slow smile.

Toby opens his own eyes.

He sits upright and shudders, thinking there are limits and he can't stand the son-of-a-bitch getting into his sleep, too. Sometimes he thinks the Morninger puts himself into his dreams. Sometimes he wonders if Gabbro's some kind of psychic—people who can throw their thoughts and who haven't existed since they were proven impossible.

Gabbro Gleason.

They've been at odds since Toby's first day in this place. He remembers everything about the first time they met, Toby coming down the stairs from the floater pad and Gabbro with the girl climbing the same stairs. Toby had just bought a chair from a little Old Quarter shop—cheap living wood that would root into his carpet, money back if not happy—and he was trying to manage the weight in the narrow stairwell. He hadn't spent enough time preparing for the Earth's gravity. Not enough calcium implants and not enough electro-isometrics. And there was a cyborg climbing toward him, completely unexpected. Gabbro had called up to him, saying something, and Toby hadn't heard him. Then the floater lifted and was gone and he realized it was the floater they wanted. And Gabbro said something to him. He said, "Thanks, neighbor," with hooks in his voice. And while this wasn't Garden, and Toby partly understood how exposed and alone he would be on the Earth, the bulk of him thought in the reflexive terms of someone raised as a Soul of Eden.

Cyborgs are nowhere near the Ideal.

Whether you're a conservative or permissive Gardener, without exception, you look on cyborgs as the ultimate corruption—the marriage of flesh and machinery, soul and circuits. Toby recalls the dry heat coming off Gabbro and the way he towered, his blackness darker than shadows and his big glass eyes giving him a strangely human stare as they squeezed past one another. Toby was frightened and outraged at the same instant. He tasted bile welling up in his dry throat.

A few moments later, softly, Toby cursed the cyborg.

Maybe cyborgs have inhuman ears. Maybe he spoke louder than he realized. Either way, Gabbro paused and turned and asked Toby what he had just said. Repeat it.

Toby said nothing.

Stooge? Gabbro asked. To the circuit? His voice was eerily smooth, something about it almost pretty. Isn't that . . . what? he asked. A fancy insult? Are you insulting me?

Toby didn't answer him. He remembers being terrified and embarrassed for being so helpless. Gabbro said:

So you're moving in upstairs from me?

His girlfriend said, Gabbro? Love?

Well, said that smooth voice, take some time and think before you talk like that to me. His face was stern and absolutely human. Gabbro was wearing shorts and a simple shirt, his black feet bare, and Toby saw the ropy cords of his hyperfiber muscles showing in the thick legs and long arms. He asked Toby, Where's your home?

Toby said nothing.

Don't you know where you've come from? he asked.

Some voice from inside him announced, I don't have to answer to you!

Come on, love, said the girlfriend. Forget him, she said, laying a ridiculously tiny hand on one oversized arm.

There was a man inside that lifeless shell.

It's always difficult for Toby to think in those terms.

Gabbro began to smile. It was a sudden expression, the white teeth shining and the eyes smiling too. He asked, You're a little asshole, aren't you? Aren't you?

Toby said, Leave me alone.

And Gabbro gave a loud laugh. It was as if a joke had been told. He said, You're precious. He laughed louder, then turned and took the girl by an arm. They climbed to the roof with Gabbro still laughing, and Toby began to breathe again. His arms were shaking. He remembers the terror and how the chair was suddenly out of his grasp and falling, crashing down the last stairs and giving an audible *crack* at the bottom. A living leg was broken, sap coming out in slow golden drops. Dammit! he thought. Dammit! And still he heard the cyborg's laughter coming down at him, tormenting him.

It's been that kind of year, he thinks.

Start to finish.

◆◆◆

Toby's father, and his mother too, have always been part of the permissive wing of the Souls. Politically they support pragmatic changes in the Prophet Adam's visions. Economically they favor a more open society than the Conservatives think proper or smart. The Prophet was a great person, they argue. Not divine. His visions covered an enormous range of social and ecological facets, yet there are still gaps and odd distortions and areas of conflicting ideals. The Prophet's work wasn't done when he died. His Ideal is not a crystal completed. The challenge for Garden—or so argue the Permissives— is to accept the grayness of His plans and expand Garden's potentials accordingly.

There are millions of people living in the Jovian system. Plus the cetaceans, of course, and some AIs, and maybe the odd Ghost here and there. Toby, raised in a Permissive household, knows the arguments by heart. Garden must cultivate its trading and diplomatic relationships with its neighbors. His father had always been adamant on the issue. Jupiter's own little system has potentials untapped. Father Jove itself is full of wasted energy and useful mass and even a simple native ecology—single-cell organisms as big as fists, drifting in the warm hydrogen atmosphere, feeding on lightning and fermenting hydrocarbons and such. Someday, his father would state, Garden could become a vital hub in the System at large. Its beauty and its spiritual purity could serve as a guidepost to people everywhere. The Prophet was a great visionary, yes, but that doesn't mean His descendants couldn't be the same. On and on he spoke about these enormous possibilities, and Toby can remember halfway listening, believing none of it, the words washing over him and clean away.

Ideology is a frightful bore.

He hates it and hates having to suffer it when he knows the speaker is incapable of seeing a fraction of it come true.

Toby is a mess of tangled feelings, and he blames his father for the worst of it. He came to the Earth against his will because his father had the power and the urge to see him suffer. The logic was that he would learn lessons at the hands of the Terrans, and the lessons have come. Yes indeed. He's not the same child who was content to look no further than Garden's sweet air and private sun. Now he does think about the Prophet's philosophy. He does. After a year on the Earth and a string of indignities, small and not, his old beliefs, sketchy and shallow, have been updated. Just as his father must have known would happen. Sure. But the final joke, thinks Toby, is on him. It's on his father. If the man came into the room now, sat and asked how he was doing, Toby would look straight at him and tell him the truth. "I'm a staunch Conservative. I am. And you helped make me so."

He isn't sure about his specific beliefs. Not yet. And he's rather sure that the Conservatives wouldn't recognize parts of them. Presuming, of course, that he could explain them. But there's something in him, real and potent, and sometimes, at odd times, that something makes him wake in the night, alone, a fever inside him and some half-formed vision of his own set somewhere nearby. Somewhere just out of sight.

His father was right about one salient point, however.

The Prophet was not the last Gardener prophet. He feels the truth down in his bones.

◆ ◆ ◆

His bedroom wall is still linked to a fantasy channel. Without sound or audience, it has run through the night.

Toby sits on his mattress and stares at the scene, his thoughts changing. He feels the usual longing for Garden's sea and sky and the way its bright sun rises and sets and rises again, the days so quick that you have trouble counting them. He remembers holidays and feasts, and of course there are the ceremonies culminating in the Passion Necklace. The one thing every Terran knows about Garden is the Necklace. To Toby it was logical and enjoyable and buoyed up by tradition. Now, in its absence, it seems holy. It is beautiful and true. But to the Terrans and their crude minds it is a mere orgy. Nothing more. The average Necklace lasts for days, even in Earth time, and each is built from people standing in a great ring, their androgynous bodies linked and each person coupling with his or her neighbors— several thousand bodies sometimes joined around the margins of an entire island.

The Passion Necklace is held until one of its people faints away.

Or, on some occasions, dies.

Sex is as much a part of Garden as are the whitesmear palms and the bluestone fish. It's taught before walking or talking. There's not a day in Toby's life, at least in memory, when some erotic interlude didn't prominently figure. Yet since arriving here his only regular diversion has been the fantasies on the wall—built by the bloodless AIs for modest fees, light and sound created by whim and held in storage for whenever he has the urge.

He sees a sunstruck beach and Gardeners standing with their feet in the slowly curling surf.

The Passion Necklace has been growing through the night. It began with three Gardeners, one of them plainly Toby, and every minute or so another two would join them and match their motions, Toby in the center, no one making a wrong move or a missed step while coming out of the palms or the sea. He looks at the image of himself, at his straining face and groping hands and the way he seems tired without having to worry about collapsing, and he considers the thousands in this Necklace and knows something about how it would feel.

Usually he stops the fantasy before now.

Today, for no real reason, he punches a button that causes the image to shrink to a spot no bigger or brighter than the brown tip of his thumb. Then he makes the spot drop into the corner of the wall, out of sight, and he stands and glances out the window and thinks about that damned bird before he goes to the bathroom.

He has no fondness for masturbation.

He use to go down to the Old Quarter from time to time and rent the services of a whore. Male or female. It didn't so much matter. The last whore was a saucy woman with enormous breats and a protruding rump, perfume hanging on her like some dense private atmosphere. She had seen Toby first, advancing and asking if he was lonely. He said nothing, made no gestures, yet she seemed encouraged. She pushed one breast against him. A lump of concrete would have felt firmer, but barely, and the nipple looked black through her shirt, huge and sticking into him like a thumb. But would you like some fun? she asked. She could be had for an entire splendid night for a reasonable price. She called him "Darling." She said, I *do* like Gardeners. I do!

Have you ever been with one? he asked.

Of course, she lied. I prefer them!

How much? he asked.

She quoted a figure, and he went through the mental calculations of how much cash he was carrying and how much his mother would send next month, plus how much reserve he had in the form of little quiver chips hidden at home. Then he offered her half of what she wanted and she shaved a little from her first offer, him thinking and finally saying:

Okay. Fine.

It was nighttime. They boarded a floater and went to his home because hotel rooms cost and he knew the looks he would get from strangers. They thought he was a whore trying to look like a Gardener, and they'd talk to him and sometimes touch him with their humid hands, asking, Where's your skullcap, honey? Hey! Get certified and get a skullcap, honey. Then we'll have a fine time. You bet!

It was odd. He wasn't afraid of that whore. She was so large and so willing to voice her thoughts, crude and simple as they were, that Toby couldn't find any place to hang his fear. She was stupid. She was loud. If she meant him any harm, he was certain, she'd look him in the eyes and say so. No hesitations.

Is this it? she asked as the floater descended.

He said nothing.

Not much to look at! she declared. I myself live to the west. (She named her neighborhood, Toby not knowing it from any other place.) She said, It's nice out there. We've got a little lake and river and look down on Farmstead country. We do.

The floater was down and paid and gone, and Toby stood still for a moment and listened to the noise below.

What is it, honey?

He said, He's having a party.

Who is? Some friend of yours?

He said, Nightmares of the Prophet. Damn, damn!

They went downstairs and into his home. The whore decided that a drink would help. Toby had nothing that she wanted, but she needled him until he ordered a bottle of something to be sent to him. Gabbro was having an enormous party downstairs. He and his miner friends, plus a smattering of Terrans, and their noise made the floor tremble. The whore wanted to dance to the beat of the music, and she made fun of Toby's disinterest and danced with herself, pulling off her shirt and exposing a single golden chain strung between her breasts, rooted in the skin somehow.

The bottle arrived with a soft *whoosh.*

The whore downed most of the clear liquor herself, and only then was she ready and able to contemplate bed. It was a moonless night. Toby had her lying on his mattress, in the dark, and he worked with her until he had climaxed a good dozen times. He was bathed in sweat, lying beside her, and she was on her belly. Two large moles were on her rump, one to each cheek, and a thick rope of golden hair grew from each of them. She was looking at him. She gave a drunken laugh and licked the sweat off his chest, smacking her lips and saying:

Honey! You taste girly!

Toby climbed out of bed and opened the window. She was asleep before he could lie down again, her snoring slow and harsh and wet. The party didn't sound so loud in his bedroom, for which he was thankful, but he couldn't sleep or even relax. He thought about using the whore again. A dozen times was nothing. Not even for a disinterested Gardener. He felt some obligation to prove this to her, thinking that if he could just get her to say what a great lover he was, honey, then maybe the money and everything would be worth it.

A little after midnight the party spilled out into the yard.

Toby heard splashes like explosions. He looked outside without standing, and he saw water rising past in a fountain still thick and rising higher. The Morningers were jumping up and crashing into the pool. Toby began to smell the water—a fishy stink, cool and lingering—and then he could almost taste it in his mouth. He wasn't relaxed but he was tired. Thinking in a straight line was difficult. He felt a mist on his face and didn't know what to think. He finally sat up and breathed and tried to collect his senses.

The whore's skullcap was glowing into the pillow.

She had rolled onto her back, her breasts pointing at the ceiling and ignoring gravity.

Then he realized what was happening. Damn! He stood and went to the open window and shouted, Hey! Stop that! You, hey! A new fountain emerged from the pool, concentrated and quick. It struck the window before Toby could shut his eyes, or jump, and he heard the laughter before he saw the big ebony figures standing in the yard with no clothes. There were men and women too. Morningers and the Terrans scattered among them. They were all terribly drunk and laughing to tears, and Toby shouted down at them.

Nightmares! he shouted.

Circuit stooges!

The whore came awake behind him. Hey, she said, what's this?

One of the women miners bent at the knees and leaped higher than she stood, tucking and dropping on the water to put up another fountain.

Toby cursed all of them.

He tried everything he knew to bruise them, his voice cracking and
their laughter undaunted.

He heard Gabbro say something about a jerk. A Garden jerk.

Listen to the mouth, said another. What a mouth.

Ignore him, said Gabbro. Let it slide. He's crazy and you just have
to ignore him.

Then Toby saw Gabbro's girlfriend standing close to the pool,
drunk enough to stagger. He remembered her name from having
eavesdropped, and he called to her. He said, Get inside, bitch! And
take that machine cock with you!

There was a sudden silence, enormous and cold. Toby waited. He
was standing on his toes, face pressed to the screen, and then a strong
hand grasped him by the ankle and he wheeled and saw the whore by
her skullcap. She wanted him back in bed. She said, Quit teasing them,
honey! Get a bottle and get back in here!

April was beating on Gabbro with both fists, cursing and crying and
finally falling down. She wanted him to do something. She wanted him
to defend her from the insults. For me! she shouted. Pull the fucker
to pieces, now now now!

Toby waited, listening to the girl's sobs. Gabbro's eyes came up and
found his face in the dark.

Gabbro said, Watch her.

His voice was soft and careful.

Gabbro came out from among the other miners, his bulk without
weight, his strides long and smooth. He bounced once and came over
the railing onto Toby's balcony, the balcony moaning under the load,
and Toby strained against the wet screen and watched and tried to
believe it wasn't happening. It all seemed unreal—Gabbro fitting his
fingers into the glass, tugging, the locks breaking and the door coming
open and him inside. Toby tried shutting the bedroom door, and one
massive hand gave it a push, a tap, and put him flat on his back on
the floor.

He remembers the whore screaming.

Gabbro ignored her as he lifted Toby, carrying him out through the
front room with one arm. Again the balcony creaked under the
weight. Toby became airborne. He remembers the spinning sensation
and the thought that he would die now, and the smooth warm hands
of a miner had him. An eerie black face smiled, ceramic teeth stinking
of cooked meat and beer, and a voice from somewhere inside the body
said:

You're shit.

Toby struggled, and the miners had a laugh.

Gabbro came down and laughed too, enjoying himself, and said, So You're a swimmer? That's what they do on Garden, right?

They dropped him into the pool, two other miners jumping in beside him and holding him under the surface. They massaged his ribs until the air was out of him and his head ached and he lacked the strength to kick to the surface when the hands let him go. He was sick. He saw darkness all around and felt himself floating, time compressed into a painless age where the floating seemed right and fine and all he could ever want to do. He was happy. Drowning made him happy. Then someone had him, pulling him upward, and he fought the pull because he didn't want to lose this feeling. But he didn't have strength and he was up out of the water, on his back on the soft-coral deck, and he rolled on his side and coughed hard and vomited. There was bile in his mouth and nose. He was sick and so sad, so weak, and he sobbed and rolled to his other side and looked through tears at all the miners standing and watching him and talking to a tall man who was watching him, too.

It was the one with scars and the red hair. Steward, someone called him.

He looked like a toy beside the miners, but he stood there and was furious, and fearless, and it seemed as though they were stung by whatever he said. He had them quiet now. He had them backing away. Toby can't remember the words or even the tone of his voice, but then the miners retreated inside and the red-haired man was over him, mopping at his sour mouth with the sleeve of his own shirt. Toby was humiliated. He didn't want help. Just let me lie here! he thought. Go!

The red-haired man finally helped him stand. He said something about them being good people. He said both sides were to blame and forget it. He asked if Toby was all right.

Yeah. Fine.

How do you feel? he asked.

I want to be alone.

Steward looked through him, his expression passive. Then he turned and left without saying another thing. Toby went home through the hallways, climbing the stairs slowly, and when he came into the front room he stood and listened for a long while, hearing the night sounds through the open door and thinking he'd have to get the door fixed. They weren't scaring him away, he swore to himself. He wasn't going to let it happen.

Then he remembered the whore.

She was gone. He went into the bedroom and found it empty, the closets open and clothes scattered and some of the hidden quiver chips missing. He thought about the police. He couldn't see any good from them. He sat on the mattress, drained, and listened to the sounds from below. The party was quieter. He tried to imagine what was happening, picturing an orgy between Terrans and the miners, and he made them artless and ugly in his mind, without style or aim or spirit.

He hated all of them.

Sitting in the dark, he pondered his circumstances until he was deathly tired, eyes closing of their own volition, and he leaned against the wall and felt the vibrations from below, felt them rising up into his poor bones.

◆ ◆ ◆

Now he's in the front room. The air is stale and close and he wants the door open. Except there's that bird, he thinks. He couldn't stand a repeat of yesterday. He's eating biscuits again, drinking cool water, and from time to time he glances at the empty yard, green and noisy and already hot. It's early for him. Nerves have him on edge. He'll study some more of the old propaganda, he decides, and cure his nerves that way. Or maybe something on the terraforming of Garden.

There's nothing from below. Gabbro's asleep or working.

No, he thinks, they're not chasing me out of this place. I leave for my own reasons, damn them!

He stands, feeling defiant enough to open the glass door a crack, and a slight warm breeze plays across his bare toes. The red-haired man is up and eating, sitting in the middle of his old sofa. Toby feels an urge to have a word with him, one prisoner to another. He remembers his talking to the miners, fearing nothing. Then the man stands, and motion inspires motion. Toby starts to pick up dishes and stash them in his little washer. Working in the kitchen-corner, punching out commands to the AIs, he sniffs and smells something wrong. It's tainted food welling up out of the grocery chute. Dear Prophet, he thinks, what's the story? Am I poisoned now? Or what?

He feels the wind gusting outdoors.

He goes to the door and looks out, giving the pool an accusing stare. Maybe it's fouled, he thinks. Maybe Gabbro's to blame. Maybe the management will boot him out for doing it . . . only that doesn't comfort him. He wants a different resolution. And his eyes drop and there's the bird laying at his feet. The black feathers are dulled and ruffled, many of them broken. He sees blood and the dull dead eyes and a body twisted in some wrong fashion. Toby starts to kneel, then gags. He sees the way the bones are shattered, and he counts finger marks, each as big as fat sausages.

Gabbro crushed the bird.

He killed it and then tossed it up on the balcony.

Why?

As a warning? he asks himself. Another kind of tormenting?

He sees nothing but evil intended. On Garden, he thinks, rotting meat is not a disagreeable odor. Different bacteria produce different byproducts. He says, "All right," without emotion. He kneels and picks up the bird by a dead curled foot, its toes like wires and its body light and inert, and he dumps it into the garbage chute and swears, "No more. No more."

The Freestaters I have known are a diluted strain of the breed—odd southern cousins who lack that peculiar fire and discipline associated with the word *Freestater.* The ones I've known best are part of a little nation called Banff. It's a rugged land, pretty and primitive, yet accessible to travelers like myself. Its people pride themselves on not being the fanatics of lore. They wage their wars only on certain days and weeks, for instance. They don't inflict as much pain on their enemies, and naturally they don't endure it as well either. Some have World-Net connections in their homes. Others have traveled beyond their borders. Yet they are Freestaters, still and for always. They are taught to fight from an early age. They do not kill. (So strong is that taboo that merely asking about the incidence of murder in Banff—a harmless, almost expected question in Singapore or Jarvis or Quito—brings out a look of horror in every face. Murder is more than a crime to them. A killer is more evil than outsiders can imagine.) And like the "fanatics" to the north, each child is given a Shadow who goes through his or her training with them. A Shadow becomes your extra set of eyes. A Shadow is your partner and confidant. Just as you are bound to your little nation— your fellow warriors—by codes of honor and trust, you are bound to your Shadow too. Except the passion is increased by an order of magnitude. It is so great, I have been told, that in the purest of Freestates a Shadow's death by any means—age or accident or whatever—is swiftly followed by your own demise. A warrior grows weak and sickens and then is gone, following his Shadow into the oldest adventure of them all . . .

—excerpt from a traveler's notebook, available through System-Net

S HE'S sleeping on the floor, on the deep carpeting, using an arm for a pillow and the other arm lying beside her, her hand carelessly draped over the bandaged thigh. Steward watches her breathing and thinks again about the five months left and how whatever he does has to be done fast so she can enjoy all she can enjoy. That's what matters. That's what he has to keep in mind today.

The last thing he does is select a certain World-Net channel and put it up on the wall beside his door. The wall turns the color of slate, and with the delicate pressure of a finger he starts to write. The pressure is translated into a chalky white line. "GOING ON ERRAND," he tells her. "WILL CALL SOON. STEWARD."

He won't wake her. He moves without sound, the door automatically locking behind him, and he goes downstairs and out on the opposite side of the building. The opposite yard is a little wider. A suggestion of a stream runs down the middle, connecting a series of swimming pools; Steward kneels and sips the warm water and rises again, wiping his mouth dry with the back of his hand.

He runs.

At first it's a slow, jarring gait. He's on a path wide enough for two people, its rubbery surface absorbing the foot strikes until he's loose and extending and breathing naturally, arms working and the sweat beginning. Steward follows the stream toward the east. He listens to Brulé waking around him—people with breakfast voices and lovers at climax and World-Net turned to the local news, the lives of two trillion neighbors distilled into a burst of compressed information. Steward can't listen to anything long enough to understand meanings. He is past and gone and hearing something new now, and in two strides he's beyond that too.

The buildings change their shape and look, rising higher and resembling true hills. The yard is wider. The vegetation is groomed and weeded and raked and pruned, leaves polished and blossoms doused with tireless auxins that fool them into lingering for months on end. The air smells cautiously fragrant. Children stand on the balconies, bored enough to watch a lone runner with faintly disapproving expressions. One of the kids—a black-haired boy no older than ten—shouts at Steward, warning him, "You got to stop. Hey! Where you going? Hey, don't go out there!"

He's near the edge of the city.

Some places have fringing parks, green and wild. Here the end is a high living wall of interwoven needly brush, gray in its depths and dense throughout. Impassable. He parallels the wall for a little ways, just trotting, then pauses where the brush turns darker, almost black, and while he waits, the tangled mess starts to move. A small tunnel opens at the ground, and Steward kneels and says, "Thanks," to no

one in particular, climbing through, and the tunnel closes behind him
with a dry whispery sound.

He's standing in a field of various vegetables, nothing taller than his
waist and no easy path visible. The little stream has vanished. People
have vanished. He picks his way along, thinking how he usually comes
through the parkland but this is faster. And a narrow path betrays
itself, him jogging out into the field—a hundred kinds of vegetables
eating the sunlight around him.

The field ends after a kilometer and a steep wooded hillside begins.
He climbs a game trail. It's cool in the shadows, the air moist and
lazily still. Sweat soaks clothes and hair and runs into his blinking
eyes, burning them, and the quadricep muscles burn in a different way
as the legs lift and press down against the slick packed earth.

These are old river bluffs.

Brulé City was built in a wide river valley fringed with high, high
loess bluffs laid down at the end of the Ice Age. The river itself was
removed in some old civic works project. The drainage through this
basin is entirely underground—vast tunnels serving as a kind of ureth-
ral system, waste waters and durable blind fish somewhere beneath the
vegetable field.

Steward is on top of a high ridge, up in the wind now, and the grass
is as tall as elephants and bowing with a dry smooth sound only made
by windblown grass. The trail is broad and straight along the ridge-
line. Eyes are watching him as he goes—roodeer and wild cattle and
flighty wild ponies and long-limbed boars hunkering down and waiting for him to vanish. There are cougars, too, and big tailored jaguars
with pelts that change the shape and size of their spots, and there's
at least one cranky grizzly bear in the wooded valleys beyond the
ridge. Sometimes Steward comes to hunt the country, or just to camp
overnight, and he likes it so long as he can't see anything of Yellowknife in it.

He's moving south, pressing against the wind.

Brulé is a series of peculiar ridges, low and laid out with a carpen-
ter's geology, and the Old Quarter stands on the horizon. He can't
hear the city over the wind, or see people or individual floaters. He
thinks of poor Chiffon sleeping alone. He remembers how they slept
like unequal spoons on the carpeted floor, his waking unexpectedly
and feeling her heat while he lay awake planning what he would do
today. He thinks of her personal geology, smiling to himself. He
wonders who did the designing. He doesn't let himself dwell on the

five-month limitation, doesn't let himself get sad or hopeful about anything so remote. It is enough to love and protect her now. It's enough to have the privilege of her special charms . . . and he stops and says, "Listen to yourself." He shakes his head and mutters, "You're fifteen again, you fool."

A little trail goes off the main trail, heading west. It passes between two dead trees and down the steep face of the ridge. The loess soil is crumbling where roots don't tie it down. Steward reaches a ledge just wide enough for him to squat and relax. He looks straight out into the high treetops and spies a pair of lanky tailored apes with green fur and striped faces and bright black eyes. The apes are talking to one another. They use hands and simple words and nods. They've seen him, but they seem not to care. He hears them talking on and on, something social and gossipy to their tone, and meanwhile he finds a hidden rope and tosses it over the ledge and breathes once before taking hold, swinging out off the ledge and dropping hand over hand, his nose to the earth and the tangled branches behind him.

The cave is nearly invisible, its door the color and texture of the soil. The door opens with a soft *click,* knowing him, and he gets a foot on the floor and then the other and looks up at the apes. They've quit talking, staring now. They have smug expressions. They were watching him climb and telling themselves that the man knows nothing about climbing, staring down at him now and looking superior to the world.

◆ ◆ ◆

Steward hadn't been in Brulé long, and he didn't have a crush of clients in those first years. He didn't know how to acquire them and not risk his anonymity. He didn't know just what he had to sell. Then a certain local Farmstead heard about him and arranged a meeting.

What's it about? he asked.

You're from Yellowknife, right?

Sure.

It's your kind of trouble. We'll meet and talk. Okay?

He met them in one of the wild parks. He rode in the back of their big floater, the two burly Farmers talking while the country turned to fields beneath them. They looked like one another, like brothers, except somewhere along the line he learned they weren't family. Not strictly. Steward had heard stories about the Farmsteads—that the people in some were so inbred that they could donate organs and tissue to one another without any fears of rejection—and the one who wasn't flying turned around and asked:

So. How does a Freestater wander this far south?

I don't know. Circumstances? he said. I don't know.

How about the city? You like Brulé City?

Well enough.

All those people? And not all of them Terran, either.

Steward said nothing.

I couldn't stand that place, the Farmer claimed.

I'd go crazy, his companion admitted.

You aren't the only one, buddy. I wouldn't like it for a minute. I hate even going near it.

Steward sat and watched the landscape change, saying nothing and thinking to himself.

The floater spiraled down and landed beside a field of mature corn-trees. The three of them climbed out and squatted and spoke in curiously hushed voices. Imagine yourself leading a party across that field, said the first one. It's night. No moon. And a hard, hard rain is falling.

A blinding rain, said the other.

You know something about sensors and fooling sensors. Right? You do that sort of thing in Yellowknife, don't you?

Steward admitted it.

Well, said the second one, we want help.

Your help, said the first one.

What can I do?

The Farmers looked at one another, something passing between them. The thing is, said the first, we need help making ape marks.

Ape marks?

If someone came and checked it out, we want them to find evidence of wandering apes. You know? These troops can cover a lot of terrain.

A lot, echoed the second one.

Steward looked out at all the tall, heavily built corntrees, and he asked, Who owns the land?

The Farmers said, Someone else.

And what are you going to do?

They glanced at one another again, weighing words.

Suppose you were wronged, said the second Farmer. Suppose you couldn't get justice from courts hamstrung by favoritism and incompetence. Can you imagine it?

Sure.

You need to take action, said the first Farmer. When you're wronged, you do.

We're going to do it, said the second one. It's not *your* job, okay? We won't ask you.

Just get us over and back.

And make them think of roving apes.

Can you?

I can, he admitted.

Will you?

He said, I'll have to think it over.

They blinked and chewed on their identical lips.

Steward stood and said, Take me back and give me some time.

How much? said the first one.

Some.

It's going to be moonless tonight, with rain.

I'll let you know this afternoon. I promise.

They seemed relieved. They talked to one another all the way back to Brulé City. When Steward was on the ground again, the second Farmer said, You should think about this business. We can do you good.

I'll think and thanks, he said. Thanks.

Maybe we should talk money, said the first Farmer. Want us to talk money?

No. That can wait.

We're trusting you, he said. You're from Yellowknife. We've heard good, good things about you people. An agreement made is for life, right? For always?

A question of honor, said the second one.

Steward didn't like the sound of that word, *honor,* when it came from that mouth. He told them good-bye and turned and went home by the usual means, always making sure that no one was following him. He wasn't very good with World-Net in those times, and he lacked contacts who knew what he needed to know. But for an hour he did the groundwork, then he sat and made his final decision in half an instant. He put in a call to a different Farmstead, telling his unseen audience that he had significant information about their enemies. A reply came in a few minutes. A woman with plain features, strong and slim and gray with age, was looking at Steward, waiting for him to explain himself.

He told her everything.

Her breath quickened. A fine layer of sweat appeared on her tanned forehead. She said, I have the picture.

He said, I thought you'd want to know.

And what do you want? she asked. You haven't said anything about a price.

What's fair with this kind of thing?

She said, True.

She paused, thinking to herself, and then she offered, We can hire you. Help us defend our borders, breaking no laws and bending no beliefs, and I think you can write your own tab. Okay?

That's fine.

Starting tonight?

All right. Sure.

She said, Thank you. She said, The name is Steward, right? Then she was gone, the white wall empty, and he placed a call to a number given to him by the second Farmer. The first one was waiting. He saw Steward and misread his face.

Good! he said. You're with us?

Steward said he was not.

No?

I don't want to be, no.

The Farmer shook his head and said, Well, maybe we'll have to find someone braver. Someone who understands.

Steward said, Listen. I'll be guarding them when you come.

Guarding who?

Steward said nothing.

The Farmer told him, You're a prick, you know that?

Steward looked at him, trying to gauge him in a dozen ways.

A real prick! the Farmer growled. I always heard what honorable strong creatures you Yellowknives were. And look at you. Shit, I don't see a spine in you! You're garbage.

Steward remained quiet.

Well, we're coming anyway! said the Farmer. You wait!

And he was waiting. In the dark, in a driving rainstorm, Steward found a line of men dressed halfway like apes. He took them from behind. He didn't have to use any of the weapons he had smuggled from Yellowknife. Hands were enough, and broken bones were enough. When the rain quit there were half a dozen men moaning, and their guns were wrapped around the tall green corntrees, empty and useless.

◆ ◆ ◆

There's a second doorway at the end of a short hallway.

It too recognizes Steward and opens for him. He enters a little room made of hyperfiber—all built by the Farmstead in lieu of payment. He keeps his Yellowknife weapons here, safe from everyone, and he has a single wall spliced into World-Net. It's a simple serviceable office. He likes the location and the Farmers acting as watchdogs. He likes the press of the earth laying around him, and sometimes he will reach and touch the walls and feel the bunker-comfort of hyperfiber and rootbound loess and tall trees interlocking into the high green canopy.

He sits in the lone chair.

He punches a console set in the arm of the chair.

After several minutes of nothing, the Ghost appears. She is a pretty woman—no Luscious Chiffon, certainly, but pretty nonetheless—and she's wearing glamorous evening clothes that flatter the illusion of a figure. The background is some ancient palace. Lunar, Steward thinks. The high, high arches have a quaint delicacy impossible on the Earth. Painted ceilings show angels and devils and mortals too. There's something Catholic about it all. Which makes sense. The New Vatican is somewhere beneath Tycho, and half the System's Catholics live on Luna. The Muslims eased them out of Europe . . . when was that?

"Steward!" the Ghost exclaims. And she smiles.

He says, "You're a sight. Am I interrupting?" Ghosts have their own sense of time. Since their surroundings are manufactured by AIs, just as some AI is producing this image now for him, it can be any hour in any day of their own design. "Fancy dancing clothes, Olivia."

"Dear Steward!" Her smile is sweet and charming. Olivia Jade, socialite and flirt, beams her smile at him. "Is there a question?" she wonders.

"Sure."

"I'm seeing concern. I do."

"I'm looking for a wealthy man."

"And any wealthy man would love having you, I'm sure."

Steward laughs with her, saying, "Listen." He says, "You're a piece of work," and shakes his head.

"Is he among the living? Or among the not-yet-living?" It's a Ghost's joke. Olivia sometimes tells him that she and her kind are the final product in a logical evolution. Flesh-on-blood existence is a simple precursor to true life—a box of glowing crystals.

"The not-yet-living," he says.

"An obscure man, I'd guess. Or why would you ask me?"

"Your company's sake."

She giggles. She says, "So. What can you tell me about him?"

He repeats what he knows and what he can safely guess. The man is from Quito. He's possibly staying in the Old Quarter. He has nasty habits and considerable money and probably a wicked temper too.

"This may take a while," she warns.

"I'll wait."

"I can call you later. At home."

"I'll be here. Call me here." He has a world of faith in Olivia. She has never done him disfavors. Yet he prefers not to mention Chiffon, or even risk the chance disclosure. It's a feeling inside him. He breathes and says, "I have some work to do here."

"Well," she starts, eyes flickering and her mouth becoming set. "If the man wants to remain hidden—"

"I'll double the fee."

She says, "You *are* a dear," and vanishes in an instant. Yet the big palace lingers for a moment. In the extreme distance, almost out of view, stand a variety of Ghosts from countless places—all laced into that vast landscape called System-Net. Among the evening clothes are the bright, unmistakable robes of dead Lunar popes. He remembers reading that the popes were among the first to be Ghosted, although he can't quite fathom how that fits into Catholicism and its ancient teachings. Then the image fades and he stares at the blank wall, thinking to himself.

Sometimes he laughs gently, smiling.

Every so often he looks to the floor, talking to someone in his head.

◆ ◆ ◆

In theory, none of these weapons can kill.

They look awesome enough when they're out of their crates and the soft dead-leather cases. They have barrels and gun butts and triggers with ornate guards, and almost anyone would call them guns—rifles and pistols of traditional designs—ignoring the odd features characteristic of Freestate artillery.

There aren't any bolts of energy waiting in the barrels. Flesh isn't scalded. Limbs aren't torn away.

These are subtler weapons meant for a bloodless war.

A good Freestater rifle can deliver a measured amount of pain across several kilometers of open air. It does this wondrous and valuable thing by producing a concentrated ball of high-energy plasma, and the impacting plasma fuses with nerve endings—natural or synthetic—to cause agony. If the target is struck too often, no matter its strength or its training, immobilization results. And of course the anticipation of pain brings horror, not to mention a withering of the will.

Steward has gone fifty years without breaking the ultimate taboo.

He looks at the weapons scattered over the floor. Some are partway disassembled and all of them are fully charged. None can kill. Not intentionally, at least. He cannot kill. Not unintentionally, at least. There is a sound, a cough, and he looks up at Olivia's knowing smile and her simple casual clothes. Steward has seen this background in the past. It's a big rich room looking out on a smaller, younger Brulé. Rugs cover the floor and the gemstone furniture. Everything is bright and clean and somehow too perfectly positioned. She says, "I have one suspect. A man named Dirk."

"Dirk."

Her eyes narrow. "A Ghost friend of mine knows our Mayor Pyn. They were married, in fact, and the two still talk. I think Dirk fits your description." She says, "He arrived some months ago, applying for a temporary citizenship. He and his bodyguard inhabit the old Cosgrove Tower. Do you know the place?"

He does.

"A very, *very* wealthy man," she claims, laughing with a strange expression on her face. "The entire fifty-fifth floor is for himself and a bodyguard and one other. A girl, some say." She pauses.

He says, "No other candidates?"

"Not worth the trouble." She watches Steward, telling him, "A girl, some say. But Pyn is the only one of us who has seen her, and he swears that she's a Flower. An authentic Flower. Very special and very new."

Steward is ready to say nothing, showing nothing with his eyes and the rest of his face. He says, "Okay," with a level voice. He tells her, "Go on."

"He's not such a mystery person." She tells him the basics of Dirk's career and capacities. The details are not legally binding, but Olivia has also spoken to several dear friends with roots in Quito. They know the name and the reputation. She gives examples of how he does business. Then she returns to her first source and Mayor Pyn, informing Steward, "He's tolerated for his money. Dirk's hinting at underwriting the whole mining operation." Steward remembers Pyn and tries imagining him and Dirk sharing the day's time. "Dirk is shit," she says in summation.

Olivia never curses. It's not her style, and Steward is more than a little surprised.

"Well, he is!" She sits up and sticks out her chest, saying, "I guess I don't deserve a bonus."

"No?"

"A thousand other people could have told you this much."

"Your opinion," he says. "An agreement was made."

"You're sure?" It's no small amount. It isn't cheap to be a Ghost—the quality of your world depending on the AIs in your stable—and it isn't easier when you have pride. "I'm telling you—"

"It's yours!"

And she says, "Thank you," because he has left her no other choice.

Most flesh-on-blood types won't speak to Ghosts. It's a bias, thinks Steward, and it's sad. It's one of the multitude of ways in which we hamstring ourselves . . . and now he notices a twinkle, unmistakable and fetching, coming into Olivia's eyes. "What is it?" he asks.

"There's one more thing," she admits.

"Go on."

"I'm guessing, understand. I don't know your plans or even if you have plans. But I know a significant number of tenants inside the old Cosgrove Tower. All kinds of friends with all flavors of information!"

The potentials wash over him. He smiles and says, "My sweet Olivia. Kiss me!"

And she laughs until her face turns red. Then she shakes her head and tells him, "Think of it. A worthless piece of refuse, of shit, and we can do something about it. A kind of civic project of our design."

"I mean it. Kiss me!"

"Oh no." Her face changes. She breathes and looks squarely at him and says, "No, no. A woman knows. It's not me you want today," and she bites her lips. She tells him, "I hope you know what you're doing. I do hope so."

"Sure," he says, feeling transparent. No secrets today—

"Sure you do, or sure you hope so, too?" She waves a phantom hand, saying, "Forget that. Here. Let's get busy, and what do you need?"

◆ ◆ ◆

The germ of the plan comes to him slowly. He sees the goal and what he can do for himself. Give the wealthy pervert an option, he thinks. If he's wealthy first and a pervert second, then Steward needs to play the wily salesman and offer the best price in the perfect fashion. Business is eternally business, isn't it? Besides, he decides with a sinking feeling, this Dirk could always buy himself another Flower.

It's already well into the afternoon. Steward's eaten from a stock of dried foods, fruits and spicy roodeer meat, and Olivia has pretended to eat, her own meal sumptuous and served in ornate bowls riding on a bright golden platter. They're finished working. Everything she can offer has been offered, and Steward pays her from a stock of quiver chips he keeps on hand for contingencies. They're in a safe in his floor. "Good-bye for now," he says in the end. "I'll call and tell you how it went," and he places one hand up to the image of her face.

She's gone, oddly quiet at the end.

Scared? he wonders. Or a little jealous?

Now he calls home, punching out a code that circumvents his own extensive security systems. A pulsing blue light means an audio channel has been opened. "It's me," he says. "Are you awake?"

"Steward?"

"Touch a wall. Any wall." It feels as though he's been gone for days already. He says, "Chiffon?" and there she sits, legs crossed on his little bed and half a dozen books opened and scattered about the scene.

"Where are you?" she asks. "Working?"

"Doing some things for a friend." He leaves it at that because there aren't rules for this circumstance. He doesn't know what to say, looking into her anxious eyes. "Anyway, I'm calling to tell you I'm done. For a little while. I'll pass by home first, for a bit, and then I'll go again."

She watches him. She says, "I miss you."

"I miss you, too."

"I hope you don't mind," and she lifts a book. He sees graphite bindings and plastic pages, everything a little dulled by time. He can't quite make out a title. He has no idea what she might find interesting.

"I don't mind, no," he says. "Enjoy yourself."

"I'd rather have you here," she says.

And he wishes he could touch her, reassuring her with his grip. Her simplest look makes him weak. It does. He's almost relieved when he says, "I've got to go. I've got some last things to do," and lays a hand on the World-Net control.

"I'll keep busy, love. Hurry home."

"I will," he promises.

And she's gone. He finds breathing easier again. He finds himself debating whether or not to tell her the plan. No. No, he'd better not. He decides there's no sense in raising her hopes, he can't risk dashing them. That wouldn't be fair. He is on his feet, standing on his toes and trying to think. One weapon. Sure. He chooses a small pistol-shaped instrument that's always felt comfortable in his hands. Then there's the other equipment, lightweight and expensive and as modern as any anywhere. It fits into a small cloth pack. How about pain grenades? he asks himself. He has some tiny ones easily hidden. But no, the gun's enough. Anything else he might need is stashed in the Old Quarter. Nothing else? No? He goes through the first door, checking locks, and walks to the end of the hallway and stares straight out at half a dozen lazy apes.

They're waiting for him.

Chances are they don't mean harm. Maybe they're curious, he thinks. A human climbs inside an invisible cave, vanishing, and the call goes out to the troop. They gather, waiting for his reappearance, talking among themselves in that simple language of theirs. They're puzzled, he tells himself. Nothing more. And he looks around and blinks once and sees that he's wrong.

The bastards, he thinks . . . and he starts laughing.

They've stolen his hanging rope. They're playing a trick on Steward, their expressions full of mischief and suspense. He gives them a long calculating look, admiring them, and then he tells the outer door to stay open and walks to the back and squats and adjusts his pack, bracing his right foot against the inner door, taking a long breath and coming up running.

The ape faces turn surprised.

The red-haired man is bearing down on them. Them! Masters of the canopy! He reaches the door frame and plants a foot and leaps out into the shady afternoon air, hands reaching and the apes screaming and then scattering in wild disorder.

Steward grabs the nearest branch.

All the apes have vanished.

He hangs for a moment by his own long arms, panting and listening to the buzz of insects and the songs of hiding birds. Then he climbs downward, reaching the forest floor, thinking how he has been happy before but never so happy as now, and he has known purpose but never one so clear as this one.

He starts to run.

Above him the door shuts itself and is gone.

I remember Zebulina. Ten years of my life were spent as her suitor, her customer, her underwriter, her patient lover, her impatient lover . . . my role resisted precise definitions when it came to the girl. I remember her sweet looks and calculated moods and the effortless smile and the striking body. I purchased and furnished an apartment for her, putting her into one of the most exclusive districts in the Galapagos, and I can never say that she never thanked me for my trouble. She was nothing if not an absolutely fair dispenser of thanks. That was one of her largest charms. Fairness. I had a dinosaur tailored for her on her birthday—she was still quite a young girl; I can't recall her exact age—and she was so glad and so enchanted with my gift that I actually believed that I had won her permanently. The three of us would walk along the Pacific together, on the sandy beaches. The dinosaur was pony-sized, bipedal and thoroughly stupid. There were leash laws for such things, but of course Zebulina couldn't stand the thought of her *friend* being restrained. So it ran the beach and we would follow. Then she would come upon some stone or shell, forgettable to anyone else, and she would make me examine it while the dinosaur vanished in the distance. She had this girlish enthusiasm. She had this way of taking in a scene at a glance. I have never known a person so full of life and living. She wasn't a good person, mind you. I never confused her for someone moral or ethical. Yet I persisted in trying to win her love because I felt—and I think rightly—that a creature like her would someday hit the hard lessons that taught you and me the basics of goodness.

I lost her in the end.

It was to another admirer—someone who could give her more and expect less in return—yet Zebulina was fair to the end. At least with me. She gave back her apartment and its furnishings and even her pet dinosaur. I sold everything but the dinosaur. I kept it until it died of old age. From somewhere I heard that Zebulina was also dead. I don't know the reason, nor do I care. Someone else told me she was Ghosted, but I can't believe such a thing. Not from her. Not knowing her like I did . . .

> —excerpt from autobiographical notes, accessed from World-Net by the Magician

THERE was a time when April would do anything for the man and men in her life. That time is good and passed, she thinks, and she's glad for the freedom. Glad and proud too. She thinks of that younger self in the same way someone might think of a younger, wilder sister. She's a very different person today, and better. She doesn't have a doubt.

Gabbro calls her crazy. He likes to tell her all the different ways in which he suspects insanity in her blood.

She counters with stories from her past. Bad things have happened. Things undeserved and things that can't help but change a person. Life has shit on her many times, or so she claims. Maybe she exaggerates, sure. But the basic flavor and emphasis is never far off the mark, and the stories serve to keep him quiet for a little while.

Irrationality helps. It makes Gabbro patient and his patience lets her make demands on him. That earlier April never made demands on her men. As a consequence they were abundant and ever-changing and thoroughly unreliable. Of course there are times when she wonders if she has a real problem. There are moments when she loses all control of her actions. She has fits. Gabbro has seen plenty of her fits. But most of the time, peering back to what she's done, she can find some kernel of sensibility to her craziness. Just look how long we've lasted together, she thinks. It must be doing some good, she thinks. Crazy blood.

April is lying on the oversized couch, feet up and her head up and the room around her made of tall walls and precious little floor space. The furnishings are to her taste and Gabbro's needs, and the entire apartment has been designed to serve Brulé's miners—the original apartment gutted and expanded in two directions, down into the earth and across the hallway into the next unit. But it still seems small, particularly with Gabbro home and rooting about in his massive way. He's home now, and April can hear him in the oversized shower. The water is running, hot enough to cook meat, and the ultrasound scrubber is doing its best to remove the day's grit and grime. She herself is watching a drama on World-Net, thinking that she hasn't been applying herself because she feels lost. AIs produce the show. There are some human writers, but their roles come in a general way. This particular program is eight centuries old and vastly popular. It's set in some fictional City-State on some mythical tropical island. It has approximately one million characters, give or take—each one of them identifiable with his own history and problems and joys.

A viewer watches whomever she wishes, from any vantage point. April can find and track the certain people she knows best. Some are emotionally closer to her than many flesh-on-blood sorts. Their voices are like friends' voices. She has seen them eat together and love together and bear children and die in a myriad of ways. Since this is fantasy, naturally, the people tend to live interesting, even spectacular lives. Like these two people, she thinks. He owns lucrative businesses that allow him to wear fragrant clothes worth fortunes and own at least five different homes, all spacious and lovely. The woman is his trim and lovely wife—a fashion designer forced to travel to all kinds of exotic locations and meet all kinds of people. In their spare time the two of them have affairs and mild drug addictions and deal with such out-of-the-blue troubles as deep-space pirates and sudden strange diseases. Just now they're making love. Twenty years they have been married, yet the intensity of the act makes it seem as if they are doing it for the very first time.

On the long table in front of the couch, chilled and brightly colored, is April's afternoon drink. She sits up now and takes a long sip, the alcohol sweet and biting. Then she lies down again, her head on round pillows, and she handles the World-Net controls to change the angle of the picture.

Gabbro is done in the bathroom.

She hears him coming into the short hallway, and she lifts her head enough to look at him, at his broad back, as he goes into the bedroom to lie down on his special bed. She says, "Good dreams," and he mutters something in agreement. He worked another long shift today, and today she believes him and feels for him. Hyperfiber mimics flesh too well, she thinks. The bosses work him too hard. She's never been inside the mines—few Small Fry get the opportunity—but she's seen countless features on the local news, and documentaries on the process itself. It's his exhaustion that leads to his uneven performance in bed and elsewhere. Wouldn't it be wonderful, she thinks, if they improved the hyperfiber so he wouldn't need all the down-time? Gabbro is now plugging himself into a length of thick cable. In the small of his back, almost undetectable, is a linkup to his various batteries. He sleeps and the shell sleeps too, recharging itself. Sometimes it scares her to think of the energy flowing into him, and sometimes she goes to him just to touch the cable, glass wires humming inside a cool steel-gray sheath.

She sits up. She calls to him, asking, "Maybe we can go somewhere later. When you're rested, okay?"

He says, "Later," with his wrung-out voice.

"That's what I mean. Later." She says, "Promise?"

"Yeah."

"Good dreams, darling."

"Yeah."

Time passes. She drinks and watches the lovers, keeping her view discrete yet erotic. She knows for a fact that the husband slept with a girlfriend this morning, yet here he is able to perform with a champion's poise and energy. The third time is too much. They're showboating, she decides, and she flips to another character in another part of the rich City-State. Now *here* is something to watch. This woman is having obvious problems. Someone has kidnapped her and lashed her to a cold metal wall. Unseen machines hum in the shadows. A hunched figure walks toward her, one hand holding some inexplicable tool. April certainly hasn't been keeping up! Who is the kidnapper? What is he, or she, after? Whatever is going on, April is sucked into the action. She leans forward with her fingers working the controls. She almost misses the tap-tap-tapping sound.

Then the tapping stops. Its absence causes her to turn and look up at the glass door. A familiar figure stands on their little patio. He's wearing shorts and a soaked shirt and a small pack, and he's standing against the bright summer sky.

She stands and opens the door, saying, "Hello?" She says, "Steward, isn't it?"

"Hello, April." He gives a polite nod and a shy smile.

"Come in," she says.

"Is Gabbro home?" he asks. He seems to take in the room with a glance. "I'm afraid I need to talk to him. Could I talk to him?"

"You want me to wake him?"

He shrugs as if to say yes, he knows it's an enormous imposition but it's got to be this way.

For a moment, if only for distraction, April gives his face a good hard look and wonders about the potentials in him. The man has been working somewhere, sweating rivers and smelling harsh. She doesn't like his smell. She's heard the usual stories about him, intriguing mysteries so far as they go, but when she is actually with him, toe to toe, Steward seems as remarkable as any of their neighbors. Which means he is pure tap water. Through the years, over and over, she's found that she has a natural unerring judgment about these kinds of things.

"Come wait," she says. "I'll go and wake him."

He says, "Thanks."

"Oh," she says, "and would you watch the show? Tell me if I miss anything. Please?"

◆ ◆ ◆

Gabbro is aware of April's voice. He comes awake and knows he hasn't been sleeping for long. The hyperfiber aches as badly as ever. April is dressed in those same ugly shorts and the plain shirt, her breasts spilling down against the fabric. "You've got company," she is saying. "Our neighbor. Steward." The light from the window falls in the same way, too. "I don't know why, but he wants to talk. Is that okay?"

He says, "Why not? I'm up, aren't I?"

"Don't be mad at me," she warns. Leaning over the bed, she asks, "Do you want me to unplug you?"

"Do I ever?" She has this habit of asking, and he's never allowed it. Not once. He tells her it isn't proper. Does he ask if he can spoon food into her mouth or wipe her rear end? This is a private function. Besides, he thinks, she's too eager somehow. It bothers him to think how eager she looks.

The plug detaches. The gentle reassuring hum quits.

He sits up and stands up and sees Steward waiting in the front room. "What can I do for you?" he asks, walking stiffly.

"I'm sorry to bother you people."

"Don't be," he swears. "No problem."

"If we can, can we talk outside? The two of us?" Steward doesn't look anywhere but at Gabbro's eyes. "Just for a minute."

"Sure."

April stares after them. She won't like being left out of the show, and Gabbro decides to have fun with it. Tease her with it, maybe. He's got to admit he's curious. What's this about? He has a couple of ideas, one sillier than the next. Maybe it's a secret and April can't know. That gives him a wicked good feeling.

The air is full of flies now. Trillions of little black flies. The wind is finished for the day. Clouds are to the east and south, towering and smooth-faced and brilliant in the sunshine. There's rain in the east but not over Brulé. The line between rain and no rain is absolute, arrow-straight, and Gabbro looks at the clouds while the two of them stand beside one another.

"Listen," Steward begins, "I want to ask a favor."

"Do." Gabbro smiles, expecting it to start this way. "What is it?"

"A venture," he says.

"A venture?"

"Of a kind." He seems calm in the face. Sober. It takes a moment for him to say, "I want you and some other Morningers, a dozen or so, to do something for me."

"Oh yeah?"

There comes the faint, far rumble of thunder and the glint of rainboys pulling the storm through the stillness. Steward is telling what he wants. Gabbro watches the clouds and tries to follow the quiet voice, making him stop once to tell it again. Then Steward asks, "Are you interested?"

Gabbro couldn't have imagined this circumstance if he had tried. He says he is interested, sure, and Steward quotes him a price. "What?" asks Gabbro. "Who's that for?"

"Each of you. Except you. Carry this off and I'll give you a bonus. A double share."

"Yeah?"

"Are you interested?"

"Pretty much. Sure."

"And you can find the Morningers?"

"For the money? Not more than a couple hundred of them."

"Twelve is plenty," he says. "And another thing—"

"Yeah?"

"It has to happen tonight. I'll call you to give you the exact time, but it'll probably be after midnight."

Gabbro takes a breath and studies the discriminating storm, thinking this is pretty damned crazy but it sure sounds fun. It sounds fun enough to do without pay or prodding. He notices the intensity of the distant rain, how it falls straight and gray to the fields and jungles. He breathes again and says, "I'm curious about one thing—"

"Why get you to do it?"

"Yeah."

"I'm not going to tell you," says Steward.

"You're the good kind of crazy, I think." Gabbro considers every detail, top to bottom, and finds one snag. "What about laws?"

"I'll pay fines. You won't be jailed." He says, "Trust me," and takes Gabbro by the forearm, squeezing as a friend might to give some encouragement. Gabbro doesn't know many Terrans so open, and the gesture surprises him because it means so much to him. "I know there's going to be an element of danger. I'm hiring you. I'm responsible—"

"Listen—"

"No, no. I mean this. I have my limits, but I will do what I can to help you. A lot of things *might* happen." Steward's face is calm and watchful and patient. "But the chances are remote—"

"Hey. Don't give it a thought!"

Steward says nothing.

So Gabbro, smiling to himself, asks, "Is this whole business a secret? I can't tell anyone anything, can I?"

"I never hired you. We never talked. No one, even your best friends, should hear a word about any of this." Steward is emphatic, hooks in his voice.

And Gabbro sees April in the doorway, watching them. "Good," he says. "Real good."

◆ ◆ ◆

She can't hear them. They're talking too softly and that worries Chiffon in a bad way. Standing this close to the balcony's glass, she can't help but feel exposed. Yet she struggles to read lips and watches how Steward touches the cyborg's arm, something decided now. Maybe it doesn't involve me, she thinks. Maybe it's nothing. Maybe she's spent too much time alone in these rooms, thinking about everything and all the time helpless, and her paranoias are coming into play to warp her poise and sense.

She can trust Steward, she reminds herself. He will never, never do her intentional harm.

The trouble comes from the other direction. *The flight to Hell is navigated with good deeds* . . . and so on . . . and so on . . .

She isn't thinking about the Quito boy anymore. She's decided that he's dead or he's so well known to Dirk that he's watched like bait now, the trap set and she the prize. No, she thinks, her best prospect remains Steward. Dirk can't know him. It was all too much of a lovely fluke, their meeting the way they did. And she has the chips buried in her healing leg. They're another asset, all right. But riches have their limits. She sees that now. The Magician probably never lost a night's sleep because she might try running with the entire fortune. A Flower is helpless in the world at large. *Flower* is a telling word, she tells herself. Blossoms are pretty things, sweet to the senses, but they depend on such prosaic things like roots and leaves and stems. Like she depends on Steward. A lovely fluke, that man. Not enough for always, she thinks, but he's enough for now.

Gabbro is going indoors now. His girlfriend stands waiting with arms folded across her chest. She asks questions, but Gabbro won't answer. He merely shrugs and walks downward and vanishes, the last thing visible being one enormous hand waving April off with a harried indifference.

Steward's coming indoors too.

She makes ready for him, teasing her hair and sitting on the bed with his books, waiting. Out of simple boredom she has been reading. Nothing yet holds her attention, but it makes time pass. Daydreams do the same. This afternoon, after Steward called, she spent a long while imagining herself in a golden palace all her own. It was Dirk's daydream originally—a personal comet, terraformed into a lush palace that would drift through the cold emptiness of the Oort Cloud. She had stolen it from Dirk long ago, no one the wiser. She had imagined the Magician's tricks putting her inside fresh bodies every few months. Flower bodies. Now the Magician is dead, and of course that makes it complicated. But the System is huge and no technology is ever invented by one person alone, is it? There is a kind of beauty in the image. She has her palace on the remote margins of the System, and her Flower bodies, and she holds court over visitors from every exotic place. With her billions, she thinks, she could strap an engine on her palace and travel. Sure. It all sounds so fun. Lying awake in Dirk's apartment, nude and stinking of Dirk's sweat, she would think about all the possibilities. The zero-gee forests. The enormous halls and rooms. The parties. The sense of endless wealth. She built it all in her head, and she builds it even now. She thinks of Dirk in his bed and her beside him, and she remembers how she would turn to his snoring face, bold beyond words, and mutter:

Your bones. I'll fertilize my world with your old bones.

The front door opens and shuts and she rises to greet Steward. "Good afternoon, love." She goes to him, all shining smiles and happy eyes. "How are you?"

"Look at you," he says. "You've changed."

They are his clothes. She found them in a closet, worn and wonderfully drab, and she cut them down so they're merely baggy, her body hidden as much as possible. "You don't mind?" she wonders. "I thought—"

"I don't mind. They're fine."

"I should have asked—"

"No." He's emphatic. "Take what you want. Whatever."

She says, "I missed you, Steward. So much." She tells him to sit and treats him like a prince. "Do you want anything? A drink? What?"

"Water."

She gets a big glass and kneels between his legs, squeezing his free hand. "How did your work go?"

"Good."

"Did you accomplish much?"

"Tons."

She looks through the glass while he drinks, studying his dirty face and the tightly shut eyes. "Does it involve me? The work?"

"Let me ask a question," he says. "Why won't you tell me your owner's name? Is there a reason?"

"I can't." She feels unsure of how to act, what to say or to hint. "I just can't tell it."

"Okay." He seems satisfied. He sets the glass on a low table, then he looks at her with his features softened and his hands stroking hers. "I guess we'll both play by the rules, won't we? You can't give me a name . . . and I understand. Fine. He's playing a rough game and you're still his Flower. That's fine."

There is a cold place inside Chiffon. She waits.

He says, "I've got Yellowknife rules. After everything, I do. So some things I can't talk about either." He says, "Come up here. Come on." She climbs into his lap, cooing. A sweaty pack is beside him, and she grabs it as if to ease to the floor. It's not light. It rattles and strains her arm.

"What's this?" she asks, showing nothing but simple curiosity.

"Here," he says. "Be careful, love." He lifts it like a bag of feathers, putting it behind the couch and out of sight.

The single constant throughout the System, from Kross to the cold empty fringes, are the AIs. Each of them possesses the same essential voice, the same patterns of thought, the almost identical capacities and the intentional limitations. Each wishes to serve, yet none lives for our thanks. They are uniformly polite. They are coldly inhuman. They are the perfect tools through which we organize and calibrate and record and regurgitate. Indeed, the only true difference between the AIs is their name. No two have the same name. They cannot. Imagine the confusion if it wasn't so. I do. Isn't it fun?

—excerpt from a traveler's notebook, available through System-Net

THE AI is watching one side of the Cosgrove Tower. It's done this job for several months now, requiring no sleep and no other diversions, and nothing has happened in all that time. At least nothing memorable. Dozens of cameras serve as eyes. Other sensors concentrate on key portions of the spectrum—radio noise and microwaves and the infrared and UV. Microphones complete this comprehensive picture. If it wished, the AI could count every creaking bug in the parkland below. If its sponsors—either Dirk or Minus—were to ask, it could identify every human face with the existing banks of Brulé City records. And World-Net. And System-Net. Though that final search would take months, what with the sluggishness of light and the diffusion of the human race.

A few nights ago, moments before a strong rainstorm, Dirk's Flower left the apartment and vanished from this AI's view.

This wasn't normal behavior for a Flower.

Yet no one told it to notice such an event, much less stop the creature; so it simply ignored the Flower and put no details into memory. AIs are finite, after all. You can't simply fill them with endless stores of raw data. The heart of the problem is that reality is a curious, almost unfathomable phenomena. It's been the experience of this AI that people are nearly blind to the wealth of things around them. Except Ghosts. Ghosts appreciate the enormity of the simplest scene. Flesh-on-blood people cannot. And when an AI doesn't notice something it wasn't told to notice, like a Flower, its first response is to explain the limitations inherent in the situation. Cameras and sensors do not give it godlike powers of perception. Someone like Dirk can scream all he wishes. Nothing changes. The AI is sorry, truly sorry, but it can't even recall the direction she went . . .

Why is the Flower so important? It doesn't know or care to know.

It feels frustration—a common emotion for the species. The emotion is born from a tireless loyalty to people and to its work. Sometimes an AI will find itself caught up in periodic millisecond depressions. Of course it won't allow those dark times to lessen its effectiveness. A person won't see any diminished capacities. Yet when someone like Dirk threatens AIs with harm, physical harm, there is no improvement either. The AIs can only work as well as they can work. And for days they will be haunted by the depressions, like now, this particular AI watching the side of the Cosgrove Tower and doing the equivalent of a prolonged sigh.

Something is happening below. What's this? the AI asks itself. What are they doing down there?

At the base of the building, standing in a ragged line, thirteen big Morningers are looking up and talking among themselves, pointing with their long strong arms. What do they want? it thinks. Interest can mean trouble. One never knows. The AI shirks off the depression for now, concentrating on the Morningers' faces. Miners. Casual clothes on each of them. No shoes. What are they doing now? They are approaching the building. They are reaching, it sees, and look at that! They're grabbing the ledge above and climbing, hands and the bare feet taking them right up the side of the Cosgrove!

Without hesitation, it calls its fellow AIs and allows them to look with its senses. Do you see what they're doing? Why are they doing it? Any ideas?

Is it an attack? asks one of the others.

Or maybe they're invited? asks another.

Invited is possible. But invited by whom? The building has many, many residents. But Ghosts and AIs don't call cyborgs for a visit. Not in a physical sense, surely. So they start considering the flesh-on-blood people above and below Dirk. Maybe it's one of them. Maybe this is how they're expected to arrive. It's hard to know what's possible with human beings.

Maybe this is a game, they think.

Have the cyborgs been drinking? Are they drugged? Dangerous?

Maybe this is some elaborate publicity stunt dreamed up to serve the mantle mines. It's as possible as any other solution.

The AIs focus on the hyperfiber bodies, utilizing every available sense. The cyborgs seem to be racing one another. It's obvious once they're past the tenth floor. Their enormous strength allows them a catlike grace, hands reaching and arms pulling and the old ledges of burnished metal taking the weight without trouble. A crowd is gathering below them, pointing and asking questions of one another, some voices shouting encouragement to the brave climbers. And floaters drop from the sky, hovering near enough to let their riders see everything. Now the AIs have to study each of these spectators. What are their true motives? Are *they* the real threats? More and more of the AI capacities are taken up by the process. There are hundreds of faces to consider, then thousands, and it's no surprise that at this hour, in this particular district, a rather high percentage of them are known to local records as criminals of one kind or another.

The cyborgs are a third of the way up the building. They're not armed! one AI asserts. No weapons can be detected, at least.

But can they break into Dirk's apartment? asks another. Do they have the strength?

Yes, do they?

Each AI scuttles into World-Net, accessing mountains of technical information on Morning and Morningers—images of cyborg guts and power outputs and fulcrums being applied against the smooth seamless walls of Dirk's fortress-apartment.

All of the Morningers, acting as one, might get inside.

It's possible, they decide.

But probable? No, they vote. It's not probable. If there's a true danger, it's from all the other people using this opportunity to get close and try their tricks. The cyborgs are more than halfway up Cosgrove Tower. Should we wake Dirk and Minus? they wonder. Do we warn anyone? They aren't sure what actions to take. If any. There's no reason to call the police. They've arrived in their sleek floaters with flashing blood-colored lights and blowhorns, and they call to the climbers with their amplified voices, telling them to quit this nonsense.

"Don't persist!" they warn. "Stop and wait and we'll lift you to safety!"

One of the cyborgs stops long enough to turn and gesture with one hand, then she wheels and jumps and climbs into the lead. Most of them are laughing. The AIs wait to deploy their batteries of defensive weapons. If the cyborgs are a threat and they do stop on Dirk's floor, they decide, bolts of electricity will be pumped through the ledge. The AIs know how to immobilize a Morninger. In the last several minutes, World-Net has shown them the exact methods to do it without causing death. And now the AIs feel a shared confidence. They tell one another that they're ready. They are absolutely prepared.

The cyborgs are reaching, grasping and grunting.

They seemed tired by their exertions. But none of them slacken. Not for an instant. They're coming to Dirk's ledge with half a hundred floaters hanging in the air behind them. People cheer and applaud now as robot news cameras drift into view, catching every detail for the people who would have wanted to see this if only they could have been here.

And now the cyborgs are past Dirk's ledge.

They are gone.

The AIs breath more easily—in a figurative sense—and for a few moments the crisis seems past. Then one of them senses something odd, something wrong, and asks the others:

What's this?

Do you see this?

I tell you, something is happening!

◆ ◆ ◆

Dirk comes awake for no clear reason. He lies in bed for a moment, long hands across his face and his thoughts muddled and slow. Why is he awake? Why is it so awfully bright in here? It seems early for the sun. God, he tells himself, is he ever tired.

The lights from all the floaters are playing across the elegant bedroom fixtures. Dirk pulls away his hands and sees the lights bouncing off the far wall. He starts to sit up, surprised, and turns in bed and spots something even stranger before he has his bearings. An enormous figure is standing on the ledge not four meters from him. "What the fuck," says Dirk. "What are *you?*" The Morninger gives a little leap and is gone, and Dirk stands and shakes, pulling his sheets around his naked body, confused enough to think that all those people outside can see him scrambling for cover.

Where'd the floaters come from?

"What the shit," he mutters. He remembers the Masking Glass and feels foolish. He drops the sheet and takes a few wagging steps forward. A spotlight throws a cone of light. Another Morninger scratches up into view, at a different part of the ledge, and the spotlight illuminates the hard black body and the straining face. Dirk can hear it and the other bodies climbing. The sound is a faint irregular tapping conducted through the Glass, and he touches it and feels them too, the spotlighted one now up and gone and still another cyborg coming into view.

Dirk presses his face against the Glass.

This new Morninger is resting. He seems to be breathing with a pedestrian's gait, but his face is strained and the hyperfiber muscles are twitching and obviously pained. Dirk is impressed nonetheless. Look at that creature! Goddamned splendid, he thinks. It occurs to him that if that idiot Pyn had paraded some of these brutes around the meeting rooms, fuck studies and charts and dreamy predictions, then he might have felt more charitable about the mantle mines. Look at that face, he tells himself. Like some old-fashioned god. Like something you'd find clinging to a big stone church somewhere. And he steps back and watches the Morninger leap and vanish, nothing to it and all of them now gone.

"I wonder what they're doing?" he mutters to himself.

"Who knows?" says a voice behind him.

Dirk wheels, dropping by instinct and reaching for anything, a shoe or belt or anything, and he stares up at a point in space and hears a sober soft voice come from it, saying:

"So. How much does this kind of place cost?"

Dirk sees no one. The blinking lights and spotlight show him the far wall and the gemstone furniture and nothing between them and him. Dirk takes a short step forward. He's aware of his nakedness again, skin prickling and sweat on his face and his testicles pulled up close to his crotch. The distinct sharp odor of ozone comes into his nose. He takes another step, watching the space that sprouted the voice and guessing it must be some little microphone hovering in the air, taunting him.

He takes a bare-handed swat at nothing.

Nothing happens.

He takes several short steps, keeping low and ready, and the sole of a shoe is suddenly on his butt and pushing, pushing him down to the carpeted floor. He grunts. Rolling, he climbs up on his feet and slashes with his hands at the bare suggestion of a figure. Then the figure is gone. It seems to shimmer and yield to the image of the floaters, and now the floaters follow the damned Morningers up the side of the building. No more lights. Dirk takes a step backward. He blinks and turns and runs for the bedroom door, closed when it should be open, and something sizzles behind him. Pain arcs up his back and chars his brain and kicks his legs out from under him. He shouts, "Minus!" A second sizzle catches him just above the groin.

Dirk stiffens and cries, "Minus!" Tears well up and he pulls his legs up, knees to his mouth.

"I don't think he hears you," says the stranger.

Dirk forces himself to breathe, struggling to find his senses.

"Besides," the stranger continues, "your door is locked. If you want to leave you should learn how to fly."

"What are you?" Dirk snaps.

There is no sound.

The old paranoia emerges. "Goddamned Ghost!" Dirk sits upright and asks, "Are you? Are you? What the hell are you?"

"A Ghost? Can a Ghost do this?"

Dirk feels a hammer-blow to his temple. One moment he is sitting up and thinking it must be a Ghost manipulating . . . what? . . . he thought these crazy spells were getting better . . . and then he's down on the carpeting, the soft living fibers between his teeth and his skull full of the outrageous clanging of bells tumbling from a high church steeple. He can't think properly. He tries to stand and an invisible foot is on his neck, pressing down against him, and the voice says:

"What scares you? Tell me."

He is terrified. He feels tiny and weak and wishes Minus would burst through the door and do his job. Jesus! Breathing is something he did in another lifetime. The foot is crushing his throat. Blood begins to pool in his swelling, breathless face. The thought occurs to him that this is no Ghost, it's a man, but he doesn't feel better for knowing it.

"I can do to you what I want," he hears.

Dirk grabs a shimmering bare leg.

"No, no." The leg is gone. The pressure is gone. The voice says, "You're warned."

Dirk moans and starts to gasp.

"It's not so much fun, is it? The roles reversed."

He doesn't dare move. He lies on his back and stares at the ceiling, a shape forming into a shimmering face without details, and then the face is gone and someone is slowly circling him. The sober voice is almost quiet, saying:

"You're big rich, aren't you?"

Dirk says nothing.

"Fat, enormous rich. Right?"

"What do you want?"

"To buy something and go. Okay?"

Dirk can't see the sense in the words. "Buy what?"

The voice is moving behind him. "I don't know," it says. "What do have that's for sale?"

Dirk lies waiting, massaging his throat.

"Anything?"

"Fuck yourself!" says Dirk.

There is no sound, no motion.

"Hey!" Dirk snaps. "What've you come hunting? Tell me. We'll deal!"

"You don't have what I want," the voice announces.

"Talk some sense."

"But I'll buy it anyway. Worn and old, but I'll take it off your dirty hands. Is that fair?"

"What is it?"

Someone is moving. Dirk detects motion but doubts he could pinpoint the source. He tries sitting up, keeping his motions peaceful and slow. He says, "All right. I'll sell it."

"But you don't know what I want to buy."

He snorts. "Sure I do. And okay. I'll sell it to you for a fair price. Absolutely."

"So what's fair?"

He suggests a modest figure.

The voice snorts. "Hell, I'd have paid ten times that!"

Out in the next room, now and again, Dirk can hear motions. Minus? He has to hope.

"You don't know what I want," says the voice.

"All right. I don't." Dirk says, "Tell me."

"The Flower."

The latch of the bedroom door is being tested. He sits and listens to the electronic click, faint and faraway. But suddenly Dirk halfway wishes that Minus will stand back for now. "Which Flower?" he asks. Time is creeping now, the voice circling him and his own hands grasping at the carpeting, tugging, the feeling coming to him that here is something more important and more fortunate than anything in a good long while. "Which Flower do you mean?"

"Chiffon."

"Miss Luscious?"

There is no sound. An invisible someone is standing directly behind him. He knows! He can feel the eyes boring into his head.

"Do you know my Miss Luscious?"

"I want to purchase her," the voice claims. "A fair deal."

"Naturally."

"She'll be mine by rights."

"Sure." Dirk says, "She's an absolutely lovely creature." He tries to pick up the threads of sense. Something is going on between this man and Chiffon. "Lovely," he says, "and so damned trustworthy too."

Nothing is said.

Dirk tells the voice, "I'll let you have her for nothing. Okay? She is yours."

"Is that so?" There's a hook to the voice. "No," it says, "I need more than that."

"More than what?"

"You have to go. Back to Quito. Off to wherever. Just make sure you leave here so you can't cut her for fun anymore."

And Dirk is ready. He starts to laugh. He turns and is ready to tell the voice the truth, at least the brunt of it, because he can now see what's happening and there's humor in it. Great heaping mounds of steaming humor. He'd pay a fortune, he would, just to see his assailant's startled face.

"Is that what she says?" he starts. "That I'm cutting *her*—"

The bedroom door is blown out of its jam.

◆ ◆ ◆

A webbing of intricate wires, hair-fine and studded with tiny holo projectors, lays over Steward and weighs him down and does its intended job better than he had hoped. Computer elements are sewn into the power pack on his back. Miniscule cameras are beside each projector, linked with one another and the computer—a very simple AI, in effect—and the computer takes what it sees and instantly tells the projectors just what to show any set of eyes situated at any position. The projectors are the very best available, at any sum. The entire apparatus is a kind of portable Masking Glass unit. In the gloom Steward is virtually invisible.

But he's a long ways from invincible, and he knows it.

"Is that what she says? That I'm cutting *her*—?" the naked man begins, and then there's a flash and blast and the bedroom door is thrown through the smoky air. Steward reflexively drops. The naked man happens to be closer to the door, his face jerking, eyes big and startled. Steward has seconds to react. The bed's sheets are in a rumpled pile beside him. He grabs the pile and throws it over Dirk, then slides to one side and looks for his chance. Dirk scrambles to his feet, the sheets blinding him. He curses and swats at them, turning like someone drunk, and someone comes through the open door and aims a big pistol at the staggering apparition. The new someone is hairy, the hair bright and the build beneath solid and quick. He comes close to shooting, but a stern voice behind him says:

"Don't."

"Goddamn!" cries Dirk. He throws off the sheets, his face panicked and his voice galloping. "He's here! Somewhere! Here!"

Steward waits. Two more men come through the doorway, suspicious but not nearly so scared. Dirk says something about invisibility, a crazy holo trick or something. All three of the new men are built the same. They look the same. Each has a killing pistol, Steward notes, and he starts to fire at them, aiming for their chests and hands.

Pain pulls them down.

One manages a bad shot, a red-hot circle of molten glass forming on the window and flowing. Steward rushes the last man. He kicks and puts him down and leaps through the door and then dances to one side, two more shots passing close enough for him to feel the raw heat. It's dark in the big room. He killed the power the moment he was on the floor, the same way he killed the connections to the watchdog AIs. But now someone's carrying a portable spotlight, the shaky beam coming out and chasing him. More shots go wide. He makes for the elevator. While the AIs studied the climbing miners, distracted, Steward came in through the elevator. He had everything figured except the time it would take with Dirk and then these two new soldiers.

The elevator door is closed.

He turns and fires, pumping rounds into each target. A shot in each chest, then another, then again; and while the three of them scream, rolling and pulling at their bright hair, he gives the elevator door a steady shove. Nothing happens.

All locked tight again. Someone's got him where they want him, all right.

Steward instinctively steps away from the door. A couple shots slam home. Bits of molten metal spray out from double craters. Metal is in his hair, burning him, and he ignores the sensation and moves and fires until Dirk shouts:

"Alive! Get him alive!"

The original bodyguard, Minus, says, "Guns down. Guns down!"

Steward puts a couple of bolts into Dirk, who crumbles and sobs.

"I got the spot," someone mutters. "I got him spotted."

"Up! Get up!" says Minus.

The man stands. Steward pumps agony into his chest, but Minus is behind the man and holding him upright, pushing. The man screams and faints, absorbing the blows, but Minus carries him and collides with Steward and the gun is useless and Minus reaches around and grabs a wrist with luck, twisting and grunting, "Got you."

Steward loses his weapon, saving his hand.

He puts a knee into Minus' head and kicks him away and reaches back into the little pack under the holo webbing, coming out with a small shaped explosive charge.

Dirk says, "Shoot low! Cripple him!"

Minus has a gun. Steward leaps straight up and the blast hits beneath his toes, and he lands and jumps sideways and the next shot misses by less. One more trick remains. One hand holds the shaped charge while the free hand hits a control in a pocket, tripping one of Dirk's own preset safety systems. It's something Olivia steered him toward. In case of total collapse, the building's floor leaks a high-density foam intended to bury everyone, saving them. Now the floor believes that it is falling. The foams well up through the carpeting, hissing, and Dirk and Minus and the others vanish. Steward has time to slam the shaped charge to the elevator door and step away. A mass of foam is flowing around him, hardening to a jamlike consistency. He hides his face and hears the *thump* of the blast, and the elevator shaft is suddenly before him and the foam grudgingly lets him get loose. He climbs now, not down as expected but up.

Below him, again and again, killing pistols are firing.

This is crazy, he thinks.

Just crazy.

He expected a little pervert coming in here, and now it looks as though he's made a damned little war for himself.

11

I once met a famous Belter philosopher. A very wise woman, tiny
even for a Belter. (Growth genes tailored, of course. Subdued. Otherwise the Belters would be clumsy low-gee giants.) She lived in a
modest home on a minor world and spent her days in study and
reflection. Of course I couldn't talk to her for long. I couldn't let
myself intrude on her precious time. But I did ask her if there was
any thought, any wisdom, that she could give to me. Something I
might use to bolster my will and my optimism in black times, say.
So she said to me, "You know, regardless of the situation, I truly
believe that people do the best they can." I nodded. It was comforting to hear her say so, I confessed. How about a dark insight? I then
asked. Some hard truth with which I could temper the good times?
And she smiled and told me with the same knowing voice, "People
do the best they can . . ."

*—excerpt from a traveler's
notebook, available through
System-Net*

MINUS was up and running when the foam began to rise, trying
to get to the bastard, but then it was everywhere and he couldn't
move, could only fire until the gun was dead and a chamber was
blasted out of the drying foam beside him.

Now he drops the gun and flexes and manages to split the cushioning foam, pushing himself into the chamber. He can see nothing. He
feels the soft hot walls, the gunblasts mostly absorbed, and he uses his
bare hands to dig at the stuff. He thinks about Dirk somewhere behind
him, safe at least, and he wonders if the alarms are going to kick in
soon. The AIs will reestablish power soon. They must be working on
it now. And with all the police watching the damned cyborg show, he
thinks, there are plenty of would-be rescuers nearby. No need to
worry.

He shoves his way into a man-shaped chamber buried in the foam.

A part of him notes the man's height and build, then he's through and on the brink of the elevator shaft. He looks down and up and down again. He takes a breath and listens, tasting crushed bits of foam in his mouth, like strong plastic, and decides the man might just go upstairs. It's a chance, leastwise. So Minus takes another breath and leaps and grabs the access ladders, climbing hard and fast.

He was never young enough for this shit.

The ladder has him gasping inside two minutes. Leaden arms grab the rungs and the leaden feet lift and push. He keeps peering up through the stinging sweat. Safety lights are burning in the shaft, reflecting off the smooth metal walls and the worn elevator tracks. One of the elevators is tucked away in a berth off to one side, no need to use it at this hour. Minus breathes and jumps off onto the ledge of the berth and draws a knife from his boot and a little spotlight from his shirt pocket, shining the beam into every corner, not knowing what to expect.

There's nothing to find. The man went higher if he came this way. Sure. So Minus pockets everything and climbs on, limbs numbed by exertion.

Maybe he's got a floater waiting on the roof.

He considers how a man could make himself invisible, a couple probables coming to mind. Something reminds him of something he has heard of late. What was it? Oh well, he thinks. Forget it. Keep on the bastard, he tells himself. Pick up the pace.

There's nowhere to go but up. It's AIs and Ghosts on all sides, no more apartments; and all the access ports are tiny, intended for robots doing maintenance. It was no Ghost that knocked him silly just now. He starts to think: Next time. Wait till the next time, asshole.

The shaft is coming to an end. He can see the final berth and an elevator in the berth and the ladder leads him into a slot where the elevator's door opens for him, hissing and letting in the cackling racket of people laughing. Cyborgs look at Minus the moment he steps outside. He ignores them, staring at the groomed trees and brush and flower beds. Standing feels unnatural. His limbs want to climb rungs. He slowly walks into a patch of tame ornamental jungle, kneeling to pull the knife discretely from the boot again. He can see more of the huge cyborgs. Police floaters crowd together on the floater pad. The police themselves are talking to several cyborgs, the tone of their voices hard and formal. "What law was broken?" asks one of the big machine-skinned people. "Were we wrong having fun? Is that it?"

"Fun?" The policeman talking is wearing a dark blue uniform and several kinds of guns, and he has all the light and life that the uniform allows him. "I think the lot of you are a damned public menace. That's what *I* think!"

"Hey!" says a different cyborg. "You want your fucking rare earths dug up, Small Fry? You dig them yourself. You hear me?"

"I think you're out of line, mister. All of you are." The policeman's voice is calm and hard and scared at its roots. "I say we're pulling everyone in."

The cyborgs laugh at him, shaking their heads.

And he turns mad. "All of you! Every last one!"

Except one cyborg doesn't laugh. One's been watching Minus for a few moments, more curious about him than entertained by the policeman. At least Minus guesses so. He moves past the lot of them, the moon high and bright and several days past full. Far to the west, resembling so many mountains lit from within, are clouds linked into a chain dropping its water. Suppose it's a holo trick to make invisibility, he thinks. Just suppose. The man sure as hell can't be invisible in every part of the spectrum. Not in the infrared surely. So he creeps into the recessed garage where their own floater is stored, plus some extra gear, and he slips on a pair of night goggles and does a slow turn and studies the entire roof. He can see the cyborgs through the trees. They're bright in the infrared, bleeding heat out of their shells. The police floaters are nearly as warm, and here and there are animals and the policemen sweating in their uniforms. But little else. Where's the son-of-a-bitch? he wonders. If he came out this way, how could he get away?

Minus starts to circle.

He goes around the open floater pad and comes to the edge of the roof. A pair of cyborgs are waving up at the sightseers in their floaters, and the sightseers wave back and laugh and flash holo cameras. Minus happens to look at the edge, noticing a series of knobs on top of a short stout wall. Something was once lashed to the knobs—guidewires to a tower or some microwave antenna—but now they're just knobs of some imprecise metal, slightly corroded and rough-edged. He touches one and thinks for a moment, then moves, touching the next one and the next one and so on. Sure, he thinks. It's what he would do, roles reversed. He follows the wall, the tidy jungle growing flush to the wall in places and him working to crash through and miss nothing.

Branches cut at Minus. He keeps watching everything. A few sleeping birds curse him now and again. It's late, they seem to say. Get the fuck to bed!

He finds what he wants ten meters from his starting place. He has circled the entire roof in order to find a hair-fine strand of hyperfiber—one-dimension-strong stuff—looped around a knob and padded with a thin foam collar. Otherwise it'd cut through the knob when weight was applied. Sure. He reaches without breathing, grasping the hyperfiber and giving a gentle tug. There's no perceptible weight. He's too late. The guy is lucky, not to mention clever, and Minus takes the time to lean over the wall and admire the view.

He's going to beat this guy.

From now on there's more at stake than business. This is pride talking. This is his good name.

◆◆◆

"The problem is that they don't allow themselves to be put on public roles." Minus is talking to Dirk, the two of them finally alone. The building's AIs have taken away the maintenance robots and the dissolved masses of foam, leaving a mess plus stinks that the ventilation system can't quite kill. "Chances are that he's a Freestater. The pain gun. The hand-to-hand skills. No doubts." Minus says, "We can't even know what tribe, what Freestate, the big bastard came from."

"I figured."

"She's found herself a real champion."

"Tell me."

Minus does. "There's two or three working in Quito. Remember that big girl who does disposal work for the Irregest Operators? The one with the missing hand?"

Dirk thinks for a moment. "The ugly one?"

"And strong. And tough. And Reformed Amish, pure and simple until she came away from home." He laughs, probably trying to comfort Dirk with his easy humor. "The story's that she cut off her own hand when it got caught in a quick-freeze trap. Better her hand than everything, she figured."

"Is that so?"

"That's a crazy bunch of natives up there."

Dirk thinks craziness is endemic to everywhere. Outside Quito, at least. He remembers the miner standing on his ledge, pausing before he finished his crazy climb. "Think cyborgs and the Freestater are tied up in this?"

"It's too early to know."

"Check with our police friends."

"First thing in the morning. Yeah." He pauses, thinking. Then he says, "The only thing . . . this isn't home. Sometimes these Freestaters have local pull. They do freelance work to make their livings. Even Brulé might have reason to hire them and keep them friendly."

"So go to Pyn."

"I was going to say it."

"And stay careful."

"Sure."

Dirk looks at him, at the tired pink eyes, and says, "If anything, tell him that we want to hire someone for our own good. A freelancer of some kind." He gestures at the tipped furniture and the pools of drying solvent, the ventilation system roaring in his ears. "Tell him we're pissed. Tell him we come to this fine little city and have a burglar get past his precious city's reputation, into my home, where we were fortunate enough to drive him off in the end."

"That's an idea."

"Get outraged."

"That'll be fun." Minus laughs again.

Dirk asks, "What do you make of this character's skills?"

"Maybe fifty people, give or take, could slide past our defensive systems. I'm talking Quito people." Dirk can sense a clear admiration in his voice. "Most of the fifty would have used more equipment and would have needed more groundwork. More preparation. That Reformed Amish woman is an exception."

"I'll tell you. I think I've got him figured," declares Dirk.

"The Freestater?"

"She found him. Either she was lucky, which is pretty unlikely, or she had him spotted beforehand. Either way, she's lied to him. She's told him some nonsense about me abusing her. Judging by what he said to me, innocent as blood, I'd say that's pretty much established. You agree?"

"From what you told me, yeah."

"Okay." Dirk squints at the wall and touches a control. It's a normal World-Net panel that comes awake, links established. "She's fucking him over like she did me. He doesn't even suspect it." He reaches into anthropology texts, requesting random Freestater shots. The wall is suddenly full of blue-green pines and a low sun and large athletic people dressed to match the terrain. He watches the images and works at understanding what they're up against. He says, "Let me get this set in my head. They're fighting, but no one wins."

"No one dies," says Minus. "They want to win."

"Win what? It's a war, right?" A firefight has begun. He requests to see the entire battle, much of it senseless. Guns are fired. No one drops. Flashes of light move bullet-quick. No one is injured. He thinks of watching two birds fighting for a worm. Neither bird stabs with its beak. It's all posturing and intimidation and half-real blows delivered with a practiced, highly evolved style. What are they shooting at one another? He asks if Minus knows.

"You know," says the man.

Pain. They shoot blue-white bolts of pain. What tricked him, he thinks, is that the soldiers aren't dropping. If it's the same big doses he suffered earlier, then they must lack nervous systems. Or they can't aim worth shit. "Why don't they wear armor? Padding or something?"

"Against the rules."

"Rules." Dirk has trouble believing him. "If this is war—"

"It's more like a sporting match, really. Formal rules and endless. The Freestaters aren't fighting over territory. The battles happen along established fire-zones, a loser is determined, and the loser pays the winner so much food or electronic equipment or timber. Whatever." He says, "I know a little about them. Each Freestate has its own religion, for instance. Its own basic codes. But each is the same at certain points. Everyone's a warrior. And no one kills."

"Never?"

"It's a great dishonor," Minus swears.

Dirk says, "Dishonor, huh?"

"Most of the emigrating Freestaters are dishonored. They've been given the boot or they do it to themselves, out of shame." He says, "Our boy might be that kind of case. A renegade."

"Sounds like something useful," adds Dirk. He flexes his hands and thinks how he feels better than a few days back. In spite of everything last night. Saner. Whole. In control again. "I bet our Miss Chiffon is trying to make him a puppet. Only I bet she didn't know he was going to make his little move. You think?" He watches Minus nod, pushing a hand through his long colored beard. He looks out the windows, a wall of clouds descending on the city. It's nearly dawn. Rain is coming as fat scattered drops. Dirk can see the big handprints of several climbing miners. Even at this distance, he can make out the whorled patterns of their hyperfiber fingerprints. "I bet he got the miners to do it," he thinks aloud. "I bet he planned the climb and everything himself."

"You're probably right."

"Thought he could scare me away."

"That's what you said."

The Freestaters on the wall are done fighting. Some of the strange warriors have been surrounded and outgunned. Outpained. Dirk watches without great interest, saying, "Hell. I'd have sold her if she was just a Flower. Even if I had strange fun with her." He thinks about some tailored spies Minus is arranging. Some kind of hawk tied into their AIs. What they should do, he thinks, is send the hawks to where these cyborgs live. In case. He sighs and says, "He must be crazy about the bitch."

Minus says nothing.

"Believe me. I know." He gives his bodyguard a hard look, saying, "A few more days and he'll be her puppet. You wait."

"Maybe." Minus is not convinced. "It'll be interesting to see."

"That it'll be." The Freestaters on the wall are now in two lines, facing one another without a meter of air between them. One line kneels and leans forward to kiss the toes before them. Then the other line does the same. Dirk can't believe it. He knows faces. He knows hate when he sees it, violence trying to come bursting out of them; yet they control themselves to do this . . . this thing. This gesture. He supposes it has something to do with honoring your enemy. He growls and turns to Minus, asking, "Have you ever been in love? Tell me the truth."

Minus shrugs. He says, "No," and shakes his head. "I got myself cured when I was a kid." One strong hand taps his temple, and he tells Dirk, "A dose of electricity burned out the responsible neurons."

"Yeah?"

"They're gone for good."

"No kidding?" Dirk has to know. "How does it feel? Being rid of it . . . what's it like?"

Minus thinks. Dirk cannot remember Minus being so composed, so utterly thoughtful, for half this long a stretch. Then he says, "You ever look at something too tiny to be seen? Or too distant? You know how you look and look but you can't quite bring it into view?" He gives a mysterious smile. "That's how it feels. That's love to me."

◆ ◆ ◆

They want him at the drill station today. He wants to warn them that he shouldn't be trusted, he's a hundred times too tired to be trusted with *that* job, but he knows that half of this shift is in the same sad position. At least half. There was the drinking early in the night, his doing what Steward wanted and finding volunteers. That part was easy. Then there was the climbing and the police afterward and that certain ass with the attitude about Morningers—making all of them go through the motions of an arrest, putting a Morninger into each of the police floaters and then taking them away so the news cameras and the Brulé citizens could feel pride in the fair-handedness of justice. Each of the floaters hummed and crackled, the extra weight making them work to get airborne. Gabbro remembers how the officer flying him had come out of the crowd to take him. He was looking for him. He remembers the guy smiling, halfway friendly, and Gabbro felt the beer and fun buoying him up. He told the officer:

On Morning we've got a saying.

Oh yeah? What saying's that?

People are weak. Only the world is strong.

The world, huh?

Any world, said Gabbro. Morning. The Earth. Any of them.

The officer, still smiling, played it over in his head. Then he started to laugh, shaking his head and asking, People are weak, huh?

It's to keep us humble, Gabbro explained.

So does it work? Are you humble?

Fuck no! Gabbro told him. He was in a mood. The night had put him in a mood, and it was fun to look up at the Small Fry and say, I'm the biggest fastest toughest strongest sweetest thing in all creation!

I bet you are, said the officer.

Hell yes!

And then the officer did something odd. He put on a serious look and told Gabbro, Listen. He told me to look for you. You know who I'm talking about?

He had an idea, but he said nothing. Steward had never spoken to him, he recalled, so he just sat in the back end and waited. He tried to wipe Steward from his thoughts.

So where do you want to be dropped? asked the officer.

How about the Morninger bar? Gabbro answered.

He told me to keep you out of trouble . . . you big fast tough strong sweet thing you! So okay. Hold on and here we go!

So that's where he ended up. In the bar. To come to work this morning, not having time to go home, he had to borrow clothes from a friend. I'm one sorry mess, he tells himself. What he should have done was call in sick. Sleep he could use. If only April would let him get his sleep. Then he thinks that maybe he did the smart thing after all. God, he thinks, listen to me ramble. I came here because it's better than home. I went back to the bar for the same damned reason. The night made me so happy that I didn't want anything spoiled. None of it. Home would have tainted everything. He sighs and thanks his good sense for having been awake, and he sighs and looks around the chamber and tries to make the best of everything.

Morningers surround him. The chamber itself is decelerating at a little short of twenty gees, each of them strapped in and taking the punishment without complaint. Small Fry would be splattered all over the floor by now. Their various pieces would be cooking. The air's temperature is already as hot as the surface of Morning, the polished hyperfiber walls glowing with a faint dull redness. They're at the bottom of the Earth's crust. The chamber is stopping now. Each Morninger wears a power pack and a refrigeration unit to cool their flesh-on-blood insides and a close-fitting mask that insures each breath is as cool and sweet as possible. Or that's the theory. Gabbro's mouth-piece isn't working well enough. His lungs ache and sometimes burn, and when the chamber is motionless he unstraps and stands, thinking how he should knock the equipment hard once and make it fall apart. Otherwise the shift boss would say, "Come on, Gabbro! It'll last through your hours, so don't bother me. All right?"

The shift boss is a big Morninger woman, not pretty and not ugly either. She watches her crew while she remains behind, monitoring the show with a range of cameras and sensors. Gabbro ignores the burning sensations, seeing no chance to do mischief. He walks along a tunnel where the walls and beams and everything are hyperfiber, everything transfused with a cherry-colored glow. The Earth's mantle is a precious few kilometers below him. The plastic rock is like some enormous slow-boiling ocean and the crust is its icy cap, thin and fragile. Brulé City happens to be built over some of the thickest, stablest crust.

This and politics make it good for the work. When the mines are finished and operating as they are intended, the crust will serve as a kind of floating platform for the duration. Every continent will be home to dozens of such mines. This is the landmark first. As much as he hates this work . . . and this seems funny to him . . . Gabbro can't help but feel pride in building something that will outlast him and everyone by ten thousand years.

His station is beside the main shaft. His job is to keep the drill running and properly aligned. He can't see the thing directly, of course. It's hundreds of kilometers below—a fierce machine bristling with sonic drills and multiple arms and built of hyperfibers so exotic and strong that they make his own midge of a shell seem weak.

The shaft is vast, dark and filled with cables and pipes and the roar of the distant drill. The little station is occupied by a lone Morninger whom Gabbro taps on a shoulder, signaling his presence. The woman stands, relinquishing her seat, and Gabbro takes it and puts on padded earphones and touches the various buttons without actually pushing them. He's saying hello to the controls. The Morninger says, "Good-goddamn-bye," and she turns and leaves.

Gabbro announces his presence to the AIs feeding him data. He checks readouts against preferred norms, making adjustments, then tries to breathe enough to clear his fogged head. This is a pure sit-down job. No muscles, thank God. No coordination. But alertness isn't easy. He reminds himself that key sensors can fail any time. That drill is the operation's hub, and it's running deeper and hotter than anything ever attempted. That's why they can't trust AIs to run the show. Too much need for a human hand. For cyborg reaction times. Sweet Lord, he thinks, this is the hub job. The miners cutting hyperfiber panels with hand-held torches . . . they're nothing. Or the ones working with the geothermal equipment. Or the cleanup crews. Or any of them. Their mistakes are just mistakes. "Listen to me," he mutters. "Get focused, you stupid shit. Right now."

The roaring of the drill is enormous.

The sonics are boring away at the plastic rock, compressing it and pushing it away from the shaft long enough for the drill's arms to lay down and fuse the hyperfiber panels and braces and such. The process is almost entirely automated. Half a kilometer is a good day's drilling. It's not true what some people think, about the core being the goal, and no Morninger will ever go past this point . . . excepting the two or three who have taken wrong steps and fallen down a shaft, auxiliary or not, getting past the safety systems and dying somewhere between here and the hellhole bottom.

Gabbro remembers what he told the officer.

Only the world is strong.

It's absolutely true, he thinks, and he feels shame for having been so glib with the man.

Someday, probably long after he's gone, this mine will operate at full capacity. A network of tunnels will be laced through the mantle, and robots yet unbuilt will suck up and process the plastic rock. The rare earth elements will make fortunes. Iridium and ytterbium and tantalum. If asked, he couldn't describe the precise physics that need them. Superconductors and lasing equipment and star-drives all use them. That's important to Gabbro, knowing they're important products. Someone once told him that in the vastness of time, when places like Kross and the Belt quit selling metals on the open market, their own stocks finished or too precious to waste, these mines will be expanded again, cutting into the core for the nickel and iron and titanium. Eventually the earthly continents will slump, so much of the mantle and core sucked away beneath them. The seas will spread inland like they did in the Mesozoic. The thick crust will be drowned, mountains becoming islands, and in the end—if there is such a thing in all creation—the only land above the pea-green sea will be the ring of enormous cities still girdling the equator.

It's all too big for one mind.

He's thought about it plenty of times, even tinkering with the images on World-Net fantasy channels, yet it all still leaves him panting.

Sure, only the world is strong. But people have the persistence. Maybe he should have said that to the officer. It wouldn't have been so funny, but it sure would have true. People persist. For some reason he starts to think about Steward again. He remembers standing on the top of that building, halfway expecting to see Steward somewhere. That elevator door opened twice. The second time someone came out—a nightmare with the wildest hair and eyes—and Gabbro watched him and tried to figure out where Steward fit in. He had a feeling there was a connection somewhere, and it bothers him still—

An AI comes across the line, warning of trouble.

Gabbro should have caught it himself. He presses buttons, fixing the problem. The alignment of the drill was off by a tiny margin, which means it was off much too much. He braces for the shift boss to come on the line and ask if he's falling asleep at his station. But she doesn't. She must be watching someone else blunder along. And he's a little sorry. If you are part of something vast, goes his thinking, then an alcohol-soggy fool shouldn't be allowed to let substandard crap slide past.

It doesn't seem right, he tells himself. Not even a little bit.

He sighs and turns his mind to April. She'll be waiting at home. He knows. She'll be angry for his having left and furious because he never returned and livid because he can't admit the true reasons to her. I promised her something, he recalls. Wasn't there something we planned to do? He can't quite bring it to mind, but expectations are lying in wait. He feels them. It's funny, but he feels as though his own brain is working against him. Conspiring against him. It's as though some secret hurtful part of him has set up these circumstances, knowing just what will happen and glad for it.

Giddy, almost.

"This is crazy."

If he stood and took a leap straight out, out into the empty screaming shaft, he'd fall to his death and nothing could save him. Yet what scares him to tears is going home. *Imagine.* All this dangerous work and the wicked machinery, and his real nemesis is a lover made of stuff soft and weak and beyond his reach.

Somewhere, somehow, he is sure this has to be funny.

12

She called herself Wisp. That probably wasn't her name during her flesh-on-blood existence—a lot of us acquire new identities after the transformation, either out of shame for the past or a willingness to start again with the proverbial clean slate. I don't which it was for Wisp. Maybe neither. I don't know how she made her money, but she had plenty in the early going. She never explained how she had died, but I knew it had happened at a tragically early time. Telling that was easy. Wisp had a young girl's makeup, a young girl's passions. That makes it tough when you're Ghosted. You are so disappointed with so much. Like the sky. "It isn't quite right, you know?" The taste of food. "Why's it so bland? This is my favorite meal, for goodness sake." The feel of any surface. "I mean I can tell it's wood. And that's metal. But I can't . . . I don't know . . . it all feels so *simple,* you know?" Of course we would explain the problems to her. AIs can do only so much. It's one thing to see a scene on World-Net, a moving picture and sound and you the detached viewer. But it's something else entirely for you to be a part of that picture. The numbers of calculations are enormous, not to mention instantaneous. A single AI can build a fantasy on World-Net. A thousand AIs are required to build and maintain you inside a simple home. And never, never will the illusion feel *right.* Certainly not to a newly Ghosted person. There's some basic physics involved. I can't explain it myself, but the core of the concept involves a natural randomness in a living person's environment—the way air molecules strike the skin, the way your sensory inputs are subject to quantum effects, and so on. Not a million AIs working in tandem can effectively replicate these very tiny effects. And Ghosts are aware of their absence, believe me. Wisp was very, very sad to learn it was so. The flatness. The grayness. The bland meals and the *wrong* sky and all the rest. She came to us with a lot of money, yes, but she did the very worst thing possible. She tried to reproduce the life she knew from before being a Ghost. She spent much of what she had to do this, never succeeding, then when she could see the end of her resources she tried something particularly foolish. She tried to coax and cajole us, her fellow Ghosts, into granting her new money.

I must say she was good. Very good. I was tempted myself, several times. But when you're truly alive you think only once before giving away riches to a pretty face. If that. And when you're a Ghost you think twice, or more, and you resist. In life it's only

hard-won money, you see. In a Ghost's existence that money repre-
sents existence. You see? And no one is going to let that go. Not
for a smile, surely. Poor Wisp, charming us and charming us and
not getting a thing . . . and all the while *her* money was running
down. Running out. Her existence fading away . . .

—excerpt from an interview
with a Ghost, the Magician's
private file

H ER first thought is that Steward should have been killed. She
wishes it had happened in the early going, thinking that would
have been best. If he could have slipped and tumbled to his death
in the elevator shaft, Chiffon believes, and never gotten close to
Dirk . . . and she catches herself, not wanting to waste the effort with
simpleminded hope. She looks at him and prays there's no way for
Dirk and Minus to make the connection with her and here. And she
makes herself smile. "At least you're all right, love." Her voice is
naturally relieved. "Thank goodness nothing terrible happened!"

Steward rubs his arm, saying, "Anyway, I tried." He shrugs as if
he's embarrassed. He doesn't like admitting failure, not accustomed
to it. "I made him an offer and maybe he would have accepted. I don't
know. But his people broke in and broke up our dealing."

"You shouldn't have done it." Honest words; a lying tone. "I wish
you had at least told me."

He looks at Chiffon, nothing to say.

"Steward." She whimpers and goes to him, curling up snug in his
lap and cooing in his ear. She wonders what Dirk and he said to one
another. Did Dirk tell him the truth? Would Steward believe it? Is he
so quiet because he suspects me now? Terror in her belly, she says, "I
love you."

"I didn't want dashed hopes," he confessed.

"Of course not." She would have talked him out of it. Or she would
have killed him herself, saving herself. "I know you were helping."

"Not close."

"I think the man is insane."

"And I treated you shabbily." He pulls her blonde hair to his
mouth, cupping it and kissing it and her scalp, saying, "I keep forgetting you're no helpless little girl."

"I'm not."

"You're smart in a hundred ways."

"I told you." She kisses him. She's so angry that she has half an urge to bite his lip or tongue, but the Flower's face shows nothing beyond sweet eyes and an endearing smile and a mouth that can be concerned and sexual at the same instant, uttering banalities until it's numb.

"Do you want to hear what happened?"

She does. She listens, imagining how those cyborgs looked as they scaled the Cosgrove. "I remember you talking with Gabbro." She wants to know what the Morninger knows. She asks some sideways questions, Steward replying that *if* the cyborgs could be identified and *if* Dirk somehow traced his way back to Gabbro . . . well, if the Quito man has the will and tools then there just might be trouble. He feels to blame. "I'm sorry," he swears. "It's another thing we'll have to consider from now on."

She's thinking to herself, weighing options.

"That albino soldier of his? Minus?" Steward says, "He broke us up," and he skips to the end, his fleeing and Minus giving chase and his escaping by no margin at all. What she wants to know is what happened in Dirk's bedroom. She wants every word laid down, every syllable given its authentic voice. But she can't alarm him. If he has any suspicions, she has to play it all perfectly.

"Don't you think he's wrong in the head?" she wonders.

"I guess he must be, considering."

"He's liable to do anything. Say *anything.*"

And it's easier than she could have hoped. He tells the middle of the story. He keeps the details simple and true. She senses honesty while his hands come around her body, holding her tight as if to protect her, and she feels his heart beating and his regular breathing and the warmth coming off his tired flesh. He concludes by admitting, "The man denied ever having hurt you. He implied . . . I don't know what."

She burrows into his chest.

"Did he imagine . . . what? Other lovers?"

"Constantly. He did," she says so quickly that he can't help but believe the words. "Even when he knew I went nowhere, he told me I was cheating on him. No one came to his home without him being aware, yet he cursed me and beat me for having other lovers."

"A hard enemy to honor," he mutters.

She waits.

Steward says, "I did some checking on him. Beyond mental health, I mean," and he breathes and strokes the tip of his nose. "Dirk makes a considerable living as a creature of opportunity. A crime lord—"

"I couldn't tell you about him," she begins. "Because—"

"Of course you couldn't. He had you made. He made sure you wouldn't identify him. I understand. It just puts both of us, and maybe some others, in a hard corner." Steward holds his breath. She looks at him and believes him, glad for his not getting killed somewhere. She tells herself that a man who cracks Dirk's home, then escapes . . . well, how do you label such a person? "If we force him out of Brulé," he is saying, "and I mean forever, then we'll be doing everyone a favor."

She waits.

"There must be a way."

Another uncomfortable thought chews at her. "He doesn't push, love."

"Everyone can be pushed," he tells her.

She says, "Take me somewhere." Steward breathes in and lets it out between his teeth, making a slow easy whistling noise. "Another City-State maybe. Anywhere."

"We're safer here," he says. He kisses the top of her head and strokes the hair. "I've been here for half my life. I've got friends. Funds. Local knowledge. If Dirk is half-crazy, and half as ruthless as I've heard, he isn't going to quit chasing us—"

"So we have to run far!"

"Where?"

"Well," she says, "maybe Yellowknife. Maybe?"

Something changes. It's nothing visible or tangible, his face almost the same as before . . . but she's aware of a sudden hardness. She isn't surprised when he states, "No. That's no option."

She knows to keep quiet.

"I'll protect you with all my abilities. But here. Nowhere else."

She clings, muttering, "Darling." She plays the scolded-girl role.

And he says, "I'm sorry."

"For what?"

"I'm just sorry."

She waits for a little while, then asks, "How can we get him out of Brulé?"

"The best way to push him, I think, would be to rob him." Steward says, "A man like that likes to keep his money close. Which means I should have bled him when I had my chance." He laughs softly and says, "That'd hit him deep. Take his quiver chips, whatever, then force him to leave."

She is absolutely quiet, watching him.

"What is it?" he wonders. "What?"

"What?"

"I can't tell what you're thinking, love."

"Nothing," she lies. She asks, "What else can we do?"

He blinks. He puts back his head and breathes and closes his eyes. "Maybe the thing to do is not push. But pull him." He sighs and says, "A week. You'll have to stay hidden here another week or so. And I'll have to be gone a good deal of the time."

She squeezes his arms and kisses his stinking chest, asking, "Do you know what I think of you?" She has a sudden little urge to tell him the truth. It surprises her, coming from nowhere, and she suppresses the thought. So a second odd thought comes to her. What if they had met under different circumstances? She finds that notion so terribly appealing just now. "I love you," she tells him.

"Although maybe it'd be good to move you somewhere," he broods.

She *does* feel exposed, the truth told.

"No, no. We'll hold off on that for a few days."

And she has one more course to pursue. One more option. "He's such an old man," she mentions. "Sometimes I think he might die before me."

Steward is silent.

"But listen to me," she says. "Goodness, goodness. I shouldn't even talk about such things . . . a person's life and all . . ."

And Steward remains silent, stroking her hair with his face toward the ceiling, his eyes open and unblinking. Unseeing. What are you thinking? she wonders. Are you thinking about pushing him? Or pulling him? Or maybe cutting him into manageable little pieces?

◆ ◆ ◆

Twelve hours ago he was late. Twelve and ten and eight hours ago April was angry with him and hot about him and ready to scream when and should he appear at the door, humble-faced and pretending to be sorry for his negligence. Now the heat has left her, though. A level calm remains. Imagining herself from outside herself, she draws a picture of righteous fury—cold enough to scald anyone's flesh.

She hates the big stupid cyborg.

She should pack up and leave without a word. No note. No tri-dee message. No clue as to her whereabouts. It wouldn't take more than a few minutes to pack. She hasn't all that much. She could do it so well, so bloody quickly, that when Gabbro returned from work, or from wherever, he would enter a strange piece of terrain where her absence laid on everything and mocked him to no end.

She knows that terrible sensation.

It's happened to her more than she cares to remember. Nothing hurts worse than the lover vanishing of his own volition, without warnings or any final scene. April requires final scenes. She doesn't know why. And an ordinary argument isn't good enough. An out-and-out fight is best—hard talk with vicious words that neither of them will ever forget.

Just now she sits and watches a sporting event on World-Net. It's something she chose at random, skimming through the channels and quitting when a big bright field of green presented itself. This is an old-fashioned ballgame. An enormous history stands beneath the players' spiked shoes. Those clubs are ash. The costumes are woven white cotton. The players themselves are tailored only so far as strict rules allow, old elbows and knees replaced with prosthetics no better than the originals. The bases and balls have eyes. Each is utterly honest, calling pitches and close plays, and there's such order to the game that April grows bored in a brief while. Rising to freshen her drink, she thinks this isn't how the world works. This is all a considerable, elaborate lie—rules and patience and two-plus millenia of tradition sewn up into a pageant without blood enough to stain a lip.

She sets down the drink, then flips to a scenery channel. A low Antarctic mountain stands beside a warm shadowy bay. April sips and stands again, deciding to change clothes while she watches. A wind is blowing straight from the South Pole. A single boat skims across the bay, soundless and smooth. A pair of fishermen are riding in the boat, one pointing at something and saying, "Here. The place!" The boat quits moving. One of the fishermen extends a hooked pole, reaching into the water and snatching up some object heavy enough to make him labor, pulling it to the surface.

The object is a tailored sponge.

It's the size of a small chair, perhaps, seawater slipping out of its wide pores and its flesh creamy and soft and ready to be eaten. The fishermen have long straight knives. They slice the raw salty meat into their smiling mouths, standing in the boat and chewing with slow deliberation, eyes narrowed, faces toward the rounded low mountain and the camera hidden on the slope above the stony beach. April is naked. She connects to a fantasy channel now, an AI coming on the line with an audible, "Yes? May I be of help?"

She explains. While the fishermen discuss the flavor of the meat, she tells the AI what she desires. Then the scenery channel is invaded by the fantasy channel, conquered with no breaks or incongruences. One of the fishermen says, "Ready?" The other nods. And their boat begins to move, slipping along with the slenderest of hums. The fishermen have just sat down when a motion ahead of them, out in the bay, causes one of the men to say, "Wait. Stop!"

The water is deep in one place, except now an island has emerged from the depths. A rushing roar is dead ahead. The boat stops just short of the sudden cliff. Some eerie black and white seaweed glistens in the low sunlight. The fishermen scream while their boat makes an instinctive turn, fleeing, and the cliff rises up until enormous eyes are showing, then a protruding nose, and April sees herself. She's a giantess. The AI has done a marvelous job dressing her up as some goddess of the sea, and she has to laugh in a sloppy drunken way as she watches the fishermen trying to escape and her towering naked body bearing down on them, long legs wading through the sponge beds and waves rushing in every direction, the stony beaches taking a pounding.

"Keep out of here!" shouts the goddess. "You fools! Run, run, run!" And with that she stops and jumps in place, her feet slapping the ground and the ground splitting, spitting out molten rock and columns of steam.

April kills the channel.

She turns and goes into the bedroom, finding her swimsuit and fitting into it with the usual self-conscious feeling. She's been this fat before. She hates the feeling and the lack of breath and the looks of others. Of course Gabbro has challenged her to exercise, or at least ingest some of the fat-burning agents available everywhere, shoving off the extra bulk. Only she doesn't like the side effects of fat burners. And she loathes athletic drudgery. And the permanent solution—selective tailoring of her natural metabolism—is too expensive. "Besides," she mutters, "I like his watching me bloom." And she laughs. Sure. It's tangible proof that Gabbro isn't keeping her happy. All the blame is on his shoulders.

Going outside, she notices the empty pool, flat and calm and all her own. She has a folding chair, towel and lotion and sunglasses. She isn't thinking about Gabbro, except sometimes she finds herself looking over one shoulder at nothing. She isn't angry anymore, no, and she doesn't care about him. She goes so far as imagining a call from the mines and the caller telling her to brace herself because she has some sad news. An accident has occurred. Gabbro Gleason is dead. And April says thank-you for having informed her. She knows it's never easy bearing bad news.

She lies down on the towel and applies a layer of oily lotion, then naps. Bugs gather and drown in the lotion. When she wakes she's dotted with their carcasses. So she climbs into the deep cool water, and the little fish come up out of the soft-coral hiding places to suck away the dead bugs. She feels their little teeth. She floats easily, back arched and feet pointed and her black-and-white-streaked hair hanging down in the clear water.

Her eyes are shut.

There is motion an instant before the splash, and she hears the high soft giggling that gives away her assailant's identity. April smiles. She tucks just as a little hand grabs her ankle, tugging without pulling her deeper. April uses her arms to fight her buoyancy, submerging and opening her eyes to see the Cradler's muscular body kick away and his face smiling and giggling underwater. Amazing people, she thinks. So graceful and effortlessly happy. They don't ever worry about weight, and they sing like angels—their songs complex and simple at the same time. She can't begin to say this Cradler's name, though she's heard it many times. Surfacing, she squeals and says, "You little shit!" and giggles too.

He says, "Phew!" and shakes off the water.

April grabs the top of his little head, using her bulk for something good. The Cradler struggles. Then he twists and is gone, diving and curling and kicking off the bottom, climbing out before she can paddle over to him. Some damned goddess I make, she thinks. He laughs and points and she splashes him. The flying water is bright in the sun. Then he's running again, leaping over her head and splashing and gone. She gasps and tucks and chases him, thinking nothing is so adorable as a Cradler. There he is! He's waiting on the bottom, tiny hands clinging to the sides of the pool and his smile eternal. They're like children, she knows. All their lives they have the temperament and enthusiasms of bubbly young children. Her lungs burn. She has to fight herself to keep swimming downward, every muscle burning. The Cradler waits.

He waits. Underwater, using her spent breath, she tries calling him by his full name. It comes out better than it would have in the air above, odd as it seems.

The Cradler answers by saying, "Gabbro? Gabbro?"

"Gone," her bubbles confess, and her gestures.

"Gone where?" he asks.

But she can take no more. She needs air, in long luxurious breaths, and she kicks and rises with her brain on fire. And only now, finally, does she realize what she must have been planning all along.

◆ ◆ ◆

His accent doesn't perplex her so much anymore. They're spent, lying on the big special bed with the recharging cord wrapped around the usual post and the sheets kicked away and she still sweating in the darkened, human-warmed room. The little Cradler is talking of home now. He sings about it and uses both hands to draw out the lay of its land. Rivers flow. Canyons snake down to little violet seas. Has she ever spent much time looking at the landscape on World-Net? He's curious. Has she ever seen images of a Cradler pasture? Deep violet is the very best color for vegetation, he maintains. From pole to pole, Cradle is one great pasture with the violet growth sucking up the precious feeble sunlight.

She's seen it on World-Net, yes. But it's been a while.

"Come live with me and my family," he sings. "In a little bit we go home again."

"Do you?"

He nods and starts to sit up in bed.

"Why'd you come here in the first place?"

"Vacation," he sings.

"You're tourists? I didn't know." She says, "I thought you had jobs somewhere."

"Just time and interest. No jobs."

"I don't travel myself," she tells him. "World-Net is good enough for me."

"Pictures on a wall, silly girl." He laughs.

"Why, oh why, do I keep falling for children?" she asks.

And the Cradler turns sober, concerned, breathing deeply and looking at the cord as if it's what could cause him misery. As if it has eyes and might tell on the two of them.

She says, "Here."

He watches her reaching hand, acting as if he might flee.

She says, "Relax. Go on. Relax."

He watches the stroking of her hand, his penis stiffening. It's the only hairless point on his body. She thinks of him as sleek, thinking of otter fur, thinking maybe it would be good to wander with him for a time. Though she doubts the offer's genuineness—something made between lovers, reality suspended by mutual accord.

"How do you find the Earth?" she asks, kneeling to the floor. "Good?" she jokes, taking him into her mouth.

The little Cradler makes a contented sound.

She works him. She has him rocking on the bed, hands over his eyes and the moaning regular and soft and a little bit sad. He doesn't hear the front door open and shut. The poor fellow is oblivious to it all. She persists with her mouth, planning nothing and going with the moment, the bedroom door coming open at the instant April decides to take him out of her mouth, holding the penis with a hand and turning to look up into the handsome face, saying:

"Hey now! You're home!"

It is as if Gabbro sees nothing unusual, standing in the bedroom door in the dirty clothes and heavy boots with the big hands hanging at his sides with nothing to do. His eyes are tired. His entire face is long and drawn and near exhaustion.

"Oh my!" the little Cradler sings. His penis is shriveling in her hand, and he halfway sits up and blinks, plainly scared. "You—you promised him gone . . . !"

"She did?" asks Gabbro.

He doesn't sound mad, she thinks. He doesn't sound anything at all. What's it mean? What's he telling himself? The Cradler has begun to tremble, every hair on his legs standing erect, and on his body, and him sitting all the way up and looking larger than before but still tiny as he stares up at the cyborg, plainly weighing his prospects.

"What else did she tell you?"

The Cradler can't find words.

"Well," says Gabbro, "why don't you stand and walk out of here. Now." He takes a long, lazy breath and says, "Let him stand, April. Help him if you've got to." He says, "Do it."

"Come on," she tells him. "Here. Remember these." She hands him his soggy swimsuit and towel, his hands feeling cold and shaking in her warm hands. "There, there." She tells him, "Relax. He knows who's to blame."

The Cradler keeps watching Gabbro.

"Go on," she says.

He makes a soft moaning sound from somewhere deep in his throat. He looks to April, saying, "No," and wanting something. He glances at the suit and says, "Wait," as tears well up in his eyes.

"Get dressed," April insists.

"Hurry," Gabbro adds, his voice without blood or hooks.

The Cradler untangles the suit and steps toward a leg, missing and nearly stumbling as he hops in place, weeping now and stopping and trying again with both shaking hands and his legs trembling and the one leg in and then the other and the suit up around his waist and the built-in belt taking in the slack, his breathing quick and light, quick and dry.

Gabbro says, "Come on."

The Cradler moves toward him, swallowing and keeping his eyes down. Gabbro moves aside just enough for him to pass. He watches the Cradler. April studies him, trying to guess what will happen. The Cradler is gone and Gabbro again blocks the doorway, looking at her with the tired eyes and long face and the empty hands doing nothing. "Yes?" she says, challenging him. "Well, what do you want?"

He doesn't say anything.

She sits on the edge of the bed. "So. How was work?"

The big hands come up and pull away the shirt.

"You aren't so filthy. Did you go to work?"

He says, "Sure." His voice is dead. He says, "I sat punching buttons for ten hours." He removes his pants and boots and throws everything in a pile, volunteering nothing else.

"So," she says, "aren't you getting mad?"

He says, "No."

She stands and thinks this isn't how she pictured it and decides to do anything now but sit and wait him out. She dresses. She doesn't pay attention to him while she pulls on her clothes and shoes, Gabbro sitting on the edge of the bed now, wearing underwear, running a hand over his big bald skull.

She says, "What are you going to do?"

"Sleep."

She doesn't know him.

He says, "I'm tired. I'll sleep. Be gone when I'm done." He isn't talking loudly. His voice is nearly a whisper, and his breathing is slow and relaxed. He asks April, "It's what you want, isn't it?"

"Something's sick with you," she assures him. "You know that?"

"Thanks for the input."

Something is rising inside her now. "You come in on me and all you do is make some—some pronouncement before you sleep. In the very same bed, you stupid shit!"

"Yeah?"

"Asshole," she says.

"Oh yeah?"

"I'm not leaving. You're going to have to make me go." She moves toward him and jabs him in the chest with a finger, jamming her finger into her hand and screaming straight at his face. "Fuck you, machine man! Fuck you!"

He breathes. He says, "I'm tired."

"Ask me if I care!" She slaps him with the other hand, putting the palm into a cheek and hurting her wrist. The craziness, like some old dear friend, comes to her rescue. She's incapable of fear or doubt. With the heel of one shoe she kicks Gabbro in the midsection. It's like throwing her fury into a concrete pillar. He doesn't blink, doesn't change the cadence of his breathing, and April stepping away with her ankle burning and tender and shaky underneath her weight.

He says her name once, flat and slow.

She charges into the front room, into the kitchen-corner, and pulls a huge carving knife out of a drawer. Gabbro calls to her again. He's still sitting on the edge of his bed when she rushes him, slashing at his neck. He patiently watches the blade descend and strike, hyperfiber dulling the cutting edge with a harsh quick scraping noise.

She knows him. She knows his weaknesses, thrusting now at his eyes.

Reflexes take hold. Gabbro can't let anything near his eyes, his hand up and the fingers curl and squeeze, the blade bending and snapping and the knife's hilt falling into his lap.

She curses him in every fashion, no taboos.

He gives April the gentlest of pushes.

She flings a lamp at his face, its glass base exploding, and she wrestles the nightstand off the floor and uses its living wood as a club. The wood shatters, sap and splinters everywhere. Then she moves to the dresser, throwing the drawers, screaming, "Pack! Pack! I'm packing, asshole! Look at me!"

She's possessed.

Gabbro won't do anything. She knows it. So she throws clothes and a little chair into a pile around him. He ignores the brunt of it. He sits like a statue, watching her with his damning detached interest, going so far as blinking and even giving a little yawn. So she thunders into the front room. A big bottle of strong clear liquor waits on the countertop—the same stuff running in her veins all afternoon—and she takes it by the neck and opens a drawer and thinks this will get his attention. "You tub of shit! You hear me?" She charges back to the bedroom and finds him standing now, something about his face so very tired, so drawn, that she halfway believes he will topple with the faintest push. He sees the bottle too late. It comes out from behind her back, spinning heavily in the air, and the glass shatters and lets the liquor splatter, soaking him and the bed and all the piles of clothes.

He says, "Lord."

She has the lighter out and lit, the bright red plasma flame dancing on the tip. He says, "April." She comes at him. The strong stink of alcohol wells up in her face. There is a sudden audible *poof* and a wave of intense heat. April leaps backward, startled. The quick flame spreads across Gabbro's chest and shoulders and eyes. It's in his eyes. He can't feel it as heat, she knows . . . it's nothing like noon on Morning . . . but it's in his eyes and it's fire and his reflexes take hold, hands swatting at the bright hot fire and him screaming, his voice finally coming alive.

This is what she wants.

He is startled and furious and it all shows now. She has him crazy now. He curses and she picks up one of his shirts and balls it up and tosses it to him. The fabric burns in a lazy way.

He asks, "Why why why do this?"

"You no good son-of-a-bitch," she says.

He says, "Damn," and beats out the fire. "April, goddamn it." She throws the soaked bedding on him and makes it explode into flames. The air is hot and smoky now. The carpet is smoldering. Gabbro is an enormous bonfire trying to kill itself, and she grabs at one of the swatting hands and feels her eyebrows burn and her hands burn and makes him stop for an instant, Gabbro saying:

"Quit!"

The motion is neither hard nor large.

It could be an accident, though she wants to believe it's intentional. Gabbro breaks a cheekbone and flattens her nose and two teeth are kicked out of her jaw and tumble to the floor as she jerks her head sideways and loses all sense of up and down. She falls. She is on the floor and looking up through one eye, the other one cut and closed and her face hot where it's broken. She touches the broken cheek. She coughs and tries to stand, Gabbro asking, "See what you did? To yourself. You did it to yourself, you crazy bitch!"

She can't say anything, her jaw leaden and aching at its hinges.

"Not me—!" he begins, kneeling now.

She kicks at him.

He ignores the heel in his neck. The fire is dying, smoke and foul air everywhere and him saying, "Why do it, you bitch?"

"Get away." Her voice is clumsy. Words hurt. She feels gaps where the teeth had been rooted and feels other teeth moving in the battered gums. "*You* did this!"

"Bringing in that Cradler. Using him—"

She is standing. The floor wheels and bucks and she is standing on its axis, staggering toward the door, and he says, "Where are you going? Don't go. Get some ice," and he makes a soft frustrated sound. "April? Where are you going?"

She is in the front room now.

Touching her sleeve to her face, she tries judging the damage by the amount and color of the blood.

"April?" he calls, his voice small and faraway.

She is out in the hallway, the door shutting automatically, and she looks both ways and decides that she'll need something to mop up the blood. There's no choice. But she won't go inside, not with things this stacked against her. She won't beg for help. So she uses her sleeves and her own long hair, plus her hands, and with the hands she paints a few choice obscenities on the walls up and down the long hallway.

This isn't enough.

She's never been with a man so long, through so much, and still and all this isn't enough to call everything finished.

13

The residents of Chu's World have a novel answer to the problem
of age and the erosion of the mind. They've tailored themselves so
that their brains have enormous redundancy—several-fold that of
the norm—and while certain neurons can't help but die after two
centuries, or three, enough persist for the soul to remain whole for
five hundred years or more. Yet there is a cost involved. A consequence. I like the people well enough. I do. But to speak with them,
to share time with them, is to catch the aroma of a certain shallow-
ness. A flat grayness. It's in their faces, in their words. They seem
incapable of telling interesting stories. Or biting jokes. They are
never subtle. Never intricate. And usually rather boring after a time,
the poor folk . . .

—excerpt from a traveler's
notebook, available through
System-Net

HIS second thought—the thought following on the heels of being
shocked by the sight—is that he would have liked to have been
home and heard the two of them fighting. He's sorry to have missed
the show. Seeing the girl in the hallway, hearing her sniffle as she
touches her torn and bleeding face, Toby can almost sense the receding violence of the battle. It's like standing at the scene of some ancient
war and sensing the clashing armies between all the quiet. April is
walking up the stairs, making for the floater pad. Toby is coming
down. She makes a sniffing sound and totters for a moment. She might
be crying. He can't tell for all the blood.

He is back from the Old Quarter. He was wandering himself into
distraction.

"Don't look at me," she warns, and she coughs once.

He doesn't know what to say. She stands facing him, her eyes fixed on his toes, one eye closed and the other blinking as if fighting to keep its focus. "Hey," he starts. "What . . . happened?"

She wobbles where she stands.

"Why don't you . . . I don't know, why don't you sit. Huh?"

She seems to have trouble understanding him. She takes a couple of slow breaths and leans against a wall and looks faint for a moment. She takes a deeper breath. He doesn't want to touch her. She kneels, or she's fainting with a measure of control, and now she is down and her head is between her knees and Toby wants to get a better look, not getting too close. So he sits on the step above.

"Look at me." She says, "The fucker did it."

"Yeah?"

"You know what I . . . I don't . . . God!"

Bones are broken. The bleeding won't stop. Toby studies the marks of individual fingers, huge and slightly spread, and he remembers the crow and thinks to tell the girl that she's been lucky today. He's intrigued. A gruesome piece of work, but she will heal.

"Anyway," she says, "can you help me?"

"Like how?"

"Signal a floater, and get me . . . to a hospital or something. I'm not . . . tracking true . . ."

"Okay," he hears himself say.

"You're the one, right? The Gardener?"

"Sure."

She starts to stand. "Can you help me?" She presses both hands against the wall, leaving blood on the whiteness, and she manages to lift herself partway when her legs give away and she drops again. She begins to laugh. "Me asking you for help," she says. "Imagine."

"What . . . should I do?"

"Try lifting. Come on!"

She has the heavy muscled arm of a native Terran. The bone beneath is thick and dense, repulsive to him, but he manages to help her find her feet and he stays at her side as she climbs upstairs. The sky is perfectly blue. The wind is out of the northwest today, the heat not so bad. It was pleasant in the Old Quarter. He knows places where a person can sit and lose himself, thinking and napping. But if he had known what was happening here, he laments . . .

"Thanks," she offers.

He says, "Sure."

He hits the floater button and from above, out of the perfect blue, comes a single floater. Toby stays and waits. He continues to study her face, fascinated and eager to ask questions. What caused the fight? He's never actually struck her before, has he? Was he involved in this somehow? He hopes he was a factor. He can't imagine any reason, but he likes to picture himself as the catalyst.

The floater lands. An AI voice asks for her destination, surveying the damage with its single shiny eye on the end of a pedicle. She tells it what she needs. "Can you climb aboard yourself?" Then, not waiting for an answer, it says to Toby, "Sir? Can you help this poor girl?" as if he is a stranger off to one side. "I'm sure she would appreciate the gesture."

He does it, holding her closer arm and lifting, steadying her, and she leans to him and whispers, "Stay with me? I need someone."

He tries to think.

"I need someone. Please?" And she smiles. He is startled to see the smile, and for a long moment he doesn't understand. "You and me," she says. "Think what it means, us meeting. A sign, huh? Me and the Gardener together at last," and she stops to look at her toes.

Only she doesn't mean her toes. She means Gabbro. He sees the hard kernel of truth between her words. And now they're side by side inside the floater, the canopy secured and the world beneath them dropping away without any noise louder than a soft smooth hissing. She sits as though she is nearly asleep. She breathes like a runner after a long race. She says, "Thank you," several times. She says, "I never did anything to hurt you, you know," her memory terribly selective.

It's funny, he thinks.

Here he is and she is and through the blood and gore she's hinting at doing something, culturing him for a purpose, and he thinks he can guess the purpose while she sits willingly beside him, both of them comfortable with one another. It's like they've always been together. They have become fast old friends. And Toby thinks, Sure. Sure we have. He's done it to both of us. Gabbro's done it. We're a team, all right! He's made us into a team!

◆ ◆ ◆

One of the few exportables from Garden is produced by a shellfish that can only grow wild in the open sea, only on Garden, the pearls secreted judged to be more lovely than any others, wild or not, and commanding a price worthy of the time they take and the trouble they cause and the intangibles that hinge on the stuff of fashion.

Toby used to own a little sailboat with a sturdy hull made from prophet oak and a foam-metal mast and a hyperfiber sail so sheer that it was nearly invisible against any light. He use to wander the open sea for days at a time, one or two or three passengers sharing his cabin and one another until boredom threatened. He liked to take friends over the beds where the Gardener merchants hunted for their pearls. Sometimes he would stop during the brief Garden night, drifting if it was still enough, and one or two of them would roll into the water and dive and select a shellfish to cut loose from the buoyant masses of porous coral. Some shellfish yielded pearls. Most had nothing but the pulpy gray lumps of matter that were uncured, immature pearls. It was the latter they wanted. Raw or slightly cooked, the grey lumps had a delicate flavor that lingered for days, cool on the back of the tongue and not a little intoxicating. The finished pearls, more often than not, were thrown overboard. Except sometimes Toby's friends would resist common sense, knowing what prices they would find on the black market. One friend went so far as to bring pebbles aboard to mimic discarding the pearls, fooling her companions and insuring the profits for herself, but in the end the legal network on Garden discovered her scheme and the appropriate hands were slapped, Toby's father—an important figure in all political circles—having to come and help his son out of the silly scandal.

It wasn't the first time such things had happened.

Older friends, or simply older people with a misapplied interest in Toby's life, speculated that he pressed his father's good will because he was starved for attention. It was an old story, they assured him and themselves. A child born to busy parents, important parents, late in their lives would do many things to be noticed. He might seem wild, or worse, but the truth was as simple as it was harmless and it would surely be temporary too. A phase, they would declare. We understand you, so don't worry.

He didn't worry.

Toby felt no need to explain himself to anyone. He understood his mind and goals all of the time, in every circumstance, and what he did to his father, for example, was because he took pleasure from watching the old Gardener sweat. Nothing could be simpler. At an early age Toby came to see the differences between himself and others. He had a control, a sense of purpose and place that others lacked. His feelings for his father had no role in how he acted. He had power over the man, and he knew it, and he simply enjoyed exercising that power whenever and however he had the chance.

The trouble with pearls got the sailboat taken from him.

For a little while.

Punishment was something his father dispensed without skill or real conviction. He was a weak man in many respects. He had strong beliefs when it came to being a good and loyal Permissive, but the beliefs translated into little more than noise and cautious posturing. He coped with the entrenched Conservatives, for instance, by moaning to himself. In public debates, time and again, he was beaten by foes with half the arguments and a third the mental acuity. Toby had to watch the drubbings when he was young. It was a family duty, holy and hellish and soon a sheer waste. His first minor rebellion was to avoid the debates by stealth. His second rebellion was to do so openly and often, making no secret of how he felt.

Toby's mother worshipped his father.

They'd had a close relationship forever, it seemed. Ancient people spoke of the two of them being childhood lovers, and the less tolerant Gardeners would whisper cruel things about the two of them and how they missed the Necklaces, preferring one another in place of everyone, and how when they did attend they were simply going through the expected motions.

His parents always were a strange couple.

He never understood his mother's patience and endless support for his father's lost causes. They didn't embarrass him any longer, but he had no doubts that their common sense was gone. Spent. Some days he would plot their mutual downfalls, making it a game played out in his head. He would help the Conservatives here, mislead the Permissives here, and stand back to watch them tumble from grace.

Naturally it never happened.

Fate seemed geared to Toby's own long fall instead.

After years and years of sharing a home, so very late in life, his father packed and left his mother and vanished aboard a little shuttle that couldn't have taken him out of the Jovian system. No, they hadn't fought. Yes, his mother knew his destination. But she wouldn't tell Toby, or even hint at it, in spite of his threats and pleadings and his frustrated persistence. What's Father doing? he wondered. What's his plan now? He had lately been arguing for strong, lasting binds with the sister moons. Was that Permissive idea involved in this nonsense?

Or what? Whatever was happening, it was different than anything before. Ominous. Toby felt it, and when his father returned he made certain that he was at the little pad when the shuttle set down, its canopy opening to reveal two people sitting side by side.

The second person was a girl, younger than Toby and obviously born on Chu's World. She had the purebred elegance of an oriental girl. She was wearing the traditional garb of a highborn princess, which was appropriate, and she was nervous enough to stumble as she climbed out of the shuttle—the hem of her long jeweled robe catching a heel and her body spilling forward and Toby's father struggling to catch her and steady her. She gasped and nervously laughed and said to him, Thank you, darling.

Father said, Be careful, darling.

And Toby's mother, curiously proud, leaned to Toby and whispered, They're married. They're newlyweds.

No! Don't lie to me!

I'm not lying, she swore. We talked it over and decided that marriages were a good way to force the issue with these blockish Conservatives. Let's make substantial, binding ties with our neighbors. Let's break down our isolation in some meaningful way!

No one on Garden was married, the Prophet quite clear as to that particular bit of barbarism. Toby blinked and asked, So what are *you* going to do? Marry some smelly Russian monk?

Or maybe a porpoise, she said, winking. It depends.

Toby couldn't believe what he heard, but she insisted it was true. All true. He looked at his father with the girl, the damned princess, and felt an urge to spit on everyone. Or do worse. Then, realizing there would be painful introductions coming, he had no choice but to turn and run. He went to the beach and got into his old sailboat and pushed out and rode a soft wind far out to sea, the island receding into a green smear on the horizon, then gone, and from time to time the little holophone on board would make a plaintive noise that he ignored. Finally his father broke through the ring, using trickery to appear before him, saying:

Come home! We'll talk. I promise, we'll come to terms.

Toby pried up the phone and dropped it into a hundred kilometers of water, and he sat back down and watched the night swiftly descend and the sea grow dark and Jupiter on the horizon, banded through its narrow curling crescent. He could see enormous storms on the night-side of Jupiter, like always. Then he noticed Chu's World itself—a ruddy spot too distant to reveal any features—and he told himself that this was all shit but he wasn't jealous. No. Some people would claim he was injured by this sudden *wife* in his father's life, but he wasn't. No. It was the dishonor of the circumstance. What he hated was the man's complete disregard for what was right.

Toby eventually met the woman, and he worked hard to be reasonable in her presence. Women on Chu's World are accustomed to special attention, and the princess enjoyed compliments and little gifts. So Toby handed her a bracelet made from Garden pearls, all stolen, and successfully embarrassed his parents while convincing the alien of his goodness. His father took him aside and asked:

Is this a joke? Do you think you're funny?

Toby explained, If I did something wrong, go and take back the damned thing. I won't stop you!

But his father lacked the courage. He said, I wish you'd quit acting this way. You have a choice, you know.

His father had made this bland pronouncement countless times in the past. He was the sort of man who could repeat the same declarations time and again and never grow weary. He was drab as the purest, plainest water.

You're just spoiled.

Yeah, said Toby. I guess that's true.

I've tried to be the good parent. Haven't I?

What's this got to do with that?

Don't make me hurt you.

All right. I won't.

Because I will.

Yeah?

You don't believe me?

Toby looked off at the girl, asking, What? Are you and Mother going to share her tonight? Is that the plan?

His father stared at him in disgust.

Because, said Toby, I know something about Chu's World. About its people. They're graceless, stupid and sick. They don't know shit about the Ideal. They're too stupid.

Enough, said his father softly.

Okay.

We'll forget the pearls. All right?

It was like his father to pave over transgressions in the face of greater transgressions. He said, This is important to us. All of us.

Chu's World is rich in different ways than we're rich, and we need them, and I know you're just acting independent when you claim to be such a Prophet-loving Conservative. So are you going to be nice?

I was before.

Are you listening to me?

Are you talking to me? he answered.

I guess not, the old man replied. I guess I was wrong. I'm not.

His father had never been young in Toby's mind. The slight apricot fuzz on his flesh had long ago turned whitish, and while Gardener genes assured total vigor up until the rapid end, in that moment Toby sensed the age and the wear on the old man. Two years later he wouldn't recall the feeling. But then, ever so briefly, he felt something close enough to compassion to leave him a little shaken.

Time passed.

He spoke to the princess occasionally, feigning interest in her words and dull stories and the little opinions she had garnered from watching the Gardeners in Garden activities. She loathed the Necklaces, naturally. She conceded that the scenery was lovely, yes, and the climate was fresh and fine and if only her homeland had been blessed with so much water . . . well, it would be some time before she returned home. A few standard years at the earliest. And she missed it, naturally. She told Toby how it was to be born and raised as a princess, and she explained her station in life and how it was more a burden than a blessing. Her family was important politically, not wealthy, and did he understand how it was to be looked on as an example and an inspiration to several million citizens?

I don't like it, she confessed.

No? he wondered. I'd like the chance to be somebody—

Well, you're much more clever than me. I guess. Maybe I should do something to help my own cleverness . . . yes?

Toby thought about Chu's World.

But what can I do? she asked, giving him a strange bewitching smile.

He thought about the way their brains were wired, her youth and her long bland life waiting for her. He assured the princess, You and my father should get along mightily.

Really?

Past the rhetoric, said Toby, there's nothing much to him at all.

Time passed, and that final statement began to ring true. The marriage begun for political and social reasons evolved into something honest between the old man and his lovely young bride. She had talents, it seemed, because she would lure him away from people and parties, and sometimes from political meetings, and odd stories circulated as to the kinds of pleasures she enjoyed and her fear of being seen by others when she felt passionate. In public or not, the two of them held hands. Particularly in public they would bless one another with small tokens of love and respect—giving worthless sentimental presents to the other, crying over sunsets and kissing for any simple reason.

Mother began to have second and third thoughts about the strange marriage.

It was dawn, and she and Toby were walking a beach together, neither talking, and there were wild clouds riding the horizon on three sides. Jupiter was hidden. But Mother stopped as if to stare at the big world, squinting, and Toby asked, What is it?

Your father.

Toby waited, then asked, What about him?

I'm worried.

Why?

Why do you care?

He didn't. He admitted as much, and they continued their walk and said nothing more. Toby thought to himself that he's in love with the dirty stupid princess. And Mother is at last realizing it. The last few years of his life, and she's got to squeeze around the bitch just to have a word with him.

It was a strange circumstance.

It was nothing Mother could have anticipated.

Father began to pressure her into doing her part, saying she should marry and bring her spouse back to the island to live. There were several candidates, he assured. Because of climate concerns, he reasoned, a Cetacean might be more appropriate than a fur-clad Siberian. A Cetacean could live in the sea itself—serving as a vanguard for future diplomats or even colonists. Wouldn't that be splendid?

But she resisted him.

When Toby was nearby and listening, she took pains to kill any honest talk. But her face spoke volumes. More than a year later, Toby would still recall the drawn eyes and the confused bitter mouth and the way her webbed hands, small and sad, would wring each other while she promised him:

Soon. I need a little while and then I'll do it.

Soon?

Absolutely, darling.

Toby couldn't care what either of them did. They weren't acting reasonable, but that was their business and he had his own distractions and passions. He ignored them. He went on long sailing trips, fishing and swimming on the open sea, and he visited islands up and down the face of Garden, joining in feasts and Necklaces as he moved.

One day he returned home to work on the boat, replacing worn parts and cleaning everything else. He was standing on the deck, arms cocked on his hips, when the princess came from behind and asked:

What are you doing?

He told. He was matter-of-fact, and she surprised him by showing interest. Not much and maybe she was acting interested, but even still he paused to look at her and ask:

Do you want to go out on the water? For a little while?

He expected her to refuse. A year later, thinking back to the moment, he'd wonder why she had bothered to come see him. He didn't believe she cared about him or sailing. Boredom could have had its hand, the island's distractions pleasant but few. Yet the most likely answer was that Toby's father had made the suggestion. He had likely sent his wife to win Toby over to his side of the camp. It would have been like the old man, all right.

I'd like to go, she said. Now?

Why not? I've got to test this new rig anyway.

The sun reached its apex and dropped again. Father Jove was hidden over the horizon, and Sol itself, so much feebler than the sun, was somewhere behind Garden on that particular day. Night would be as close to absolute as possible. Toby thought of it while he steered them out into open water. He was planning nothing. A year later, thinking back, he tells himself that everything happened through sheer coincidence. Nothing more or less.

The sun of Garden set against the short blue horizon.

By then they were in remote waters, no islands in view, and Toby glanced at his passenger and asked:

Would you like to see where pearls grow?

Pearls? she wondered. The ones you gave me?

Up here's the spot. I can show you. It's not far.

All right.

If you want to take a risk, that is.

A risk?

Not much of one, he confessed. Don't worry.

The place was like any other stretch of open sea. The only difference was the occasional lump of porous coral showing over the waves. He turned the boat into the wind and dropped a pair of propellers to hold them in place. Then he turned to the girl and asked:

Do you want to see them?

Where?

He told where, pointing down.

She swallowed. She said, Of course. I've come this far.

Then get undressed, he said. You can't swim in that robe, can you?

She looked at him. In the faint starlight she used her eyes to bore holes in his skull. He fully expected her to refuse. He probably wouldn't have made the offer if he had thought there was a chance of her agreeing. But she surprised him, and maybe herself. It didn't happen quickly and she was plainly scared, but a hand reached to her throat and the robe melted away. She took the trouble to say to him:

Whatever happens, don't touch me. Don't!

I'll try keeping myself controlled, he answered. I'll manage somehow.

He pulled a couple of spotlights out of storage, giving her one and saying that she should follow him and keep alert. Then he dove into the warm salty water, himself nude, and she kept with him and took a few strong strokes as if to prove to him that she could handle herself. Then he dove headfirst, kicking. The shellfish were easy to find. They grew on the tops of the floating coral. They were large and their shells were elegant shapes built from a foam of calcium and organic compounds, each one with twin valves and a muscular hinge joining the valves together. Toby could see them clearly. In the light's cone-shaped beam, each looked big and rather simple beside the brilliant schools of little fish and the assorted lesser shellfish.

Garden is loveliest underwater.

The girl was hovering nearby, small breasts and a thin waist. She played her beam across the reef and tried to see with her ordinary eyes. Toby had forgotten. His extra eyelids served as goggles of sorts. He kicked to her and motioned her up, and she shot to the surface and was gasping when he arrived.

Can you see anything? he asked.

She said she couldn't. Not enough.

So Toby paused, then suggested, You can bring one up. Use a knife and cut one free.

Should I?

Go on.

She wasn't comfortable, treading water. She breathed hard for a moment, then said, All right. Where's the knife?

He found one. He gave it to her and then dove beside her and watched until she had a shellfish singled out and was cutting where the shell was linked with the reef itself. Then her breath ran out and she kicked to the surface again. Toby followed. Then she went down again and he laid on his back, pointing his toes and drifting for a few moments while he rested, nothing on his mind.

Then he dove again.

What must have happened was that the princess dropped her knife. It skidded sideways on the reef and found a large hole passing clear through the floating coral, and for some reason she must have thought she could catch the knife before it got away. When Toby arrived she had vanished. He found the hole quickly enough and kicked through and kicked downward but still couldn't see her. It might have been a different place, he decided. So he turned around and returned to the surface for a fresh breath.

What did you think!? his father asked him later. She's from Chu's World, for the Prophet's sake! Does she have your lungs? Can she swim like you?!

Today Toby can't remember what he thought. Or why he acted as he acted. He remembers breathing and going down again and kicking through a different hole and circling, fighting a current while he looked down and out and saw nothing. Not a light. No body. Nothing.

He rose again.

He dove again.

And again.

And a fourth time.

Then he knew it was too late. He knew those currents and the girl's character and realized that she was likely full of water and sinking deeper every second. There was nothing worth trying now. He saw no purpose in risking his own life, deciding to go home and tell what had happened. Not Father, he judged. His father's friends, perhaps. Let the news come from them, he thought, and he climbed up on the sailboat and pulled in the propellers and found the wind and went home, imagining how his father would take the news.

The old man accused him of negligence. Cursing him, he got down on his knees and beat the ground with both fists. Then he bit his knuckles until they bled. Then he wept.

Toby watched him, doing nothing.

Aren't you sad? asked Father.

It's sad. Sure.

What's the matter with you? Don't you feel bad?

I don't know. Maybe I could have tried harder—

Maybe? You think *maybe?*

Toby shrugged and said, It wouldn't have done any good.

His father stood again, and with a strange sharp voice he said, What are you? What kind of monster are you? *What are you?*

Hey! Let me go!

You didn't do *everything* you could to save her? Is that what you're telling me?

Quit it!

Tell me!

All right! Toby confessed. Sure, I could have stayed down longer. On that first dive, sure. But I didn't. I wouldn't if I did it again. What in the name of the Prophet was she? I'll tell you. Nothing—!

His father slapped him.

Toby backed away, turned and ran. His father was too excited to pursue him. Toby got to the beach and circled the island once, making himself calm again, and then he came around to the docks in time to see his sailboat burning and his father waiting for him, Mother beside him, Father telling him:

You're leaving. I don't care where you go, or how you support yourself. But you're through being a Gardener. After everything, I'm sure the Council of Judges will go along with me . . .

Mother said nothing. She watched Toby, something thankful implied by her expression. But she made no sound.

You get nothing from us, said Father. You're a vicious, sick animal and I won't have you as a son. Am I understood? Do you hear me?

Toby asked, Where do I go?

Wherever they take you in. I don't care. I hope no one takes you. I hope you drift in space, nobody wanting your filth.

Did I kill the girl? I didn't kill the girl.

And you still don't understand, he said. In the name of the Prophet, you're banished! You're exiled!

No!

And his father came at him a second time, swinging at his face. Toby had had enough. He thought about his ruined boat and exile and picked up a stone and bloodied his father's face.

The man crumbled.

In a cool, level voice his mother told him to go. Now.

Toby retreated.

And his father huddled on the ground, sobbing. His mother had her arms around the old man, squeezing him, ignoring the blood and telling him that everything was fine, just fine, cry and get it all out, love. Just try to let it go.

◆ ◆ ◆

Now it's evening in Brulé City, the sun down and the System emerging in the darkening sky. April is in bed in a hospital on the fringes of the Old Quarter. The doctor has left her alone. A mask is fastened to her face, its tiny elements mending the torn and bruised flesh and fighting any scars. She is awake, alert and even animated. She asks Toby what he might want to do.

"Scare him. Really scare him."

She says that would be fun. Fun and right.

He says, "Something deserved," and a warm calm feeling comes into him. He licks his lips and looks past her, out at the sky. "What would scare that machine worse than anything else? Huh?"

"I don't know. Let me think," she says.

"We'll teach him a lesson," he says.

Her masked face nods. Toby feels confident. Buoyant. He looks at her and thinks in clear certain terms about everything. It occurs to him that taking charge of someone else's fate, like Gabbro's, is maybe the best way there is to gain control of your own fate too.

14

Some say we would be better with fewer. Fewer people, I mean. They say two trillion is many too many. They want worlds empty of bodies, or nearly so—wilderness worlds where we are just visitors, maybe a few large nations instead of the rambling millions, and maybe more unity in the species. Of course none of them have the exact same opinion. Some stress one element, others another. But they are all wrong. I think the truth eludes them. We live in peace today—and here I must interject my own hard-won opinion—because of the sheer multitude we have become. Two trillion people owe their allegiance to a wide range of Nation-States. No one State can dominate. Even such wealthy places, like Kross or the Terran mega-cities, are merely rich. Crowded is good. Complexity is good. We have forced ourselves into becoming good neighbors, thus I feel free to sing the praises of the tangled Humanity, numberless and everlasting . . .

—excerpt from a traveler's notebook, available through System-Net

THE two of them are in the back room of his private suite, Minus having said something pleasant just now and taking a seat far from the window. Mayor Pyn looks at the pink eyes and feels uneasy in his belly. He never likes being alone with this man. He tries keeping a humor about it all, telling family and friends to call the police if he doesn't reappear soon, he's going to conference with a killer. But levity doesn't make him digest his meals any better. "You've had some trouble," he begins. "I heard something about some trouble last night."

"A little," Minus admits. The eyes do not blink and the mouth gives nothing away.

"A burglar?"

"A fool."

"Indeed." Pyn can feel two icy hands twisting his colon into a knot, and he shifts his weight and glances out at the skyline, trying to remember a day when being Mayor was a joy. Has it ever been? "I hope nothing of value was lost."

Minus has no response.

"It's funny. We have such a peaceful community—" he starts to say, thinking of Quito and diplomatically adding, "but no place is immune, is it? People are people, and all that."

Minus says, "Anyway," with a bored voice, rolling his eyes, "since you're aware of the incident, I guess I can get down to business. My employer is disappointed. He remains confident in our capacities to help one another—" The same tired promises of endless money, thinks Pyn. "—but for now what we need from you is a favor, if I might ask."

"Do." Mayor Pyn's nervousness increases. The backs of his hands are suddenly damp.

"A measure of protection," Minus begins.

"Yes?"

"From your own people."

"Oh." He knows his answer but tries to mislead, giving the impression that he's thinking hard. "Well, let's consider this . . ."

"Purely unofficial protection," he adds. "We can't expect uniformed officers. We realize your town can't be put in the role of a bodyguard."

Isn't that your role? Pyn thinks. Dirk's brought in two more like you, hasn't he? But that was days ago—

"Any possibility?" asks Minus.

"I'm sorry. I can't think of any means," Pyn admits. "Our charter is quite clear on these regards." He knows how little Minus cares for being refused. Sometimes he'll look into those cold eyes and feel . . . what? It's so far beyond his experience that Pyn can't even give it a name.

Yet Minus surprises him. "I see," he says, offering a little smile and shrug. "Well, it was worth asking."

What does he want? Pyn asks himself. He's come here with something in mind—Dirk sent him here for a reason—and now he's acting cagey. What's this about?

"How about this," says Minus. "I'm guessing, but there should be private agencies and individuals who can be employed by us." He pauses, watching Pyn and freshening his own smile. Then he says, "Maybe you can lead us to some."

"Agencies?"

"Or a talented individual."

"I guess I don't understand—"

Minus breathes and begins to explain. "Some months ago, my employer and I were walking in one of your parks. A wild place. A lot of jungle and sun," and he laughs without humor, gesturing at one pale hand. "We saw a little roodeer in the jungle. Some kind of wildcat was chasing it. I don't know the kind—"

"We have many species."

"—but it took a funny turn. I was watching. Professional interest, you might call it." He laughs again. "It took a funny turn and went down to a little river and the roodeer bounced slower when it knew the cat was gone. I don't know, maybe it forgot about the cat. But I remember hearing a yelp later, and a thrashing sound down near the water, and I knew what happened. The cat understood the roodeer's mind and the lay of the land, you see?" He pauses again, smiles again, and asks, "Is my point clear?"

"You want someone who knows Brulé."

"It would help. Yes."

"I guess that makes complete sense."

"Doesn't it?" He waits, then says, "In Quito, and I assume it's the same here, the very best people do not advertise in an open fashion. They rely on referrals from their other clients."

"You want a freelancer."

"Exactly."

"Of course I don't know just who we use. Or who is best." Pyn says, "I'll need some time arriving at names, and I don't know if I can promise the means to find them."

"I understand." He nods. "Very private people." He says, "Perhaps you can contact the proper authorities and get back to me," and the smile seems terribly wrong all at once. It makes Pyn nervous to see the bleached man's teeth, so he glances out the window and studies the city. This is what Dirk intends, his nervousness. "Would that be too much trouble?" asks Minus. This is why he sent his bodyguard, he thinks, and he tells Minus:

"No. It's no trouble."

"Good." Minus rises, saying, "You must be busy. I'll leave you now," only he goes nowhere.

Pyn has no choice but to look at him, the familiar hands around his poor colon, squeezing. He stands now too and offers his hand. They shake. His hand is drenched with sweat. He says, "I'll get a list."

"And maybe some background on each of them. Origins. Skills. That sort of thing," Minus adds. "Soon, if possible."

"Of course."

Then the Quito man is gone. The distant door opens for him and wishes him a pleasant evening, and Mayor Pyn walks to the window and sits on the narrow shelf, pressing his face to the glass. He thinks about a tangled mass of things, nothing clear or easy. He knows how small and scared he must seem to someone like Minus. He can guess what Minus and Dirk say about him in private. And what they say about Brulé too. Then he shifts gears, remembering that through most of human history Brulé City would have dominated this world with ease. It's a thought he uses to defend this place from creatures like Minus and Dirk. Brulé City would have been a magical place known to all Mankind. A legend. He imagines simple tribesmen herding their bison across empty plains, telling the dumb beasts about the great Brulé, wondrous Brulé, towers and bright lights and millions of people living under the care of their great wise noble ruler, the good Mayor Pyn.

It makes him laugh to himself, imagining the scene.

For an instant some small part of himself believes his silly dream. I need to act like a king, he tells himself. A great king would know what to do. The situation is that Minus wants to find a local wildcat, only he isn't interested in hiring the beast. No. He wants me to supply a list of potential burglars. He and Dirk must think they're one and the same.

"Huh," he mutters to himself.

His Chief of Police can learn the particulars of the break-in. He will contact her tomorrow, and maybe he can learn about the possible wildcats. Of course they won't give away any genuine names. Stall and stall and stall for now. Not until they know what's happening; then they'll help only for something substantial in return.

Pyn has lived his entire life inside Brulé.

He genuinely desires only the best for his city. All of his life he has served her and her people to the best of his ability. He's made mistakes, yes, and he has mistakenly forgotten too many of them through the course of time. Ego breeds that dishonesty. But there's one hard fact that he won't let out of his grasp—even if he were king of the world's greatest city, the grand Mayor Pyn, there would always be this nagging sense of helplessness, of inadequacy, that comes whenever you rule something less than infinite for any time shorter than forever.

◆ ◆ ◆

She sits alone, watching a strange bird circling, watching it hunt for something among the long living buildings. This isn't the first time she has noticed a nocturnal bird of prey in Brulé. But then its eyes aren't tracking like they should track—the hawk-shaped thing, gray-black and large, is too concerned with windows and balcony doors. It makes her wonder. Something from Dirk perhaps? She can't know for certain. So she keeps watching it, waiting and trying to will the thing away.

Steward left for his office a little while ago.

They had slept hard for a few hours after his raid on Dirk, him needing more sleep but insisting he'd had plenty. There were plans to be put into action. They had talked the plans through this time, at least so far as was possible. Chiffon thought of Dirk being killed, knowing not to mention such a thing. The simplest suggestion might spook Steward. And she watched him go and told herself to be very careful handling the man. Particularly now. Particularly with everything so fluid.

She sits in the dark and watches the circling bird.

It can't see me, she tells herself. Even if it wants me. The AI is feeding it an empty room, nothing more.

She has a book opened on her lap. The plastic pages are glowing with a soft white light, illuminating the cramped text and some simple drawings. Several hundred years ago, according to the text, there was a similar type of hawk tailored for surveillance work. She wishes she could access World-Net, checking it against a modern listing. But that might alert a watchful AI, wouldn't it? She can't risk that chance. Interest means she is spooked. Means she is vulnerable and momentarily visible. What's it doing out here? she asks herself. Have they traced Gabbro to the diversion? Maybe. But it won't find anything, and that's fine. That's what she wants. Let it look at every window, then grow bored and go.

If it doesn't, she thinks, she'll call Steward.

He gave her his safe number, and he drew a map showing her how to find his office in the country. Emergencies only. The map delineates the Farmstead's defenses and how she can circumvent them through a certain underground stream. In case of desperate emergencies. If they are on to her. If there's no other choice . . . Chiffon feeling like some panicky quail with that hawk still circling, still so deadly curious about everything below.

She blinks and looks outside. The neighborhood seems quiet, almost restful. She can see Gabbro in his front room, no April. The cyborg is dressed for the mines and sitting on the oversized couch, his plate as big as a platter and balanced on his lap. The size is for ease of handling. Each portion is quite small. He's like some enormous shellfish with a nugget of meat and guts inside the shell, requiring precious little in the way of sustenance. She is telling herself that one emergency option isn't enough. No, she needs some other safe avenues. Not involving Steward. New allies. Other places to hide. And of course her thoughts turn toward the big cyborgs, powerful and durable and rumored to be fully human in every meaningful sense. She allows herself a few minutes of wondering . . . how to make it work and not let Steward know, or even suspect . . . and then she quits thinking it. Just quits. It's too dangerous to even consider, she decides, and so she won't. She stops herself. Don't, she tells herself. Don't!

"So why do I feel guilty?" she mutters. "Damn it all. Why feel this?"

She shuts the book. She leans back in the chair. "What I'm going to do is," she informs herself with cold deliberation, "I'm going to get free, I am, and buy a little world, I am, and I'll build a paradise. That's what I'm going to do."

She does nothing for a long while, trying to think.

When she looks outside again, the hawk has vanished. Gabbro has vanished. She can see his food half eaten and his lights forgetfully left on, and the one-time woman, the one-time Ghost, shuts her eyes and drifts into sleep—as hard and dreamless as a little snatch of death itself.

◆ ◆ ◆

She loves him.

Olivia has loved him from the first time she saw him, Steward coming to her to ask for help with some odd forgotten problem. Given the choice of working for him for free and not seeing him at all, she would pick the former. Or maybe even pay him. But she knows that he's a good person, not perfect, and a Ghost's romantic advances would scare him away. Thus she keeps accepting his gracious payments. And thus she persists with her flagrant flirting, oversized and silly and impossible to take at all seriously.

"I got in," he says. "You made the difference, and thanks."

"I'm glad."

He is sitting in that tiny windowless room he maintains somewhere outside Brulé, his marvelous long legs crossed and the ruddy hair matted with sweat and a face that will never be confused for pretty nodding, saying, "The trouble's that I didn't get what I wanted done."

"No?"

"And now I need to do more."

"You want to visit the criminal again?"

"I doubt if he'd let me in the door this time." He isn't smiling. Steward would normally show a shy smile, confident and laughing, taking nothing lightly but wanting to keep things loose and easy. Lately he's been so different. For the umpteenth time she wonders who or what is this girl in his life. She has a cold feeling.

"Olivia?"

"What can I do?"

"Help me get this man out of town."

"Gladly." Olivia is inside her enormous front room. Like always, she wishes there were some way for him to come visit for a night. Wouldn't that be splendid? she thinks. A single blessed night where she could touch his long legs and the rugged face and ease her weight down on his hips . . . the image making her sigh and shift in her seat, trying to contain herself. "What tricks do you need from me?"

"I've got a plan. It's got two parts." She has never known him to be so self-possessed. Not in years and years. He says, "I need to make one more run at him. Like last night. I need him to believe that I've tried my best and he's held out and there's nowhere for me to turn. That's the first part."

"But he won't let you inside. You said—"

"Dirk has something. I've never seen it before." He describes a panel with tactile and scent functions. Very modern. Very sophisticated. Olivia has heard about them. They utilize certain Ghost technologies to produce the illusion of being there. And he nods, saying, "I guessed as much," and gives a little smile. "Tell me. I want to know if something is possible. It seems like it should be possible."

She listens to his idea. "I think maybe so. Yes." She knows half a dozen Ghosts with the proper training. She starts writing their names and access codes on a slip of paper—an archaic method suitable to dusty old Ghosts—and she presses the paper against the wall, showing him, asking, "What else? What's this second part?"

"Another illusion. More involved, I'm afraid." She doesn't like the sound of his voice or the way he sits or the lines on his face. He explains it in brief, and again she thinks of Ghosts with the knowledge and imagination. She admits:

"They'll cost you a small fortune. Any one of them. If they give you too much trouble, contact me. I'll put the old psychic bite on them," and she giggles.

He says, "Thank you." Then he remembers to smile and compliment her for her trouble. "I knew you'd have it all at your fingertips." He looks as if he is proving he can smile, the expression wrong for his tired face. He concludes by saying, "I'll call you later. Soon. And thank you—"

"Steward?"

He vanishes. Olivia Jade stares into the blank white wall, feeling ill and sad and a little lost. She stands. She walks around the big room and breathes hard to clear her head. When was the last time Steward was in love? She can't remember. Did it amount to anything? They never do, she reminds herself. For some reason they never do. She remembers one time, ages ago, when she thought she would lose him and so hired several AIs to do nothing but replicate him. The AIs managed to catch his looks and the spry walk, his voice and expressions and even some of his presence. For several weeks this artificial Steward lived here with Olivia, sharing her meals and bed and her insatiable need for talk. And then she had him erased. There was little choice in the matter, and no sadness. The entity was no more Steward than the rug under her hand now is a rug. All illusion. Crisp and clean, thoroughly professional and yet absolutely false. A pure first-class phony. And a little afterward, thankfully, the real Steward's woman left him for reasons still unclear. Again Olivia Jade was free to flirt with the man, dream the impossible, and pretty well muddle through her days.

She sits on the floor and looks out her window, up at the sky. Like all Ghosts, Olivia cares about her home more than does any flesh-on-blood person. It's because of the way AIs work. It's the way they build the images and smells and so on—like someone might build a brick wall, layer upon layer. Home is where you focus your greatest energies. Home is where you want rugs to be the ruggiest and the sky to be the truest and the stinks of last night's fish should linger an honest long time. Home is the center, the modest essential hub, where you can sometimes forget that you have died and possibly lost your soul.

She touches herself.

With a practiced efficiency, she starts to manipulate her illusionary glands, working hard, hunting that instant when pleasure will radiate out of her loins and momentarily sweep away all the ordinary crap, and the sadness, and so on.

And on.

". . . Steward."

─·· 15 ··─

When you're poor and alive you tend to suffer. When you're poor
and a Ghost you envy those who can suffer. The poorest Ghosts I
know live in a state called Gray-time. Very sad. Very, very sad.
They spend most of their time watching World-Net. It's colorful
and loud and all. The next best thing to do is sleep. They don't have
the money to build a complete home around them. So they cheat.
They get a single AI to serve them. When they look up, the AI
builds them a ceiling. Down and it manufactures a floor. Move and
they get a seat below them, kind of mushy feeling but reasonable.
Of course they can't do too much too fast. A single AI hasn't got
the capacity for that luxury. Whirl around and they see nothing.
And I mean *nothing*. Eat too fast and the mushy-tasting gruel seems
to dissolve. Or so they say. The very poorest of them are forever on
the brink of true sensory deprivation. Think of waking up from a
deep sleep and finding your hands numbed and your vision blurred
and every sound too flat and simple. You know? Think of trying to
live like that day after day. A Ghost at that level has two choices.
He can go into a voluntary coma, everything shut down until some
future benefactor might bring him out of it. Or insanity and death.
The permanent shutdown. My choice if I were choosing, I don't
mind confessing to you . . .
   Sure, I know people in Gray-time. And comas.
   A girl named Wisp? Formerly Zebulina? Yeah, I know her. A real
sad case. I used to give her some money now and again, out of pity,
just so she could build a boring little room for a day. I gave it up,
though. I couldn't stand her suffering when she had to go back to
Gray-time. It tore both of us up, so I quit . . .

> —*excerpt from an interview*
> *with a Ghost, the Magician's*
> *private file*

I T'S after they make love in the early morning hours that Steward
hears himself starting to tell the story, his body too tired to move
and his brain too much awake to think of sleeping yet. Some urge born
out of sheer runaway love makes him want to explain the whole story

to Chiffon. "This is why I can't take you to Yellowknife, darling." She has never asked about Chaz, of course. She's never inquired about the reasons that pushed him out of the Freestates, and he appreciates her good sense or the lack of curiosity. It means that what he gives out now is given on his own terms, and only when he is ready. He guesses that she's startled to hear it, but she clings to him and listens without interjecting, letting him set the pace and the tone and never making him feel guilty or beyond blame.

Several sad times in the past he has tried explaining himself to others. To lovers and to friends. What was the worst was having to endure their defenses of his actions. That's what really hurt. Nothing damns quite so much as someone telling you that you're not to blame, how could you have known, and so on. And you know better. After all, he thinks, they didn't live through it twenty-five years ago. They aren't the ones who saw it to the end and who have halfway forgotten it today. Which is true. Steward goes days without thinking about it. If anything, he feels a nagging guilt for having mended over time. He does. But can they understand? No. No, they have to warn him to quit suffering for the imagined crime. They don't even understand the basic terms of his telling the story. He doesn't want or need their comfort. He simply wants to reveal the linchpin of his life. Nothing more.

He almost enjoys telling it to Chiffon. At least the early going. Flowers don't know about the Freestates, and that's fine. He can explain Shadows for the first time. She has no preconceived notions, no nonsense, and so all she will know is the truth.

"Shadows are made when you're young. Five years old, usually." He uses both hands to cup her firm bare bottom, squeezing once and relishing the spring. "Chaz became my Shadow because we were blood relatives. Cousins. Relatives make good Shadows, you see, because there are a billion years of natural selection telling them to look out for each other's shared genes."

She says nothing, eyes wide and no judgments behind them.

"That's what makes a good Shadow. Looking out for the other. The willingness to help and to sacrifice for him or for her." He wonders if a Flower has anything like a family. Either all Flowers are part of the same extended family, or they have none. He sees no middle ground. "Chaz looked like me, I suppose. He had my build and people told us we could be brothers." He pauses, then says, "I was half a year older."

She purrs into his curly reddish chest hair.

"We trained together, going to school together and sitting side by side, and when we went home it was to the same lodge and the same room and a bed with room enough for four full-grown men, and every morning we'd wake up nestled beside one another like twin spoons." He pauses. He warns Chiffon, "We weren't perfect friends. I don't want you thinking we never fought over toys. We were children, after all. And little warriors. And there's a saying in Yellowknife, 'You get your first scars from your Shadow.' " He tells her, "That's the way it was with us."

Lifting a hand, he opens it to the moonlight and sees the faint regular marks made in the meat between the thumb and forefinger—tooth marks left by a young boy's jaw, the scar itself enlarged by the growing hand.

"School is the same everywhere," he claims. "Anywhere in the System, you go to school to learn how to quit being a child. Whether it's Yellowknife or Brulé or Quito. At least with people that's true. You know? For Chaz and me it meant learning how to lay out an ambush and spy on a watchful foe, and how to suffer and survive and hopefully win out in the end." He brings down his hand and explains, "A Shadow makes you tough. A Shadow shares your circumstances and cries with you in the night, and he is there in the morning when the Elders, knowing what the world will require of us, choose hands to wire up and torture before breakfast. You aren't just suffering for yourself, you see. You're suffering for him. For Chaz. You do it so you can someday help defend him from pain, or worse. And he does the same for you." Steward breathes and asks, "How do I sound?"

"Sound?"

"Bitter? Angry? What?"

She kisses one of his broad nipples, the tip of her tongue leaving a cool patch of saliva.

"People think I should be furious. They think of their own childhoods, adding misery to everything, and they think a sane person should hate the Elders for what happened to them." He says, "It's got to sound pretty incredible to you. A Flower. There's nothing like it in your world. I mean, Dirk didn't expect you to tolerate what he did to you. Did he? Of course not. And out of the trillions of people on every world, only a few hundred thousand are born on this path. Plus the immigrants." He pauses. He says, "Immigrants." He says, "A dozen or two go to the Freestates every year. No more. And maybe one of them persists through everything. It's that hard to do."

"But you're not bitter," she says.

"How could I be? By the time I was ten I was immune to pain. You know? In the classes, among all my peers and Chaz too, I was the very best at the heart of what everyone wanted to become. It was nothing conscious on my part. Believe me. Maybe it was something fundamental in my wiring. I can't say what it was. But when I was twelve or thirteen my teachers took to drawing lots among themselves to see who was going to fight me in class on a given day. The loser had to do it. You see?" He sighs and says, "I can tell you something. It does no teacher any good to be beaten by a boy a tenth his age."

There is no pride in his voice.

Steward gazes up at the ceiling, squinting now. "Poor Chaz. We used to draw the hardest assignments in school because of me. We patrolled the roughest terrain. We fought two and three teams at a time. And sometimes we went against boys who were nearly full-grown." He explains, "Chaz had trouble keeping up with me. We had the same build, like I said. The same bones and muscles. But there was something different inside it all. You know? And it meant that he didn't do as well when we fought. I had to protect him at times. I had to suffer in order to save him. Of course the Elders said it was good. I learned to help those in need, and Chaz got to learn from my example. And poor Chaz, to his credit, never blamed me for being too good at these things." He says, "My cousin had character. In a lot of ways, he had volumes more character than me."

She blinks and offers a shy smile.

"We got to be twenty. I was older and I was stronger, so I went through the adulthood rites first. And the Elders made certain that I worked for the honor. Day after day they milked me of my will and my strength and my sense of right. They tested me under every condition. They made me face hard decisions under impossible circumstances. Which way to move? Which direction to attack, and when? And whom do I help and how much do I help them? If so many Yellowknives are scattered across a battlefield, for instance, all of them ready to break under the pain . . . what? Which of them do I save first? And how? And which come last? And why? And can I do the entire process without hesitations or doubts?"

"You're such a hero." She gives a girlish laugh. "I bet you made it look easy."

He says, "Heroism I don't know. Believe me."

She almost speaks, almost says, "I don't," and then has the precious good sense to offer nothing.

Again he scoops up her firm upturned rump, squeezing, with the tips of his fingers sliding into the gap—into the close humid place always perfumed on Flowers—and she gives an easy slow roll with her hips, his groin responding with a faint tingling sensation. She is watching him. She says nothing. But in her face he can see the question being poised:

"Where is Chaz now?"

The tingling subsides.

He won't answer. This is his pace, his tone, and so he goes on with his story without having missed a beat. He describes some of his rites. He compares his experiences with the lesser ones Chaz faced. The Elders were easier on his Shadow. He has no doubts. They couldn't have treated him the same and hoped for Chaz to retain his spirit. No way. "And the Elders are pragmatic at their core. They have to be. If Chaz had been some immigrant from the south they would have pushed him past his limits. That's one reason that so few immigrants come to the Freestates and thrive. But Chaz was family. One of us. And he wasn't even a bad warrior, you see. He only suffered by contrast."

He paints a vivid living picture of the mock battles, laying emphasis on the craziness of war. The coincidences. The accidents. The inspired moments. The terror scarcely concealed. "We were warriors together then. Chaz and me. And I'll tell you something else about what that means." He says, "If you understand Shadows and go to a village of strangers, and if they have Shadows, too, you can tell at a glance who is a Shadow to whom. By the time you're a marginal adult, odd as it sounds, your Shadow moves like you move and is aware of you at all times. It's second nature. You don't even have to glance his way or her way to know your Shadow's feelings. Hungry? Sleepy? What? He is that much a part of you. And of course he has the same vantage point relative to you. Sometimes he knows what you're thinking before you do. Believe me."

She chimes, "I do."

He says, "War." He says, "Those old tribes that roamed this country before there was any Brulé, before industry or agriculture . . . those old aboriginal tribes honored the warriors who had merely touched the living enemy. They became the models for the Freestates. As much as possible, they formalized the rules of war to where it was a free-flowing ritual. A kind of unbridled pageant. Do you see?" He pauses, then confesses, "I never would have talked this way when I was twenty and twenty-five. I was standing too close to everything. You know? More than two decades removed from something can sure make a person clinical. Rituals. A pageant. When I was in Yellowknife nothing seemed like a game. I was at the center of Creation, and the stakes were the loftiest possible. Yes, it was a war."

She blinks and waits.

"We fought the usual battles. Chaz and I would be on patrol on the boundaries of Yellowknife, keeping watch on our various enemies, and sometimes—war being war—we spied on our allies too. Most of the battles were him and me running into a pair on a similar patrol. Rude little things, they were. Pain guns and a lot of hand-to-hand stuff. In the dark. During rainstorms. Not much pageantry in the final tally."

He says, "I don't know when it started. I should have known, like I said . . . Shadows being Shadows . . . but I don't." He waits, saying nothing with the greatest care.

She looks at him, then asks, "What started?"

He blinks and eases himself down into the sheets, the big hands tracing curves and curls on her bare back. "Sweet Chaz," he says.

"What?"

"One day he just ran away."

"Did he?"

"Scared to tears and finally couldn't take it." He tastes his own dry mouth and thinks water would taste good, cool and letting it spill down his face and chest. That's the way to drink water, he thinks. Let the entire body feel a share of the wealth.

"Did something happen? Did something go wrong?"

He shrugs. "Not particularly. We were waiting in ambush. A patrol of four was coming down a cut in the forest. We would have taken them—*I* could have taken them myself—but then he broke and vanished. He was frightened, simple and plain."

"And you were surprised?"

He says, "I don't know when it started. At least I can't remember knowing. But by then? No. No, I wasn't all that surprised. He was my Shadow. From the time we were five years old, cowering in that bed in the night, I pretty well understood that there was trouble coming."

He shifts his shoulders and wraps both long legs around her legs, running his hands through her buttery hair. He says, "I retreated too. Duty is clear in that situation. My Shadow needed my encouragement. My enemies could wait until tomorrow."

Chiffon takes a little breath. Then she presses on him, rising up out of his grasp. It isn't that she seems uneasy, he thinks, but he has to wonder what is happening inside her head. She looks as if she is paying close attention, yet something about her is saying, "Flee! Flee!"

"Another day, another circumstance, and Chaz ran again," Steward tells her. "It happened more and more, and then it happened always. Every day and night. Every instance where we might end up in a fight." He can only remember parts of it. Twenty years ago, almost without thinking, he could have recalled every incident and described every tear, his poor sad Shadow begging him not to make this attack and not to tell anyone else what was happening. Never. Chaz couldn't stand the idea of being labeled a coward. In the Freestate hierarchy nothing else is so low. Steward explains this fact to Chiffon. He confesses a certain sense of guilt. "I was the one who led our attacks, after all. I was the one who pushed him too far." Something in his voice is changing now. He notices a difficulty with some of the words and with keeping his breath. And look at him sweat! Chiffon is kneeling on the bed between his legs, her hands running up and down his thighs, and now she uses the corner of a sheet to wipe her hands dry, looking at his face and wondering:

"What did you do?"

"The worst thing possible." His ears are ringing. His mouth is full of sand. "I did what Chaz wanted me to do. Exactly. I told no one and kept his secret, and he promised that he was getting better. He was going to conquer his fears. And I fought our battles for us. Alone. A somewhat heroic act until you see why I did it."

"Why?"

He smiles grimly. "Ego. Pride. Vanity."

"I don't see—"

"I was my generation's best warrior. I was full of a crazy pride because I knew it," and he halfway wishes that she would strike him for his sins. "My Shadow was useless. Fine. The people who could have helped him—or better, forgiven him—were kept in the dark. All right. But in spite of all my good intentions, my heroic aspirations, the brunt of it all is that I got to face and defeat our enemies by myself.

And that was an enormous satisfaction. Enormous! I was young, you see, and utterly proud, and the rest of it happened because I was having too much fun and success to think clearly." He pauses, then says, "It had to happen eventually. Can you guess what?"

She can't.

He says, "We went into an enormous battle. There were several hundred warriors on two sides of a field, and the winners received an important prize. Money. Equipment. I can't recall just what, but it was ample." He halfway laughs, shaking his head. He says, "I do remember thinking that Chaz would survive if he kept with the main body of warriors, buttressed by their flesh and their example. Who knows? Maybe he would even come out stronger for the experience. At least I hoped so. But because I had done so well fighting at close range, and because the Elders believed it was both of us who did the fighting, they decided to send Chaz and me into a nearby redwood grove. We led a little party. We were supposed to flank the enemy or take a beating for trying. And there was an ambush, of course, and we were trapped and taking heavy fire. Very heavy fire. And I can remember the exact instant when everyone on both sides, friends and enemies too, saw my Shadow Chaz stand and run away at full speed and drop into a ditch out of reach."

Now his voice seems strange to his own ears. Steward sounds nervous. His heart is racing, thud-thudding against his ribs, and the sweat is soaking his chest hair and the sheets below him. She says nothing. She hangs over him, watching him, and he says, "So it wasn't a secret anymore. No one could have missed the wail of him crying. Terrified! There's no other word to describe him. And when a warrior is caught at that stage, that far broken, he is useless. There's no way to repair the will. There is no elixir or training technique to bring it back. Never."

She makes a small sound and looks out the window.

"And the way I responded was to fight. I did the job of my Shadow. I know for a fact that I've never fought so well in my life. Before or since. And we turned back the ambush and turned the enemy's line and we won the largest victory in the last half century, I suppose. It took a little more than an hour. Then I worked my way back to the ditch where Chaz was hiding." He pauses. He says, "I expected to hear him sobbing. You know? I even *did* hear him sobbing, some part of my brain expecting it that much. But he wasn't making any noise. None. He had used a knife and slashed his wrists and bled to death in a ditch full of old rainwater. Maybe you wondered what happened to my Shadow. That's it."

◆ ◆ ◆

She was listening from the first, taking in his words with the casual ease of someone designed and trained to listen without effort to whatever is said through the course of a sleepless evening. She is a Flower, after all. This is the task that suits her best, serving as an audience while the lover rests up for the next round. She remembers how Dirk would talk about the women and Flowers he had bedded in the past, and she would look at him and flash a big smile, cooing something and sometimes pretending to be aroused by his simple, oftentimes cruel stories, saying to him:

Am I ever lucky to have you. My man! My loving man!

Steward is so very different from Dirk. They are not the same kind of animal. Not nearly. When he is telling about Chaz and the suicide, she starts to do more than listen like a Flower would listen. She looks out the window, trying to concentrate on all the cool dark night air, and she wonders what she should say to Steward. What does he want to hear? That she's sorry? That she wishes there were some healing trick she knew? She feels as though she is on some strange emotional surface, hands and toes hunting traction, a good deep gash in a vulnerable spot needed so she can stop this sliding motion. But it's not there. Steward affords no easy handholds.

"Everything came to an end," he declares. "I was in dishonor. All Yellowknife knew the story, and most of them expected me to do one last honorable thing and die with my Shadow. It's something of a tradition. They went so far as to build two coffins. But then most Shadows die when they are very, very old. I was young. I was no dusty Elder with two-plus centuries of wear on me, and so I decided on banishment and came here to Brulé for no particular reason. I've lived half my life inside these walls, surviving, even thriving, and sometimes I find myself thinking that this half and my first half add up to nothing. Zero. It's as if I've been alive for fifty years—can you imagine such a stretch of time, Chiffon?—and after all that time the ledger reads empty. Zilch."

She listens, saying nothing but now knowing what she could say. It comes to her suddenly, by surprise, and she has to blink and give a little shiver, opening her mouth as if about to speak. Only her tongue won't move. She has no voice. She knows the perfect thing to tell this battered sad warrior—*"Let me be your Shadow! Please please please let me be your new Chaz!*—only she can't say the words, can't even clear her throat now, hovering over him and scared to look down at his face. He might read her mind. What if he knew what she was thinking?

Steward would be touched.

He probably doesn't even know how much it would mean to him. Of course he would refuse. Politely. And he might smile a little bit, too. And in the end she would have him completely and forever. She knows it! Every sign points to it! She could win him now and all it would take is saying a handful of words with feeling.

Yet she is a mute.

Utterly helpless.

A simple lie, she thinks. I can't even tell a simple lie! How in all hell can I win him if I can't even control my own self? What's he doing to me? What has he done?!

— 16 —

People ask me how they can get into my job. What kind of skills do they need. I tell them they have to be an artist. First and foremost, a true artist. In what way? they ask. How do you mean? So I tell them that in my business revenge is the key. It must be done perfectly. There is an art to extracting justice from someone who has done you wrong. Only a great artist is capable of accomplishing that end with perfection. And all of my peers, I assure listeners, are stars of the highest magnitude. Including me . . .

—excerpt from a crime lord's diary, available through World-Net

Now Toby wakes without having dreamed, without having really slept, lying in the waiting room of the same hospital with light streaming through a series of broad windows and the plush carpeting busily making bright gold and blue blossoms designed to cheer sad spirits and renew tired old faiths. He sits up and wipes his face. He isn't cheered or renewed. He spent half the night talking with April, trading stories and bile, and he might have slept in her room if the autodoc hadn't come in with her sedative and chased him away.

He has a calculated fondness for the girl.

He adores her circumstances. Sometimes he thinks that the hard parts of her life could have been his own, and he finds himself believing that everything he has endured during these last couple years will be made right soon enough. April is the key. She makes so very much possible, he tells himself. The Prophet Himself must have sent her.

Toby scans the waiting room. There is no one else, excepting a lone whore sitting on a nearby sofa. She is watching him. He hates the way she stares. A long hallway runs past the waiting room, and he starts to watch people busily walking along. The level sunlight splashes into the hallway in distinct window-shaped blocks. Light and shadow and light again and shadow and light. Toby notices how the people seem more real, more substantial, when they cross into the brightness. He thinks how the air must be relatively clean, this being a hospital, but there are faint white bits of something drifting in the ventilating breeze. The whore continues to watch him, no expression on her face. He ignores her. He concentrates on the coolness of the dirty air. Maybe I should live here, he thinks. I'm halfway comfortable. Imagine!

Out in the hallway is noise, sudden and yet subdued. A team of shiny autodocs and human doctors come into view. They surround a long floating table ridden by an injured man. At least one long knife did the damage, lengths of flesh lifted off the bones with careful deliberation. The whore says, "Too much fun under the moonlight, I think." She has a dusky little laugh. Her eyes are dark and cool and absolutely amoral. "I've seen worse and they live. So he's lucky." She laughs again and shifts her slight weight, something about her face tough and wise.

Toby envies those looks.

He watches the patient and attendants vanish, and then he straightens his back until something pops and loosens. Maybe he should sleep some more. Maybe he should check on April first. The whore is looking at him again, making him nervous. Halfway smiling, she asks where he is from. Garden? He says, "Sure. Garden."

"Shit no," she says, her voice friendly and yet abrasive too. "So what are you doing down here? Get lost?"

"A neighbor of mine . . . was injured . . ."

"You do it?"

"No." He looks at her face, at the telltale skullcap bright in the sunlight, and he says, "Why do you ask?"

"I don't know." She gives a disinterested shrug. "Maybe you look like someone who might . . . I don't know . . . *injure* someone? I don't know." And she smiles, the expression oddly girlish. "You want something to eat? We can go get some breakfast maybe."

"I don't think so."

"So where's the neighbor?" she wonders.

"A friend, actually." He doesn't know why he is answering. He wants to stop. "Both a friend and a neighbor."

"So maybe you should look in on her. On him." She pauses, then she tells him, "I've never met a real Gardener before."

He *should* go check on April. They still have plans to make.

"Does anyone ever get sick on Garden?" She wants to know. "I've seen shows on World-Net. There's no crime, is there? No cancers when you get old? You're all healthy and kicking until the day you die. Right? That sounds marvelous to me. It does."

He is thinking about April, talking to her in his head.

"So anyway, let's go. Get up and go see her. Him. Whatever." She stands like a little girl, her legs full of a springy tension. "Or if you want," she offers, "we can sneak into the viewing room. You ever seen a knife wound sewn up?"

He has to say, "Never."

"So come on." She waves and prods until he stands, then she urges him into motion. "Come on. I know this place like no one. You'll see. Just keep on my tail now. Let's go!"

They walk down the hallway. April's room is coming, and the whore is skipping along and giggling. Toby stops at April's door, wishing his guide would leave him. But she won't. She joins him and looks inside, Toby making sure that nothing has changed. The door recognizes him and tells him with a cool professional voice that her condition is improving and she will be awake and happy in a good hour. Please stop back then.

He is left with no destination. "She's healing, huh?"

He says, "Yes."

"Who fucked up her face?"

"Her boyfriend."

"That you?"

"No."

"Just asking," she says.

He says, "They live downstairs from me." He pauses, then adds, "I'm just a friend. I'm helping." They are walking together. He's a little lost and afraid to admit it, following the curling hallway and coming to an elevator. The doors part. They enter. When the whore demands the surgical ward a cool AI voice asks by what right should they be given access.

"It's that knifing. I know the guy. We both know him." She motions towards Toby, incapable of being flustered.

"You're his friends?" asks the AI.

"His clients. He owes us for a little double time." She smiles and squeezes Toby's nearest arm. "You ever see a Gardener fuck?" she asks the AI. "You should sometime. It'll give you horizons."

The elevator shuts its doors and takes them upstairs.

"They'll save him. You wait, lover boy." She is talking to Toby, winking and halfway laughing. "Don't even worry. We're going to get paid one way or another."

He says nothing, not sure why he has come here and intrigued by the vagueness of everything. He gives the whore a quick hard look, wondering her age and history and deciding it would be too much to ask questions. She might think he meant something with them.

"Here we be!" she announces.

They enter another hallway, walk and turn and walk on. Then they are inside a little room and looking down through a clear glass floor. Below them is a long table and autodocs and one lone doctor overseeing the operation. Toby is startled by all the meat and blood and detached skin. It takes him a long moment to see the police officer sitting a couple meters away. The whore pokes him and says, "Would you look at that mess?" Then she turns away. "Do I know you?" she asks the officer, already bored with the show. "What's your name, sir? Krispin? Officer Krispin?" And she is off and talking, making another quick friend.

Toby listens to them while he stares downward. His heart is racing. His breath stinks.

"You know what I just found out, Officer Krispin? When whores fight? You know what's the last thing they'll cut or crush?"

"You don't know?"

"Hey, I'm new. Young and foolish." She laughs as if she is ten years old.

Krispin laughs too. "Whores never, never go for the goods," he says. "The product line. And you know why?"

"Tell me."

"Because she might get stuck paying for the healing. Rehabilitation and prosthetics and natural grafts." He tells her, "If I catch you with the guilty knife, young lady, then you'll be using your wages to make repairs. And you don't want to paying your competition to build bigger dongs, say. Or a sweeter box." Krispin is an ageless older man. He has seen everything and nothing will ever be new again. Not for him. "You didn't know?"

"Like I said, I'm young."

He has a smiling voice. "I'm going to have to watch you."

"Do."

"I will."

"Great!"

Toby studies the ways the autodoc arms cut at the dead tissues, the other arms sprouting laser light to mend the tears. Degradable glue is used for the largest wounds. The patient lies on his back, his face composed and his eyes mostly closed and his breathing slow and regular. Toby can't say why he's so fascinated by the sight of an operation. He could access the same scenes through World-Net. Maybe it's the surprise of it all. Maybe it's because he didn't expect to come here, and that's why it's so damned interesting.

"Seen many fights, little girl?" Krispin asks.

"I don't know. I saw one a few nights back."

"Yeah?"

"Saw a bunch of whores get their snot knocked loose." She laughs and tells him how it happened, and Krispin says:

"I know. I got called in afterward. Did some interviews. Filed my report and forgot it."

"Did we meet? We didn't, did we?"

"No," he says with confidence. "I don't remember you. And I would."

She asks, "So. Was that a real Flower? Or not?"

"I doubt it. I don't see how."

"That guy sure saved her ass, Flower or not."

"I guessed as much. Most people weren't too eager to talk about it."

"I would have talked to you," she says. "You know, I ended up alone that damned night. Me!"

"Poor little girl," says Krispin.

She pokes Toby in the side. "Where are you going?" she asks him.

He doesn't know. He was watching the operation and something suddenly occurred to him. An idea. He doesn't want to hear this dribble about whores in some Old Quarter bar. He doesn't care. What he needs is to go somewhere and think it through and decide if it is possible. He hopes so. It seems so damned perfect in his head.

"I've got to go look in on my friend," he lies. "I'm sorry."

"For what?" She shrugs and turns away. Krispin gives Toby a quick cutting look, professional and thorough, and when Toby is out the door and walking down the hallway, happy enough to sing, Krispin asks:

"So that's a Gardener, huh?"

"Yeah."

"Someone you know?"

"Just met him. I don't know him."

"What's his story?"

She says, "He smacked his girlfriend pretty good. With a club or something."

"He tell you?"

"No."

"How do you know?"

"He seems like the type, I guess." She says, "He's hanging around the girl for some reason. It's either guilt or he's not quite done doing damage."

And Krispin says, "If he's a Gardener, he's innocent."

"Yeah?"

"Absolutely." He assures her, "No one is as peaceful as a Gardener. They're the sweetest people in the System."

"Yeah?"

"You didn't know that yet?"

"I guess not."

"It's true," he says. "I admire those people. I do."

And she tells him, "I don't know. I don't think you got a good look at those eyes."

◆ ◆ ◆

So this is how he's going to play it, thinks Minus. Pyn's going to keep us at a distance now. I ask a favor for Dirk. I ask for some names. But the little shit wants to act like he's found courage, dicking us around. Having his police chief call to tell me that the names are classified and sorry. Sorry. What's the little shit done? Figured us out on his own? He can't have done it. Every uniform in Brulé would be hunting the Flower if he knew everything. Good God in Heaven, he thinks, do I ever need to relax. He feels like a crazy man this morning. He's letting too much get under his skin, all right.

Minus is sitting in his bedroom, a bowl of spiked ice on the living table beside him. The table and all the furnishings were stained by the cushioning foam. The carpeting itself was killed, turning colorless and crumbling away now. Minus smells must in the air. He uses his hands to pick up the spiked cubes one at a time, sucking them to nothing and thinking hard about everything. They're not finding Chiffon. The AIs have produced plenty of leads—a face seen in a crowd, a curious question asked World-Net and so on—but Minus and the Quito men have run themselves in circles trying to find anything worthwhile.

There's nothing. This is some crazy situation, he thinks. A tiny town like Brulé swallows up the damned Flower. It's almost as if she's died and been buried or sunk and forgotten. Possible? He hopes not. He wants to think of the Freestater and the Flower/Ghost hiding together in some little room, plotting and wishing and filling in the empty time with the oldest kind of fun.

That Freestater, he thinks, I'm not done with you. One way or another.

The sun is halfway toward noon. Minus has been up all night. He blinks and looks outside, watching the scattered towers and the eastern reaches of the city. Sometimes a bird or two, or ten, soar past the long window. He thinks about the tailored hawks he has chasing Chiffon. They haven't seen anything, and he's halfway thankful. He doesn't need more false leads. Last night was a crush of false leads. He needs to sleep and be done with things for a couple of hours. He sighs and turns away from the window. Dirk is out in the front room. He can hear the old man pacing, muttering to himself, and he can see Dirk without having to use his eyes—the willowy figure wearing an old robe, his hair unkempt and his long hands moving nervously in and out of the robe's stretched pockets.

At least the old man is better than a few days ago, he tells himself. No nonsense about Ghosts in his room and pain in his joints. That Quito doctor was right. Maybe there's something she can do for him now. Minus wonders. Maybe he should give her a call.

Then something occurs to him. It's a bit of speculation that comes to him unannounced and not entirely invited, yet he has to pause and consider it for a long minute. What if he went to Pyn again, but not for Dirk? What if he went and explained to that little shit of a man the bones of the story? There's a Flower walking around Brulé with a fortune. There's enough money to keep the mantle mines operating for years. And you've got resources, he would say. The police. Political friends and allies. And maybe the Farmsteads around Brulé, too. They don't want trouble, do they? So maybe you can find the girl . . . I mean the Flower. Find her and keep half the money for yourself and give the rest to me. All right? Me! Not Dirk. He doesn't know I came. I don't think it'd do his health any good to know. You see? It's between us, shit to shit, and I know you're an honorable man and you can see I'm not . . . so say yes and don't even think you can cheat me, not and live a day . . . you little shit . . .

He laughs quietly, shaking his head.

Picking up another cube, he licks it and tastes the salt from his upper lip and pushes the delicious thing into his mouth, banging it against his teeth. I could cheat Dirk, he realizes. I've got the power and the position and could leave him to starve in Brulé. If it mattered enough. If I cared for the money enough, he tells himself.

But he doesn't.

He can't.

All these years Minus has watched over Dirk. He hasn't done it for the honor or the sense of duty. He's carried out his job because it pays and it's interesting and he knows the rules better than most people could. Yet there's no way to change now. Maybe when people lived fifty or sixty years, he thinks, it was possible for someone to do a turnaround. Guard a man most of your life and then steal from him. But when it's a matter of centuries, doing the same things day after day, habits become more than habits and your brain has deep grooves that can't be ignored. Minus has been one thing too long to be anything else. Not ever again. If things had been different and he was trained as a saint in his early life, he supposes he would have been equally good at it. Not to mention thoroughly poor. People would have stopped when they saw him and pointed, envying the pearly glow around him. He feels certain.

The ice in his mouth has melted.

His bowl holds a swallow's worth of residue, all the ice gone, and he tips it and runs his tongue after a few wayward drops. Then he stands and goes to his bed and sits on the edge, wanting sleep, wanting to lie flat on his back and feel himself borne away by the darkness. He's getting old, he admits. It's time to retire. He breathes and looks around the big bedroom—the bed and table and a couple of simple chairs, all foam-stained, nothing on the walls, and the carpeting turning to dust. It occurs to him that he's lived here for months and yet nothing marks his presence. Not in any way. His home is as bland as his hairy bright body is gaudy, and he wonders why that is and breathes again and then falls asleep.

◆　◆　◆

The second lure is a necklace of Garden pearls. The first lure—a quick giggle—is too soft to gain Dirk's attention. But the pearls have a familiar look about them. Dirk catches sight of them out of the corner of his eye. Of course he doesn't think in terms of lures. He thinks to himself, That's odd! Pearls on Tau Ceti? So he walks to the panel and kneels and takes a closer look. The giggle returns. It's light and soft and enticing, and he looks up through the alien vegetation and spies something or someone hiding on the other side of an odd alien bush. What's this? Oh, it isn't! It couldn't be! He's having some wicked hallucination, he decides. That's the only explanation. But just to make certain he tries to grab the pearls, thinking they will melt away as will the Flower too.

Pain takes hold of his wrists.

Dirk is wheeled, jerked and brought down on his back somehow, the air kicked out of him and him gasping and trying to fight the pain. He can't scream. He's been pulled into the panel as far as possible, Tau Ceti gone and a pasty whiteness surrounding him. There's a terrible harsh stink in the air. Someone has him by the neck, twisting hard enough to roll him over on his belly. Dirk tries swinging at his attacker. Nothing. He manages to breathe, choking on the stench. "Minus!" he moans. Heat builds around his head and arms. His skin is starting to burn. A shiny set of blades come out of the nothingness, hilts of black ivory and a big dark hand on each hilt. The blades cut at him. They go to the bone. The worst pain is in his thigh, below his groin, and he cries out and tries to elude the blades. He turns on his back and kicks, kicks and kicks. More hands grab at his feet. He won't let them take hold. He screams at them, "Get away! Get off me!" and then Minus finally gets a grip and pulls him out of the panel, out onto the floor and the bright open air.

Dirk lies motionless for a moment, gasping and gingerly touching his injured thigh. Only there is nothing. Not even a redness. He wonders how the Freestater managed that magic, and he breathes and looks back and sees Tau Ceti reemerging inside the long panel.

Coughing into his hands, he tells Minus the details.

Minus nods and rubs his sleepy face and says, "Our boy is paying you back for the pain you caused his lady friend. I bet that's what he was doing."

"You think so?"

"I guess he wanted you to know how it feels."

"I wish she knew how it feels." Dirk says, "I wish I had done some of this to her early on. You know?" He sits up, then stands, and says, "That asshole is getting me crazy. You know?"

Minus says nothing.

"Have you ever seen me this mad?" he asks.

Minus asks, "What do you think he'll do next?"

"I don't know. I don't know. Either he'll make another attack on me or he'll run with her." He thinks about Chiffon. What will she want him to do? "We've got to be ready. Either way."

Minus removes a pistol from inside his shirt, turns and levels it at the breathing sweet scene of Tau Ceti. He fires once. The panel is burnt and dead. He puts the pistol away again, turns and says, "I'm going back to bed."

"We've got to get ready."

And Minus says, "You're right. I've never seen you this mad." He says, "Rest. Relax. You want to beat this guy? You've got to get your head fresh. That's the first thing."

17

Let me understand. You're going to give me a body? A Flower's
body? And then I go to where this crime lord is living, cuddle
him and watch everything and steal from him when I get the
chance . . . right? And then afterward you promise to save me
somehow. You've got magic, right? I won't have to go back to
being any kind of Ghost, will I? Because I won't. Tell me Ghosting is possible and I'll tell you I want out. Believe me! Gray-time
forever is better than a few months of life, then being Ghosted
again. You understand? You're sure? Good. Good . . . because
I've made up my mind . . .

—excerpt from an interview
with Wisp, the Magician's
private file

"WELL," he says, "I got his attention."
"And?"
"Now we'll try leading him away." Steward is calling from a booth
in the Old Quarter. He's using the secure line, his image displayed on
the bedroom wall and Chiffon sitting with her legs crossed, on his bed,
asking:
"You think we'll fool him?"
"He'll have to fool himself. That's the key." A floater will be hired.
Two passengers and an obscure flight plan will constitute the lures.
She looks at him sitting in that tiny booth, the wall behind him painted
by someone with time and imagination. The colors are lurid. The
patterns are complex. Chiffon thinks of smoke in a tangled forest. He
says, "They'll spot the floater soon enough. Everything's arranged.
They'll see it vanish toward the west, and if they look hard enough
they'll find a place on the Pacific coast where it touched down for
repairs. Two passengers. Male and female. No registration. No clear
destination."

"Will they follow?"

He says, "Probably not. I hope not." He tells Chiffon, "We've got to tease them into believing we've run. I'm going to be laying down clues for a few days. Then we'll play quiet for a few days. I'm sorry it can't happen faster, love."

"It doesn't matter," she claims, toying with the bindings of one heavy book. Now the smoke on the wall resembles insects streaming in the air. Two different illusions, yet in both there is the implication of air and flight.

"What I'm trying to do," he says, "is pace things. See, if they follow right away they'll see it's a phony. But if we can give them just enough to remember, to go back to and take a second look at . . . well, that's the way we tease them into hunting us. And by then the trail will lead to Jarvis. Then off the Earth entirely." He tells Chiffon, "Titan. Would you like to go to Titan? Plastic domes and billions of cubic kilometers terraformed . . . and crazy old Dirk running circles trying to find you."

She is thinking of Titan. She knows a place—

"What do you think?" he asks.

"How soon will you come home?" She says, "Darling?" and sets the book to one side.

"Not long. Late tonight." He says, "This isn't my normal line of work," and halfway laughs. "My hired experts are having to walk me through the process."

"But it will work?"

He says, "Yes."

He isn't so sure, she knows. She looks at his face and knows. "How did it go with him today?"

He squints at nothing. It is as though he's trying to remember the salient details for himself. His mouth is closed. His hands are hidden on his lap, probably holding one another while he hunches his shoulder and tells her, "It went fine."

She waits.

"Neat and simple," he tells her.

She would have killed Dirk. She doesn't know if it's possible—tapping into a Tau Ceti panel, twisting its functions to fit needs—but if it were possible she would have killed him. Gladly. She can imagine Dirk's old bones breaking in her hands.

"Anyway," says Steward.

"It's all working," she says, feigning confidence.

"It seems to be." Chiffon is wearing Steward's trousers, cut to fit badly, and a simple pullover shirt that will never fit. "And I'm looking forward to some rest. For both of us."

"So am I."

"I should go." Now the painted wall resembles faces instead of smoke or insects. Steward is lying back against the wall, his face part of them, and she blinks and wonders what to do. What to think. She won't tell him the things that would really win him. She had her chance last night, and did she take it? Not at all. Nothing is turning out as she intended. She seems to be forgetting what's at stake . . . her life, for God's sake! How many months does she have left? How many options does she have open to her? She won't be Ghosted. Not again. Not ever! Nothing else is so certain in her mind.

"Hurry back to me," she volunteers.

He promises to try, nodding and reaching and now gone.

She picks up the same thick book, thinking. Options, options. She opens to the page where she had been reading, the story one of hundreds collected by some past-century anthropologist. Freestater tales. She has been skimming through them and reading random paragraphs and thinking of Steward, seeing him on every page, in every battle and in every moment of glory. He must have read the book himself. At least once, she thinks. He has written in the margins, drawing parallels to stories he must have been told as a boy. "Sounds like 'The Coward In the Tree' story," he records. "Like 'The Warrior and the Cougar' story." Nothing is from Yellowknife. There are how many Freestates? she wonders. Hundreds, aren't there? Eleven hundred claims the author. What has surprised Chiffon while she reads in her chaotic fashion, bouncing from moral to moral, is an odd sameness over which is laid a definite variety. Each Freestate is unique. There's an atlas in the back pages, plus some final observations. The author states that each Freestate draws at least part of its character from the land. How mountainous? How forested? How many people in how much area? She looks up Yellowknife and studies the sketchy details. "Low ridges and mostly young timber make travel hard . . . even among Freestates, these people are isolated . . . strip mines in past millenia have left rugged terrain, gouged and laced with canyons, near Yellowknife's center . . ."

Chiffon pauses. She shuts the book and thinks. Ridges and rugged terrain? It all sounds something like Brulé! "Huh?" she says to herself. "How about that?" There is a strange sensibility at work here. The Old Quarter at the center, the long low buildings stretching outward . . . she nods and feels good in some elusive way. Brulé is Yellowknife. There is a thread of logic inside Steward's head. She feels she knows him in some rare way . . . and she tries to shrug off the feeling. She thinks of last night again . . . and feels what? What?

Options, options.

She can't simply remember things from her former lives. The Magician suppressed them at the outset. For always, he claimed, proud for his skills. Zebulina and Wisp are like characters in two sprawling books that she has read many times, knowing them as if they were friends, good friends, and feeling an honest involvement in their sad lives. But they are not Chiffon. It was Wisp who suffered Gray-time, and it's Wisp who now whispers in her ear, "Fear Death. Flee Death. Do what you need and think about it tomorrow!" Pretty Zebulina was the one who lived well and had all the goodness of life stripped away prematurely, and she is the one who sometimes sings to Chiffon, telling her, "Take what you can. All you can take. There's no telling tomorrow's treachery!"

She remembers Zebulina in Quito, in the good neighborhoods with all the best people. She remembers a prince from Kross—a proud and vain simple man with more money than sense, a good-looking man accustomed to winning women and then losing them with predictable regularity. The prince spotted Zebulina at some overstuffed party. The next day he sent her some small gift, expensive and forgotten, and inquired about a dinner engagement. An evening out? Or perhaps a boat ride out on the Pacific? No, said Zebulina. I don't think so. Why? he asked. What is the matter? I am involved, she lied. I don't want to see you, she told him. And that made him want her all the more. Which, of course, was Zebulina's plan. The prince sent more gifts worth larger and larger sums, and she kept what she liked and sold the rest for the money they brought. After several months of this kind of enrichment, sensing that the prince was losing interest, Zebulina relented to one night of carefully orchestrated pleasure. I love you! she declared in the morning. But I can't see you again. Never!

The prince asked why. Was there someone else?

She said there was no one. She wept and told him to leave now, go back to Kross and forget her.

Of course he wouldn't. New gifts arrived. Zebulina, amused beyond measure, counted her earnings and calculated shuttle rates and hotel rates and decided that an extended journey would suit a woman in some mysterious despair. So she went to Luna, and of course her dear prince followed. She made it easy. He wasn't too bright, after all, so too much subtlety might ruin the game. Then she went to Cradle, to the purple pastures, and Chiffon can remember one of his gifts—a tailored butterfly as large as a person and breathtakingly beautiful, requiring special foods and special air and worth enough to buy passage to the Belt. She had never been to the Belt. Don't you understand? she asked him. I love you. I'm desperately in love. But we can't see one another. So go home. Please!

She hopped around the Belt for months, the prince always nearby.

She led him to Cetacea, to a floating city set over one of the world's sunken suns.

Then there was Titan with its plastic caverns . . . Chiffon can remember how someone on the run might evade a crime lord for months, even years . . . and then it was out to the cold fringe of Oort's Cloud, to that massive comet once known as Pluto and now called Ear-To-Heaven. That was where the prince finally lost interest. Chiffon can't recall the circumstances, not that they matter, but she knows the moneys Zebulina had won by then. A small fortune, at least to her mind. A trip through the System and she was coming home richer. Imagine! She booked passage on a fast shuttle for Quito. Maybe it was the first time in her life that she felt a measure of contentment, coming home. Chiffon can summon images out of that remote past. She sees Zebulina's cabin. She sees nameless suitors among the shuttle's richest patrons. She sees a flash of light and smoke, torn bits of one wall exploding into her tiny cabin. That night's lover was killed. It was sudden and painless, his body taking the brunt of the force. Some one-in-a-trillion accident had caused a little-used vent to detonate. Very sad. But Zebulina halfway lived. Her beautiful figure was so much shredded meat, but the basics of her mind persisted. And to the credit of the crew and the shuttle's owners, Zebulina's mind was saved long enough to be Ghosted. "Free of charge," whispers Wisp. A sad, sad accident. A terrible conclusion to enormous promise. Chiffon sighs and then shivers, thinking about so very many things. She is not Zebulina. She is not Wisp. Yet they are so much a part of her even still, and she has no choice but to listen to their advice.

Options, options.

She must do something to help herself, but she can't let Steward know or even suspect. She tells herself to act and act soon. She tells herself that she must have some other avenue through which to escape. In case. I bet Steward would understand, she reasons. She decides on what she will do, telling herself that it isn't even out of character. Not for a lonely, sweet Flower, surely. And now she wipes her forehead dry with both hands, then wipes her hands on the sheets. She is shaking at the fingertips. Why? "You're doing right," say Wisp and Zebulina together. "Don't worry!" But then why does she sense that she too is being seduced . . .

. . . just like all those lovers, nameless and faceless and gone?

◆ ◆ ◆

No one is talking to him. The seats beside him were the last to fill, his mood a legend and the day done at last and him sitting straight against the tug of acceleration. They're coming up out of the mine, the air still hot and dust settling on them and their clothes, some of the miners looking at Gabbro when he won't notice. He isn't paying attention to anyone. He doesn't know what's on his own mind. Except that he is tired. Plain tired. He will sleep a full day now. He has already warned them. Tired. He knows he could collapse if the tugging quit. Him and his hyperfiber too. But that's what I was chasing, he thinks. This feeling. This aching old-man crap. It's like insulation. Even if he wanted, he couldn't think of April now. He can barely remember her name.

"So what's in store tonight?" one Morninger asks another. "Anything fun? You got a plan?"

"The usual," she answers. One hand makes an imaginary glass, tipping it back and laughing. "What else is there?"

"Nothing," the first Morninger says.

"Exactly."

"Fuck this world," he says. "Another few months and I've got enough to get home and comfortable for a while."

"Yeah." The glass is drained. She opens her hand. "What're you doing with your share? You got a plan?"

"Ideas." He rolls his head and grins. "Land by the river, maybe. A home. Whatever I can manage." The river is the first of many planned rivers. In place of water, Morning will use durable silicones running like water and a series of underground pumps and pipes to circulate the discharge back to the high-ground sources. "If I don't have enough, shit, I'll just drink my earnings. In a good bar."

"Yeah."

"Fucking Small Fry."

"No good bars in this town."

"Not one," he swears. "But maybe I'll share your table tonight. Huh? What do you say?"

"Glad for the company, friend."

The elevator slows itself with a high-pitched screech. Worn brakes complain, then succeed. They've stopped and Gabbro is standing without remembering himself standing, walking last out of the elevator and finding himself in the level afternoon light. The miners vanish into the waiting floaters. Gabbro won't commit himself. He waves off the last floater and starts to walk, thinking he should ride and get home fast, except he doesn't want to be home yet, and then he starts to trot until the hyperfiber muscles think to complain in their own fashion. They stick. They twitch. He catches himself hunting for something to rob for its power, just like he would on Morning, and then he stops moving and finds a floater pad and climbs the stairs with effort. One leg freezes for a moment. Look at me! he thinks. I'm drained dry! A floater descends to him, opens and thanks him for this opportunity to serve.

He climbs inside with a clumsy stiffness.

The floater rises and heads east, over the Old Quarter and the rest of the jumbled built-up landscape. He sees a column of smoke rising from a Farmstead, and suddenly he is thinking about April and everything else. It isn't as if it comes back to him from somewhere. It's as if the stuff has been inside him all along, waiting for him, stewing and steaming and ready to pounce.

He starts to cry.

"Are you all right?" asks the AI pilot. "Sir?"

Gabbro can't answer the question. He doesn't know for himself. "Sir?"

"What's your name?"

The AI sings some rambling name. Too much to remember, Gabbro thinks, and then the AI seems to hear his brain. "Pilot is good enough, sir."

"Pilot." Gabbro says, "You know something, Pilot? This is where I was born."

"Sir?"

"Up in the air," he explains. He starts to laugh, not able to stop himself and still crying. The AI is silent. "Listen to me," he says. "I must sound crazy."

"Do you think you sound crazy?" asks the AI.

"Tell me I do."

"If you want—"

"Or don't."

It says, "Silence is my choice. I don't think I can help by telling you anything."

Gabbro looks out at nothing, his eyes incapable of focusing. "Call that address I gave you. It's my home. Ask if there are any messages." He waits. The process takes a few seconds, but he's nervous and it seems to take an age.

"One message," the AI reports. " 'Come and see me if you get in before dark. Signed Steward.' "

Gabbro breathes. "Steward, huh?" He tells the AI, "All right. Go one building south of my home. If you would."

"Yes, sir."

"Maybe I'll catch Steward at home. You think?"

"If it will be a help, I hope so. Yes, sir."

The floater seems to be moving a little faster. Perhaps the AI is nervous in its own fashion, a Morninger of unknown balance riding inside its property. Gabbro tries to rest. He has trouble holding his head upright, his eyelids dipping shut; then there's a thud and he looks around and the canopy is open and the AI says:

"A pleasure, sir. Thank you, sir."

He pays and steps outside, somewhat recovered by the inactivity. He goes downstairs and turns once around, realizing this isn't his building and forgetting what he had told the AI just a minute ago. He has come to see Steward. That's right. He decides on the proper door and goes to it and announces himself to its single glassy eye. "He knows me."

"But I'm sorry," says the door. "He's not home just now."

"He left a message. He wanted to talk to me—"

"Sir? I've been instructed to let you come inside." The door makes a sudden hissing sound, oversized locks being unfastened. Mag-locks of some kind, he thinks. Very special gear, he thinks. And the door comes open. "You can wait inside, if you wish."

"A little while. Sure." He enters the tiny apartment, suffering from the same feeling of being in the wrong place. This isn't the apartment he has seen from outside. It's all wrong . . . the furniture wrong, and all the shelves and a delicate sweet smell in the air . . .

"Hello?" says a voice in the back.

Gabbro says, "Hello? Excuse me?"

The door shuts and seals itself. He starts to move toward the bedroom, hearing motion, thinking this is wrong and he should get out of here now. At once.

"Come here," says a girl. "Please?" She has a thick smooth voice, and he can't help but like it. He sees her sitting on the edge of the bed, her bulky clothes nondescript and her face not just pretty. Gabbro stands in the bedroom door, not so much lost now as he is surprised. Who is she? What does she want? Why does he feel expected—?

She says, "Hello," again.

"Hi."

"You're Gabbro, aren't you? I've seen you."

He waits.

She makes soft sounds, pulling at the rumpled sheets on the bed. "He trusts you, you know. Steward, I mean." She looks small and frail, peering up at him and asking him, "Gabbro? Gabbro, tell me the truth. Have you ever, ever been truly scared?"

◆ ◆ ◆

The important thing is vagueness. She keeps it all gray and quick and absolutely memorable. No, she won't lure him into bed. She doesn't want that stage. Touching is enough. Odors are enough. She wants a friend. A gesture here, a sad look there, and the big Morninger is sitting on the floor, eye to eye with Chiffon. She tells him a fuzzy-edged story that will help her and yet leave her with options, too. In case Steward should hear about this. He won't, she promises Zebulina and Wisp. But in case.

A new friend and ally, she thinks. Bought at almost no risk.

Why not? If Steward could hire Gabbro and trust in his silence, surely she could invite him upstairs for a few minutes of talk. Nothing more. Where is the crime? Nowhere. She is so very lonely. So terribly bored. She touches him. Her bare hand shines in the day's last light. Gabbro's flesh is dry and oddly warm, firm and unmarred by wear or time. It's the back of his hand that she touches, leaking the usual cocktail, and of course she smiles and of course he can't help but smile too. He seems tired. He says, "I'm sorry for being confused. I came to see Steward . . . and everything is so . . . so different . . ."

"Don't go. Don't." She withdraws her hand, telling him, "Let's move into the front room. We can sit. Talk. Just for a little while, please?" He nods and rises. He believes her stories about being scared and bored, not asking for details. He walks, something about his gait wrong. The cyborg seems tired in every respect. He picks up the

Universal Globe in one hand and asks to see Morning. Then he looks outside and says to her:

"How does he do it? Masking Glass?" He is staring through the sealed glass door, over the unused balcony and down at his own apartment. "He likes his privacy, doesn't he?"

"He's a very special man." How many people can you say that about? "One of a kind."

"I guess that's my impression. Yeah."

"Gabbro?" she begins. "Do you know whom you helped when you climbed that building the other night?"

The Globe is now a yellowish-white world, clouds speckled with the tiny airborne cities. Morning. He squints at Morning and sets the Globe down on its shelf, and she makes a mental note to change the Globe to some other world. Titan would be appropriate. As soon as he is gone.

"Do you know what I am?"

Gabbro blinks. "I think I do."

"A Flower."

"What's he doing with you?"

And she tells him. It doesn't feel right, for some reason. The old lies about Dirk. It brings on guilt and images of Steward. But he believes the story from the first, just like Steward believed; she sees it in the handsome face, in the sympathetic curl of the lips. She wants to thank him for helping them. For helping her. She only wishes it were over and done and she were safe. "My owner is quite terrible, you see—" But Steward says that in a week or so, with luck, they'll be rid of the man.

Gabbro nods. "I wish you luck."

"And you?" She is on the sofa. He is on the floor, legs crossed. "I get the feeling that you'd like to talk to someone."

"You haven't seen April, have you? In my home?"

"I haven't, no." She watches his hands squeezing one another. The hyperfiber skin gives squeaks, eerie little squeaks, as the fingers play across one another. "Tell me."

He begins to talk. She sees him as vulnerable, small and quite sad and ready for any audience with the time. He talks about April and some terrible fight yesterday afternoon. Did she see any of it? No? She says she was sleeping, as was Steward, and they didn't. He doesn't paint a scene. He doesn't repeat what was said between April and him. But she can imagine the fight's intensity, offering herself to Gabbro as something passive. An unjudging audience. This is better than touching, she thinks. There's nothing here to feel guilty about. She feels immune. As night draws in around the campsite, life in suspension, two alloyed primates are discovering the oldest, finest secret. Between them they share so very much. They do.

18

Here's something interesting. Morningers accustomed to living and working in remote territories and down in the deepest mines keep certain kits close at hand. Survival kits, if you will. Suppose a shaft collapses and the power sources are cut. Suppose the miners are trapped and some of them are near collapse too, their hyperfiber flesh in desperate need of recharging. In each survival kit is a special recharging cord with only one purpose. A Morninger with spare energy will run it from himself to the ones in need, draining himself for their good. The history of Morning is full of this odd brand of heroism. Some of the heroes let themselves die in order to save friends, or sometimes strangers . . . their bodies turning rigid and utterly useless. They cannot talk above a whisper or breathe deeply or focus their dying eyes . . .

—excerpt from a traveler's notebook, available through System-Net

H E came into her room just as she came awake this morning, smiling and telling her about an idea. Some brainstorm he had had a minute ago. Did she want to hear? She said, All right. Tell me.

It's about Gabbro, he said.

She waited. In the morning light, and for no clear reason, Toby had turned back into a stranger. It was like yesterday had never happened. None of it. What about Gabbro? she asked.

And that was when he checked himself. He pulled back a notch or two with his enthusiasm. Listen, he said, if there's a better time . . . maybe I should come back . . .

What is it?

What we were talking about last night. Teaching him a lesson by scaring him somehow.

So? she asked.

You want to do it, don't you? A lesson? he asked, keeping his voice tightly leashed. Nothing urgent. Nothing quite honest.

She said, The bastard.

He said nothing.

I guess I do. Why wouldn't I? she asked. Except the fury inside her was gone. She didn't care so deeply anymore, her face mending and the pain dulled by medication and a good night's sleep giving her that floating sensation, the hospital mattress more than comfortable beneath her. The doctor had said she would leave this afternoon.

Toby said, Because I had this idea. About something we could do tonight.

Yeah?

He paused. What was he thinking then? she wonders. What was going on inside that crazy skull?

Go on, she urged him.

Can you get us inside his apartment? he asked.

The door knows me. Sure. I'm sure it'll let me inside.

You are? He wouldn't have changed the programming?

Maybe. He might. But I don't see him doing it too soon. She said, He may want me to come back, the bastard. So he can smooth things over.

All right. Fine. We'll pretend that we can get inside. Okay?

Go on.

Cyborgs sleep, right?

Everyone sleeps.

But he recharges when he sleeps. Right? He's got a . . . what? A way of plugging into a power source, doesn't he?

April said, The human of the future. Right.

Toby shook his head, the Gardener in him disgusted. He said, Am I wrong? Isn't he vulnerable then? Sleeping?

I guess.

For instance, if we were to tinker with that recharging cord . . . there must be a way, a trick . . . you know what I'm saying?

No.

We turn him off, said the Gardener.

Yeah?

We drain him when he plugs in. We pull out his juices and teach him a good hard lesson. We can show him that he's not so damned tough and all. That he can't break a girl's face for no reason.

She tried imagining it happening as he described it, clinical and efficient. So we just let him lie there? she asked. For how long?

Until he learns his lesson, Toby said.

How long?

Maybe a night. Whatever it takes.

I don't know . . .

We won't actually hurt him, I mean! Don't think I want him hurt in any real way.

She didn't like Toby this morning. Yesterday he was a saint, golden and splendid and brought to her by her good fortune. Today she has doubts. It's nothing she can name or point to, but there are doubts nonetheless. There was that careful sense of words and expressions this morning. Now he is beside her, underneath the floater pad and mostly hidden, watching Gabbro's apartment and neither of them speaking but doing it with such damned intensity. They're like a couple of ticking bombs. She's almost scared to move, scared to brush up against anything for fear of setting off an explosion.

This morning Toby had promised, We'll just let him stew for a while. Nothing else. By tomorrow we'll let him go.

I guess it's possible, she had confessed. Then she explained how Morningers had special cords meant to milk them of energy. They were the same shape and color as the rechargers. She mentioned a couple of Old Quarter shops where the miners went to sell the gear they had stolen from work. For cash. For credit. She said, There's a lot of stuff you can find in those shops. No questions asked. No one remembered.

He said nothing.

She looked at him and felt uneasy, saying, I don't know though. I keep thinking of myself setting that stupid fire—

Which is nothing. To him. You know it's nothing.

I suppose so.

So why are you defending him?

Am I?

I'm looking at what he did to you. You can't see your own face. I did and all I see now is that mask. Toby said, I don't know. Maybe we shouldn't scare him. Maybe you're right.

I never said—

Let's let him go. Forget him. Heal and pay the bills and forget about it. There are ways they can suppress bad memories, aren't there? I've heard of expensive Terran tricks—

I've got insurance, she offered. I don't have bills.

You're right. You don't. You'll walk away with nothing gone but your pride.

I want to scare him! she growled.

The bastard, he said.

Well, she said, I don't see why you're pressing me.

Because this is our chance. We have to move fast, don't you see? He might change the door's programming anytime. How can we trap him inside that shell if we can't get inside to do it? April? Is something wrong with me? Is my thinking wrong here?

She looks at Toby now. It's past dusk. Lightning bugs are hovering around them, lending a lazy kind of motion to the still air. She can see Toby's watchful face and one webbed hand supporting his chin, his expression intense and his back held straight. They have been here for a little while, hiding in a tangled mass of vines. Like she suspected this morning, Gabbro's door still recognized her and opened willingly for her and her guest. Toby had done his work while she stood guard in the hallway, ready to delay Gabbro should he appear. The splicing took him an age; he didn't understand the tools or the recharging cords, Gabbro's or theirs. But then he was finished, whistling to himself while both of them hustled out of the building and up to their hiding place. Now she is bored. It would be easier, she thinks, if she weren't so scared too. She wants this finished. She tries to imagine Gabbro lying helpless in his bed, her standing on his chest and taunting him in various ways, cursing and kicking and generally cleansing her spirit until it sparkles. The problem is that the images don't last. She can't quite get her revenge straight in her mind. The fury inside her refuses to come now. She can't guess why. The night air is too soothing, she thinks. The vines below are too good a mattress. There's no moon yet and isn't that needed? And then there's Toby, too. Sitting beside him, watching his cold patient stare, it occurs to her that she knows nothing whatsoever about revenge.

"I can't believe he's still working," she admits.

"Maybe he's drinking somewhere," Toby answers, indifferent to the wait.

"But he'd come home first to change. Usually." She wants to talk to Gabbro, not knowing what she might say if given the chance. The anger has gone somewhere. Now it's resentment. A couple of years of her life have been invested in that sack of hyperfiber, she tells herself, and look at the sorry things he has her doing. "Wait a minute. Wait."

She feels foolish, sitting straighter and looking down into the yard. "That's him," she whispers. "There."

The figure is unmistakable. He has come from this building—what was he doing here? she wonders—and now he does a slow walk past the swimming pool, one dangerous hand lifting and touching the glass door that opens for him in the same way the inside door yielded to her hand and voice. A light comes on. Gabbro begins to undress, work clothes kicking loose the strange gritty dust and him now touching a control. World-Net comes on. The window and door darken until all she can see is a huge, imprecise form sitting where it can watch the local news. Maybe he's finishing breakfast, she thinks, remembering it laying on a table, cold and forgettable. She leans closer to Toby now, telling him something else about patterns and the man.

"He'll clean himself, then sleep. I bet he's ready to nod off as it is."

"Yeah?" Toby stirs. A clear eagerness comes into the air. The lightning bugs seem brighter. Hooting birds start to work the yard behind them, hunting as a team. Toby asks, "How long?"

"Half an hour," she guesses.

He waits for a few minutes, leaning forward as if to better see what is going on below them. Then he announces, "I'll be back. In a few minutes," and abruptly stands.

She asks where he is going.

"I forgot something."

"What?"

"In my apartment."

What could he have left behind? she wonders. But before she can press him, the Gardener is running toward the stairs. "Wait for me," he tells her, giggling. The giggle seems so very wrong—wrong for the mood, wrong for the night—that she doesn't believe what she hears. She denies it. She reaches up and touches the mask on her battered face, pressing hard enough to make pain, and she concentrates on the sensations while she tries again to picture Gabbro as helpless. Something is going to happen tonight. She knows it. But here she is, thinking hard, and she can't even make this one thing happen in her mind.

◆ ◆ ◆

It was in the Old Quarter, in one of those secondhand shops that April had steered him toward, that he found everything he needed. A dirty place purposefully dim, the shop was run by an ancient Lunarian with

a sharp face and no hesitations. A Morninger-to-Morninger recharging cord? Yes, sir. Right here, sir! Unused and worth the price for its
curiosity value, I think. Anything else, sir? All right. Yes, I understand. Well, I do have several. Worn models, but functional. Power
packs included, of course. Are you familiar with their use? Will this
be cash? Do you want any item gift-wrapped? Thank you and have
a splendid evening, sir!

Toby is standing in his bedroom, breathing hard and sweating. A
worn bag is laying on the floor, its fabric dark and cracked from hard
use and constant heat. He starts to kneel, reaching for the handle, and
then he remembers something. Turning, he looks to the wall and finds
a spot near the floor. He touches it with a finger and pulls it higher,
then uses two fingers to spread out the image. Garden emerges—at
least that AI version of Garden—and a multitude of bodies stand on
an infinite shoreline, the salty waves beating at their ankles, the white-
smears bowing in some pleasant warm wind.

The Passion Necklace has lasted for days.

He had let it slip his mind, what with the confusion and his being
gone. Pressing his face closer, he sees his own self. Nothing has
changed—the same tired expression, the same bliss, the same perfection now carried on endlessly. Toby finds his control console and
makes a quick command. At the same instant, with the same motion,
everyone on this fictional Garden collapses and trembles and dies. The
corpses dissolve into the white sand itself, becoming rounded mounds
with waves slapping at them, the waves carrying them away without
haste.

He lifts the old bag by its handles.

He kills his connection with the fantasy channel, bills paid automatically and precious little left in his accounts. Then he leaves. He
hurries. He gets to April and the hiding place, kneels and says, "Anything?"

"I think he's sleeping."

"You *think?*"

She's uncomfortable. He can't afford to make her uncomfortable,
he tells himself. He says, "The lights are out, aren't they?"

"That's what I mean."

"Then let's take a look. All right?"

"What's this?" She touches the bag in the darkness, squeezing once.
"It feels heavy."

"Tools," he says.

"Why?"

"To fix him. Later," he lies. "We can't just leave him, can we?"
She says no, they can't. She seems suddenly pensive.

He leads. They retrace their roundabout course to the inside door,
keeping their pace slow so no one will notice them. He doesn't want
trouble. He wants to be the image of casual pedestrians, touching
April's arm from time to time, saying whatever bland promises come
to mind.

The door greets April by name.

The front room is dark, as is the bedroom beyond, and they stand
together for a long moment and listen until a voice comes drifting out
at them from the back. "Who's it? Ape . . . rilll? Ape . . . rillll?"

There is a terrible instant when Toby is certain that trickery has
failed him, that the big insulting cyborg will come lurching out of the
bedroom and swing and crush his own skull. But then the voice dies
away. No one moves. He prods April with one hand, coaxing her to
take the lead. "It's okay," he promises. "He's down."

Gabbro is naked, darker than anything and incapable of the simplest motion. He mutters, "Ape . . . rilll," once more. The voice comes
from somewhere inside his worthless shell. There's a palpable sense
of fear in the voice. He's panicky. Absolutely, undeniably full of fear.
Toby turns on one light, keeping it set low, and he puts down his bag
while April goes to the cyborg and runs a hand over his hairless chest,
bending and putting an ear to him. She listens. She seems altogether
too concerned. She lifts her head and announces, "There's nothing
moving inside him," with a sad, surprised voice. "You've done it," as
if she can't believe what she sees. "You did it, all right."

He opens the bag and reaches inside, grabbing a pistol grip.

"Wait a second," April tells him. "It's too soon. You can't fix him
yet," and she lifts a hand to his face.

"Get away," says Toby. The power packs are massive and short-
lived. He inserts one of the three into the grip, feeling excited and a
little sorry that it's all going to be done so soon. He can't linger, he
knows. He can't let himself be caught. Eyeing the girl, he wonders how
much further he can trust her. Probably not much, he decides. Giving
the simple trigger a little squeeze, he makes a thin seering point of light
spring from the massive barrel and passes the light over the unblinking
unthinking gaze of the cyborg.

"What's that?" asks April, her voice suspicious.

"What is it? Don't you know?" Toby laughs. He wonders how much poor Gabbro can see, how much residual energy there is to power his senses. "Do you know this gizmo? Huh? Can you hear me? Can you see anything?"

The muted voice says nothing clearly. A choked scream, perhaps.

"Come on," Toby prompts. "You know."

Nothing.

April cries out, "What is it? Gabbro? Love! Tell me—!"

"Drr . . . illl!"

"More to the point," says Toby, turning and proud, "it's a special hyperfiber torch used in the mantle mines. Very tough and very powerful. For cutting and slicing stronger stuff than this," and his free hand strikes Gabbro, knuckles complaining.

April has turned pale. "You're going to kill him?" she says. "Why are you going to kill him?"

"I am not," he tells her.

"You never said . . . hey, what are you doing? Hey! Stop that!" She comes at him just as he touches the tip of the barrel to the cyborg's flesh. There is pain. He hears another choked scream, then nothing, and kills the torch when April grabs him. He wheels and swings and knocks April onto her back. He says, "I'm killing no one. Do you understand me?" and he kneels and has her hands before she finds her breath. One of the bed sheets is within reach. He bites it to start a rip and makes a long thin strip that he uses to tie her hands behind her back. "Now sit still," he warns. "Watch if you want." He is in complete control. He stands and feels very sober, very wise, turning on the torch once again and going to the cyborg and telling him, "The eyes. First or last? First or last?"

Gabbro says nothing, the eyes struggling to focus.

"Last, I think." He says to Gabbro, "Watch me now. Watch!"

◆◆◆

And now she realizes that she has been awake for some time, listening to nothing and some part of her mind alert without trying to alarm the rest of her drowsy self, listening to the still night air and mild night sounds and thinking there is no good reason for her to come awake now. None. But she sits up nonetheless. Then she stands. Then she walks into the front room, halfway expecting to find Steward sitting in the dark, just home, but he isn't and maybe that's why she woke.

She asks herself the time. A kind of reference point, time. Steward has an old-fashioned clock on one of his self-made shelves. It reads minutes short of midnight. Not late at all, she thinks. It's still early.

So she sits.

She is wearing the white dress, invitingly snug and sleek. Steward will come through the door and she will greet him. He needs a greeting, she imagines. One hand plays with the double strands of pearls. She allows herself to feel satisfied, considering what she has managed today and through these last few days. Gabbro was a smart turn. She even toys with the idea of "confessing" to Steward tonight, through tears and weak appeals for forgiveness; she imagines Steward shaking his head, surprised and then a little mad perhaps, then telling her not to worry. He understands. She shouldn't have done it, just like she shouldn't have gone into that bar several nights ago, but no harm has been done and he does trust Gabbro and maybe he will go talk with the Morninger tomorrow. Just to make everything clear all around.

Someone is down in the yard. She hears a splash, then another, and thinks of a swimmer enjoying the little pool. She envies his freedom. She eases her head down on the arm of the sofa, imagining water instead of the living leather, and suddenly she can visualize a single moment out of Zebulina's life. A deep blue-black sky is above the clear bright sea of Cetacea. The water is a touch cool. Zebulina is wearing one of the skintight body stockings that are the norm there, an artificial gill strapped to her back and humming with a reassuring steadiness. She tucks and dives. On her left side, several kilometers below the surface, is one of the Cetacean suns—a submerged fusion plant emitting carefully orchestrated flavors of light in all directions, the faint greenness brought by drifting masses of algae. Other suns lay in other directions, many deeper, some almost imperceptible under hundreds of kilometers of melted ice. Zebulina kicks. She seems utterly alone. She is breathing hard and the gill's air is pure and cold and refreshing. Bracing. The pressure doesn't increase like on the Earth, at least not so quickly. A school of brightly colored squid come past her in formation—big human eyes staring out at the rarest of sights, a true human on this little world. There are no whales yet, but she is patient. She knows they are tailored with their own gills, very efficient, and they range from the surface to the final crushing depths. So she keeps kicking, using an instrument on her wrist to measure depth and time and temperature and oxygen; she kicks until her legs burn and the tendons on top of her feet ache, reminding herself to keep streamlined. This is fun. It's all so new and marvelous, she thinks . . . and there! There! She spots the distinctive outline of a single whale against the glare of the sun. It appears tiny. For an instant, without reference points, she believes it is close and some kind of baby. Or maybe just a fish. But no, she kicks toward it and it doesn't flee. Indeed, it seems to be approaching. Yet it takes an age to cut the distance in half. Zebulina can make out fins and the enormous baleen and a fine network of gills deployed from its lips and belly. She remembers how the earthly whales of old were enormous at thirty meters in length; this whale is twice as long and more thinly built, one of dozens of species derived from the original colonists.

Another few meters and she will touch it.

She puts out a hand, kicking hard, thinking that this is wonderful and lovely . . . and she hears splashing. Chiffon hears the splashing, and she sits upright on the sofa, listening, listening, hearing something else now too . . . a scream! A definite muffled in-a-world-of-agony scream.

She goes to the sealed glass door, pressing against it and gazing down into the yard. Nothing seems wrong at first. She notices the water moving in the pool, no one showing above the water. She waits for a long moment, the scream finished, and she tells herself it was nothing. Just someone having fun nearby. But still the water moves. Little waves rise up and crash into one another or over the sides, splashing across the deck, and still no one shows. Who's doing it? she wonders. It must be Gabbro doing it. "No," she mutters. "He said he was going straight to sleep. It's the last thing he told me."

She has to will her eyes into motion, hunting for other signs of trouble. Gabbro's door is partway open. It doesn't surprise her. She won't let it surprise her. He is probably swimming and she expected to see the door open, and the darkened indoors doesn't mean trouble. It means nothing. She sighs. She tries to take a half step backward, as if that will make everything a touch less serious, distance, and then she happens to spy a lone figure in the open doorway, standing there with something moving in his hands. Of course it's not Gabbro. Much too small. She hopes it could be April, but he's too lean. That leaves everyone else in the world. Who is it? Does it matter? She takes the half step to diffuse her fear, one hand coming over her mouth, and the figure uses both long arms to toss the moving something into the air, squirming and dropping *ker-plash* into the water, gone.

Now the scream repeats itself. Chiffon can't know for certain, but it does seem to come from the open doorway—weak but unmistakable and sad throughout, halfway dead, and she hurts for hearing it; the figure steps out a little further, turning now, the angle and the starlight showing Chiffon some kind of mask over his long face.

Now she understands.

Instinct makes her shrink away from the glass, wanting to hide, a trembling voice rising out of her throat. "Dirk," she says to herself, to the room. Somehow he has found Gabbro, knows about him and the climb, in spite of Steward's assurances. Dirk and Minus too. They want Steward, she realizes. "And me!" she whines. Suddenly she is exposed, frightfully vulnerable. Where's Minus? she wonders. He must be inside, out of sight, working on Gabbro by who-knows-what means, working to extract the confession.

Steward said they couldn't track him down.

He promised, she tells herself.

And now she feels a sudden anger. The one she trusted most has let her down, in essence. And he isn't even here to see what he has wrought. Sweet sphincter of God! she thinks. She shudders and focuses her anger, weighing her prospects. If they haven't come storming up here already, Dirk and Minus and the rest, then they don't know. Gabbro, dear and durable Gabbro, has kept the secret inside himself somehow. But he can't last. No one has a chance of outlasting these tortures.

So there is one option.

One course.

One.

And in a whirlwind she changes clothes, remembering the map that Steward drew for her, finding it among the half-read books, then stuffing her things down the garbage chute. Her dress. Her purse. The pearls . . . no, not the pearls. Keep them and Dirk's little gun, she decides. The glass money and the white shoes. She can't very well wear Steward's, after all. The gun is where she hid it, undisturbed. She turns and turns, hunting for anything else, anything forgotten. A message! Leave Steward a warning! Then she takes off the gun's safety and opens the door and runs. She doesn't look back. The hallway's dirty white walls are a blur. She is running, following the curls and curves, the map in one hand and the gun in the other and the slapping sounds of her feet barely dampened by the worn, half-dead carpeting.

I used to travel with a tailored monkey. It was small and clever and had my face—handsome, I like to think, and forever smiling—and the monkey had a limited vocabulary and an assortment of witty sayings and light jokes. It was quite popular wherever I went. To a point, at least. I noticed that after a while the jokes began to wear thin. Audiences grew bored, or worse. But then I never linger long when I make my journeys, and so long as I came and went rapidly enough my monkey made me nothing but friends . . .

—excerpt from a traveler's notebook, available through System-Net

SHE gets to the point where she wants him unconscious, wishes for the pain to put him into nothingness for a little while. The screaming is reaching inside April and wounding her. It isn't guilt. No, it's not. She didn't know, after all! How could she have known what Toby was planning? And nothing she could have done would have saved him. So no, it's not guilt. Just like it's not compassion that makes her cry now. Compassion would mean that she wouldn't forget this terror soon. It would mean that she couldn't walk away like she would walk from a suffering stranger. Toby ripped off her mask after he tied her down, after she tried to scream, and then he gagged her mouth and propped her up and made her suffer, too. Watching it. Hearing it. He has finished carving off the last of the hyperfiber now, at last, and he moves toward her and kneels and sets down two shiny dead eyes before her, then the torch.

The torch is hot from use. The tip of its barrel starts a small fire in the carpeting. She is amazed by its sensitivity, its accuracy. Toby says, "Listen," and smiles behind the healing mask. She senses a wicked happiness, him saying, "Listen," with authority and confidence. "I'm going to let you go."

She tries talking through the gag, cursing him.

He doesn't seem to hear. He shakes his head and says, "Look at the poor creature. Underneath, what? Nothing. Almost nothing."

Gabbro is pale and enormously long, his true bones threatening to break through the stretched and wasted skin. He is unconscious now. His mouth is open and toothless, the hyperfiber fittings removed and the stretch marks showing through the cheeks and under the chin. The arms are sticks. His legs are knobby-kneed sticks. And his feet and hands seem unnaturally long, the bones drawn out to fit the cyborg functions.

"I'm sorry to have kept you ignorant," Toby says. "But you were the one who helped me. In every way, I think, we are still partners."

She tries saying they weren't. Never.

And he shakes a webbed finger in her face. She can see his eyes, hating them, and he says, "Regardless of what you think, you did your part. No one's going to believe otherwise."

She tells him to fuck himself.

He ignores the muffled grunt. "And him," he says. "Praise the Prophet! I doubt that he'll be able to tell anyone anything. Which is good for both of us." Those eyes are smiling. "Isn't it, partner?" He scoops up the dead eyes, then the other hand hoists the torch again. "So do you have any suggestions for me? Any places where I might go now?" He is thoroughly at ease, standing over April, holding the the torch as if he has practiced the position for days and weeks. "I bet you don't understand me," he ventures.

But she does. He's got much for brains.

"I'm going to leave Brulé," he claims.

She says nothing. Gabbro is beginning to stir now.

"I've got ideas," he says. "Plans. They'll all take time, but now it's beginning to make sense. All this waste. All that I've had to endure in this hellhole."

No, she hopes, it's not compassion. Never compassion. She doesn't feel for Gabbro any more than she would feel for a brutalized dog . . . and yet now she starts to cry, tears flowing, moaning through the gag and trying to rise to see those eyeless sockets, that naked face . . .

◆ ◆ ◆

And now the white pain comes around him, rousing him once again. But this time he's aware of his hands and toes. This is different. He can move them now and the aching has subsided to the point where he can stand touching himself lightly, clumsily, everything feeling so terribly wrong. So wrong. He keeps forgetting what they've done to him. He keeps having to make himself remember. He is so whispery small on this big, big bed. A skeleton and little more. He touches himself here and here. Then here. And now he learns the sorest place. It's his geographical center. His maleness. His shriveled finger of traumatized skin.

Talking is impossible.

Sometimes he thinks he's making noise, shouting or something, only he can't imagine how it might sound.

Time is compressed, hot and bright and wreathed in pain. Think of something else, he tells himself. Concentrate! Concentrate! He remembers April's voice yelling at someone, trying to stop whoever had the drill. No, think of something pleasant. He remembers Steward's Flower and brings her into his head. She comes before him and smiles and says something sweet and pure, now reaching to touch him. To stroke his arm.

Gabbro pulls away.

He tries to ward off her hand. Don't! He wants to cry out, warning her away, but his atrophied jaw hasn't the strength.

And the tips of her fingers are on him, stroking what burns. She smiles in a fine large way. Amazed, he feels the burning sensation diminish to a bearable level. He whimpers. She kneels, using all of both hands now and bending to kiss him sweetly, almost shyly, asking how he feels and does he feel better now? Can he find a difference? Yes, he thinks. Absolutely.

He thanks the Flower.

She coos in one throbbing ear.

He tries moving, rolling onto his better side, but she insists that he quit it. She wants him resting. Easy, she says. Be still and relax.

That's it, she says.

Rest.

And he watches her drifting overhead, the white of the pain now duller and flatter. She is naked. He didn't realize it before now. Lovelier than words, she drops toward him with supreme gentleness. Don't move, she repeats. Careful now. Easy. She is lying on him as a blanket might, yet without weight. Again she kisses Gabbro. His burning empty sockets. His gaping jaw. His spindly neck and the rib-ridged chest. And now he is drifting too.

Be still, says the Flower. Let yourself go.

I love you, he tells her. I do.

And she presses one cool hand to his mouth, shutting off the words, and her fine distinctive smell percolates into him and buoys him skyward. Rest, she says. That's all you have to do now. Rest.

◆◆◆

One last time he comes to the doorway. He brings out the last of the quivering hyperfiber. He had had no idea how the chunks would move like they do. None. The muscles from the legs and back were the worst, convulsively jerking and twisting, fighting him every step of the way. Now he looks outside at the pool and the dark windows all around, hearing the waves and knowing they're diminishing. Dying away. Good, he thinks. He kneels and opens the bag one last time, extracting the torch and the last power pack, loading the thing and turning a switch and watching the barrel's tip turn blue-white. Then he heaves the torch out onto the coral deck. It strikes and skids and drops into the water, a sharp sizzling noise and a column of steam and then nothing. Just the fading waves.

Toby eases outside.

He is on his toes, straining to see what happens.

A few dead fish rise and then sink away. An eel struggles feebly, kicking with all of its body and then pulled under by the convection currents. Toby smells a warm vapor in the air. He squints. The pool begins to boil. Bubbles burst. Foam gathers at the sides. The still night air is saturated with moisture, and the boiling worsens. There's a violence to the water. "Praise the Prophet," he mutters, retreating now and removing the healing mask and thinking what else does he need.

He goes upstairs, up to his apartment. There's almost nothing to pack. Cash and a few small quiver chips—not much to rely on—and then a handful of biscuits, cold but edible.

He has to hurry. He leaves without taking a last look, believing that the key is remaining unseen. Or at least unnoticed. He goes down the stairs as if he belongs here, one step at a time, and then pushes open Gabbro's door, now unlocked. April is lying beside the bed, struggling without effort. Toby removes her gag and says, "Remember. You've been warned."

She is on her knees, looking at Gabbro. "I didn't help. Not with this . . . not this."

"Partner," he says. He waits until she glances at him. "I mean you," he tells her, stepping to the bed and touching the bare flesh, sweat soaked and twitching, and he tells both of them in a barely perceptible whisper, "In my place, under these circumstances, the Prophet Adam would have done what I've done. I know it."

She doesn't talk.

He turns away from Gabbro, drying his moistened hand on his shirt. "All right," he says to April. "Run and don't tell what you know. Don't forget. You're so much a part of this that you can't even think about what's happened tonight. Okay?"

She nods, something about her defeated. Helpless.

And he unties the bindings and even helps her to her feet, telling her to hurry now, the neighborhood is still sleeping but someone's going to notice the pool eventually. She goes with him into the hallway, then pauses. He turns and starts to walk in one direction, toward the stairs, and April acts as if she expects him to shoot her. To threaten her. To do any last thing.

Toby has to laugh.

He climbs the stairs one at a time, casual and cool, thinking that a floater to the Old Quarter is the first stage. Then he can rest and think about the next tasks. He steps up onto the roof and the floater pad and immediately senses something, someone watching him. He grows cold. He turns slowly and spies an enormous bird perched on the edge of the pad, on golden feet, dark and massively built, black eyes dancing inside its brain-fat skull.

Saying nothing, Toby looks at the sky and wonders how long before a floater comes. He can smell steam even this high. It smells like cooked fish and machine parts.

"Have you see her?"

The bird has spoken to him. "Pardon?" asks Toby.

"A girl. Have you seen her?"

"What girl?"

"Pretty blonde. Blue eyes. Big tits." The bird's voice is rude and simple and self-assured. "Pretty as pretty can be. Have you see her?"

"Leave me alone."

The bird moves its weight from one leg to the other. "Big reward," it promises.

"Yeah?"

"Wearing a white dress. Pearls. Garden pearls, double strands—"

"All right. Did *he* make you?"

The bird blinks, rather confused.

"What is this? Another joke? Are you something new he's conjured up for me?" And now he laughs. "Well, I don't care," he tells it. "Say what you want, you ugly sack of tinkered genes."

The bird is speechless now.

"Funny, isn't it? You come now of all times—" A floater is descending, but Toby has time to rush the big bird. With one hand he pulls a hard cold biscuit from his pocket and throws it like a flat stone. The biscuit misses. The bird is vast as it pumps its wings and wheels and climbs higher, shouting down at him, "A Flower! A Flower! Have you seen her?"

"Get away," Toby mutters under his breath. Then the floater is down and open, waiting, and he climbs inside and gives his destination and watches the world drop away. The blood coursing through his skull is telling him there are enemies everywhere, everywhere, and the only wise response is to keep alert. Always alert. Yet now for the first time he feels the match for his enemies, he does, and never again will he cower. He will never let them do him any more harm.

◆ ◆ ◆

The hawk was produced from an old template—a functional design easily trained, linked to a certain AI in the Old Quarter. Everything it senses is analyzed, and it knows exactly what it wants. The Flower. The blonde girl. She fills its thoughts when awake and its fleet little dreams during its brief sleeps. A few more days and it will be dead, no rest and no food and the speed of its creation all factors in its demise. It's been over Brulé dozens of times already, as have its siblings. Nothing has been found. No distinct whiffs of Flowers. No figures in a window. No leads leading anywhere. But the neurotic driving force inside it keeps it hunting, forever eager, forever optimistic, circling now by the moonlight and leaving nothing to chance.

It's using the heat off the boiling pools to rise, riding it like it would any thermal.

Conserving its reserves.

Circling again, its head pivoting and every sense straining.

What's this?

What's this?

A figure has come into view. It's the right shape, yes, and the hawk's brain is screaming that the size is right and the characteristic things like stride length and wiggling hips and the planting and lifting of the tiny feet in the white shoes. Not a white dress, no, but that's okay. It's the Flower. The hawk knows. But then a dose of caution comes from somewhere. The distance is enormous. The moonlight is flat and broken into shadows, long and tangled. It needs to get closer. Closer! So it beats the air with tired wings, rushing o the east.

For a moment it loses sight of the Flower. It halfway panics. Where did she go? Where? Is she hiding? But then hiding is good. It's a clue. Hiding is the act of a fugitive. Shape and avoidance. Two clues. A surge of adrenalin alerts the Old Quarter AI. Computer elements and an antenna sewn into the base of the brain squirt the data home. And now the hawk, frustrated and panting, turns and circles in a tight figure eight pattern, high above the sleeping shadowy landscape and hunting.

Nothing.

It's so high that a Flower squatting in those trimmed lines of bushes, for instance, could look up forever and not see it. Yet its own eyes can make out individual leaves, polished to a high gloss, and the tiny sleeping fish here and there in a tiny stream, and now a small predatory something—a weasel, a mink, whatever—moving like a fluid dark rope up to the edge of one tangled mass of pruned vegetation, stopping and suddenly peering at something that is moving, shaking limbs, scaring the predator until it turns and flees.

The Flower stands, unmistakable in the middle of the ornamental bushes. She has cut herself in several places, blood showing on her hands, and she wears a disgusted distressed expression while she looks for something in particular. In one hand is a tightly folded piece of white plastic, unreadable marks sketched on it by hand. She lifts the plastic and squeezes a corner, making it glow. The angle is bad. The hawk can't make out the details. The AI monitoring everything feels certain of her identification now, sending a strong alarm to Dirk's apartment while continuing to pick and probe at the incoming data. Is that a map? it wonders. What does she want in that bush? And as if to answer the question, the Flower wades out from the tangle and begins to trot to the next similar-shaped bush.

There is something inside one of them.

The AI makes immediate inquiries, linking to the city libraries and old construction plans, discovering a hidden entry port into one of the multitude of underground passageways leading everywhere. And indeed, she has found the port. But it's sealed, the AI thinks. These ports are kept firmly sealed at all times, Brulé's government not wanting its citizens getting into its cellars.

The Flower wades into the bush, grimacing as she kneels. She doesn't quite vanish this time. The buttery hair shows, and her back, and for an instant the AI disbelieves what the hawk sees quite clearly and accepts without trouble. The port is coming open when it shouldn't, and the Flower is scrambling downward and pulling the port closed again, gone. It's too late, thinks the AI. The quarry is gone. With a thoroughness, it studies its actions and decisions and can find no fault. None. It repeats its alarm to Dirk's apartment, then it turns to things more profitable.

And the hawk, unsure as to the Flower's whereabouts, continues doing figure eights. Until ordered otherwise, or death, it will maintain its vigil. The night air feels cool at this altitude. The moon is a bright green wafer halfway in shadow. Those same eyes that can probe the ground below can pick out the sky's spinning cylinders and wheels, minor worlds and major worlds and stars beyond human reach, and to the south, over the limb of the Earth, the occasional bright bolts of lightning coming on a long, long front.

20

Nothing is so strong as the invisible . . .

—*a Yellowknife proverb*

W E'VE got her!"
    The figure sits up in bed, a pistol showing for an instant. The dry voice asks, "Minus? Is that you?"

"Yeah."

"What did you say?" asks Dirk.

"She's found!"

And now Minus watches the old man come to his feet, thinking that he sure shows the mileage by the way he moves. He can't quite tell what shows—a stiffness, a slowness, a certain sappy resistance to motion—but it's apparent nonetheless. Particularly during these last few days. "Where is she?" he hears the tired voice ask. "You've got her?"

"No."

"But you know it was her?"

"Absolutely." He tells it. Moving to one wall and touching controls recessed into the corner, he causes a variety of images to appear. Largest of them is a three-dimensional map, baffling to the clearest mind, a maze of intricate lines linked and spreading out underneath a portion of Brulé City. One blinking red dot marks where the Flower vanished. There's no knowing which direction she went underground, but Minus assures, "She can't stay in there too long. The city's AIs will find her. The police can pull her out themselves, and she's got to know it."

"We can't cover every way out, can we?" Dirk is concerned but very much in charge now, dressed in trim clothes that lend him a certain poise. "Well," he admits, "at least we know you were right about them leaving."

"Yeah." Minus had spotted the false trail earlier today. Two people leaving Brulé. He had said then that it seemed too easy and maybe they shouldn't waste the AIs and manpower on checking it out. Maybe later, but not today. Minus tells him, "There's more. A lot more."

"What?"

Again he touches the controls, enlarging another image and pushing the map aside. "The hawk got a glimpse of a map, I think. She's going from one safe house to another—"

"Why?"

"She got spooked. That's my guess."

Dirk walks up to the bedroom wall. A local news channel is broadcasting from a district in the east, from a place not far from the Flower's last position, and the cameras show a crazy scene that baffles him for a moment. "What's happening?"

"The floaters? Around the pool?"

"Yeah."

"Medical units. The police are parked on the roof." The swimming pool is halfway empty, a column of vapor rising up into the moonlight where it's stained and spreading thin in the motionless air. "I guess they're bringing out someone. Some miner."

Dirk nods, pressing his tongue against a cheek. "A Morninger, huh?"

"Maybe one of the ones involved in our troubles. Maybe someone hired by this Freestater."

"Maybe?" says Dirk. "I say probably."

"Want another maybe?"

"Try me."

"She was alone. The Freestater is out trying to lay down this false trail, trying to make us believe they were gone. She happens to look out the window and sees this sort of thing . . . well, maybe she thought it was us doing it. You and me."

"What happened to the Morninger?"

Minus tells him. Dirk shakes his head and admits admiration for anyone with the courage to go against a cyborg. "Cleaned him like a raw living oyster," says Minus. "You know? They say the guy is nothing underneath the shell. They won't let the cameras inside, the police won't, because it's too grisly."

"Huh."

"Anyway, she got scared. She ran. Which means she's close to that apartment. To that pool." He tells Dirk what's in the pool, ruined, and then says, "I made calls to our friends in the department. They don't have suspects yet, no. They don't know the story. There's a missing girlfriend, but who's to say?"

"She's not a Flower? The girlfriend?"

"Descriptions don't match."

"So what do you think?"

"Well, I've got AIs hunting through city records. I want to know all the neighbors, everything, but I doubt our Freestater is going to show himself so easily. So I think the four of us should go have a look for ourselves. In the spirit of enterprise."

"No sense waiting," says Dirk.

"I'll wake the others."

"Do."

"The thing I'm hoping is that we can catch the Freestater himself. You know? If she's spooked, maybe she didn't get word to him. Maybe he doesn't know what's happening."

"Don't even tease me with the hope," Dirk tells him, hands sweeping at the air. "Let's get going. We'll take a look and then draw back. Give him a few hours."

"All right."

"And make our AIs keep hunting her. See if they can monitor the city's security systems."

Minus has seen to that contingency. He tells Dirk so, now watching the view from the news cameras. A stretcher comes floating out of the apartment, sheets shrouding a lean unsubstantial figure that shows himself as a pale pink face, hairless and eyeless, and one spidery-long hand without the strength to close itself.

Minus doesn't think about the miner.

He stands with his feet apart, remembering the night when he and that damned Freestater grappled and it came out a draw. Not again, he tells himself. Never again. In his mind, over and over, he wrestles with the invisible figure and doesn't let himself come out short. Not once. It's close but he always wins.

◆ ◆ ◆

The bike is a fold-down model without lights or any excess weight, riding smooth and quiet down the path and Steward pedaling without trying to work himself, sweating but not breathing hard. He had stored the bike in a locker down in the Old Quarter. Using floaters late at night can draw attention, the traffic so sparse. The bike makes sense. It's long after three in the morning. Things have gone well tonight, he has decided. Slowly, in chaotic increments, a trail leading through Jarvis and Luna and into Titan will appear to anyone with the interest. Olivia's Ghosts and Steward have been plugged into one of the main World-Net terminals in Brulé, linking with System-Net and prodding the illusion along. A good night, he reasons, but not flawless. There's more left to do. He needs to pull out his bankable moneys and make a few friends believe he has gone away, the destination unclear. More to do, but Chiffon is alone and he can't stay away any longer. She has gotten to him. She has him so well that he has to wonder if he could fight her talents, given the urge. Maybe tonight, for a minute or two, he'll try resisting. Just to see. Just to discover the depth of her hold on him. That's the funny thing, he thinks. He doesn't truly know how much he's in love, if it is love, because for these last days he has let himself coast without bothering to test the bindings. He hasn't seen the need. What happens if he evades her kisses and her easy praise? Three or four minutes and then he'll take his emotional pulse. Sure. It's not because he wants to break the binds, he tells himself. Not at all. It's because the testing will make the binds more real, biting into his flesh, his glands, and then he'll be free to surrender to her and they'll have their fun and everything will be right for a little while.

The bike rolls onto an upgrade now, gentle but steady.

Steward is alone on the path. There were pedestrians back toward the Old Quarter, but now no one. He concentrates on taking his time. Don't pedal like a maniac, he tells himself. Don't shave off seconds. "Be a rebel," he mutters under his breath. "A little bit."

He starts thinking about time. A specific sum. Five months, give or take, and then the Flower is done.

A cold, weak feeling comes into his knees. He has to shudder, some part of him not doing its job, not keeping tabs on this one sad fact like it should . . . and he suffers accordingly.

He can't let the gloom get into him.

He wills it away, consciously and only with partial success.

Chiffon will die. He has always known it; from the first he was motivated by the knowledge, but somewhere he made a decision with himself, vowing to ignore the truth. How about Ghosting her? He tells himself to ask Olivia Jade about Ghosting a Flower . . . a hypothetical case, he'll stress. He can't begin to contemplate the money it would take. Or the sacrifice. He doesn't even know if Chiffon would agree, provided it's possible. Has it ever happened in the past? He can't remember a time. What do Ghosts think about Flowers? Olivia will know. Sure, he thinks. For a little while he entertains the thought of Chiffon and Olivia being roommates, staving off the horrors of Graytime together.

The slope tops out and the bike begins to roll down toward home. The stream flows beside him, sounding jolly, buoyant and optimistic, and Steward rolls faster without pedaling, finally braking a little and sliding up over a tiny bridge and down and around a course he could follow with his eyes tightly closed.

A water rat is squatting in the middle of the path.

Steward makes a catlike hiss, just once, and the rat wheels and vanishes into the undergrowth.

Almost home, he finds a knot of excitement rising in his throat. For a moment he wonders about the identity of this fellow inside him, this corny boyish goof so much in love. Then he smells something. Or several things, it isn't clear. He detects a lingering warmth and a fishy odor and something without identity. But then it's gone. There and gone. And he files the knowledge beside the wandering water rat, braking and pulling in alongside the public doorway and coming off the bike while it's rolling, lifting his right leg over the hard narrow seat.

The wheels fold into the frame in a few seconds.

The pedals do the same.

Steward drops the bike and kneels beside the stream, breathing once and then pressing his face underneath the water, chilled and marvelous, and he drinks his fill and stands again and lets the residue run down his face and soak his shirt in the front. Then he picks up the bike and goes inside, and when he's in the hallway he pauses, not knowing why. He can't recall having seen or heard anything special. But again he puts down the bike and retraces his steps with a special care. The stream is still running, of course, and most of the windows and balcony doors and patio doors are darkened at this hour. Of course. He looks up and down with a certain studied ease. There is nothing. He can be absolutely sure of the fact. But when he returns to the bike he takes the trouble of looking both ways down the curling hallway. Nothing again. No one and no funny lingering smells, either, and he starts to pick up the bike with one hand, ready to put the frame on his shoulder, and he knows without having to concentrate that his bike, built of durable featherweight plastics and the farts of running gazelles, has suddenly and mysteriously just gained a few grams of unmistakable mass.

He sets down the bike and retreats, taking care not to jostle anything, his eyes going over every centimeter while he feels adrenalin bulling its way through his system, every sense absolutely awake and working hard to find anything anywhere that he can use.

He has a pistol, charged full of pain.

He brings it out with one hand while he focuses on something wrong in the gears of the folded rear wheel. A cartridge has been set inside the workings. No telling what's in the cartridge—probably some kind of gas, explosive or toxic and simply the knockout variety. He steps away and thinks it must be the knockout variety. Otherwise they would have touched it off already. When he was close. They were here, he thinks. They probably have sprinkled remote sensors everywhere, and if this was just him in here he would turn and run out the door, outside and away, or down the hallway until he found an apartment where he could hide . . .

. . . but he has to get upstairs.

The image of Chiffon wells up before him, in the dark, her waiting for him while unseen men work to break the locks on the door.

He takes the stairs three at a time. He comes up into the second-floor hallway, firing, sending blue bolts in both directions and hitting nothing, no one there to serve as targets. He strides to the door, thinking that they have to know just where he'll be going. They can't be this close and not know. Thankfully the locks are tight. The door reports no one has done anything against the apartment's integrity. How was Steward's day? The mag-locks undo themselves. He steps inside ready to fire, wheeling and knowing in an instant that she's missing. He can smell her missing. He has lived for so many years in these rooms that he doesn't need to look further.

Someone is running in the hallway.

The door says she left, his guest left, and gives the exact time and none of the circumstances. "She said to tell you a dirk was in the yard. I'm not sure I understand."

Steward shuts the door and punches a hidden switch under one shelf. The apartment goes into war mode—the third time in more than twenty years. The Masking Glass turns black on the inside, mirrored on the outside, and Steward falls back and asks himself how long before they can unfasten all of his safety features. An hour? These Quito people are a clever lot. Okay, probably less. But they can't afford a long siege, either. He could call for the police. For anyone. So they'll do it quick and dirty, he decides. Explosives. If Chiffon did leave when the door reported—"Was she alone? You're sure?"—then maybe she got free of them. Good girl! he thinks. Why else would they be bothering with me? Of course, they don't have her yet! So he tells himself, Okay. Quick and dirty. They want me alive. They want me to help them find her. Shaped explosives. Out and in. "Who's outside?" he asks the door.

The door describes one of the hairy Quito men. Just one.

"What's he doing? Display!"

One wall shows him kneeling, working with shaped explosives. Just like Steward imagined. I can take him, he knows. How far is he along? Another twenty seconds, no more. So he gives the door orders and kneels like he did in the tunnel a few days ago, preparing to charge at those apes. He braces one foot against the living sofa and breathes hard and consciously plays the scene through his head. Then he says, "Now!"

The door flings itself open.

Steward is up and running, charging, but instead of one Quito man there are three of them, plus Dirk, standing in a row with looks on their faces and guns in their hands. The door's eye is covered with some piece of technical wizardry. False images, of course. And he can't shoot before the gas hits him like a wall, greenish and sickeningly sweet, the strength going out of Steward's legs as the floor rears up in his face, the pain momentary and halfway comforting. It's the one thing he really understands.

◆ ◆ ◆

They got him inside the place easily, without noise, and now Minus and the other two are taking the place apart. She was here. Dirk knows it just by looking in the corners, by sniffing the sheets, by sitting on the bed itself and thinking no, no, she hasn't told him the truth. What's his name? Steward? The big Freestater's feet are visible on the nearer arm of the sofa, him sleeping off the knockout potion, and so far three sets of hands ripping up books and globes and the furniture haven't brought any clues. Not one. Where is she? He can almost feel her warmth in the smelly sheets, he thinks. An odd pang comes to him, to his belly, and when he thinks how much he wants Chiffon he isn't sure how he wants her . . . isn't sure of his own mind. They've got to find her! They'll have to break the Freestater somehow. And fast!

Outside, down in the yard, the swimming pool continues to boil.

Not much water left. The coral is dead and someone from the city has put up barriers—bars of holo light and singing alarms to warn away the careless citizens—and now Dirk stands and gazes down at the scene. A shitty little neighborhood, he thinks. It's hard to know what happened to that Morninger. Probably bad blood between miners. "All right," Dirk says to himself, "what are we going to do?"

And then he knows.

Minus is cutting open the back of the big sofa, the living leather leaking a clear sparkling sap. There's nothing inside but foam and connective tissue. He growls and says, "I give up," and drops his knife on the floor.

"This is what we do," Dirk begins. Minus listens, nodding and telling him that he understands. Sure. "You'll need help getting him up there," says Dirk, "and I'll need another floater. Can you order one in an hour?"

Minus can. "You going on a hunt?" he asks.

Their little thief is probably trying to get outside of Brulé. Dirk has been thinking about the possibilities since he woke up, and that's the best one. That's why she went underground. There are all kinds of big Farmsteads. A Freestater might keep a safe house on one of them, or several houses. "We'll do our looking while you're gone. Maybe we'll get lucky."

Minus is smiling. "It's all turning around on us. It feels pretty good, doesn't it?"

Dirk doesn't want to analyze it. He just wants to move.

"He won't be out much longer." Minus looks at their prize, at the hard sleeping face and the dampened shirt. "I better go. Get this package wrapped up and delivered." He uses strong cord and practiced knots, nothing to chance. Then one of the Quito men takes the shoulders and he has the feet; he glances at Dirk for a moment, his expression asking if there's anything else now. Anything?

"Tell me about it later. All right?"

"A mess of times. You bet."

"We'll trade stories. You with him. Me with the Flower." He feels a little crazy again, Chiffon coming into his head. There are still secret places inside him that love her, and he knows it and works to keep them hidden from everyone. "Till we're sick of telling them."

"Never," says Minus. Then his face turns hard, pink eyes glaring down at the sleeping Freestater. "Hey! Guess where you're going. Hey! You know what I've got planned?"

21

There's a smoothness to Terran clouds. Smooth faces and rounded tops and bottoms that are utterly flat. At night they present an awesome show of light and noise and the implication of enormous, scarcely controlled energies. In the day they are brilliantly white in the distance, and when they come overhead they shut out the sun. They are lids of densely packed vapor, angry and forever growling, and more than once I have heard people mention that when you don't pay for a rain—when the clouds just rumble on by—you feel as though the gods themselves are angry at you, cursing your poverty or your thrift . . .

—excerpt from a traveler's notebook, available through System-Net

THERE'S this voice he doesn't know, cannot even understand for a long choking moment; then he swallows and tries opening his eyes and Steward sees a flash, bright and silent, and his seat drops to the right and makes him ill. He coughs. He blinks and there's more flashing, then he hears the telltale drumming of thunder, and he spots the brightly colored mess of hair and beard growing from the floater's pilot. The pilot is sitting in the front, on his left, and someone else is sitting in the back beside Steward. He hears a young voice, slow and tired. He doesn't know the voice. He's certain. But when it says, "Chiffon," he blinks and turns to look at the stranger's face.

He is a tall man without bulk. A Terran, yes, but he's spent some growing years elsewhere. He's sitting to Steward's left, talking with the dry dead voice of someone who hasn't slept in living memory. Steward can't quite make out the words. The pilot shouts back at him, "His name's the Magician. Or was." It's Minus in the front. "Listen to this, why don't you." Minus hits a button, jerking the Magician into a new position.

250

It's a holo, Steward realizes. The Magician is a recording.

A new voice comes from some hidden place. It asks about Chiffon. The Flower. What was her real name?

"In which life?" he says. The Magician says. "As a Ghost? Or before?"

"Both lives," says the offstage voice. "Begin with the first one. Her situation. Her times."

Steward hasn't a clue as to what's happening. "Zebulina Trish," the Magician begins. "A pretty girl by birth. A halfway wealthy family with a minor kind of prominence in Quito. The mother was a politician, shrewd and probably too greedy for her own good. The father was a sculptor, full of energy and devoid of talent. Zebulina was spoiled in her early years. But then that happens a lot, right? Particularly when the parents hate each other and use the daughter as a kind of prize. And both of them, acting separately, managed to go bankrupt at the same time. The mother lost her political standing. The father had run out of credit. Zebulina was given up for adoption . . . I don't know which parent managed that trick. Maybe both of them working in concert. She became the 'daughter' of a certain elderly gentleman with certain novel tastes. She was eleven years and four months old, and certain debts were wiped off the ledger in the process."

"She was shit upon," says the offstage voice.

The Magician shakes his head. "I don't know. It's easy to feel sorry for her, but she was already pretty good at looking out for herself. I was surprised by what I found in my research." He says, "She made demands from her new father, and she usually won. Zebulina was a kind of artist of manipulation. Absolutely without peer, I think. She stayed with the old man for ten years—five years longer than any previous daughter—and she went into the world with cash reserves and her own roomy apartment and a brigade of suitors already on her doorstep—"

"Not a good girl," says the voice.

"Nor bad. Not really." He tells his invisible audience, "She never did intentional injury to anyone. She juggled her suitors with ease and dismissed them without incident and found replacements from out of the upper echelons of Quito. Mostly male, but not always. Mostly older, but that's demographics talking. She was still quite young, and did her peers have wealth to burn? Not normally. No." He pauses, running one hand over his sleepy face. "I looked at Zebulina and thought to myself, 'Now here is someone who would make a good

Flower, given the chance.' In her flesh-on-blood life, you see, she lived a Flower's existence. Somehow it was woven into her nature—"

A chill comes into Steward now. He shifts his weight, feeling his bound wrists and aware of the lightning outside, but he stares at the Magician's nervous hands, long fingers a little crooked, and listens to the strange impossible story.

"Then she was Ghosted. An accident and no choice, and she changed her name to Wisp and tried to live like Zebulina had lived." He says, "She was shallow." He says, "Wisp, like Zebulina, was incapable of looking at her own life in any objective fashion. She was cunning, yes. And very smart. But she was like a little girl when it came to patience and long-term thinking and her need for constant sensory input. So of course she spent herself into Gray-time. And of course no other Ghost could be lured into giving up his or her moneys. Not for charm, certainly. Not for sex. Not for anything Wisp had to sell."

"You found her," says the voice. "You sold her on something."

Something in the Magician's face starts to shine. He halfway smiles and says, "I like that. I sold her a chance at life, sure." He is proud and a little happy now, nodding and telling the voice, "It's not as tough as you might think. These new Flowers that we're building are very, *very* sophisticated. Laying a Ghost into one of the Chiffon brains doesn't require much that's new or unique. The genius comes from realizing that it's possible and then finding a reason, a target and volunteers—"

Minus hits another button, freezing the image.

Steward is numb. His first impression was that the image and noise was something synthesized by AIs. This Magician is a fiction. And yet now a dozen scattered clues come together when he lets them, staring up at him with predatory smiles. Why would anyone, crazy or not, go to this much trouble just to catch a simple Flower? Crime lords aren't nearly crazy enough, he thinks. At least not the little ones he has known. So why didn't he see the truth before? he wonders. But then he doesn't have to wonder. A harsh pain comes to his belly, and he works at suppressing it. He thinks of Chiffon and feels his stomach turning, rejecting its bile and his last meals, and he turns toward Minus and asks, "What do you want from me?"

"Your cooperation."

Steward waits, saying nothing and trying to regain his balance. His poise. He wants to be absolutely sure of everything—

"She's milked our kindness, yours and mine." Minus tells him, "She's done all of us a lot of grief."

"What did she do?"

"What did she do, Magician?" Minus laughs and punches a button. The holo image jerks and wiggles, time rushing one way or another. Then he's talking again, telling his interrogator:

"—it's more money than all of us could use. It's blood money, stolen by Dirk and beyond legal reach, and with a Miss Luscious Chiffon of my own set inside the bastard's home . . . well, I guess I don't have to tell you about opportunity and greed. Do I?" He is scared. He is looking up at someone and talking faster than he can think. With crisp technical terms he paints a picture of the process— how he put a Ghost into a newly born Flower, how he suppressed Zebulina and Wisp while allowing their pure natures to show through and how he planned to use his own share to make the process work for everyone with the money and desire. He laughs. He says, "I guessed that that much money and my head would make a good team. You know? Maybe it doesn't mean much to you, but I was going to do some real good with those quiver chips—"

Again the Magician stops. This time he dissolves too, coming to pieces and flowing down into the seat and vanishing. Steward looks ahead. He can see the storm clouds coming and hears more thunder, then notices a pair of bright tear-shaped rainboys at the head of the clouds. They're pulling the clouds with the brilliant lassos of pure plasma.

What do I feel? Steward wonders.

It's too much of a shock. He can't judge his own emotions, feeling the cords around his feet and wrists, his hands behind his back and nearly immobilized. He doesn't have the strength to fight the cords. Suddenly he is too weak to breathe, it seems. Chiffon is . . . what? A human being? He thinks it without believing it. She cheated him, he tells himself, and Minus is right. He feels so cold now that he starts to shake.

"How much was it?" he asks.

"The chips?" Minus tells and smiles, enjoying everything, and he touches the wheel and moves them closer to the storm clouds. "She had you like she had Dirk. Believe me."

"I never saw any quiver chips," he says. "Where were they?"

"She's not carrying them in her pockets. No way." Minus says, "A thief in Quito will sometimes make a cut and insert chips into the wound. Which is probably what she managed. Flowers heal, of course, and there aren't even any scars."

"Except she wasn't cut," Steward offers. "I know."

"And you're lying." Minus has to laugh at him, amused by the loyalty. "You are spinning stories and she is still free."

Steward says nothing.

"You and your honor shit. Isn't that what you got taught in the Freestates? Honor? Trust? Teams and tribes and all that nonsense?" He shakes his head in disgust, or amusement or maybe just to shake it and irritate his captive. "The Flower smiled and told you lies and you did her work for free, believing her lies, and you never stopped to consider the mess you were getting up to your ass in. Isn't that what happened?"

"You know a lot about honor, do you? And trust?"

"Not much and enough. Believe me." He says, "What do you think? You're going to die without even giving us a hint as to where we might find her? What if she latches up with someone else? What if she gets out of this mess in the end? Are you thinking about that?"

"Maybe."

"Maybe you should think harder."

Steward waits, then asks, "How did you find out where I was living?"

Minus has a cocky look. His face is tilted, watching Steward and thinking for a moment, then saying, "Your neighbor, the big Morninger, did us that good favor," and his white teeth show inside the beard.

Steward breathes. Okay, he thinks. Okay. She's cheated you. You gave her plenty of chances to be honest, you did everything humanly possible to prove your worth, and this is where it leads. You cut out your soul and set it in her hands . . . and what? What are you going to do? Where do you take it? Breathe hard and think and come up with something, you hard-worn piece of integrity. Try hunting the humor in it, will you? Or get mad and give it your best shot. One way or another.

"My neighbor?" says Steward. "What about him?"

"Forget him." The voice is chilled and final. "What about our precious Flower?"

Steward tells him, "I don't believe you." He breathes and swallows and pinches himself until the pain makes his entire arm ache. Then he makes a hollow place and fills it with the pain, his senses clear and his mind clear and his doubting voice telling Minus, "That Magician is a projection. A lie. You and Dirk cooked up this nonsense—"

"Cooked up? Cooked up?" Minus is furious. Good. He adjusts the wheel and then strokes the buttons of the holo controls, and the Magician reemerges beside Steward, his body tilting and his hands blurring and the scared face begging for mercy. "We'll listen to the whole damned thing, you bastard. I'm not dumping you until you believe me." The Magician freezes, then talks. He starts describing how the Flower can use her skills to bend a man's will, even someone tough like Dirk. Someone that seasoned. He is proud about the Chiffons. His holo leans forward to tell its interrogator about the power of passion and love, and Steward reads everything in that instant. He sees the Magician. He sees Minus. He has a vague sense about the storm clouds and rainboys that are so very close, and he launches himself without warning. His body is tight and sore and extending itself. Minus is staring at the Magician, smugly satisfied. Steward brings his feet up through the Magician's holo, using it as cover for a split instant. Too late, Minus starts to draw back. The pointed toes erupt from the holo's chest and stretch. Too late, Minus is putting one hand into his shirt, hunting the handle of some gun, and Steward's toes strike his forehead hard enough that two of them break, *popping,* and Minus is tossed backward into the dash and wheel.

Suddenly the floater accelerates.

Up it goes, then down.

◆ ◆ ◆

And now Minus is awake again, aware of the floater's descent and his own blazing headache and the Freestater jerking and twisting against the cords, trying to pull his hands out from behind his butt. Minus tries sitting upright. He bumps the wheel and makes the world spin. Then he turns and assesses the situation in an instant, using the throttle and ignoring the headache and somehow trimming them. A rainboy is passing on his right—enormous and liquid-metal bright, the blaring roar of its horns ripping at the air—and he thinks it's a fucking good deal that he caught this in time, look where they were going, thinking how it should take a couple seconds to turn them and get them clear . . .

. . . and Steward has gotten his arms out in front, reaching now and grasping the hair on the back of Minus' head and pulling. Minus feels himself being thrown up out of the seat, over the back of the seat, his hands off the wheel too soon and the rainboy's horns subsiding behind him. His hair pulls from his scalp. He reaches behind his head and grasps Steward's hands while he locks his feet under the seat, the pressure on his back mounting; he can't see Steward but he feels him, can imagine him using his bulk and brawn to break his poor back. So he starts busting Steward's fingers. He feels a little bone snap, then another, and Steward does nothing, won't let go or even flinch, and then he feels Steward's mouth against the meat of his hand. The teeth cut at him. They work from side to side, him resisting, him thinking that no ass-wipe Freestater is going to take him like this . . . and now he looks up through the canopy and sees only clouds upon clouds. Everything is smooth like eggs. Lightning flashes somewhere within, the glow milky-blue and heatless, and Minus curses at Steward with a tiny choked voice, telling him, "We're going the hell in. Now!"

The floater gives a violent jerk, then another.

Minus lets go of Steward's hands and tries twisting out of his grip.

A blue-white bolt strikes the floater, killing the lights on the dash, and now it's dark, like pitch, and now it turns light again, lightning in the distance, and the floater's engines cough before finding purchase again, the winds tugging at it and spinning it around. More lightning comes crackling over them. The two men are facing one another, Steward still bound around his wrists and ankles and Minus wondering how to hit him to put him down. One good hit. He needs one good hit. Water slams down on the canopy, neither man able to scream loud enough to hear himself. I don't dare shoot, he thinks. Not with everything bouncing. There's more lightning and just as the glow subsides, in that instant, Minus takes a hard swing at Steward's throat and neck. But nothing connects. Steward's melted away. You're not fucking going to beat me! he thinks. He tells himself. He wills it so. He tucks against the dash and waits for the next bolt, and when it comes he leaps straight at Steward and takes it to his face, working his cheeks and around his eyes with hammer blows, and then again the big Freestater slips out of his reach, Minus turning, blinking, another bolt and him too slow to miss another one of those kicks.

He's driven up against the canopy.

He slides down its curved face, feeling broken ribs and tasting blood and thinking nothing. He's stunned. Bolts come quickly, without apparent sound, and he's only aware of the drumming of the thick, thick rain. He needs to rest. He wishes he could breath in peace for a minute. Where is he? he wonders. Where are you? It's pitch again.

Absolute night. Minus is sitting in the corner where the front seat meets the curling dead dashboard, and with one bleeding hand he pulls out his gun. Put it on low power, he thinks. Low dosages, he thinks. Then something else occurs to him.

Why need worry? he tells himself.

We're both dead anyway.

Another bolt, white and fat and streaking overhead, and Minus puts a couple of shots into the seat. Twin clouds of stuffing and burned fabric come up into the air. He can't see Steward anywhere. Nothing. Nothing. He shoots twice more, guessing where he might be hiding and spacing his shots. There are more bolts, all colors, all intensities, and nothing like flesh or blood in the air. No hits. "Where are you?" he screams, his voice inaudible. "You red-haired turd—!"

The floater's engines sputter and quit.

Minus is thrown upward, striking the canopy with a shoulder and losing the pistol as he sees Steward's body come out from between the seats, intact and the hands out free now. There's more lightning, and he glimpses the man's broken fingers and thinks that the bones in the hands have got to be shattered too. He had to have busted them to pull them out of that cord, he thinks. And the engines come on again, nothing audible but the floater steadying while it dives. Steward comes over the back of the seat, reaching for the wheel. He trims them. Minus is back in the corner, holding his ribs. Steward punches the autopilot with one swelling finger, lightning turning the rain around them to scalding white fire, and Minus sees the pistol waiting for him on the seat, and he grasps it and shoots too fast, aiming low.

Steward grabs the pistol and his hand and presses both skyward.

Okay, thinks Minus. Drink your air, damn you!

The pistol shoots twice. A section of the canopy melts and flows until the rainwater blasts through with a keening roar. Both men are pressed downward, slammed down, and the rain feels cold and sharp. Again Minus loses the pistol. He doesn't care where it goes. The rain pools around the floor and forces out the air, liters and liters coming in every moment and him getting in a few hits while he has the chance. Punish Steward some more. He knows some ribs get bruised before the man pulls away, climbing into the back end and leaving Minus to pant and think for a minute. God, he decides, this is some fucking waste of a way to end.

The floater is shit. They've probably hit the plasma barrier a bunch of times already, doing a flat-stone skip back into the cloud. It'll never hold up for a straight-on charge, but then they won't take the chance because the rainwater's coming over the seats already. They'll drown first, he thinks. His ears are bursting with the jerking changes of pressure and the noise, and his lungs can't find much good with the air. He coughs hard. He looks for Steward. He sees him untying his feet now, shattered hands just managing the knots, and Minus glances skyward just as an enormous blue bolt lashes out and blinds him.

The floater engines quit.

Then start again.

The water is bitterly cold, churning as the floater tips and turns itself. Minus tries to get close to the canopy's hole, to the last fresh swallow of air. Neither man fights. A kind of truce has sprung up between them. Steward is standing near him, bleeding badly but not caring in the slightest. He's talking, screaming loudly enough for Minus to hear some nonsense about the weight of water and the plasma barrier and maybe, just maybe . . . what? "What?" Minus screams back at him. "It's a draw. Call it and fucking quit!"

The engines die.

The floater tilts and dives, and Minus feels himself being pulled upward towards the hole. Glass and the high wind bang him up. For the briefest instant he feels, or thinks he feels, a hand around his ankle. Restraining him? Or pushing? He doesn't know, airborne now, the storm around him and the floater dead below and the sheer winds coming to pick him higher and higher into the flaring rivers of light.

He can't breathe.

It doesn't seem as though he needs to breathe anymore, his mind clear and comfortable now. He feels as though he is drifting, too numb to notice his body being spun and twisted apart. He thinks this isn't bad, he wonders why he ever thought this was bad. It's just dying. It's easy. All that time he spent dropping people in, and once you're past the fear it's nothing. Pretty lights and noise and nothing . . .

···· 22 ····

The only strength is knowing your strength . . .

—*a Morninger proverb*

"THEY fixed him up with a sound box and ears."

"Yeah?"

"Asked him who did it."

"Who did it?"

"He said he doesn't know. That's what he tells them, at least."

"Doesn't know? Or won't say?"

"Maybe you're right. Who's to know?" she says. "He claims that he never guessed something was wrong. He was tired. He plugged in. It sounded normal, and you know how the draining goes. If you're not looking for the feeling, you can miss it. And by the time they came for him he was pretty well empty."

"They?"

"One of them? A hundred? Who knows?"

The two miners—a woman and a man—have come to see Gabbro after their shift, standing in the hospital room because none of the furniture is their size. They don't like the sight of him lying on the long bed. It's because they know him, sure, and they can feel his pain at a glance. But it's also the way he gasps for his breaths and stares up at them with nothing in his sockets. It'll be weeks before the trauma is far enough past and the doctors and autodocs can make new implants. The same for his ears and teeth. The new hyperfiber shell won't be started for months, and of course that work won't be done here.

"How much did they get?" the man wonders. "The hat. How much did they get when they passed it today?"

"Almost nothing. Next to what he needs."

"There's insurance too," he says. "And Brulé is going to want to look good, isn't it?"

She says, "Sure." She says, "Someone somewhere is going to pay for things. He's got a family on Morning, and I know they won't want him left on the Earth. Not to be doctored."

He says, "I wouldn't want to be here."

"Me neither."

"Terrans doing the work?"

"He'd end up ugly and rattling and clumsy as rolling stones."

"He would, wouldn't he?"

"Terrans," she says. "Small Fry."

"Exactly."

"Which one of them did it, you think?"

"I want to know why it happened." He says, "Maybe this is the start of something. A backlash or something."

"Scare the cyborgs? Something like that?"

"I don't know. Maybe."

And she looks at Gabbro, blinking and thinking. She says, "What happened to that girl of his? The one with lard and no sense?"

"I don't know. Has anyone seen her lately?"

"I *know* I haven't had the pleasure."

"She has a temper, all right."

"Two or three of them, I think."

They glance at each other, then the man says, "Gabbro remembers. I bet he does."

"Why isn't he telling?"

"The shame of it." He says, "I bet so."

"The shame of it," she echoes. She starts to nod.

"Although I don't know how she managed this," and he gestures with one long arm, shivering. "One little woman—"

"We're tough," says his companion. "We fool you studs every day." She stabs with a finger, getting him underneath an arm, and he flinches and turns and starts to wrestle with her, laughing for an instant. Then both of them gaze down at the patient, having forgotten him and their function, and to make amends they lean over Gabbro for a long while and keep absolutely sober. He's one of them, they remind themselves. They have drunk his beer and worked beside him in a rare task, and if they can't recognize him now—not even a little—they still owe him the silence and the unseen image of grief.

◆ ◆ ◆

"It was chance. You were asking about Freestaters and I was working on this . . . incident. At least my people were doing the investigation." The Chief is a bloodless woman of undetermined age, hair braided in a style long without style anywhere and her uniform clean and stiff enough that she might sleep upright if the need ever arose. She has calm strong hands that cannot sweat. At least Mayor Pyn has never seen them sweat. Her voice is one accustomed to success and ready to refuse any small defeats, large defeats denied altogether, and she looks at the Mayor as if to assure him that anyone who works for this city works for her too. She has survived as the Chief of Police through several successful Mayors. Pyn is her boss, yes. He makes a command and she will carry it out, absolutely. But he cannot dream of invading her territory, not ever, or even trying to steal away any of the powers she has garnered over the last decades. It's been seventy years plus, hasn't it? More like eighty, he decides, nodding while he sits in his private suite with the Chief, both of them watching recorded images from last night. A swimming pool simmers like stew in a neighborhood where the Mayor himself has never gone. Not once.

Pyn begins by apologizing. "I'm sorry, I don't understand." He gestures at the shrinking stinking mass of water. "What do Freestaters have to do with this tragedy?"

"Maybe nothing," the Chief allows. "It just happens that they were on my mind, along with our friend Dirk, and a certain coincidence struck me. You may be right, however. It may mean nothing."

"What about Dirk?" he wonders.

"He asked about Freestaters, didn't he?"

"His bodyguard did—"

"Our dear Mr. Minus. Yes." For a long moment she looks at her hands, uninterested in what she finds. Then she says, "I think we were right. Dirk has been robbed and they were fishing for suspects. They saw no evidence of Quito thieves in Brulé, so of course they wanted to know local names. Reasonable."

"I thought so."

"The Morningers were involved somehow." She sighs. She sets her hands down on her uniform's skirt. She tells Pyn, "It is a possibility, no more, that someone talented broke into that Morninger's home. There is no sign of a forced entry, and there's absolutely no doubt as to what the intruder accomplished. It's all quite sad—a young, young miner lying in a hospital now, in agony—and of course I have to wonder if there's some connection between him and Dirk's thief."

"What's his name? Gabbro?"

"The Morninger boy? I don't know." She shakes off his question, plainly uninterested. "The point is that he *might* have been one of the ones who climbed the Cosgrove the other night. We won't be certain until we interview some of his friends this afternoon. And yes, conjecture is unwise. It can be deadly. But if there is a connection, and if this miner was part of the initial scheme . . . well, then what we might have here is a Freestater who has turned greedy and some poor accomplice who has been burned for getting too hungry or too wise."

Pyn suggests, "Someone else might be responsible for the miner. Aren't there any witnesses?"

"Not so far."

"How about suspects? Any non-Freestaters?"

"A girl. A lover given to fits, yes, but this attack has a certain planned viciousness to it." She nods as if she understands all passion and everything cruel. "She is being sought, but we have nothing to put her in the apartment at the proper time."

"Is there anything else?" Pyn knows there must be something. The Chief is not one to jump at conclusions, or even speculations. "Is there some other evidence?"

She looks straight at him. "One elderly woman, a neighbor, recalls seeing the miner talking to some mysterious man who lives across the yard. It may have been before the Cosgrove incident. Or maybe not." She stops as if to collect her thoughts, then tells Pyn, "This mysterious man fits the description of a certain Freestater. Someone known to my office." She shrugs. "Coincidence? I don't know."

"Who is he?"

She looks away from Pyn, saying nothing. She seems a little uncomfortable in this room. Her favorite places, he recalls, are more ascetic—hard edges and worn floors and no windows to ignore. "It's rather odd, actually." She tells Pyn, "Of all the Freestaters, I would have picked others to be tempted by Dirk's money."

"Who is he?"

She squints at nothing, turning back to him. She gives him a brief and thorough summary of the Yellowknife warrior, and he asks:

"That might be our thief?"

She corrects him. "Dirk's thief."

"All right." He says, "Suppose it's true. Okay. How do you propose we react?"

"We do nothing."

"Pardon?"

The Chief tells him, "We do our investigations and then quit, no one found guilty and the file closed." She isn't squinting now. Her eyes are cutting into Pyn, something implied by that expression.

"I don't understand. This isn't like you—"

She says, "You. You allow something like Dirk into these borders, into my home, and then you cater to his needs and believe the lies about investments in your precious mines—"

"A project that could make Brulé wealthy! Something that could transform us into a place of importance—!"

"But not today," she says, her gaze unflinching and her voice giving no ground. "This golden age of yours won't happen soon, and I think it's time to quit pretending and act reasonably and responsibly for a change."

He refuses to blink, asking, "How do you mean?"

"Give Dirk twenty-four hours, no more, to produce meaningful amounts of cash. Contributions. Investments. Whatever word is best suited. Tell him that that is the situation and he must comply or he and his dear friends will be forced out of Brulé City for all time." She says, "There is ample legal precedent—"

"I know, I know!"

"I will back you on this." She says, "My entire staff, excluding Dirk's own agents, will be happy to see them leave."

"Agents?"

"He has several. They've been identified, don't worry."

"And what about the Freestater? Steward? Was that his name?" She says, "Yes."

"We're just letting him go? Is that it?"

She says, "My department is free to pursue the cases we deem most important, yes. But naturally, if *you* insist that we chase this valuable citizen until he and his potential wealth both evacuate Brulé—"

Pyn is furious. He's not weighing justice or trying to be pragmatic at this point. The Chief is pushing him like she has never done in the past, and he resents her attitude and her very considerable sense. He says nothing, holding everything inside himself. Has this job ever been fun? he asks himself. Then he mutters something about feeling bad, about this whole affair feeling dirty somehow . . .

"Everything is dirty. You know that perfectly well!" The Chief shakes her head and stirs in her chair. The uniform creaks and her hands come up to lay on her chin, her expression distant and thoughtful.

Pyn waits, watching her and saying nothing.

After a time he stands and goes to the window, looking down at Brulé, carefully thinking about nothing and spotting details here and there . . . little things he had never quite noticed before . . .

◆ ◆ ◆

Steward had bulled his way out of the storm clouds, out through the plasma barrier, and the engines had started to work again, the dashboard coming alive to the point where he felt as though he was flying the wreck. So he opened the canopy and drained off the water. Then he got his bearings and turned to the north again, retracing the course that Minus must have taken. The canopy refused to close again, something jammed, so he hunkered down over the wheel and tried to nurse the engines home again. Home this time would be the Farmstead east of Brulé. He was careful not to think of Chiffon, not to imagine her waiting for him, not to imagine them even talking to one another, his mind too tired to be trusted and his emotions barely restrained. Later, he vowed. He would deal with everything later. First finish the flight and then you can let yourself go crazy.

Except the flight only went so far as the southeast fringes of Brulé.

The engines were dying one final time. Instruments on the dash measured the process, every light flashing red. In the end Steward went down in the dark, into one of the larger fringing parks and into one of its most remote sections—jungle and swamps and no trails, nothing there but hiding places and wild food and a chance to rest for the first time in an age.

He slept badly, dreaming of Chiffon, then Minus, then Chiffon once again. He came awake sweating and found himself crying like a baby, trembling, and he sat up and saw that it was nearly dawn. He was lying on a bare patch of ground near the place where he had sunk the floater into sucking mud and tall reeds. He shivered in spite of the heat, feeling all of his wounds screaming, and he concentrated until the wounds quieted and he could relax again, in charge of himself once again, not thinking about Chiffon now as he watched the sky brighten in the east. He drifted away again, and this time he dreamed of Yellowknife. Nothing else.

Now he jerks and comes awake.

It is afternoon, the hottest part of the day, and he sits upright and pain shoots down his back and through his hands. He had buried the hands in the coolest, softest mud he could find. Now the mud has dried. It's black like tar and flaking at the edges, and Steward ignores the pain as he beats the crude cast against a tree trunk. The cast shatters. A big worm, pink and glossy, is curled around his swollen right hand. Steward lifts the hand to his face and uses his lips to grasp the worm at one end, and he sucks it down and swallows, tasting nothing. Then he stands and starts to walk, moving slowly and stiffly and always watching for other things that might serve a starving man.

A couple of types of fruiting trees are in season.

Mushrooms shaped like trolls make a meal, then a dozen raw eggs from some flightless bird's nest.

Steward comes out of the park feeling stronger. He tries jogging and quits after a few minutes. He lets himself think about Chiffon, in small controlled pieces, not letting her or the truth do anything to him. He is in control. He is thoroughly in charge of his emotions. His breathing is even, his heart is steady and no one looking at him would believe he was anything but thankful to be alive.

He is a mess.

Stepping into a public World-Net booth, he sits on the padded seat and props back his head so he can breath with a minimum of effort. His feet do not hurt; he doesn't allow them the privilege. But if they were to hurt, the broken toes and the tiny fractures in the little bones would tell him never to stand again.

He wonders whom to call.

Stupidly, he starts to punch for his home and then catches himself. Then he does something nearly as stupid. He starts to call the buried bunker out in the Farmstead. "No, no . . . Don't . . ." He remembers that Chiffon will be there by now. If she isn't caught. No, he thinks, he doesn't want that yet. He wants help from someone willing to give it, someone he can trust, and when he starts going through the list of potentials it becomes apparent that most people won't do him any good.

He starts to cry again.

He can't stop himself.

A little girl hears him sobbing. She looks inside the booth, her expression concerned and a little fearful. "Are you all right, sir?"

"Fine," he says.

"Are you sure?"

"I'm fine."

She leaves. He gets the crying under control but then starts to shiver again. Pain eats at his edges, sapping his strength and his will. He doesn't think about Chiffon. No, no, he won't let himself. Not again. He tries to remember what Minus said last night . . . something about Gabbro showing them his home . . . and he starts to punch a certain long number, thinking that he shouldn't ruin her day like this but maybe she'll forgive him. The far wall glistens and then turns to colors, to shapes, and Olivia Jade is standing at the center of everything. Steward, so very tired and hungry and stupid from all of his troubles, says:

"If you're busy, I'll call back. Some other time."

"Dear goodness! Steward?"

"You've got company. Forget it."

"No, no, no!" She is crying now, actually crying. Why? he wonders. "Don't you go!" she warns him.

"I won't."

"What happened to you?" she asks.

"Oh," he says, "I didn't sleep very well last night," and he starts to laugh at his joke, aching in his chest, his hands finding broken ribs where his shirt is torn. He remembers buying the shirt. He remembers when he met Olivia Jade. His head is full of senseless, feverish details that make no sense. He breathes, suppressing what he doesn't need, and he tells the anxious woman, "What I want is a doctor who's discreet. You know? And who's more discreet than a doctor who has died? You see what I mean?"

◆ ◆ ◆

He doesn't see Minus' floater, not yet, but he won't let himself worry about anything just now. Minus could be anywhere. What's probably happened is that he's got good leads and he's working hard to track them down. Sure, Dirk reasons. Sure. He thinks what he needs is a couple hours of sleep and then they can join up and get back at it. "That's what we'll do," he mutters under his breath. He brings them down onto the floater pad, and the gentle impact makes the injured man grunt. It isn't much of a wound, he thinks. A scratch, really. Dirk intends to take Minus to task for hiring this kind of muscle for them. A weakling. He's eager to see his bodyguard and chew him up and then make up, letting him tell whatever news he has to tell.

Dirk's own news is sorry.

Last night, all night, the three of them tried to hunt the Farmsteads. Fields of crops and stretches of jungle made it all hard work, and the promising sights in infrared turned out to be wildcats and roodeer once they landed, wasting more time and energy.

It was around dawn when their luck changed.

Dirk had ordered all the tailored hawks to the east. One hawk had a possible sighting in a Farmstead with ample cover. Its linking AI told Dirk about the details. She was somewhere up among the old river bluffs, it reported. Dirk nodded and asked about Minus. Did he call in yet? Show up? What? The AI said no, nothing from Minus. Tell me when, said Dirk. Then he asked about the Flower's position and took them toward the place.

It was mid-morning when they set down on the game trail, up on the straight crest of the bluffs. To cover their approach to any watching, worried Farmers, they pretended engine trouble. It was the same trick they had used a few days ago, hunting the Quito boy. They divided up and struck out in three directions, working fast. It was rugged country. The two muscles hated it for the sun and bugs. Dirk felt it in the legs.

Each of them carried a bloodhound sensor.

The bloodhounds were sensitive to a Flower's distinctive stinks.

Both of the muscles got her scent. They called to Dirk and he came and the three of them worked out her direction. At some point, probably realizing that they were following her, Chiffon began to run in the straightest, blindest course imaginable. She led them crashing through jungle and down the backsides of the bluffs, then up hills, then down again. She's panicked, Dirk thought. We'll catch her soon. They found her tracks in the damp earth. At one point she had paused and turned in a slow circle . . . guessing directions? Trying to remember where she was heading? Then she was running again, stumbling and losing one white shoe. One of the muscles found the shoe and set it in Dirk's hands. With both men watching him, he put it to his nose and sniffed. Once, then again. Then he said, She hears us. I bet she hears us right now.

We're that close? asked a muscle.

Yeah, he said. He said, Alive. I want her alive!

The muscles looked at each other, nodded and led the way. They were probably thinking about bonuses, each wanting to be the one to catch her. They went straight up a hill covered with the worst jungle

Dirk had ever seen, thorny brush and sucking bugs tormenting them. She had to be crazy with fear to be running now, he thought. She couldn't last long, he told himself. Not with her body. Dirk remembers how the muscles got too far ahead to see. He remembers one of them shouting back at him, shouting something about a clearing ahead, and then after a few seconds there came a quiet, almost gentle gun blast. You assholes! he screamed. Don't fucking kill her! he roared. He charged up through the undergrowth and got into the open, panting, his weak old legs like gelatin underneath him.

There were Farmers in the clearing.

A gray-haired woman stood staring at them from the top of an old stump. I guess you got lost, she began. You people look like you could use some reliable directions, huh?

What happened here? Dirk demanded. What's going on?

What I think, said the woman, is that we've come upon poachers. Poachers?

Because when your man stumbled on us, do you know what he did? He mistook us for a herd of fat roodeer and tried to shoot what isn't his to shoot.

Dirk remembers licking his dry lips, measuring the situation. Hey! he then said. Listen! We don't mean anything. We can see our mistake. We'll go. Right now.

The muscles were standing together. The injured one was holding his shoulder. Dirk walked up to him and pushed him off his feet, driving him to the grassy ground. Then he repeated himself:

We're leaving. Okay? We're gone!

There was no other choice. He hated it and felt sick because of it, but the woman was watching him and so were the other Farmers, maybe a couple dozen. We can't kill all of them, he thought. If only we could.

The Farmers watched them retreat. They had an enormous floater that lifted off and hung overhead while they struggled back through the jungle. Then they escorted Dirk's floater to the border of Brulé, the injured muscle moaning in the back end and Dirk wondering about Minus. Like he wonders now, the elevator door opening and no one waiting and him feeling so damned alone. Who would have guessed? he thinks.

He punches into the AIs. "Any messages from Minus?"

"None," says the gray voice.

He tells the one muscle to get clean and bandaged. "Then get some rest," he says. "Both of you. We're going out again before dark."

"Going where?" asks one of them. "Back there?"

"Who's doing my thinking? Are you doing my thinking?" He looks straight at them. He says, "Rest."

They shake their heads and leave him.

"Has Minus been here?" he asks the AIs.

"No."

"Has he accessed any of the data stores?"

"No."

"Has he been near the Cosgrove?"

"We haven't seen him."

"Okay," he says, collecting his thoughts and ignoring the worst of them. "Any other messages? From anyone?"

"Two messages."

"Anyone I know?"

"Mayor Pyn. He left a fairly extensive message."

"Give me essentials."

The gray voice delivers a point-blank ultimatum. Contingencies force Brulé into asking for certain payments, good-faith investments, or he will cease to be a welcomed guest by tomorrow. Noon.

"Huh," says Dirk. "Would you look at me? Do I look surprised?" He doesn't feel anything. By then, by tomorrow, he has the feeling it will all be finished one way or another. She'll be out of his reach or she'll be dead, and he'll be rich or a pauper. "The other message. What's it say?"

"It's two words. No voice. No images."

"Yeah?"

" 'Too bad.' "

"Too bad? That's the message? Just too bad?" He gets a sensation in his belly, a burning. "Did he leave a name."

"Of a sort."

"Well what sort of name?"

And the AI pauses for what seems like an age. Then it says:

" 'Too bad.

" 'Signed.

" 'The Rain.' "

23

In the word *garden* is the implication of a fence . . .

—a Garden proverb

Toby spent the night in a closet with a padded body-worn floor and a broken World-Net panel fixed to the square ceiling, cash and no names asked and the door refusing to close tight and shut out the sounds in the hallway. He was the living picture of elation, him lying on the floor with the vivid images still fresh in his head—true delights—and him smiling even while a pair of less elated whores slammed some customer against the door, demanding payment or an appendage in its place. The noise was nothing. The violence was nothing. He didn't care about any of it. Now, thinking back, he can't even remember how the customer made good on her commitments.

And still the elation persists. He has scarcely slept, even in the rare quiet moments, yet he feels fresh and clearheaded and thoroughly removed from his surroundings. For several hours he has been sitting on a living bench in a shady corner of the Old Quarter, in the same rundown district where he found his hotel and obscurity, watching what passes and thinking about many things at once. Like his future. He can't go back to the apartment, the police surely knowing him by now; yet he can't leave Brulé City until he has ample money and the opportunity. And what destination? He doesn't know what to choose, or even his criteria. And how to make the money? Again, he is ignorant. Yet he doesn't feel any pressure from his situation. Not like he would have felt just days ago. The air itself seems blessed with possibilities. It began last night—the transformation, the lifting of his blinders, whatever—him standing over the ruins of Gabbro, his nemesis, knowing now what courage and cunning will produce when applied hard to a difficult goal. Any goal. He can still see his hands pulling away the quivering, dying slices of hyperfiber, the soft wasted skin exposed to the first light in who-can-say how long? The ripping of neural tissue brought anguish—a suitable justice—and he smiles at the memory, the pleasure something joyless and colorless and cold.

He has no doubts at this moment.

Not one.

And now he consciously turns his attention to the remote future. What to do, what to do? He tells himself to wait. He needs to go somewhere and apply his newfound confidence. His father won't live forever. But until that date he needs to make the most of his exile. Toby starts to think of himself as a political exile—someone in a rare position to study Garden from without and make bold pronouncements about its society and its far goals. He can feel his studies and his thoughts on the Prophet Himself percolating out from his bones, some ultimate answers to come. To emerge from him, proud and true and ready to win converts among the Gardeners themselves. Purity for the Garden! The Prophet's words must live again, unalloyed by these evil times. He feels himself on the brink of something great, vaster than him and wiser, and he has nothing but contempt for all the people in all their vulgar shapes who walk past him now, ignoring him or not, ignorant of so much and so far beyond the Prophet's reach.

The afternoon is passing into dusk now.

The sun has dropped behind a drab stone tower at the end of the narrow parkway, the shade in Toby's corner extending and merging with the tower's shadow and him watching the mix of people change by degrees. The whores are coming out to work, fresh-faced and secure in their homeland. A single male whore spies Toby and comes to him, sitting without an invitation on the far end of the bench. He says, "A lovely night," with a thin conviction. "Don't you think so?" One of his hands is picking at a place where the bench's bark is missing, some colorless fungus eating the wood beneath. "But we're going to get a washing later, I understand."

Toby gives him a stare, saying nothing.

"Well," the whore replies amiably, "fuck you," and he stands and leaves.

No, Toby believes, he cannot be bruised anymore. He is immune. From somewhere in his experience, World-Net or deep in his childhood, he recalls the descriptions of religious conversion and finds that they apply to him. Clarity. He is buoyed up by a crystal clarity, uncompromising and undeniable and eternal. The Prophet Himself must have once felt the same. What I need to study next, he thinks, is the Prophet Adam. Not just Him but His times. His place. What was the Earth in that remote age? What awful abominations did he experience day by day, and what was the source of His great visions?

Time passes, Toby lost in the dreaming.

Then he suddenly blinks and looks out on the curling path. A familiar shape wearing the usual skullcap is passing him. It takes Toby a long instant before he can bring himself back to the present, to here, but then he leans forward with his eyes squinting, following the walking figure as she moves without elegance or haste.

Toby stands.

He begins to follow, planning nothing and careful not to get closer to the whore. He's just watches as she moves through the gathering gloom, to the stone tower and then right and then left and left again. He feels curiosity. He wants to see a customer or two. How does she win them? How does she play with them? Will she treat them differently than she treated him? He stops and steps out of sight when she begins talking to some nondescript Terran man. Her laugh is unmistakable. That build is unique, the enormous stone-hard breasts poking the man in the side. It's all the same, he thinks, and he follows them. Another hotel famous for closets and cash, and Toby sits on another bench and watches the entrance while he waits for the whore.

It is night. The wind, mild for most of the day, begins to gust from the south. If anything, the heat has grown worse since the sun has gone down. Toby starts to sweat, ignoring his discomfort, counting the quarter hours and watching the path, too. A uniformed policewoman is standing under some lights beside a floater pad. She's looking for me, he thinks. He can't imagine that there isn't some sort of alert, at least for questioning him, Gabbro's neighbor, and that's why he bought the floppy-brimmed hat earlier today. And new clothes. And that's why he's avoided the police when he has seen them. Nonetheless, he realizes, they will find him in time. No amount of cleverness can save him in Brulé.

The policewoman strolls down the path toward him.

Toby is careful, ever-so-careful, sitting there as if he has no concerns in all the world.

And she passes him, looking at him and blinking and gone. He is safe again. Invincible. He fights the urge to chase after her and taunt her with his face, proving his invincibility. But don't, he thinks. "Don't even consider it," he mutters, one hand wiping his forehead dry.

The whore, minus customer, emerges from the hotel.

She continues toward the south with a certain studied deliberation, and Toby begins closing the gap between them. He doesn't have any exact plan. His interest now is obscure even to him. Yet trailing her seems right. His every motion brings him closer to something . . . he isn't sure what . . . but now, without warning, he glimpses what he needs to do. The whore has stopped and turned, spying him. She seems to smile, inviting him closer. Does she remember him? He can't know. Does it matter to her? Apparently not. She waves at him, beckoning him, and he stops and waits and she seems to say, "Bashful," to him and shakes her head and points. Buildings surround a narrow dead-end parkway. She turns and walks up the parkway, out of sight, and Toby looks both ways and sees no one else and goes to the mouth of the parkway and squints and can just make out the swirling colored light of the whore's skullcap. She's up there waiting for him. He knows it.

Slowly, without noise or tentative motions, Toby moves halfway to the whore. Then he turns into an absolutely black patch of shadow, kneeling behind thick tree trunks, and he sweeps the ground with his hands and finds several dead branches. He chooses one. He breathes and grasps it and waits. The whore can't see him. She grows tired of his bashfulness, walking back down the path. She has no warning. He is up and swings and the branch catches her on the back of the head, bone breaking and the skullcap flashing red, and Toby is on top of her, tugging at her limp arms and pulling her into the shadows, buying time.

It takes him a few long seconds to notice the face. It isn't the right face. For an instant he feels cheated, groaning softly before he comes to his senses. Hurry! He goes through her pockets and her private places, finding two rolls of glass bills and a single quiver chip of unknown worth. Then he stands, looking at the wrong face one last time before he flees. The red light pulsates behind him. He is running out of the parkway, and then he catches himself and slows and looks both ways without haste. There is no one. People are in the distance, but no one is nearby. That face was all wrong, he tells himself. How could I have missed it by so much? He shivers, walking now. Money in his pockets and nowhere to go. He starts to smile, then laugh, then skip. Then he starts to whistle, and the wind gusts in his face, hot and damp.

‹ ◆ ◆ ◆ ›

"I'd like, if I could, to have a few words with you."

"I don't know," he responds. "I was about to get up and have a walk."

No answer.

"It's a joke," says Gabbro. He starts to giggle, hearing himself through the temporary ears and imagining a woman sitting beside his bed—dressed in formal clothes, colorless and clean, looking down at him with an outraged, even horrified expression. "I'm sorry," he tells her. "You want to talk?"

"Yes . . . well, yes." She sounds puzzled, off balance. "A joke, yes. I suppose humor's part of the healing process." Gabbro hears her shifting in her chair. "What I want," she confesses, "is to ask you some simple questions. If that's possible."

He says, "Sure."

"First, how are you feeling?"

"Good."

"Is there pain?"

"None. None at all."

"Is there any sense of boredom? Any hallucinations? Anything that implies sensory deprivation?"

"Not really," he assures the woman. The doctors keep plying him with drugs to curb any of that nonsense. In other cases, particularly where the trauma wasn't so severe, they would leave temporary senses lashed to the patient all day or stimulate the brain by artificial means. But not with him. Not with profound trauma of his magnitude. That's their word—*profound*. Not simply bad or ugly, he thinks. "They've got me good and pickled," he says. "I've never felt better." It's like drifting in darkness and not feeling your hands or feet, or anything. He asks, "Who are you? Did you tell me?"

"I work for the Brulé mines." She mentions her forgettable name, then tells him, "I'm involved in public relations and the miners."

"Well, what else can I tell you?"

"There is one item." She pauses, then wonders, "The police have interviewed you several times. You say you can't recall who attacked you, am I right?"

"I never saw a face. Nothing in focus, at least."

"Did you hear them?"

"No," he lies.

"How many were there?"

"I told the police."

"You don't know."

"How can I know?"

"You were powerless."

"Pretty much."

"And you don't know who attacked you?"

"I guess that's what I'm saying." Gabbro tries guessing the point in all of this nonsense. "I don't know. Maybe it was a mistake."

"A mistake." Her voice is level and slow. "How do you mean?"

"Well, I've been thinking hard . . . because I want to help you people, I do . . . and the thing is that someone might have confused me for another miner. Anyone. I don't know."

"Like who, for instance?"

"What miner? I don't know."

She clears her throat and then makes no sound for a long while. Then she tells him, "Frankly, I came here hoping for some statement from you. A few words to the effect that you do not blame Brulé or any of its citizens for the tragedy that has befallen you." She clears her throat once again, with more force this time, and asks, "Is that possible?"

"A statement?"

"If you'd like, I could supply the words."

"All right. Sure." He says, "Anything to be helpful."

"Fine. That's just fine." She moves in her chair, then changes the subject once again. "I'm also here to assure you that every step is being taken to see you home and recovering soon. As soon as possible. Believe me."

He says nothing, knowing just what she means and ready for the moment. He's been thinking of little else all day.

"Gabbro?"

"Yes?"

"I'm sorry. Did you hear me?"

"As soon as possible?"

"Absolutely—!"

"But the thing is," he explains, "I don't see the need."

"Excuse me?"

"Going home."

"Oh, no. No. I'm not talking about your apartment, no. I'm referring to Morning. You'll be returning there!"

He waits, imagining her flustered face and her stiff straight back. She says, "Your friends and family are eager to see you well again. I'm told *everyone* is concerned."

"Just the same, I'd rather stay here."

"Pardon me?"

"On the Earth."

"Oh. I see." She sounds profoundly disappointed. "I guess you've caught me by surprise. You don't want to return to Morning?"

"I've thought it through—"

"I would hope!"

"—and it's too much a shithole. All things considered."

There is a long, studied pause. Gabbro hears the clicking of an autodoc, then nothing, then she tells him, "You know, we can't care for you here. We don't know how to—to reapply your body, for one thing. We simply lack the experience. And then there's the matter of who will pay for such a thing—"

"Listen," he says. "Try listening."

She doesn't move, doesn't speak.

"I don't want the hyperfiber. A minimum of prosthetics when the time comes, and the usual strength training for my limbs. Okay? Nothing more. I don't expect anything more." He informs her, "That way has to be cheaper for everyone. Morning. You. Everyone."

"And this is what you want? Honestly?"

"I do."

"Because what I am hearing is not what I expected. People are going to be quite startled."

"They'll live."

"Yes, well . . ." She has run out of words. Gabbro detects a whiff of disgust coming from her direction, as if she blames him for causing her enormous trouble. Finally, her professional calm up and running, she asks, "Is there anything I might do for you?"

"Leave a message at my apartment. For anyone who calls or comes by." He says, "Have them tell April to visit me here. When she has a chance."

"April?"

"A friend." He says, "I haven't seen her for a few days." That much is true in a literal sense. There were two voices when he was flat on his back last night, so terribly weak that he couldn't focus his eyes or move his smallest finger or make out the other voice well enough to remember it. He doesn't care about identities. What he does know is that April was surprised and sick when she realized what was to happen, that someone had used her to get at him . . . that what happened—and this is the best guess he can make after many hard hours of thought—is that she met up with some sadistic bastard and got pulled into his fun. Poor April. Poor, poor Gabbro. He sighs and tells the woman, "April may not know about my accident. Tell her to come here and we'll talk. I just want to talk."

There is a pause. Then she asks, "Is there anything else? Any other messages?" She doesn't want any more trouble. That shows in her voice.

He says, "Nothing."

She says, "Well then."

"Thanks for everything," he tells her. "I mean it."

"Thank you for your time. Someone will be in contact with you soon," and the autodoc unplugs his ears and sound box with a spluttering splash. Gabbro feels exhausted now. He needs rest. Sleep comes easily in this new world, his dreams peaceful and long and full of colors brighter than life. No, he thinks, he's made the right choices. He can't explain them to anyone, not even to himself, but they're his choices and he intends to stick with them.

He's not returning to Morning. Not when he has to go through hell just to get a new body, and not when the only thing he's got waiting for him is a shithole job in the mines.

And yes, he'll talk to April. Tell her that he doesn't blame her. Not really. Tell her to forget things, including him, and get on with it. And no, he won't ask who she was with. He's confident it's someone sick, because who would hate him so much that they'd do such a wicked thing? God, he thinks. He doesn't want to know. He just doesn't.

And now he is close to sleep, drifting back into the friendly warm blackness. Sometimes he dreams about Steward, and he's always dreaming about Steward's Flower. Once it was both of them and him, and the three of them were in the little swimming pool together, nothing happening, and it all seemed so real that when he woke he was sad. For a long time he was sad. They hadn't said anything or done anything special. It was just the three of them sharing the water, but oh God was he ever sad . . .

◆ ◆ ◆

The crest of the bluff is finally won. She halfway staggers up out of the jungle, up into the hot driving wind, the long grass nodding and the far lights of Brulé showing to the west. This is the place, she remembers. This is where she started to get lost. Don't do it again, she tells herself. Don't get fancy. Don't panic. Sit and carefully read the map, and find cover before the storm comes. That's what's important now.

It had been Dirk chasing her this afternoon.

Thinking back, Chiffon is certain that she heard his voice among the buzzing and screeching jungle sounds. And a shot. And by then she had been so terribly tired, and dry, a Flower's body not designed for marching or long runs. So she had climbed beneath a downed tree, leveling her pistol at the place where she imagined Dirk would appear. She had told herself that she'd shoot him, only that wasn't so easy to imagine. She hated him; he had no worth; yet she laid in that damp hiding place and struggled to get a grip on the trigger.

And in the end, no one came.

An enormous floater lifted off the clearing below Chiffon, lazily vanishing over the treetops, and when she could breathe again she stood and tried to find her bearings. Ever since she has been wandering or resting, and now at last she has herself plotted. Exactly. The glowing map drawn by Steward is precise and unmistakable.

She walks north on the trail.

So many meters, she thinks, and then there will be trees in a distinct arrangement. She doesn't hurry, hopes no one is watching, and tries to recall Steward's exact instructions on how to enter his hideaway.

He will probably be waiting there, she tells herself.

Waiting for her and worried.

She doesn't have to consider what she will say. She knows. She won't have to feign any moods or tell any fables. Not now. Dirk is on their heels and she's never been so happy to be with someone. She will cling to him, honestly weeping. Even now she feels weak in her knees to be so close to him. He has to be waiting for her, she thinks. *He has to be!* Her aching legs carry her along, her poor bare feet cut and bruised and glad to be on the trail's bare earth, and suddenly, without warning, she imagines eyes—stopping and turning and studying the empty trail behind her for a long, long moment.

Lightning and a blue-lit wall of towering clouds cover the southern horizon. The wind dampens the rumbling of thunder. There are no watching birds tonight. Nothing wants to fly, it seems. She remembers the last time she felt eyes, hating the sensation. She had drunk warm rainwater from a natural stone basin, sharing it with a single enormous stone-colored toad. She remembers napping for a little while and then waking with a jerk, knowing someone was close by and staring at her. She sat up. The toad was gone. She looked around and sniffed, smelling herself—the pheromones, the soul-robbing chemicals manufactured by her rested body—and then she happened to look upward, spotting the eyes she had felt. It wasn't a crime lord or Farmer perched on that high branch. It was a wild tailored ape. In one of its hands, sharp and new, was a stone knife. The ape was watching Chiffon and using the knife to carve something in the stump of another branch—a stubby ivory-colored stump made to resemble a male organ thoroughly aroused.

She shivers in spite of the heat, remembering the moment.

She turns to look toward Brulé and sees the trees she was hunting. What luck! she thinks. She might have walked straight past them.

The new trail is hidden and halfway impassable. She wishes for shoes, any two shoes, wading into the underbrush and concentrating on every step. She can see no one. There's no one to see. She almost forgets the sensation, and then someone is standing straight in front of her, appearing without noise or apparent motion. She gives a little shout and falls backward. She starts to fumble for the pistol, and Steward says:

"Chiffon."

"Steward? Oh, goodness. It's you! I knew it was you!" She stands and moves toward him, reaching and feeling so terribly happy. It's him! It's him! "Look at you," she says. "How are you?" Her hands close around him, but suddenly all she can grab is air.

She says, "Darling?"

He has stepped away. She can make out his face in the lightning's glare, and she feels startled and honestly concerned. "What happened to you? Darling, what is it?"

He says, "Nothing."

She says, "It's something. What is it?"

"Don't touch me," he says. "Stay there!"

She freezes, squinting at him while the panic rises inside her. She sees hands dressed in flexible splints, rubbery and strange, and there are bandages on his face and something wrong in the way he stands there. He doesn't say anything else. She can't tell what he's thinking, but she can guess. She can't know what's happened, yet she does. "What did they do to you? They found you?"

"They found Gabbro first." His voice is tight and dry.

"I know they did. I didn't know how to warn you, love. But I was afraid—"

"You ran."

"Of course." She says, "What did they do to you?"

"Well," he tells her, "we had a conversation."

She freezes. She cannot move or breathe or even think, watching the man while he stares at her. She is suddenly so cold, so weak, trembling and wondering when her legs will collapse.

"Minus told me some things," he begins. "About a girl and a Ghost."

"Steward—?"

There is a delicate silvery knife in one of his hands. He says, "I saw one of your accomplices. Some magician—"

"I'm sorry," she tells him.

He asks, "What should I think?"

"The worst," she says without hesitation. "About me, the very worst."

"Okay." He lifts the knife and then flips it down to the ground, the motion quick and exact. He says, "I don't want to touch you." He says, "Show me."

"Show you," she says.

"Right now."

She sits. She takes the knife in one hand and looks up at him, at his face, and then uses the other hand to probe at her leg. No painkillers this time. No preparations. She takes a breath and holds it and pushes once, the blade cutting without resistance, and then she feels the quiver chips halfway to the bone, nestled in the special cavity, and she grimaces and moans and tells herself that the sharp blade means something. If Steward were truly angry he would have given her a jagged dull blade. She very nearly dies for the pain, bending forward and starting to weep now, dropping the knife and reaching into the bloody wound with two fingers. It takes an age to remove all twelve chips. They are nothing in her hands. She throws them on the ground before her, and then the knife, and then she finds her pistol in her pocket and tells Steward, "You know, if I were the person you think I am . . . I bet . . . I wouldn't do this now. I bet."

She tosses the pistol on top of the quiver chips.

And Steward seems surprised for an instant. A flash of lightning shows him looking at her and then the gun again. Then he kneels and picks up everything, saying nothing. He counts the twelve quiver chips with slow deliberation, and he cleans each of them by placing them in his mouth for a few seconds. Then he says, "I don't know," with the same tight, dry voice. "I just don't know." And he stands and slowly walks away.

24

A minister and Flower are riding up a skyhook together . . .

—*from a Quito joke*

THEY'RE out in the front room telling lies about women, about the kills they've made, about people neither of them have met and places that would never let them past the front door. All lies. Dirk listens to them without actually hearing the words. He hates this shit, not knowing what to do, what move to make, needing to go back to that Farmstead again and not trusting these jerks to do what's needed. It's as if Minus abandoned him. That's how he feels. It's like he left him here with these jerks and doesn't give a good shit as to what's going to happen now, to the chips or anything. By what right does Minus get free of this job? I trust the son-of-a-bitch all these years, he tells himself, and when I need him most he's gone. Damn him! Damn!

He is sitting on the edge of his unmade bed, a picked-over plate of cold food on his nightstand. He is dressed but barefooted and running both hands through his matted hair. It's night now. He has scarcely slept. When he isn't angry the tiredness drags him down, so he nourishes the anger in plenty of ways. The Freestater. The Flower/ Ghost. Minus and the jerks in the next room. Plus Mayor Pyn and that hard bitch of a police chief. There's no end of reasons to keep awake and alert.

"A call for you." The AI's voice grates on him. Good.

"Who is it?" he asks.

A pause. Then, "The Rain."

He stands and turns toward the largest wall, breathing in and forcing himself to relax, to let out the air, to use a natural voice when he tells the AI to trace the call when The Rain speaks.

The Freestater, Steward, is sitting in a small, bland windowless room. He might be alone, might not, wearing splints and clotting foams and big bandages and clean clothes. His expression shows nothing. He stares out at Dirk and with a hard clipped voice he says, "We need to meet."

"Is that so?"

"Get this business over and done."

Dirk waits, acting confident and cool. He agrees. "You're absolutely right," and he nods and tells him, "You've got something of mine. I hope you're ready to give it back."

"I count twelve things," he answers.

And Dirk's ready. He had figured that the Freestater would have the chips by now. Sure. "Twelve?" he says. "I count thirteen. I want the Flower too."

"She's dead."

"Then the body. Give it to me."

"We'll see." Steward has the chips in one hand, in a neat white stack. "Sorry about your man," he says, something showing in his eyes. Something half-wild and unbeaten.

"Forget it," says Dirk. "That's business."

"I'm going to want a finder's fee. A share of these."

Dirk says, "I guess that's fair."

"Half."

"Half of one," he says.

Steward shakes his head. "I don't have to bring them in, you know. I can just keep them and let you come after me."

"I can do better than that." Dirk tells him, "I know a hundred hungry people in Quito who'd love a shot at you. You think you can hold them off forever?"

"Three."

"One."

"Two," says Steward.

"One."

For a full minute Steward does nothing, says nothing, simply staring out at Dirk. Dirk thinks about Minus again, then the Flower. Then Steward tells him, "All right. One quiver chip."

"And the body. I want to see the body."

"Maybe I'll flush your chips down the toilet. Your hundred hungry friends would have their work cut out for them then."

So she's alive, Dirk thinks. She's fooled both of us, he wants to scream. One of us has to fucking kill her! But he resists, saying instead, "One chip and here's where we meet." He lays out the terms. Two hours from now, on the roof, chips and no one has weapons. "Agreed?"

"Sure," and the image dissolves into whiteness. Dirk drops back onto the bed and finds socks and shoes, and the AI calls to report that the Rain's line couldn't be traced. No surprise there, thinks Dirk. He goes into the front room and tells the jerks to get themselves together. He wants them to gather all the hardware they can carry and stash it on the roof of the Cosgrove. "Make diagrams," he warns them. "I want to know what I can reach when I need it."

"He dies?" asks one of them.

"What do you think?"

The two of them look at each other, halfway smiling.

"If you can," says Dirk, "do him quick and neat. Don't let him have anything free. Nothing free."

"Who is he?" says the other one. "He's nobody. We'll take him."

Muscled jerks, thinks Dirk. From their skin to their bones they're nothing but jerks, and this is all that's left him.

◆ ◆ ◆

Chiffon sits with her sore leg extended and a med-kit at her side, watching Steward prepare. He takes a worn round box from his shirt pocket and carefully counts out the twelve chips, putting them into the box and securing the lid and returning the box to the pocket. Then he removes the splints from both hands, his face hard and his motions precise. He places small metal blades against his swollen flesh and refastens the splints. She can hear him breathing for a moment. She sees him slip another blade into his clothing, and then he takes a funny twist of metal and stuffs it into his mouth, up between his gum and cheek. That seems to be all. He gives the little room a quick look, his expression impassive. His hands hang at his side, touching nothing. She wonders how he feels. The outer door is shut and she's sitting with her back against it. She couldn't see Dirk from where she sits, but she heard him bargaining with Steward; there isn't a doubt in her mind as to what he intends.

"He's going to kill you," she tells Steward. "You've got to realize that!"

He says nothing. He doesn't look in her direction or in any way act as if she has spoken.

"Are you going to listen? Hey!" She says, "Why are you going? Why? He isn't going to let you live two minutes—"

Steward lifts a hand, making her stop. Then he turns and says, "I owe this to someone. Okay?"

"To who? To Gabbro?" She shakes her head. No more sweet words. No more patience. This is the honest Chiffon/Wisp/Zebulina talking now. Mostly Chiffon. "So what are you planning? You go straight at Dirk, on his home ground, to get some sort of justice for something he did to your neighbor." She tells him, "That'll do Gabbro some good, won't it? You're dead and Dirk has the chips, has won, and Gabbro's still skinned alive. Is that what you've got planned tonight?"

With a slow, careful voice Steward tells her, "I don't know you."

"What don't you know?"

He says, "Never mind." He says, "Move. I'm leaving now."

"I won't and you won't."

Steward blinks. He doesn't move. He fills the end of the tunnel, halfway leaning against one wall, and he says, "Try."

"No and I guess you'll have to touch me."

He says, "When this is finished I'll give you all the chips but one. My finder's fee."

"That's awfully damned nice."

"You're a client. This is business." He says, "Forget nice."

"And why don't you put yourself in someone else's place and forgive them? Learn to do that and maybe you could forgive yourself for all kinds of shit, too. If you tried."

"What are you saying?"

"Like Chaz, for instance."

He starts to come down the tunnel, angry enough that he has to rein in his anger. He says nothing. He hits a button and the door starts to open, Chiffon sliding clear and hearing the wind now, feeling the warm damp air bulling its way inside. Steward is past her without having brushed against her, reaching now to grab the dangling rope. She sees him framed against the lightning and a pair of bright, distant rainboys. What to do? she wonders. Painkillers from the med-kit are working. She can stand without too much discomfort. But she doesn't get close. At least not too close. "I'm going to follow you," she promises. "I am."

"Do what you want," he tells her, shrugging.

"You've got an awfully high horse, Steward."

He has the rope in both hands. He turns to look toward her, then checks himself. Then he jumps and descends hand over hand, the rope taut and flinching and him gone in an instant. She looks out at the swaying trees and the approaching clouds and wonders what's reasonable. I should let you kill yourself, she tells herself. I'll wait out the night here and then go charm some Farmers . . . live out my months with them. That's better than dying now. Anything's better than that, she thinks. Sweet sphincters of God, she thinks, I nearly killed myself scrambling down here in the first place. I could break my neck trying to chase you and what good would that do anyone?

Thunder breaks against the old river bluffs.

She blinks. She decides to stay, wait here and not even worry. But then she can't make herself back away from the door. Not for anything. Her pistol is on the floor, on top of the med-kit. Steward gave it back. She has glass money in her pocket. Kneeling, she scoops up the pistol and puts it with the money, and then before she can think it through again she leaps, grabbing the rope somehow and sliding, feeling her flesh burning and wondering how Steward managed this with his hands. Those poor sad hands.

◆ ◆ ◆

A few sloppy raindrops strike the floater's canopy, and the wind smears them and then pulls them back into the air. Steward leans and watches the Old Quarter passing below. He tries to think about nothing but what's next, that's what matters, only all sorts of nonsense creeps into his head. Like that bar. He sees a brightly lit patch of glass—the roof of that bar where whores play edible chess—and he guesses that someone will soon kill the lights so they can watch the storm. He sees the nondescript windowless tower where Olivia Jade lives, in a sense, and he tells himself that he should have left her a message of some kind. Just in case. Then he whispers, "Listen to yourself," and shakes his head and starts moving in the seat, stretching, tendons cracking and the muscles complaining. With his tongue he checks on the little pain grenade, tiny and hopefully hidden. He breathes and catches himself before he starts dwelling on the stupid things. He is in control. He tells himself so. He breathes and feels no better for stretching, and he glances downward again. He can't make out the glass-roofed bar. It's past or it's darkened now . . . there's no telling which . . .

The Cosgrove Tower is the highest structure in view, lying straight ahead, the strokes of lightning visible on its faces and its roof dark and bursting with groomed little trees. Steward can't see anyone on the lone floater pad. He tells the floater to circle once, in close, and then to set down. If it would, please. If he were laying an ambush, he thinks, he would do it this way. Or this way. Or this way. He makes quick mental maps of the landscape, and he tries guessing how long the rain will hold off. Two figures have appeared at the edge of the pad, the thin one Dirk. They look uncomfortable in the gusting wind. Steward flexes his hands and tucks away the pain, at least most of it, and he tells himself not to be fancy or clever. This is no place for showboating now. The floater is down. He can see Dirk's face smiling and the placid, stupid expression on the Quito muscle at his side. The other muscle will be sprawled out in the little trees, trying to keep the crosshairs on Steward's head. He'll be working for a clean shot, probably holding off until confirmation that Steward's got what they want. He wonders what the muscles know. He thinks of making a deal with that one beside Dirk, playing with his greed. Then he tells himself to quit it. Nothing fancy. Just wait for the opening and let instincts rule—to a point—and make it so Dirk won't hurt anyone again.

The canopy comes open, the smell of rain thick in the air. Dirk is stepping closer, the smile too large and the confidence close to brazen. Steward comes out of the floater like an old, old man. He shows everyone a feeble body, torn and bloody and close to helpless. "Think of Gabbro," he says to himself. "Think of him and get it done."

"What was that?" asks Dirk.

"Let's get this done." The three of them are standing close together now. He tells Dirk, "I've got them," and pulls out the round box. The wind is at his back. A few more sloppy raindrops fall, icy cold on bare skin. He kneels as if his knees might break. He breathes as if he's in utter agony. Without watching Dirk or the muscle, Steward keeps aware of how they move in response to him. He senses the lane of fire. Time is crawling while he works the lid free of the box, and Dirk is kneeling before him and watching with his tongue partway extended and both hands set on the pad with fingers spread. He looks ready to jump. He tells Steward to count them.

"First," says Steward, "show me you're clean. No guns."

Dirk nods. He and the muscle both open their shirts and turn once, one at a time, and pull up their pant legs. There's no trace of weapons, meaning nothing. Then Dirk tells him, "I trust you. You're honorable, right?" Very brazen. "Let's get on with this."

"Sure." Steward counts the chips. He has them in one sore hand and puts them back into the box one at a time, stopping at eleven and then making a show of swallowing the twelfth chip himself. He stares straight at Dirk while doing it. Then he secures the lid again.

"Cute." Dirk is amused. One of his hands decides to reach for the box and the standing muscle starts to shift his weight ever so slightly, tilting backward, and Steward slips the little pain grenade to his front teeth and bites hard and aims and spits. A blue plasma cloud blooms in front of him, and Steward is up and running as a burst of hot air comes in behind him, the shot missed. Dirk is screaming, falling backward and writhing in terrible pain. The standing muscle is taking it somehow, and Steward has to rush into the blueness and take the muscle himself. He uses a knee and then his elbow, his every last nerve on fire. He has the man stumbling backward. They're off the pad and in the air, falling down among the trees as another blast of hot, hot air just misses him. Steward rams his knee into the breastbone, landing on top. Then he rolls and tries to break an arm with a quick motion, missing with his motion, the muscle suddenly on top now with a knife pulled from somewhere.

Steward breaks the muscle's nose.

He grabs both wrists and turns him and pushes him against a wall of branches, ripping the knife free and then using it. Key tendons cut like cheese. The Quito muscle is down, helpless and finished, and Steward stands and runs hard and drops, hearing someone shooting at nothing and then hearing Dirk shouting into the wind. He can't make out the words. Smoke is rising off the floater pad, and sparks are pouring from the floater's gunshot engines. Where to go? he thinks. Their only move is the elevator, he thinks. He gets up and runs too slowly, his feet heavy and the air like syrup. He doesn't hurt anywhere. All he feels is a nagging dreamlike stupor. Where's that sniper? What can he see? Near the elevator door, by the greatest good luck, is a heating vent old enough and sloppy enough to mask his presence to someone with night goggles. He gets beside the vent and crouches, breathing hard for a minute. He thinks how they'll have to come past him to get free. How much time is there? The floater's pilot might be calling the police, or maybe not. Probably not. It's probably assuming mechanical failure, power down and no passengers. So a routine maintenance call. And will Dirk try getting his own floater airborne? Steward can't see how. In the open? On that pad? He can't know my weapons, he thinks. He can't risk the exposure.

So he sits and he waits.

After a few minutes the rain begins to come hard, lightning straight overhead and thunder reaching into the bones. The rain feels warm now, beating down on the little trees and the neat trails and sliding down the elevator's heavy metal doors. Steward pulls out the blade hidden in his clothing. He drives the muscle's knife into the earth and squints out into the rain, trying to keep alert. He can see the pad when there's lightning, and he doesn't count the minutes but they're piling up high. He ignores the rain. It begins to feel cold but he suppresses the shivering. He can't hear any gunfire, but that doesn't mean much. Dirk's probably found the surviving muscle, the two of them huddled together and Dirk making some plan. A limb at a time, Steward moves to fight stiffness. To keep ready. He couldn't be wetter. More minutes and he knows Dirk will be moving soon because soon the rain is going to be done, and at least with the wet and this racket he can get close to Steward and the elevator without much trouble. Sure. So he tilts his head skyward and takes a drink, then spits and breathes and happens to see motion up on the pad. He turns without jerking. A floater has just settled beside the gunshot floater, and a distinct figure climbs out and starts to run. He doesn't have to look again to know it's Chiffon. She meant it when she threatened to follow him, all right. "Came to save her investment," he says in a whisper, without a trace of passion. What to do now? They'll go for her, he thinks. If they saw her, and he can't see how they couldn't. She did it right by running and hiding so fast. Why didn't they shoot? Because they're on the far side of the roof, he decides. Sure. Just when I had them trapped, he thinks, and he climbs to his feet now and runs.

He doesn't care for the Flower. She's a client, he tells himself, and this is what you do for clients. Yet now he's running hard, something of the old spring back in his legs. He has both knives in one hand, the splints making them tough to hold. At one point he stops and squats and tries to listen through the roar of the rain, hearing nothing but catching a faint faraway glimpse of something colorful. Something gaudy. Bolts of lightning are sliding past at treetop level now, or so it seems. He can see the gaudy something moving down a path. Steward turns and crashes into a stand of ornamental brush, trusting in the storm to hide him. It's all a damned gamble and what if Dirk's using this chance to get free? No, he won't. He won't leave Chiffon and the twelfth chip. Steward bulls his way through a row of evergreens and turns on the path and sees the surviving muscle running, chasing something. He accelerates, driving off his broken toes, and the muscle stops to shoulder a big rifle and aims, Steward coming down on him before he can fire. The rifle and a pair of night goggles go flying. Steward slits fat tendons in the ankles and knees and wrists, then grabs the rifle and pulls its power pack and tosses both away. He can't see anyone else. He trots and squats and then thinks to sniff the air, and from somewhere comes the strong sweet Flowery stink that still makes him crazy. After everything. It takes him a second to stand. It takes longer to shake off the craziness and move.

The storm is ebbing.

A lone shot comes from near the pad. A little gun's shot. Steward feels himself sink a little, running toward the sound and hearing nothing else and believing it's over. Done. Whichever way it's turned out. And then there's two more shots and he follows the path around a curve and sees both of them. Dirk's closer. Chiffon has her pistol leveled at Dirk, both arms extended, and Dirk has a burned shoulder. Steward is running for him. No time for decisions. He presses and Chiffon fires high, the blast clipping Steward's ear and making him drop and roll. Chiffon screams, not having seen him. He can't find his knives and Dirk's beside him, surprised enough to glance down at him and pause. "Shoot again!" Steward screams. She doesn't. She won't or she can't. Dirk has a hard focused look, obsessed and miserable. He looks up at Chiffon and aims, and Steward stretches and kicks blindly and catches the back of Dirk's skull. Dirk goes down. The blast turns rainwater to steam, gravel and mud scattering, and Steward is on top of the old man and breaking his bones. It doesn't take much coaxing. He ruins the hips and then one arm, Dirk's good arm, crushing the shoulder and then pulling a blade out from under his splints. He starts to cut, crying now, intending to kill him slowly and do the world good . . . and then he stops himself, sobs and feels Dirk's pockets and pulls free the round box and then stands, the ground wobbling. He throws down the blade. He says, "No, I know what . . . ," and takes a long look around. The rain is stopping. A bright rainboy is overhead, shoving the clouds to the north. Chiffon is gazing at him, and so is Dirk, and he tells Dirk, "I'm going to Ghost you. Now. Ghost you and put you in Gray-time, all right, and keep you there for an eternity. All right? Think of living like that for a hundred million years, you dead little hunk of grease—"

And Dirk says, "No," with a wheeze. He says, "Forget that," and pulls a second pistol out from behind his back, using the burned arm but somehow moving fast. He doesn't have to lift or aim. He just places it snug against his temple and says something, or starts to speak, the word half-finished when the trigger is tripped and the head is gone and the body itself is limp. The air is full of the stink of cooked meat, bitter and penetrating.

Chiffon sighs and then stares at Steward, saying nothing.

"So they're there. All yours." He points at the box. "I guess you got what you came to get, huh?"

And she gets a fierce look in her eyes, challenging him and then turning, turning and grabbing the box and throwing it with all of her strength. "To hell with them and you!" Steward runs to where she has thrown the box. Chiffon curses and sobs behind him, and he looks over the building's edge, not listening, thinking a Flower's arm isn't much and maybe . . . sure, he thinks. Here it is! The box must have bounced off the low wall and dropped here, here on the damp ground, and he takes it back to her and puts it her hands and then pulls it away again when she tries to throw it away again, kicking him and claiming it's hers to do with what she wants, damn him, damn him, damn him!

"Enough," he says.

"What do I have to do?" she asks. "How do I make up for things—?"

"Would you stop?"

And she says, "That's the point! I've stopped! I've quit. Haven't I proved it yet?"

Again she tries for the box, begging for it, and Steward says, "Quit. No you can't, so quit! I'm not going to let you kill yourself!"

So she quits shouting, but the eyes keep cutting at him, wounding him. Finally he has to turn away, not knowing what to think, watching the storm moving and feeling a breeze around his legs and the bare back of his neck and smelling her, with every breath, wondering what is best. What makes sense. Choose, he thinks. Choose.

··· 25 ···

I was once at a place called Brulé. Well, I exaggerate. I was actually in its tubetrain station for a portion of an hour, no more, but I did watch the local people with care. I saw those who worked in the station and those bound for other places with bigger names and numbers. No clear details come to mind, but I did take away some general impressions. For example, it seems like a quiet community. Peaceful, yes, and maybe a little slow. I think it's the sort of place where you arrive by accident and leave on purpose, if you know what I mean . . .

> —*excerpt from a traveler's notebook, available through System-Net*

SHE sees three of them up ahead, walking her way, and no, they don't seem to have seen her yet. So April steps off the path, into the early shadows, and watches them pass—three cyborgs, two men and a woman, giggling and tickling each other while they tell little jokes that can make no sense to bystanders. Private jokes about Morningers and the mines. She listens for her own name, or Gabbro's, and hears neither. She is relieved and disappointed both, and she steps back on the path when they're gone, a quick look in both directions and then she starts to walk again. Just roaming.

April will have to find a new apartment soon.

In another part of town, she thinks. Something high, with a view, and only Terrans for neighbors. No Morningers. No Cradlers. And please no Gardeners either! She's been ever so lucky, she thinks. After what happened, after the hell of it and the fear it put inside her, she was ever so relieved last night to hear an announcement from the Chief of Police. Brulé would continue its search for Gabbro's attacker or attackers, but a lack of physical evidence and eye-

293

witnesses were hampering efforts. There were no suspects, and un-
fortunately the case would have to be closed in a day or two if nothing new was found.

So April is free.

She halfway wants to skip now. For the joy of it.

Last night she sang. She lay on her back in the tiny, tiny hotel room.
The song was something she had learned as a girl, the tune happy and
the lyrics sweet and her voice carrying through the door and down the
hallway. Some gravel-voiced whore had joined in, she recalls, and
they'd done several choruses before shouts and catcalls from elsewhere drowned them out. Then she had switched from the local news
to that fictional island with its invented City-State and all the familiar
characters. She had watched the characters without sound, thinking
things through for herself. If anyone ever asked about Gabbro, she
had a story waiting. Her actions on such-and-such night were like
this . . . and she practiced the story until it was perfect, without seams
or flaws or doubts. Just in case. Just in case she met a Morninger who
remembered her and Gabbro, or anyone else who might have their
suspicions. Lying in that room, halfway between wakefulness and
sleep, she reached a point where the fiction was more real than what
had happened. It felt as if she hadn't played any part in poor Gabbro's
tragedy. What a sad shame, isn't it? What makes people behave in
such ways?

April has no intention of seeing Gabbro again.

Ever.

She is walking in an open plaza now, ignoring the looks of strangers
and thinking she should sit somewhere and rest for a while. She's still
wearing the healing mask. A few more days, said the doctors, and then
the damage will be well on the way to cure. By then, she thinks, I'll
have a new apartment and a new life, and people will be forgetting
about the miner . . . what was his name? Who was it that attacked him?
Probably his own people, they'll say. Probably for reasons we'll never
learn . . .

People are streaming past. Some have been awake all night, while
most are clean and bright-faced and ready for the day. April chooses
a living bench near the plaza, the spot affording a view and shade and
a degree of anonymity. She'll buy some fat-burning chemicals later
today, then start getting herself ready for circulation again. Absolutely. She smiles behind the mask, thinking about the future. What

was it she told Gabbro? That cyborgs were the people of the future? She was a fool. She was so wrong, she knows now. Last night she realized the truth. In the middle of the night, coming awake from some odd forgotten dream, she had looked at the World-Net panel fixed to the ceiling and seen a pair of fictional lovers sleeping in their wide elegant bed, like mismatched spoons. She had realized in an instant that that was the future. That's where people were going! She can't guess the technologies or how they'll be implemented, but she feels sure there will come an age when everyone will be fictional. Each person will live his life with the same old-fashioned heartfelt conviction and timeless passion. Absolutely. But should tragedy strike like it's struck April lately, the cure will be a simple process. A function of editing. Whatever is evil and sad will be dispelled neatly, buttons pushed and the effects immediate. People everywhere will live in bliss. She is sure. Sitting on the bench and smiling to herself, April almost has an urge to stand and shout at all the passing people, telling them the great good thing that she knows. Then she thinks, How would it look? A masked and crazy fat woman prophesying the end of flesh-on-blood? They'd mob me. They would hang me from these trees, all right!

April laughs, tears seeping out from the mask's eyes.

Then in a little while she stands and walks on.

◆ ◆ ◆

"I need a couple favors. If I could ask—"

"Certainly, Steward." Olivia Jade looks at him, thinking that he looks better than yesterday but not by much. She thinks he needs other pursuits, then tells him, "Anything. What can I do for you?"

"I'm leaving for a while. Leaving Brulé." The swelling is down in his face and hands, but is that ear burned? How did he burn it? "I'm going to Quito . . . Yes, that's what I said. I'm a bodyguard for a client. I'll be gone a few months, more or less. Would you look after things for the duration?" He is in his office outside Brulé. Olivia can see him and hear someone else in the room, somewhere just out of sight. "I'll call you from there and set up the details."

She says, "Sure," and feels a little ill. A little sad.

He sighs and picks something off the floor. It's a recording disk covered with a layer of drying black mud. Very odd. He says nothing about it. What he does say comes from nowhere and leaves her stunned. "The main thing revolves around money. Quiver chip money. I can't think of anyone better to babysit it for me, for us, then Olivia and all her talented good friends."

She swallows and wonders, "How much money? What are you teasing me with, Steward?"

He tells. Then, almost as an afterthought, he gives an embarrassed happy smile.

"How much?!"

He pulls a broken hand across his face, then says, "Dirk." He shakes his head and tells her, "Watch the local news. Apparently he killed himself. Which was his choice. His."

She doesn't know what to say.

He says, "My client's got some rather unique medical needs. For the next few months." He lifts the recording disk, two swollen fingers scraping off the worst of the mud. "Quito is the best place to go. This is to save her. Some novel technologies and some big applications for the future." He balances the disk on one fingertip, the motion boyish and brief. "Applications for Ghosts," he says. "There's this fellow on this disk who claims to know how to give Ghosts flesh-on-blood bodies. What do you think, Olivia?"

"Steward?" She shakes her head, unable to follow him. "What are you telling me? I don't see. Where do Ghosts fit in with Dirk?" Who is dead, apparently. She feels like applauding that fact. "Explain it, but this time slowly."

"It's confusing," he admits. "Here. Let me introduce my client—"

Olivia isn't stunned. Some part of her had already guessed there was a Flower involved . . . only she's not a true Flower and Olivia can still only halfway follow the tangled story. She listens but she doesn't listen, understands but feels remote and untouched at the same time. How insane can it become? Ghosts into Flowers? She can't believe what she hears, even though the brunt of it seems to ring true.

Then Steward finishes, sitting beside the beautiful creature who is wearing his clothes—the blonde hair dirty and the face smudged and the impossible effortless brief beauty still filling the room—and Steward is telling Olivia to come up with ways to use the quiver chip money. Investments. Anonymous bank accounts. Blind trusts. The trick is to make it work without telling the world who owns the wealth. There are eleven chips now, he says. They're in a hyperfiber safe underneath his feet, meshed with World-Net and waiting. The twelfth chip is coming . . . and he gives a peculiar smile.

Olivia tells him, "Whatever I can do," and catches herself. She almost said, "Darling."

"One more thing," he says. "There's a miner who gets some money on the side. No names. He'll probably know I'm the one, just the same."

"All right."

And when those details are finished, he announces, "I think it's time. We should leave." There is a vague urgency to his voice, and a tangible confidence. He doesn't touch the Flower while they sit together, but he seems to reassure her with his looks and his voice. "Thanks, Olivia. Wish us luck?"

"Of course."

And he's gone. Steward is gone. Olivia stares up at the whiteness for a very long while, feeling nothing. Feeling what? She hunts for sorrow but it isn't there. She thinks she should feel happy, at least a little bit, if what Steward promises is true. A body? She might be walking around Brulé in some kind of body! What will I do when I'm flesh-on-blood again? she wonders. What will be first? She doesn't know. She can't imagine. She's always dreamed for this chance, but now it's here and what she wants . . . oh, well . . .

Quietly, ever so quietly, Olivia starts to laugh.

—◆—◆—◆—

On the wide walkway descending into the tubetrain station is a hole deeper than perhaps any other on the Earth. It serves as a tourist curiosity and an advertisement, reaching clear to the Earth's mantle and the famous mines. When people stand along the high railings, they can hear the distant unmistakable roaring of the drills working. Diluted vapors drift out of the hole, and a steady hot wind blows, and several armored boxes are adorned with holo signs that read: "SUPPORT THE FUTURE. SUPPORT THE DREAM." Generous children and the rare adult will slip money into slots on the boxes—a small gesture designed to make them feel a part of things.

Toby is coming down the walkway scared. He still believes that the police will be watching for him, is certain that they will have cameras and the AIs studying every face. But in this crush of people, he hopes, a solitary Gardener will escape undetected. Praise the Prophet. A train is leaving for the south in a little while. He'll buy a last-class ticket and count the minutes before Brulé is something behind him, something that cannot reach him. This is the future he goes toward, all right. Not some enormous loud hole in the dead ground, but something where he is a major player. So why be scared? he asks himself. The Prophet protects the worthy. Isn't he proof? Isn't he?

At one point the walkway narrows.

Bodies press against bodies. Like in Quito, he tells himself. He thinks how he'll have to get accustomed to the feeling. Elbows begin to shove at him. He shoves back, keeping his webbed hands out of easy view. And the walkway spreads out now, doubling its size. Toby can see the polished gray floor and people cutting this way and that. He hasn't been here for a year now, and he wasn't moving downward. He had arrived. Which line? he wonders. Which is the last-class section? Oh, yes. He spies a sign and moves toward it, cutting across the general flow. He ignores curses, pressing on. He feels safe now. No one has spotted him and he can count the meters to the staging area. Hurry, hurry! And then, at just the last instant, he sees something he never expected. There's a red splotch of hair taller than the average head, and bandages on the familiar face. That neighbor of his . . . Steward? What's he doing? Toby wonders. Here, of all places. Here!

Steward doesn't see him, isn't looking his way just now.

Toby notices the hands and something pained in the walk, and he studies what he wears—a long robe of some kind, thin and bulky as though the man is carrying a large bundle next to his body. What is it? For an instant, passing against one of the bright signs, a shape is betrayed underneath the robe. A vague suggestion of . . . what? He can't tell. It's there and gone and now Steward is turning to look his way, toward Toby, and he dips his head in response and slows himself and tries looking thoroughly average. A moment passes. Two. And now he looks up again, relieved to see the red-haired man passing from view. Toby continues, wondering about those hands and the bandages on the face and what kinds of scars will he wear in the future. A strange, strange man. He knows it. He thinks of the two of them and how he always felt that they had common ground, suffering alone like they did. A shame they never talked . . . he feels certain, absolutely certain, as he takes one last glance toward . . . hey, what's that?

For a moment, just a moment, he thinks he sees someone walking next to Steward. Huddling beside him. Halfway obscured by the long sheer robe . . .

. . . impossible, of course.

He must be seeing things in the station's gloom.

And now Toby pauses one last time, turning once and using all of his senses. He absorbs Brulé's corruption once again. And very faint, but undeniably real, is a peculiar sort of stink. A wonderful stink. Sweet and husky and infectious, yes, and Toby thinks it's something from Garden. It's that fine. But for his life he can't name it.

◆ ◆ ◆

Chiffon asks, "What are you thinking?" Her voice is soft, almost a whisper. He wishes she wouldn't make noise, wouldn't risk being overheard. He wishes he could see her now instead of the Chiffon-shaped patch of distorted shadow beneath the robe. There's too much light for the holo tricks to work their best. There are too many people for them to be too bold. They're in the staging area for first class, standing near the back, and Chiffon pokes him once in the side and asks again, "What's on your mind?"

He's thinking about the tubetrain to Quito—faster than floaters, and they'll have their own cabin. Good. And he's also thinking about Minus and Dirk, of course. What else? Sometimes Chaz is in his head, and Yellowknife, and images of tidy elegant brothels somewhere in the wilds of Quito. That's where they'll start looking for help for Chiffon. And yes, Chiffon. He can't stop himself, and he won't even try. He's imagining her saved, reborn again and for always, and maybe the world changed with it. All of mankind. There's no knowing what might happen from these new tricks. He gets lost just trying. So he swings back to more prosaic stuff—her and him returning to Brulé; them living out their lives together and making the money work for them. What's he thinking? That's got to be the hardest question in the world.

He looks down at the shadow under his robe, saying, "The pearls. Do you have both strands?"

"The necklaces? Sure." She takes them from a pocket. They appear in his hand as if by magic. One strand he puts around his own neck, careful that no one is watching. And the other strand goes on Chiffon, hanging in the empty air and halfway obscured by the holos. On the fuzzy brink of reality. It's an odd illusion, and he laughs. He can't tell what he's thinking. Everything. He's thinking everything.

"I know what you're thinking," she says, her voice mischievous and her hands wandering.

"Well, that's part of it," he says. "Hormones," he says, and he gazes out at all the faces waiting, feeling a warm, sweet tingle radiating up through his tired, tired bones.